CW01084499

The Association of American University Presses

Directory 2013

The Association of American University Presses
28 W. 36th Street, Suite 602
New York, NY 10018
Phone: 212.989.1010
Fax: 212.989.0275
Website: www.aaupnet.org
Email: info@aaupnet.org

Published by the Association of American University Presses
28 W. 36th Street, #602 New York, NY 10018
© 2012 by the Association of American University Presses, Inc.
All rights reserved.
Printed in the United States of America

International Standard Book Number 13: 9780945103295
Library of Congress Catalog Number 54-43046

Distributed to the Trade by:
The University of Chicago Press
11030 South Langley Avenue
Chicago, Illinois 60628
USA

Publication of this *Directory* was assisted by a generous grant from Thomson-Shore.

Contents

PREFACE

This *Directory* serves as a guide to the publishing programs and personnel of the 130 distinguished scholarly presses that have met the membership standards of the Association of American University Presses. Updated annually, the *Directory* provides the most comprehensive information on these publishers available from any source. It belongs on the reference shelf of anyone connected to scholarly publishing: scholars preparing materials for publication, booksellers, librarians, scholarly presses interested in joining the AAUP, and, of course, AAUP's own members.

The *Directory* is organized particularly for the convenience of authors, librarians, and booksellers who require detailed information about AAUP members and their wide-ranging publishing programs. The "Subject Area Grid," for example, provides a quick overview of the many disciplines published by the presses, indicating those most likely to publish a work in a given area. "On Submitting Manuscripts" gives advice to potential authors on preparing and submitting a scholarly manuscript for publication.

For further detail, individual press listings provide information on their editorial programs, journals published, and key staff members. Addresses, ordering information, and information on sales representation for Canada, the UK, and Europe are also included.

The last section of the *Directory* focuses on the association and its purposes, and includes its by-laws, guidelines for admission to membership, and the names of the AAUP's Board of Directors, committees, and staff.

GENERAL INFORMATION FOR AUTHORS

What University Presses Do

University Presses perform services that are of inestimable value to the scholarly establishment, and also to the broader world of readers, and ultimately to society. If you are considering publishing with a university or other non-profit scholarly press, the following list should give you a good understanding of the scholarly publishing community.

• University Presses make available to the broader public the full range and value of research generated by university faculty.

• University Press books and journals present the basic research and analysis that is drawn upon by policymakers, opinion leaders, and authors of works for the general public.

• University Presses contribute to the variety and diversity of cultural expression at a time of global mergers and consolidation in the media industry.

• University Presses make common cause with libraries and other cultural institutions to promote engagement with ideas and sustain a literate culture.

• University Presses help to preserve the distinctiveness of local cultures through publication of works on the states and regions where they are based.

• University Presses give voice to minority cultures and perspectives through pioneering publication programs in ethnic, racial, and sexual studies.

• University Presses bring the work of overseas scholars and writers to English-language audiences by commissioning and publishing works in translation.

• University Presses rediscover and maintain the availability of works important to scholarship and culture through reprint programs.

• University Presses encourage cultural expression by publishing works of fiction, poetry, and creative nonfiction and books on contemporary art and photography.

• University Presses sponsor work in specialized and emerging areas of scholarship that do not have the broad levels of readership needed to attract commercial publishers.

• University Presses, through the peer review process, test the validity and soundness of scholarship and thus maintain high standards for academic publication.

• University Presses add value to scholarly work through rigorous editorial development; professional copyediting and design; and worldwide dissemination.

• University Presses are based at a wide array of educational institutions and thus promote a diversity of scholarly perspectives.

• University Presses encourage and refine the work of younger scholars through publication of the first books that establish credentials and develop authorial experience.

• University Presses make the works of English-language scholars available worldwide by licensing translations to publishers in other languages.

• University Presses commit resources to long-term scholarly editions and multivolume research projects, assuring publication for works with completion dates far in the future.

• University Presses add to the richness of undergraduate and graduate education by publishing most of the non-textbook and supplementary material used by instructors.

• University Presses collaborate with learned societies, scholarly associations, and librarians to explore how new technologies can benefit and advance scholarship.

• University Presses extend the reach and influence of their parent institutions, making evident their commitment to knowledge and ideas.

• University Presses demonstrate their parent institutions' support of research in areas such as the humanities and social sciences that rarely receive substantial Federal or corporate funding.

• University Presses help connect the university to the surrounding community by publishing books of local interest and hosting events for local authors.

• University Presses generate favorable publicity for their parent institutions through news coverage and book reviews, awards won, and exhibits at scholarly conferences.

• University Press staff act as local experts for faculty and administrators, providing guidance on intellectual property, scholarly communication, and the publishing process.

• University Presses provide advice and opportunities for students interested in pursuing careers in publishing.

On Submitting Manuscripts

JOURNAL ARTICLES

University presses have always been associated with publishing books of merit and distinction. This remains as true today as in the past, but less well appreciated is the extent to which university presses are active in publishing scholarly journals.

Journals form a major part of the publishing program of many presses, and more than half of the Association's members produce at least one periodical. (See page 18 for a list of presses publishing journals.)

Authors submitting papers to a journal should check a current issue for information on where to submit manuscripts and for guidelines on length and format. Editors of journals often have very precise requirements for manuscript preparation and may return articles that do not meet their specifications.

BOOK MANUSCRIPTS

Selecting a Publisher

If you are looking for a publisher for a book-length manuscript, do some research on which press may be best for your book. You should consider the reputation in your field of various presses and their editors, the design and production quality of their books, and the range and strength of their marketing efforts. To take advantage of group promotions and past experience, presses tend to specialize in certain subjects. Occasionally a press may take on a title in an unfamiliar area, but you are more likely to be successful in your submission if you choose one that knows the field. Use the "Subject Area Grid," which begins on page 9, to find out which presses publish titles in your field. You can then find more specific information about their interests under the listings of individual presses or by consulting their catalogs. If your book has a strong regional interest, consider the lists of the university presses active in your state to determine what types of regional books they publish.

You can also learn more about the list of each publisher by reviewing press websites and blogs, reading book advertisements in journals, and by visiting press exhibits at academic meetings. At these exhibits you can meet acquisitions editors from the presses most active in the discipline and talk with them about your manuscript. Such talks can be very helpful to you and the editor in deciding if your manuscript would be suitable for a particular press. If you have already decided which press you would prefer for your book, call the appropriate editor before the meeting to make an appointment.

Preparing a Manuscript Prospectus

If you have selected a publisher but do not know an editor, you can use this directory to find the appropriate editor at that press. If you are not sure which editor to approach, write to the director of the press or to its editor-in-chief. Many AAUP member presses describe their submission guidelines on their websites. It is best not to send the complete manuscript until you have been invited to do so. Presses vary in the amount of material they want to receive on a first submission, but some or all of the following materials are usually provided:

- a short, informative cover letter including a clear and concise description of your book and its notable features, your opinion of the audience for the book, information on the current status of the manuscript and expected completion date, and some details on the physical characteristics of the manuscript, such as length, number of illustrations, tables, appendices, etc.

- a table of contents

- a preface, introduction, or other brief sample of your manuscript

- a curriculum vitae or biographical notes

If the press is interested, the editor will invite you to submit the complete manuscript or inform you that he or she can proceed to review the materials you sent.

Preparing Your Manuscript for Review

Presses vary in their requirements for manuscript preparation. In general, the manuscript you submit for review should be as accurate and complete as possible. If a manuscript is carelessly prepared, reviewers may take offense at typographical errors or careless citations and spend precious review space discussing these problems instead of attending to the substance of your manuscript. If, for good reasons, your manuscript is incomplete, you should indicate what material is missing and provide your schedule for completion.

Although some presses will accept a single-spaced manuscript for review, it is best to double-space your text. A double-spaced manuscript is easier to read and may be required when your manuscript reaches the copyediting stage. For book publication, every element of the text should be double-spaced (including quotations, notes, bibliographies, appendices, figure legends, and glossaries). Once your manuscript is accepted for publication, your editor will advise you on any special requirements imposed by that press's house style.

The Review Process

Some university presses may give advance (i.e., conditional) contracts to experienced authors on the basis of incomplete or unreviewed manuscripts. Most, however, must obtain one or more reviews of a completed manuscript before presenting a project for the approval of the press's editorial board. As review procedures differ from press to press, check with the editor when you first submit the manuscript to find out what will be involved. He or she should be able to give you a tentative schedule for the review process. It is difficult to predict exactly how long it will take to reach a decision, since often readers' reports encourage authors to make further revisions to the manuscript and the manuscript is usually reviewed again after the author makes the revisions. If your manuscript is also under review at another publisher, be sure to let the editor know. Some editors will not review manuscripts that are under simultaneous consideration elsewhere; others will not object.

Preparing Your Manuscript for Publication

Most publishers will want an electronic version of your manuscript. Your manuscript should be keyboarded as simply as possible. There is no need to change fonts, type styles, and formats to differentiate between sections; in fact, this is counterproductive. The press's copyediting or production department will insert the proper typesetting codes for formatting extracts, different levels of headings, and so on. And keep in mind that your book will be designed by a professional. Many presses will send you their own guidelines for submitting manuscripts.

FURTHER READING

Abel, Richard, Lyman W. Newlin, Katina Strauch, and Bruce Strauch, eds. *Scholarly Publishing: Books, Journals, Publishers, and Libraries in the Twentieth Century.* Indianapolis: Wiley, 2001.

American Psychological Association. *Publication Manual of the American Psychological Association.* 6th ed. Washington, DC: APA Books, 2009.

Appelbaum, Judith. *How to Get Happily Published: A Complete and Candid Guide.* 5th ed. New York: HarperResource, 1998.

Becker, Howard S. *Writing for Social Scientists: How to Start and Finish Your Thesis, Book, or Article.* 2nd ed. Chicago: University of Chicago Press, 2007.

Belcher, Wendy Laura. *Writing Your Journal Article in Twelve Weeks: A Guide to Academic Publishing Success.* Thousands Oaks, CA: SAGE Publications, 2009

Day, Robert A. and Barbara Gastel *How to Write and Publish a Scientific Paper.* 7th ed. Westport, CT: Greenwood Publishing Group, Inc., 2011.

Derricourt, Robin. *An Author's Guide to Scholarly Publishing.* Princeton: Princeton University Press, 1996.

Germano, William. *From Dissertation to Book.* Chicago: University of Chicago Press, 2005.

Germano, William. *Getting it Published: A Guide for Scholars and Anyone Else Serious About Serious Books.* 2nd ed. Chicago: University of Chicago Press, 2008.

Hacker, Diana. *A Writer's Reference.* 6th ed. Boston, MA: Bedford Books, 2009.

Harman, Eleanor, Ian Montagnes, Siobhan McMenemy, and Chris Bucci eds. *The Thesis and the Book: A Guide for First-Time Academic Authors.* 2nd ed. Toronto: University of Toronto Press, 2003.

Huff, Anne Sigismund. *Writing for Scholarly Publication.* Thousand Oaks, CA: SAGE Publications, 1998.

Katz, Michael J. *Elements of the Scientific Paper: A Step-by-Step Guide for Students and Professionals.* New Haven: Yale University Press, 1986.

Kasdorf, William E. *The Columbia Guide to Digital Publishing.* New York: Columbia University Press, 2003.

Luey, Beth. *Handbook for Academic Authors.* 5th ed. New York: Cambridge University Press, 2009.

Luey, Beth, ed. *Revising Your Dissertation: Advice from Leading Editors*. 2nd ed. Berkeley: University of California Press, 2007.

Modern Language Association. *MLA Style Manual and Guide to Scholarly Publishing*. 3rd ed. New York: Modern Language Association of America, 2008.

Moxley, Joseph M. and Todd Taylor. *Writing and Publishing for Academic Authors*. 2nd ed. Lanham, MD: Rowman and Littlefield, 1996.

Mulvany, Nancy C. *Indexing Books*. 2nd Ed. Chicago: University of Chicago Press, 2005.

Parsons, Paul. *Getting Published: The Acquisition Process at University Presses*. Knoxville: University of Tennessee Press, 1989.

Powell, Walter W. *Getting into Print: The Decision-Making Process in Scholarly Publishing*. Chicago: University of Chicago Press, 1985.

Schwartz, Marilyn and the Task Force on Bias-Free Language of the AAUP. *Guidelines for Bias-Free Writing*. Bloomington: Indiana University Press, 1995.

Strong, William S. *The Copyright Book: A Practical Guide*. 5th ed. Cambridge, MA: MIT Press, 1999.

Strunk, William J. and E. B. White. *The Elements of Style*. 4th ed. New York: Pearson Higher Education, 1999.

Swain, Dwight V. *Techniques of the Selling Writer*. Norman: University of Oklahoma Press, 1982.

Thompson, John. *Books in the Digital Age: The Transformation of Academic and Higher Education Publishing in Britain and the United States* Cambridge: Polity Press, 2005.

University of Chicago Press. *The Chicago Manual of Style*. 16th ed. Chicago: University of Chicago Press, 2010.

University of Chicago Press. *The Chicago Manual of Style Online*. 16th ed. Chicago: University of Chicago Press, 2010, http://www.chicagomanualofstyle.org/home.html

Zerubavel, Eviator. *The Clockwork Muse: A Practical Guide to Writing Theses, Dissertations, and Books*. Cambridge, MA: Harvard University Press, 1999.

SUBJECT AREA GRID

This eight-page grid indicates the subject areas in which each press has a particularly strong interest.

Some presses are prepared to consider manuscripts of outstanding quality in areas other than those listed. For more detailed descriptions of press editorial programs, consult the individual listings in the "Directory of Members" section and contact the presses that interest you.

Subject-area availability by publisher. Dots (●) indicate coverage.

Subject	Abilene Christian	Akron	Alabama	Alaska	Alberta	A. Historical	A. Psychiatric	A. School Classical	Amsterdam	Arizona	Arkansas	Athabasca	Baylor	Beacon	British Columbia	Brookings	Cairo (American)	Calgary	California	Cambridge	Carnegie Mellon	Catholic	Chicago	Chinese	Colorado	Columbia	Cork	Cornell	Duke	Duquesne	Florida	Fordham
African Studies																●			●	●			●						●	●		
African American Studies	●		●							●	●		●		●				●	●			●		●	●			●	●		●	●
Agriculture			●	●						●	●				●			●	●	●			●			●			●			
American Indian Studies			●	●						●	●	●		●	●			●	●	●			●		●			●	●		●	
American Studies			●						●	●	●	●	●		●				●	●	●		●		●	●	●		●	●		●	●
Anthropology			●	●					●	●	●		●		●	●		●	●	●	●		●	●	●	●		●	●	●		●	●
Cultural			●	●					●	●			●	●				●	●	●		●	●	●		●		●	●		●	
Physical			●	●											●	●	●				●		●		●					
Archaeology			●	●		●	●	●	●		●		●			●	●		●			●		●		●	●	●	●		●	
Architecture			●			●	●	●			●			●		●	●		●	●	●		●				●				●	●
Art & Art History			●			●	●	●		●		●		●		●	●	●	●	●	●		●				●	●	●		●	●
Asian Studies									●				●	●	●	●			●	●			●	●		●		●	●		●	
Asian American Studies										●					●				●	●			●		●		●		●	●		
Bibliography & Reference						●									●		●		●	●			●		●	●	●		●	●		●
Biography	●		●	●	●				●	●			●	●	●	●		●	●		●		●	●	●	●	●	●	●	●	●	●
Business									●					●	●	●		●			●	●	●		●		●					
Canadian Studies			●	●										●				●	●									●				
Caribbean Studies			●						●				●	●	●		●		●			●						●	●		●	●
Child Development			●			●					●	●			●				●				●	●								
Classics						●	●	●				●							●	●	●	●	●	●				●				●
Communications/Media			●						●		●	●	●	●	●		●	●	●	●	●		●		●			●	●			●
Computer Sciences									●										●													
Creative Nonfiction	●		●	●						●		●		●				●	●	●												
Criminology									●						●				●	●			●					●	●			
Demography									●						●	●			●	●			●									
Economics			●						●					●	●	●	●	●	●	●			●		●		●		●	●		●
Education			●		●					●			●	●	●	●	●	●		●	●		●	●				●				●
History				●									●	●	●	●						●						●	●			
Learning Disabilities			●		●									●											●							
Theory & Method	●				●										●								●	●								●
Engineering																		●														
Environment/Conservation		●	●	●					●	●	●	●	●		●	●	●	●	●	●			●		●	●		●	●		●	●
ESL																		●														
Ethnic Studies			●	●				●	●	●	●	●		●	●			●	●	●			●			●		●	●	●	●	●
European Studies									●			●		●		●			●	●								●	●	●	●	●
Fiction			●								●		●				●				●											
Film Studies			●		●				●			●			●	●	●	●			●				●	●	●	●	●			●
Folklore			●						●	●	●								●				●				●	●	●			●
Food Studies													●	●					●				●				●		●			
Gay and Lesbian Studies			●										●	●				●	●	●			●				●		●			●
Gender Studies						●			●	●	●		●	●			●	●	●	●			●	●		●	●	●	●			●
Geography			●						●	●	●	●		●				●	●	●			●		●		●		●			
Gerontology	●				●								●						●				●	●			●					●
History		●	●	●		●			●	●			●	●		●	●	●	●		●	●	●	●	●		●	●		●	●	
African					●								●	●			●	●	●		●						●					
American	●		●	●	●				●	●	●		●	●			●	●	●		●	●	●		●	●		●	●		●	●
Asian					●				●				●	●			●	●			●	●		●		●		●	●			
British					●								●				●	●	●		●	●					●	●	●			
Canadian			●	●	●							●					●		●													
Environmental		●	●	●	●				●	●	●		●	●			●	●	●		●			●	●		●	●		●		
European					●				●		●		●				●	●	●	●		●	●	●	●	●		●			●
Latin American			●		●					●			●				●	●	●		●			●			●		●	●		
Middle Eastern					●					●			●			●		●	●					●		●	●					
Ancient					●		●	●											●	●		●	●			●						
Classical					●		●	●											●	●		●	●			●						●
Modern			●	●		●			●		●			●				●	●	●	●	●	●	●	●	●		●	●		●	●
World																			●							●		●	●			
Law			●						●			●		●	●	●	●				●		●	●	●	●			●			●
Language			●						●	●					●		●			●			●	●		●						●
Linguistics			●						●	●					●		●			●			●						●		●	●
Speech																		●														
Latin American Studies			●							●			●		●		●		●	●	●		●		●				●		●	
Library Science									●										●				●									

10

Subject	Abilene Christian	Akron	Alabama	Alaska	Alberta	A. Historical	A. Psychiatric	A. School Classical	Amsterdam	Arizona	Arkansas	Athabasca	Baylor	Beacon	British Columbia	Brookings	Cairo (American)	Calgary	California	Cambridge	Carnegie Mellon	Catholic	Chicago	Chinese	Colorado	Columbia	Cork	Cornell	Duke	Duquesne	Florida	Fordham
Literature			•	•	•				•	•			•			•			•	•	•	•	•			•		•	•	•	•	•
Literary Criticism	•	•	•						•				•					•	•	•	•	•	•			•	•	•	•	•	•	•
Literary History			•						•										•	•	•	•	•			•	•	•	•			•
African																			•													
African American		•																	•				•					•	•		•	•
American	•	•	•									•	•						•	•	•	•	•			•		•	•		•	•
Asian																				•	•	•	•	•		•		•	•			•
British																			•	•		•	•			•		•	•	•	•	
Canadian					•						•								•				•						•			
Classical								•	•										•	•		•	•			•		•	•			•
Eastern																			•				•									
European									•										•	•		•	•		•	•		•	•	•	•	•
Medieval									•										•	•		•	•			•		•	•	•	•	•
Renaissance									•										•	•		•	•			•		•	•		•	•
Modern	•		•						•										•	•	•	•	•		•	•		•	•		•	•
Contemporary			•						•	•									•	•	•	•	•			•		•	•		•	•
Mythology			•	•					•	•									•				•					•				
Translations			•									•						•	•	•	•	•	•		•	•		•	•			
Maritime Studies			•	•					•						•				•												•	•
Mathematics																			•				•									•
Medicine			•						•	•	•								•				•					•				
Ethics		•						•											•							•		•	•			
History		•	•					•										•	•				•			•		•	•			
Medieval Studies									•										•			•	•		•			•	•	•	•	•
Middle East Studies									•	•			•		•	•	•		•			•	•		•			•	•		•	•
Military Studies		•	•						•		•	•		•	•		•	•					•			•		•			•	•
Near Eastern Studies									•				•		•	•	•		•	•		•	•			•		•	•		•	•
Performing Arts									•				•					•	•	•		•			•			•	•			•
Dance													•										•		•			•	•			•
Music									•				•					•	•	•		•	•		•			•	•			•
Theory & Method									•		•		•	•								•				•		•	•		•	•
Theatre																			•									•				
Pacific Studies					•				•				•	•					•				•					•	•			•
Philosophy									•		•		•					•	•	•		•	•		•			•	•	•		•
Ethics									•			•	•						•	•		•	•		•			•	•	•		•
History of Philosophy									•			•	•						•	•		•			•			•	•			•
Photography			•	•														•	•				•		•				•		•	•
Poetry	•	•		•					•	•	•	•	•						•									•	•			
Political Science/Public Affairs		•	•						•	•			•	•	•	•	•	•	•				•		•	•		•	•			•
Popular Culture	•	•	•						•				•	•					•		•	•	•		•			•	•			
Psychiatry							•												•				•	•				•	•			
Psychology		•		•	•				•				•	•					•				•		•			•	•	•		
Public Health			•							•			•	•	•	•			•				•		•			•	•			
Publishing									•										•			•							•			•
Regional Studies	•	•	•	•	•				•	•	•		•	•	•	•		•	•	•	•		•	•	•	•	•	•			•	•
Religion	•								•	•		•	•	•	•		•	•	•	•			•		•	•		•	•	•	•	•
Buddhism																			•	•			•			•						
Christianity	•											•							•	•			•			•		•				•
Islam																			•	•			•			•		•				•
Judaism																			•	•			•	•		•		•				•
Science		•		•					•		•		•	•					•				•		•	•		•			•	•
Biological Science			•	•					•				•	•			•		•				•		•	•		•			•	•
Botany			•	•						•			•	•					•				•		•	•		•				
Genetics					•														•									•				
Earth Sciences			•							•			•	•			•		•				•		•			•			•	
Geology			•							•				•					•				•					•			•	
Physical Science			•						•				•						•				•					•				
Astronomy										•									•				•									
History of Science		•	•						•	•		•							•				•		•			•	•		•	•
Slavic Studies			•										•		•	•			•				•		•			•	•		•	•
Social Work				•					•		•		•	•	•								•	•	•			•				
Sociology		•		•					•		•		•	•	•		•	•	•	•	•		•	•	•			•	•		•	•
Sports	•	•																	•				•				•	•			•	
Urban Studies									•		•		•	•	•	•			•				•					•	•			•
Veterinary Sciences																											•	•				
Women's Studies			•					•	•	•	•	•	•	•			•	•	•				•		•		•	•	•		•	•

	Gallaudet	Georgetown	Georgia	Getty	Harvard	Hawaii	Hong Kong	Illinois	IMF	Indiana	Iowa	Island	Johns Hopkins	Kansas	Kent State	Kentucky	Leuven	Lincoln	Louisiana	McGill-Queen's	Manitoba	Marquette	Massachusetts	MIT	Medieval Institute	Mercer	Michigan	Michigan State	Minnesota Hist.	Minnesota	Mississippi	Missouri	MLA	MOMA
African Studies		●			●					●																				●		●		●
African American Studies	●		●		●		●			●	●			●		●			●				●				●	●	●	●	●	●	●	●
Agriculture												●					●																	
American Indian Studies					●									●								●	●				●	●	●	●	●	●	●	●
American Studies			●		●	●		●		●	●		●	●	●	●		●	●				●				●	●	●	●	●	●	●	●
Anthropology	●				●	●	●			●	●								●				●						●	●	●	●	●	
Cultural	●				●	●	●			●	●						●		●				●						●	●	●	●		
Physical					●																													
Archaeology				●	●	●					●			●			●	●	●				●			●		●						
Architecture			●	●	●	●			●					●			●	●	●			●	●	●	●	●				●	●	●		●
Art & Art History	●			●	●	●	●			●				●			●		●			●	●	●	●	●				●	●			●
Asian Studies		●			●	●	●			●							●	●	●											●			●	
Asian American Studies			●		●	●	●	●															●					●		●	●		●	
Bibliography & Reference	●				●	●	●			●		●		●																●			●	
Biography	●		●		●	●		●		●	●	●		●	●					●	●		●	●			●	●	●	●	●		●	
Business					●	●	●																	●										
Canadian Studies								●												●	●												●	
Caribbean Studies		●																		●	●									●	●		●	
Child Development	●				●								●						●															
Classics			●	●	●		●	●					●						●								●			●			●	
Communications/ Media			●		●	●	●	●		●	●						●		●	●		●	●	●			●	●		●	●	●	●	●
Computer Sciences				●													●						●											
Creative Nonfiction	●		●		●	●				●	●			●					●									●		●		●	●	
Criminology													●				●		●		●		●							●				
Demography	●				●								●				●		●															
Economics			●	●	●	●		●		●							●	●	●				●											
Education	●		●	●	●					●			●				●		●							●			●	●			●	
History	●		●	●	●								●				●									●							●	
Learning Disabilities	●		●																															
Theory & Method	●												●				●																●	
Engineering			●		●												●																	
Environment/Conservation		●	●	●	●	●	●			●	●	●	●	●		●	●	●	●				●	●		●	●	●	●	●	●	●		
ESL	●	●			●	●											●										●						●	
Ethnic Studies			●		●	●	●			●	●						●			●	●		●				●	●	●	●	●	●	●	●
European Studies					●					●	●		●				●	●	●								●			●	●	●	●	●
Fiction					●					●	●	●							●				●							●			●	
Film Studies		●			●	●	●	●		●						●	●		●				●				●			●	●	●	●	●
Folklore					●	●			●	●						●		●					●						●	●	●	●	●	●
Food Studies			●			●			●		●								●												●			
Gay and Lesbian Studies					●	●	●			●									●				●				●			●		●		
Gender Studies			●		●	●	●	●		●	●		●				●		●				●				●			●	●	●	●	
Geography			●		●	●		●	●	●							●	●	●											●	●	●		
Gerontology					●								●																					
History	●		●		●	●		●		●	●	●	●	●	●	●	●		●		●	●	●	●		●	●	●	●	●	●	●	●	
African					●	●		●		●									●											●				
American	●		●		●			●		●	●	●	●	●	●	●	●		●		●	●	●	●		●	●	●	●	●	●	●	●	
Asian					●	●	●	●		●						●			●										●					
British	●				●		●									●			●						●							●		
Canadian																	●	●			●	●							●	●				
Environmental		●		●				●		●	●	●		●		●	●	●	●		●	●	●							●		●		
European	●				●					●			●			●	●	●	●		●			●		●		●		●			●	
Latin American		●		●						●						●			●		●	●								●	●			
Middle Eastern					●					●			●			●	●																	
Ancient				●	●	●	●			●			●				●			●		●					●							
Classical				●	●		●			●			●				●			●		●		●			●							
Modern			●		●	●	●			●			●				●	●	●		●					●						●	●	
World																	●																	
Law	●				●	●	●					●		●		●			●	●							●			●		●		
Language	●	●			●	●	●						●				●			●				●			●						●	
Linguistics	●	●			●	●							●				●		●	●			●				●						●	
Speech																							●											
Latin American Studies				●						●							●	●												●	●	●	●	●
Library Science				●		●										●																		

	Gallaudet	Georgetown	Georgia	Getty	Harvard	Hawaii	Hong Kong	Illinois	IMF	Indiana	Iowa	Island	Johns Hopkins	Kansas	Kent State	Kentucky	Leuven	Lincoln	Louisiana	McGill-Queen's	Manitoba	Marquette	Massachusetts	MIT	Medieval Institute	Mercer	Michigan	Michigan State	Minnesota Hist.	Minnesota	Mississippi	Missouri	MLA	MOMA
Literature	•	•		•	•	•	•			•	•		•		•					•	•			•		•	•	•	•	•	•	•	•	
Literary Criticism		•		•	•	•	•			•			•		•		•			•	•					•	•	•		•	•	•	•	
Literary History		•		•		•	•			•			•		•		•			•				•		•	•	•		•	•	•	•	
African										•							•													•	•	•	•	
African American		•		•						•	•		•						•				•				•	•		•	•	•	•	
American		•		•				•		•	•		•	•			•		•				•			•	•	•	•	•	•	•	•	
Asian				•	•	•	•			•							•										•			•			•	
British				•		•				•							•	•	•				•			•		•		•	•	•	•	
Canadian																				•	•									•	•	•	•	
Classical			•	•						•							•			•							•			•			•	
Eastern																	•			•										•			•	
European			•														•			•							•			•		•	•	
Medieval			•	•													•			•			•			•				•			•	
Renaissance			•	•													•			•			•	•						•			•	
Modern		•		•	•					•			•		•		•	•		•							•			•	•	•	•	
Contemporary	•	•		•	•					•			•		•		•	•		•							•			•	•	•	•	
Mythology				•													•			•							•						•	
Translations	•			•	•	•		•	•	•							•			•						•				•		•	•	
Maritime Studies						•	•			•										•								•						
Mathematics										•			•				•			•														
Medicine		•		•		•				•			•				•			•							•							
Ethics		•		•		•				•			•				•			•							•							
History		•		•	•	•	•			•			•				•			•	•						•			•				
Medieval Studies			•	•													•			•		•		•			•			•			•	
Middle East Studies		•		•						•			•		•	•	•			•							•					•		
Military Studies		•		•	•	•	•	•		•			•	•	•	•	•		•	•				•				•		•	•	•	•	
Near Eastern Studies		•		•						•							•			•							•						•	
Performing Arts	•			•	•	•	•			•	•									•						•	•			•	•	•	•	
Dance				•			•			•										•						•				•				
Music				•			•			•										•						•					•			
Theory & Method				•			•			•							•			•							•			•				
Theatre				•	•					•	•				•					•						•	•							
Pacific Studies				•	•					•										•										•			•	
Philosophy		•		•	•	•	•			•									•			•	•	•					•	•		•		
Ethics		•		•	•	•													•			•	•	•	•				•	•		•		
History of Philosophy				•	•	•	•												•			•	•	•						•		•		
Photography	•		•	•		•													•			•	•	•		•		•		•	•	•		•
Poetry	•		•			•				•									•	•			•		•			•					•	
Political Science/Public Affairs		•	•		•	•	•			•			•	•	•	•	•	•	•	•	•			•			•	•	•	•	•	•	•	
Popular Culture			•	•	•	•	•	•		•	•			•	•	•				•							•	•	•	•	•	•	•	
Psychiatry	•			•									•				•			•														
Psychology		•		•	•					•			•				•			•		•					•				•			
Public Health		•		•		•				•			•				•			•							•				•			
Publishing																							•										•	
Regional Studies		•		•	•			•		•	•		•	•	•	•	•	•	•	•	•	•	•				•	•	•	•	•	•	•	
Religion		•		•	•	•	•	•		•			•				•	•		•		•			•		•	•		•	•			
Buddhism																																		
Christianity										•										•					•	•								
Islam										•										•														
Judaism										•																								
Science	•		•		•	•				•	•	•	•				•						•											
Biological Sciences		•		•	•	•				•	•	•	•				•			•			•											
Botany			•		•	•					•	•											•											
Genetics	•				•						•	•								•			•											
Earth Sciences					•	•	•			•	•	•					•						•											
Geology					•						•	•											•											
Physical Science					•	•				•	•						•						•											
Astronomy					•	•					•																							
History of Science					•	•		•		•	•	•					•						•	•						•		•		•
Slavic Studies					•					•							•			•										•				
Social Work	•					•	•										•			•										•				
Sociology	•		•		•	•	•			•							•			•										•				
Sports	•						•			•					•					•			•			•	•		•	•	•			
Urban Studies		•	•		•	•	•	•			•			•	•			•								•	•	•						
Veterinary Sciences																																		
Women's Studies	•		•		•	•		•		•	•		•	•			•			•	•				•			•	•	•	•	•	•	

13

	National Acad.	National Gallery	Naval	Nebraska	Nevada	New England	New Mexico	New York	North Carolina	North Texas	Northern Illinois	Northwestern	Notre Dame	Ohio	Oklahoma	Oregon State	Ottawa	Oxford	Pennsylvania	Penn State	Pittsburgh	PISA	Princeton	Puerto Rico	Purdue	RAND	RIT	Rochester	Rockefeller	Russell Sage	Rutgers	St. Josephs	Soc. Biblical Lit.	South Carolina
African Studies				●										●									●					●						
African American Studies	●		●	●		●		●					●		●			●	●	●	●							●		●	●			●
Agriculture	●		●							●					●			●		●				●	●	●								
American Indian Studies				●	●	●	●		●						●	●		●												●				
American Studies				●	●	●	●	●	●	●				●		●		●	●	●	●									●	●			●
Anthropology				●	●	●	●		●					●	●	●		●	●	●		●	●	●				●		●	●			
Cultural				●	●	●	●		●					●	●	●		●	●				●	●	●					●				
Physical				●		●												●					●											
Archaeology				●	●	●								●	●	●	●	●	●				●										●	●
Architecture		●	●	●	●	●		●						●		●		●	●	●	●		●		●	●	●	●		●		●		●
Asian Studies				●					●					●				●		●			●								●			
Asian-American Studies						●		●										●										●		●	●			
Bibliography & Reference			●	●									●		●	●			●	●			●	●	●					●				
Biography	●		●	●	●	●	●	●	●	●	●	●		●	●			●	●	●	●		●					●	●	●			●	●
Business	●			●	●	●		●	●	●	●							●	●				●	●	●	●	●							
Canadian Studies				●													●																	
Caribbean Studies				●			●	●				●						●			●		●											
Child Development	●																	●						●				●						
Classics				●					●					●		●		●	●				●	●	●									●
Communications/Media				●	●	●		●		●								●		●			●	●			●	●		●				
Computer Sciences	●																	●					●	●			●	●						
Creative Nonfiction				●	●	●		●	●		●	●				●		●		●														●
Criminology	●		●		●		●		●	●	●	●					●						●	●			●			●	●			
Demography	●																	●					●	●	●	●		●			●			
Economics	●																	●	●	●			●	●	●	●	●	●			●			
Education	●				●			●		●							●						●	●	●			●		●	●			
History						●	●			●													●	●										
Learning Disabilities																							●					●						
Theory & Method	●	●																					●	●	●	●							●	
Engineering	●	●										●						●					●		●									
Environment/Conservation	●			●	●	●	●		●	●				●	●	●		●		●			●	●	●	●				●				
ESL																		●																
Ethnic Studies				●	●	●	●	●	●	●	●		●		●	●		●		●			●					●		●	●			
European Studies				●	●						●		●		●			●		●	●		●		●			●						
Fiction	●			●		●		●	●	●	●	●		●	●	●							●											
Film Studies				●		●		●										●			●		●		●						●			
Folklore				●	●	●		●								●	●						●											
Food Studies	●					●		●					●																					
Gay and Lesbian Studies				●		●		●												●			●								●			
Gender Studies	●			●	●	●	●	●	●		●							●		●	●	●	●					●		●	●			
Geography	●			●	●	●		●						●	●			●		●	●		●							●				
Gerontology	●																	●					●	●	●						●			
History				●	●	●	●	●	●	●	●	●		●	●		●	●	●	●	●	●	●		●			●		●	●			●
African															●			●										●						●
American				●	●	●	●	●	●	●	●	●		●	●	●		●	●	●			●					●		●	●			●
Asian				●		●					●				●			●					●											
British				●		●			●			●		●				●		●														
Canadian				●	●													●																
Environmental				●	●	●	●		●	●				●	●	●		●		●										●				
European				●		●	●		●		●		●					●	●	●	●		●		●			●			●			●
Latin American				●	●		●		●					●	●			●	●	●				●										
Middle Eastern				●			●		●	●					●			●					●										●	
Ancient									●				●					●	●				●		●								●	
Classical				●					●				●		●			●	●				●	●	●								●	
Modern				●		●	●	●	●	●			●	●				●		●			●	●							●			●
World																		●				●												
Law	●				●	●	●	●				●	●		●			●					●	●	●			●			●			
Language				●	●				●		●			●				●		●	●		●								●		●	●
Linguistics				●					●		●	●					●	●					●								●			●
Speech											●																							●
Latin American Studies				●			●	●		●				●	●			●		●	●				●			●			●			
Library Science																									●									

14

	National Acad.	National Gallery	Naval	Nebraska	Nevada	New England	New Mexico	New York	North Carolina	North Texas	Northern Illinois	Northwestern	Notre Dame	Ohio	Oklahoma	Oregon State	Ottawa	Oxford	Pennsylvania	Penn State	Pittsburgh	PISA	Princeton	Puerto Rico	Purdue	RAND	RIT	Rochester	Rockefeller	Russell Sage	Rutgers	St. Josephs	Soc. Biblical Lit.	South Carolina
Literature			●	●	●	●	●		●		●	●	●	●		●	●		●	●			●	●	●						●			●
Literary Criticism			●	●	●	●	●				●	●	●	●					●	●		●	●	●	●	●					●		●	●
Literary History			●	●	●	●			●			●	●		●	●			●	●	●		●	●	●						●			●
African												●	●						●		●		●					●						●
African American						●			●			●	●						●				●					●			●			●
American			●	●	●	●	●		●		●	●	●	●	●	●			●	●			●					●			●			●
Asian									●										●				●											
British			●								●	●							●	●			●											●
Canadian																	●																	
Classical							●				●	●		●		●			●	●			●								●			
Eastern																			●				●											
European			●									●							●	●			●	●										●
Medieval												●	●						●	●	●		●											
Renaissance						●			●			●	●						●				●											
Modern						●			●			●							●				●	●										●
Contemporary			●	●	●	●	●		●	●		●				●			●				●	●	●									●
Mythology						●								●	●	●			●				●											
Translations			●	●		●	●			●	●			●		●	●		●	●			●	●							●			●
Maritime Studies	●	●		●		●			●		●					●			●				●		●			●						●
Mathematics	●			●		●													●				●	●	●									
Medicine	●			●	●	●			●						●				●				●					●		●				
Ethics	●			●	●	●			●				●						●				●					●	●					
History				●	●	●			●										●		●							●	●		●			
Medieval Studies												●	●						●	●	●		●	●										
Middle East Studies						●			●				●						●				●		●						●			
Military Studies	●		●	●			●	●	●	●				●	●				●				●		●									●
Near Eastern Studies									●										●	●	●		●								●			
Performing Arts				●			●		●		●		●						●					●	●	●								
Dance													●						●															
Music				●			●	●	●	●									●				●	●	●			●						
Theory & Method				●				●		●		●							●				●					●						
Theatre									●	●									●															
Pacific Studies									●			●		●		●			●				●											
Philosophy				●					●	●	●	●	●				●	●	●	●	●		●	●	●	●		●	●	●	●			
Ethics				●					●	●	●		●					●	●		●		●	●	●			●	●					
History of Philosophy									●	●	●							●		●			●					●						
Photography		●		●			●	●		●							●						●	●										●
Poetry					●				●	●	●	●	●	●									●											●
Political Science/Public Affairs	●			●	●		●	●	●	●		●		●	●	●	●	●	●	●	●		●	●	●	●	●		●		●			
Popular Culture				●	●	●	●	●				●							●				●							●				
Psychiatry	●																		●				●											
Psychology	●						●			●									●				●		●					●				
Public Health	●			●	●	●		●								●	●			●	●		●	●	●	●		●			●	●	●	
Publishing						●								●																				
Regional Studies				●	●	●	●	●	●	●	●	●		●	●	●		●	●	●	●		●	●	●	●	●		●		●	●		●
Religion				●	●	●	●		●			●		●		●		●	●	●	●		●	●			●				●	●	●	●
Buddhism									●																									
Christianity									●		●		●																				●	
Islam									●																									
Judaism									●																							●		
Science	●		●	●	●	●			●					●	●			●					●	●	●	●	●			●				●
Biological Sciences	●			●	●	●			●					●	●			●					●	●	●					●		●		●
Botany	●			●		●			●						●			●					●	●	●						●			
Genetics	●																	●					●	●						●				
Earth Sciences	●			●	●	●									●			●					●	●			●							
Geology	●			●	●	●									●			●					●	●										
Physical Science	●			●	●	●												●					●	●	●		●							
Astronomy	●					●												●					●	●										
History of Science	●		●			●			●				●			●			●				●					●	●		●			
Slavic Studies									●	●		●						●		●		●	●						●					
Social Work	●				●													●				●	●	●	●		●			●				●
Sociology	●			●	●		●	●										●		●	●	●	●		●					●	●			
Sports				●			●		●		●																							
Urban Studies	●			●	●		●	●								●			●	●			●	●	●		●			●	●			
Veterinary Sciences	●																						●				●							
Women's Studies	●		●	●	●	●	●	●	●		●			●	●	●	●	●	●	●	●		●		●			●		●	●	●		●

	Southern Illinois	S. Methodist	Stanford	SUNY	Syracuse	Teachers	Temple	Tennessee	Texas	Texas A&M	Texas Christian	Texas Tech	Tokyo	Toronto	United Nations	U.S. Inst. Peace	Upjohn	Utah	Utah State	Vanderbilt	Virginia	Washington	Wash. State	Wayne State	Wesleyan	West Indies	West Virgina	Wilfrid Laurier	Wisconsin	Woodrow Wilson	Yale
African Studies	●												●		●	●					●						●		●	●	●
African American Studies	●		●	●	●	●	●	●	●		●	●								●	●	●	●	●	●	●					●
Agriculture									●				●		●								●						●		
American Indian Studies			●	●	●			●	●	●	●	●		●				●	●		●	●	●								●
American Studies	●		●	●	●		●	●	●		●	●	●						●	●	●	●		●		●		●	●	●	●
Anthropology			●	●	●		●	●	●	●			●	●				●		●	●		●		●		●		●		●
Cultural			●	●			●		●				●	●				●		●	●	●	●	●	●		●		●		●
Physical									●				●	●				●			●						●				●
Archaeology							●	●	●				●	●				●		●	●		●				●				●
Architecture							●	●	●	●	●		●	●						●	●	●		●							●
Art & Art History			●		●		●		●				●	●						●	●	●	●				●	●			●
Asian Studies			●	●			●				●	●	●	●	●	●					●							●	●	●	●
Asian American Studies			●	●		●	●						●	●							●										●
Bibliography & Reference	●												●	●						●		●				●					●
Biography			●	●			●	●	●		●	●	●	●				●		●	●	●		●				●	●		●
Business			●										●	●	●												●		●		
Canadian Studies													●	●						●		●	●	●			●		●		
Caribbean Studies							●						●							●	●					●					●
Child Development					●								●	●																	●
Classics	●							●					●	●													●	●	●		●
Communications/Media	●			●		●		●					●	●									●				●		●		●
Computer Sciences													●																		●
Creative Nonfiction	●	●		●				●			●	●									●	●					●				●
Criminology	●		●				●						●								●										●
Demography													●													●					
Economics			●						●				●	●	●	●	●									●			●	●	●
Education			●		●	●		●					●	●		●		●	●		●					●	●				
History			●		●	●							●	●				●			●					●					
Learning Disabilities					●									●																	
Theory & Method			●		●	●			●				●	●				●								●					
Engineering													●																		
Environment/Conservation			●	●		●	●	●	●	●	●	●	●	●	●			●	●	●	●	●	●	●		●		●	●	●	●
ESL				●																											●
Ethnic Studies			●	●	●		●		●	●		●	●	●		●		●	●	●	●	●	●			●				●	●
European Studies				●				●				●	●								●								●	●	●
Fiction	●	●							●	●	●																●	●	●		
Film Studies	●			●		●		●					●										●	●			●	●	●		
Folklore				●			●	●	●	●	●		●					●	●					●	●		●				
Food Studies								●					●																		
Gay and Lesbian Studies	●		●		●								●							●									●		
Gender Studies	●		●	●	●		●	●	●				●	●	●	●			●	●		●	●			●		●			●
Geography				●		●		●	●				●	●	●			●			●					●		●	●	●	●
Gerontology	●												●	●						●											
History			●	●	●		●	●	●	●	●	●	●	●			●		●		●	●	●	●	●	●	●		●	●	●
African	●												●			●					●					●			●	●	●
American	●		●	●	●		●	●	●	●	●	●	●	●			●		●	●	●	●	●	●			●		●	●	●
Asian			●	●							●	●	●	●		●						●							●	●	●
British			●								●	●	●	●		●										●			●	●	●
Canadian													●								●	●	●	●			●		●		
Environmental			●	●			●	●			●	●	●	●		●		●		●	●	●	●	●					●	●	●
European			●	●							●	●	●	●		●					●		●						●	●	●
Latin American			●	●			●		●			●	●	●		●				●						●			●	●	●
Middle Eastern			●		●		●					●	●	●		●													●	●	●
Ancient							●						●	●																	●
Classical	●						●						●	●														●	●		●
Modern			●		●		●					●	●	●		●												●	●	●	●
World													●																		
Law	●		●				●				●	●	●	●					●	●						●	●	●		●	●
Language	●						●						●					●						●					●		●
Linguistics													●					●						●		●					●
Speech													●											●							
Latin American Studies			●	●			●		●		●	●	●	●	●	●			●							●			●	●	●
Library Science													●																		●

16

	Southern Illinois	S. Methodist	Stanford	SUNY	Syracuse	Teachers	Temple	Tennessee	Texas	Texas A&M	Texas Christian	Texas Tech	Tokyo	Toronto	United Nations	U.S. Inst. Peace	Upjohn	Utah	Utah State	Vanderbilt	Virginia	Washington	Wash. State	Wayne State	Wesleyan	West Indies	West Virginia	Wilfrid Laurier	Wisconsin	Woodrow Wilson	Yale
Literature	•		•	•			•	•	•	•	•	•	•	•				•		•	•		•	•	•	•	•		•		•
Literary Criticism		•		•			•				•		•	•						•	•	•				•	•		•	•	•
Literary History			•				•		•	•	•	•	•	•						•	•	•							•		•
African														•						•		•									•
African American				•										•						•	•				•	•	•	•			•
American	•		•	•	•		•	•	•	•	•	•	•	•						•	•										•
Asian			•	•							•	•	•							•			•								•
British			•								•		•							•	•										•
Canadian														•											•				•		•
Classical								•						•																•	•
Eastern				•										•																	•
European			•	•							•			•						•	•										•
Medieval														•														•			•
Renaissance														•																	•
Modern	•		•	•			•	•			•			•						•	•								•		•
Contemporary	•		•	•			•	•						•						•									•		•
Mythology				•				•						•				•	•						•				•		•
Translations			•	•				•			•	•		•										•	•	•			•		•
Maritime Studies								•					•	•	•									•	•						•
Mathematics		•												•						•									•		•
Medicine														•	•					•											•
Ethics			•				•							•	•					•							•		•		•
History				•										•	•					•							•		•		•
Medieval Studies														•	•					•								•			•
Middle East Studies			•	•	•			•						•	•	•	•		•										•	•	•
Military Studies	•		•				•	•	•	•	•			•	•	•													•	•	•
Near Eastern Studies			•	•	•			•						•	•	•	•												•	•	•
Performing Arts	•				•									•											•				•		•
Dance																									•				•	•	•
Music				•	•			•												•					•			•	•		•
Theory & Method	•	•			•								•																•		•
Theatre								•						•																	•
Pacific Studies		•												•	•	•	•						•	•						•	•
Philosophy	•		•	•	•									•	•											•			•		•
Ethics		•	•	•	•									•	•	•						•							•		•
History of Philosophy				•	•							•	•	•																	•
Photography							•		•	•	•									•		•						•	•		•
Poetry	•				•									•	•			•	•					•	•			•	•	•	•
Political Science/Public Affairs		•	•	•	•		•		•	•			•	•	•	•		•	•	•	•		•			•		•	•	•	•
Popular Culture	•			•			•							•					•	•				•	•			•	•	•	•
Psychiatry				•										•	•					•								•			•
Psychology				•	•									•	•					•							•		•		•
Public Health				•										•	•	•		•		•									•		•
Publishing		•												•	•																•
Regional Studies	•	•	•	•	•		•	•	•	•	•	•	•	•	•	•	•	•	•	•	•	•	•	•	•		•	•	•	•	•
Religion		•	•	•			•	•	•				•	•	•	•	•		•		•			•			•		•	•	•
Buddhism				•																											
Christianity				•																											
Islam				•												•															
Judaism				•								•												•							
Science								•					•	•	•	•		•				•	•								•
Biological Sciences								•					•	•	•	•						•					•		•		•
Botany	•			•			•	•	•				•	•								•									•
Genetics													•																		•
Earth Sciences				•			•	•					•	•		•		•				•									•
Geology													•	•		•		•													•
Physical Science													•																		•
Astronomy													•																		•
History of Science													•	•								•	•	•			•				•
Slavic Studies													•	•															•	•	•
Social Work													•	•		•		•									•				•
Sociology		•		•	•		•						•	•		•		•		•						•	•		•	•	•
Sports		•		•			•		•		•																•	•			•
Urban Studies				•	•		•						•	•	•		•			•	•			•					•		•
Veterinary Sciences													•																•		
Women's Studies	•		•	•	•		•	•	•		•	•	•	•	•	•	•	•		•				•	•	•	•		•	•	•

17

PRESSES PUBLISHING JOURNALS

University presses have always been associated with publishing books of merit and distinction. This remains as true today as in the past, but less well appreciated is the extent to which university presses are active in publishing scholarly journals.

Journals form a major part of the publishing program of many presses, and more than half of the association's members produce at least one periodical. University presses publish several hundred scholarly periodicals, including many of the most distinguished in their respective fields.

Each individual press listing also gives the number of journals, if any, that a press publishes and usually lists the titles of journals under the press's editorial program. Many journals are available in both print and electronic versions. For information concerning a specific periodical, readers are advised to consult a copy of the publication before communicating with the press concerned.

The following AAUP member presses publish journals.

> University of Akron Press
> The University of Alabama Press
> American Historical Association
> American Psychiatric Press, Inc.
> The American School of Classical Studies at Athens
> The American University in Cairo Press
> Amsterdam University Press
> The University of Arkansas Press
> Athabasca University Press
> Brookings Institution Press
> University of Calgary Press
> University of California Press
> Cambridge University Press
> The Catholic University of America Press
> The University of Chicago Press
> The Chinese University Press
> Cork University Press
> Duke University Press
> Fordham University Press
> Gallaudet University Press
> Georgetown University Press
> University of Hawai'i Press
> University of Illinois Press
> Indiana University Press
> IMF Publications
> The Johns Hopkins University Press
> The Kent State University Press
> Leuven University Press

Lincoln Institute of Land Policy
Marquette University Press
The MIT Press
Medieval Institute Publications
Michigan State University Press
Minnesota Historical Society Press
University of Minnesota Press
Modern Language Association of America
Naval Institute Press
University of Nebraska Press
The University of North Carolina Press
University of North Texas Press
Northwestern University Press
University of Ottawa Press
Oxford University Press
University of Pennsylvania Press
Pennsylvania State University Press
Pisa University Press
University of Puerto Rico Press
Purdue University Press
RAND Corporation
The Rockefeller University Press
St. Joseph's University Press
Society of Biblical Literature
State University of New York Press
University of Texas Press
Texas Tech University Press
University of Toronto Press, Inc.
Washington State University Press
Wayne State University Press
Wesleyan University Press
University of the West Indies Press
West Virginia University Press
Wilfrid Laurier University Press
The University of Wisconsin Press

DIRECTORY OF MEMBERS

This section includes a wealth of information on AAUP's member presses, including current street and mailing addresses, phone and fax numbers, and Website and e-mail addresses. Most presses also list their sales representatives/distributors for Canada, the UK, and Europe. (Addresses for these representatives are included on page 227)

Each entry contains important information describing that press's editorial program. This includes a list of disciplines published, special series, joint imprints, copublishing programs, and the names of journals published, if any.

Press staff are listed, wherever possible, by the following departments / order: director and administrative staff, acquisitions editorial, electronic publishing, manuscript editorial, design and production, marketing, journals, business, and information systems. In most cases the first person listed within a department is its head. Readers should note, however, that this method of organization is intended to promote ease of use, and is not always indicative of the lines of authority within an individual press.

Information on each press's membership status follows the staff listing. This includes date of press founding, type of membership (full, international, associate, or introductory), year admitted to AAUP, title output for 2011 and 2012 the number of journals published, and the total number of titles currently in print.

Abilene Christian University Press

1626 Campus Court
Abilene, Texas 79601

Phone: 325.674.2720
Fax: 325.674.6471

Orders:
Phone: 325.674.2720 or 877.816.4455
Email: orders@acupressbooks.com

Websites and Social Media:
Website: www.abilenechristianuniversitypress.com;
www.leafwoodpublishers.com; www.acupressbookclub.com
Facebook: Facebook.com/ACUPress
Twitter: ACUPress
YouTube: www.youtube.com/user/leafwoodpublishers

Staff

Director & Acquisitions Editor: C. Leonard Allen (325.674.2720; email:
  leonardallen1@cox.net)
Editorial Coordinator: Robyn Burwell (325.674.2720; email: robyn.burwell@acu.edu)
  Editorial Assistant: Mary Hardegree (325.674.2761; email: mary.hardegree@acu.edu)
Director of Sales & Operations: Duane Anderson (325.674.2720;
  email: duane.anderson@acu.edu)
Director of Trade Sales & Special Acquisitions: Gary Myers (325.674.2720;
  email: gary.myers@leafwoodpublishers.com)
Marketing Manager: Seth Shaver (325.674.4978; email: seth.shaver@acu.edu)
Publicist: Ryan Self (325.674.4976 email: ryan.self@acu.edu)
Sales Associate: Philip Dosa (email: phil.dosa@acu.edu)
Office Manager: Lettie Morrow (325.674.2720; email: lettie.morrow@acu.edu)

Full Member

Established: 1984

Title output 2011: 28
Titles currently in print: 456

Admitted to AAUP: 2008
(as introductory member)
Admitted to AAUP as full member: 2012
Title output 2012: 36

Editorial Program

Religion in American culture; biblical studies and Christian theology; Texas regional studies; history and theory of higher education (with an emphasis on faith-based education); international and multicultural studies; literary works.

Special series: Christianity and Literature; Faith-Based Higher Education; History and Theology of the Stone-Campbell Movement; Texas History and Culture

The University of Akron Press

120 E. Mill Street, Suite 415
Akron, OH 44308

Phone: 330.972.6953
Fax: 330.972.8364

Customer Service/Order Fulfillment:
Phone: 419. 281.1802
Toll-free: 800.247.6553
Fax: 419.281.6883
Email: orders@atlasbooks.com

Websites and Social Media:
Website: www.uakron.edu/uapress
Blog: uakronpress.wordpress.com
Facebook: www.facebook.com/UAkronPress
Twitter: uakronpress

Staff

Director & National Marketing: Thomas Bacher (330.972.6202; email: bacher@uakron.edu)
Editorial & Design: Amy Freels (330.972.5342; email: afreels@uakron.edu)
Production & Manufacturing: Carol Slatter (330.972.2795; email: slatter@uakron.edu)

Full Member

Established: 1988
Title output 2011: 15
Titles currently in print: 154

Admitted to AAUP: 1997
Title output 2012: 15
Journals published: 2

Editorial Program

Regional trade books, scholarly books, and poetry, with special interests in applied politics, business, multi-disciplinary studies, and regional culture and history. The Press distributes the publications of Principia Press and The University of Göttingen Press.

Journals: *The International Journal of Ethical Leadership*; *Journal of Economics and Politics*
Special series: Akron Series in Poetry; Akron Series in Poetics; Center for the History of Psychology Series; Critical Editions in Early American Literature; & Law: Legal Issues Across Disciplines; Ohio History and Culture; and Ohio Politics
Other imprints: Buchtel Books and Ringtaw Books

The University of Alabama Press

Street Address:
200 Hackberry Lane
Tuscaloosa, AL 35401

Phone: 205.348.5180
Fax: 205.348.9201
Email: (user I.D.)@uapress.ua.edu

Website and Social Media:
Website: www.uapress.ua.edu
Facebook: www.facebook.com/
 UniversityALPress
Twitter: univofalpress

UK/European Distributor:
Eurospan

Mailing Address:
Box 870380
Tuscaloosa, AL 35487-0380

Order Fulfillment:
The University of Alabama Press
Chicago Distribution Center
11030 South Langley Avenue
Chicago, IL 60628
Phone: 773.568.1550
Fax: 773.660.2235

Canadian Representative:
Scholarly Book Services

Staff

Director: Curtis L. Clark (205.348.1560; email: cclark)
  Assistant to the Director: Rubye Harrison (205.348.5180; email: rhharrison)
  Rights and Permissions Coordinator: Claire Lewis Evans (205.348.1561; email: cevans)
Acquisitions Editorial: Dan Waterman, Editor-in-Chief and Acquisitions Editor, Humanities
  (literature and criticism, rhetoric and communication, African American studies, public
  administration, theater, environmental studies) (205.348.5538; email: waterman)
  Senior Acquisitions Editor: Joseph Powell (archaeology, anthropology, ethnohistory, Native
  American studies) (205.348.1568; email: jpowell)
  Acquisitions Editors: Elizabeth Motherwell (natural history and the environment)
  (205.348.7108; email: emother); Donna Cox Baker (history) (205.348.7471; email:
  donna.baker@ua.edu)
Electronic Publishing: Claire Lewis Evans, Associate Editor for Digital and Electronic Pub-
  lishing (205.348.1561; email: cevans)
Manuscript Editorial: Crissie Johnson, Managing Editor (205.348.9708; email: cjohnson)
  Assistant Managing Editor: Joanna Jacobs (205.348.1563; email: jjacobs)
  Project Editor: Jon Berry (205.348.1565; email: jberry)
  Editorial Assistant: Carol Connell (205.348.5183; email: cconnell)
Design and Production: Rick Cook, Production Manager (205.348.1571; email: rcook)
  Designer: Michele Quinn (205.348.1570; email: mquinn)
Marketing: Shana Rivers, Marketing Manager (205.348.9534; email: srrivers)
  Publicist: TBA
  Marketing Coordinator: Latasha Watters (205.348.5181; email: lwatters)
Business: Rosalyn Carr, Business Manager (205.348.1567; email: rcarr)
  Accounting Specialist: Allie Harper (205.348.1564; email: aharper)

Full Member

Established: 1945
Title output 2011: 58
Titles currently in print: 1,600

Admitted to AAUP: 1964
Title output 2012: 52
Journals published: 3

Editorial Program

African American studies; American history; American literature and criticism; American religious history; American social and cultural history; anthropology; archaeology, American, Caribbean, southern and historical; creative non-fiction; ethnohistory; Judaic studies; Latin-American studies; linguistics, esp. dialectology; military history; Native American studies; natural history and environmental studies; public administration; regional studies; rhetoric and communication; southern history and culture; sports history; theatre. Submissions are not invited in poetry, fiction, or drama. The Press distributes for Samford University Press.
Journals: *Journal of Community Engagement and Scholarship*; *Theatre History Studies*; *Theatre Symposium*
Special series: Alabama: The Forge of History; American Writers Remembered; Atlantic Crossings; Caribbean Archaeology and Ethnohistory; Classics in Southeastern Archaeology; Contemporary American Indian Studies; Gosse Nature Guides; Judaic Studies; Library of Alabama Classics; Modern and Contemporary Poetics; The Modern South; Public Administration: Criticism and Creativity; Religion and American Culture; Rhetoric, Culture, and Social Critique; Seeing the Elephant; Studies in American Literary Realism and Naturalism
Imprints: Fiction Collective 2; Fire Ant Books

University of Alaska Press

Mailing Address:
PO Box 756240
Fairbanks, AK 99775-6240

Street Address:
794 University Avenue, Suite 220
Fairbanks, AK 99709

Phone: 888.252.6657; 907.474.5831
Fax: 907.474.5502

Orders Outside Alaska:
Chicago Distribution Center
11030 South Langley Avenue
Website and Social Media:
Website: www.uaf.edu/uapress
Facebook: www.facebook.com/pages/
  University-of-Alaska-Press/44832289241
Twitter: ualaskapress

Chicago, IL 60628-3892
Phone: 800.621.2736
Fax: 800.621.8476

Staff

Director: Joan Braddock (907.474.2776; email: jfbraddock@alaska.edu)
Assistant to the Director/Marketing Manager: Amy Simpson (907.474.5832; email: amy.
  simpson@alaska.edu)
Acquisitions Editor: James Engelhardt (907.474.6389; email: james.engelhardt@alaska.edu)
Production Editor: Sue Mitchell (907.474.6413; email: sue.mitchell@alaska.edu)
Marketing Assistant: Dawn Montano (907.474.6544; email: dawn.montano@alaska.edu)
Sales and Distribution Coordinator: Laura Walker (907.474.5345; email: laura.walker@
  alaska.edu)

Full Member

Established: 1967
Title output 2011: 17
Titles currently in print: 214

Admitted to AAUP: 1992
Title output 2012: 20

Editorial Program

The University of Alaska Press is recognized as the premier scholarly publisher of books relating to Alaska, the Pacific Rim, and circumpolar North. The Press publishes on topics that include history, politics, and literature; anthropology; Native American studies and art; science and natural history; energy and conservation; environmental studies; geography; biography and memoir; humanities and health; poetry and international poetry; photography; field guides; and children's literature. Submissions are invited in poetry, fiction, and literary nonfiction and should have a strong connection to Alaska or the circumpolar North.

The Press distributes publications for the following University of Alaska entities: UA Foundation; UA Museum of the North; Alaska Sea Grant College Program; Alaska Native Knowledge Network; and Alaska Native Language Center. The Press also serves as a distributor for various independent publishers.

Special series: Alaska Literary Series, Alaska Writer Laureate; Classic Reprint; Oral Biography; and Rasmuson Library Historical Translation

Special imprints: Snowy Owl (trade books)

The University of Alberta Press

Ring House 2
Edmonton, AB T6G 2E1
Canada

Phone: 780.492.3662
Fax: 780.492.0719
Email: (user I.D.)@ualberta.ca

Website and Social Media:
Website: www.uap.ualberta.ca
Blog: holeinthebucket.wordpress.com
Facebook: www.facebook.com/pages/
   University-of-Alberta-Press-UAP/
   18764314500
Twitter: UAlbertaPress

UK/European Distributor:
Gazelle Academic

Canadian Distributor:
GTW Limited
34 Armstrong Avenue
Georgetown ON L7G 4R9 Canada
Phone: 905.873.9781
Fax: 905.873.6170
Email: orders@gtwcanada.com

US Distributor:
Wayne State University Press
The Leonard N. Simons Building
4809 Woodward Avenue
Detroit MI 48201-1309
Phone: 800.978.7323
313.577.6120
Fax: 313.577.6131
Email: bookorders@wayne.edu

Staff

Director: Linda D. Cameron (780.492.0717; email: linda.cameron)
   Administrative Assistant: Sharon Wilson (780.492.3662; email: sharon.wilson)
Senior Editor (Acquisitions): Peter Midgley (780.492.7714; email: peter.midgley)
Editor (Production): Mary Lou Roy (780.492.9488; email: marylou.roy)
   Editorial Assistant: Duncan Turner (780.492.4945; email: duncan.turner)
Design/Production: Alan Brownoff (780.492.8285; email: alan.brownoff)

Sales & Marketing Manager: Cathie Crooks (780.492.5820; email: cathie.crooks)
  Sales/Marketing Assistant: Monika Igali (780.492.7493; email: monika.igali)

Full Member

Established: 1969
Title output 2011: 24
Titles currently in print: 250

Admitted to AAUP: 1983
Title output 2012: 25

Editorial Program

The University of Alberta Press (UAP) publishes in the areas of Canadian biography, history, literature, natural history, regional interest, travel narratives, and reference books.
Special series: Mountain Cairns—a series on the history and culture of the Canadian Rockies; Wayfarer—a literary travel series

American Historical Association

400 A Street, S.E.
Washington, DC 20003-3889

Phone: 202.544.2422
Fax: 202.544.8307
Email: aha@historians.org

Website and Social Media:
Website: www.historians.org
Blog: blog.historians.org
Facebook: www.facebook.com/AHAhistorians
Twitter: AHAhistorians

Staff

Executive Director: James R. Grossman (202.544.2422 ext. 100; email: jgrossman@historians.org)
Controller: Randy Norell (202.544.2422 ext.109; email: rnorell@historians.org)
Editor, American Historical Review: Robert A. Schneider (812.855.7609; email: raschnei@indiana.edu)
Deputy Director: Robert B. Townsend (202.544.2422 ext. 118; email: rtownsend@historians.org)
Internet Projects Coordinator: Vernon Horn (202.544.2422 ext. 122; email: vhorn@historians.org)
Editor, *Perspectives on History*: Pillarisetti Sudhir (202.544.2422 ext. 121; email: psudhir@historians.org)
Production Manager: Christian A. Hale (202.544.2422 ext. 133; email: chale@historians.org)
Publication Sales: Matt Burruss (202.544.2422 ext. 108; email: mburruss@historians.org)

Associate Member

Established: 1884
Title output 2011: 11
Titles currently in print: 102

Admitted to AAUP: 2005
Title output 2012: NR
Journals published: 2

Editorial Program

The AHA publishes a wide variety of periodical, annual, and other publications of service and interest to the historical profession and the general public. Primary publications are the journals, the *American Historical Review* (published by the Journals Division of the University of Chicago Press) and the monthly news magazine *Perspectives on History*. The Association's other major publication is the annual Directory of History Departments, Historical Organizations, and Historians. Beyond that, the AHA publishes a wide range of topical booklets on the practice of history and historical topics. On the Web, the Association publishes articles, directories, and documentary materials. The AHA also maintains a daily blog for those interested in the study of the past and the practice of history, and a wiki on archives for history researchers.

American Psychiatric Publishing

1000 Wilson Blvd., Suite 1825
Arlington, VA 22209

Phone: 703.907.7322
Fax: 703.907.1092
Email: appi@psych.org
Indiv: (user I.D.)@psych.org

Orders:
Phone: 800.368.5777; 703.907.7322
Fax: 703.907.1091

Website and Social Media:
Website: www.appi.org
Facebook: www.facebook.com/pages/American-Psychiatric-Publishing
Twitter: APP_Publishing

European Distributor:
NBN International

Canadian Representative:
Login Brothers Canada

Staff

Publisher: Rebecca D. Rinehart (703.907.7876; email: rrinehart)
    Executive Assistant: Bessie Jones (703.907.7892; email: bjones)
Editor-in-Chief: Robert E. Hales (703.907.7892)
    Editorial Director, Books: John McDuffie (703.907.7871; email: jmcduffie)
    Book Acquisitions Coordinator: Bessie Jones (703.907.7892; email: bjones)
e-Publishing Manager: Melissa Coates (703.907.7870; email: mcoates)
Managing Editor, Books: Greg Kuny (703.907.7872; email: gkuny)
Director of Production: Andrew Wilson (703.907.7882; email: awilson)
Assistant Director of Marketing: Christie Couture (703.907.7877; email: ccouture)
Editorial Director, Journals: Michael Roy (703.907.7894; email: mroy)
Director of Finance and Business Operations: Kathy Stein (703.907.7875; email: kstein)

Associate Member

Established: 1981

Title output 2011: 29

Titles currently in print: 745

Admitted to AAUP: 1993

Title output 2012: 21

Journals published: 6

Editorial Program

Clinical books and monographs in psychiatry and related fields; research monographs; medical textbooks; study guides; nonfiction trade books in mental health; annual review; and journals.

Journals: *Academic Psychiatry; American Journal of Psychiatry; FOCUS; Journal of Neuropsychiatry; Psychiatric News; Psychiatric Services*

Special series: Concise Guides, Clinical Manuals

Special imprints: American Psychiatric Association; Group for the Advancement of Psychiatry; American Psychopathological Association

Copublishing programs: The World Health Organization

The American School of Classical Studies at Athens

Publications Office:

6–8 Charlton Street

Princeton, NJ 08540-5232

Phone: 609.683.0800

Fax: 609.924-0578

Email: areinhard@ascsa.org

Website: www.ascsa.edu.gr/publications

Orders:

Phone: 800.791.9354

Fax: 860.945.9468

Email: queries@dbbconline.com

UK Representative:

Oxbow Books

Canadian Representative:

David Brown Book Company

Staff

Director of Publications: Andrew Reinhard (ext. 21; email: areinhard@ascsa.org)

Managing Editor: Carol A. Stein (ext. 16; email: castein@ascsa.org)

Editor of *Hesperia*: Tracey Cullen (ext. 22; email: tc@ascsa.org)

Editor of Monographs: Michael A. Fitzgerald (ext. 17; email: maf@ascsa.org)

Editor: Timothy D. Wardell (ext. 19; email: twardell@ascsa.org)

Production Manager: Sarah George Figueira (ext. 18; email: sgf@ascsa.org)

Print Designer and Website Managing Editor: Mary Jane Gavenda (ext. 20; email: mjgavenda@ascsa.org)

Associate Member

Established: 1881

Admitted to AAUP as Associate Member: 2012

Title output 2011: 8

Titles currently in print: 136

Admitted to AAUP: 2008

(as Introductory Member)

Title output 2012: 4

Journals published: 2

Editorial Program

All fields of Greek archaeology, art, epigraphy, history, materials science, ethnography, and literature, from earliest prehistoric times onward. A particular focus is on publishing the work of the American School of Classical Studies at Athens, a research and teaching institutions founded in 1881 and based in Athens, Greece.

Journals: *Hesperia, The New Griffon*
Special series: Agora Picture Books; Ancient Art and Architecture in Context; The Argive Heraion; The Athenian Agora; Corinth; Gennadeion Monographs; Hesperia Supplements; Isthmia; Lerna

The American University in Cairo Press

113 Kasr el Aini Street
PO Box 2511
Cairo, Egypt 11511

US Office:
420 Fifth Avenue
New York, NY 10018-2729

Phone: 202.2797.6926
Fax: 202.2794.1440
Email: aucpress@aucegypt.edu
Indiv: (user I.D.)@aucegypt.edu

Phone: 212.730.8800
Fax: 212.730.1600

Website and Social Media:
Website: www.aucpress.com
Facebook: www.facebook.com/pages/Cairo-Egypt/The-American-University-in-Cairo-Press-
    AUC-Press/26100067607

North American Distributor:
Oxford University Press
2001 Evans Road
Cary, NC 27513
Phone: 800.445.9714
Email: custserv.us@oup.com

UK and European Distributor:
Eurospan

Staff

Director: Nigel Fletcher-Jones (202.2797.6888; email: nigel)
    Assistant to the Director: Tawhida Sherif (202.2797.6926; email: tina)
Associate Director for Editorial Programs: Neil Hewison (202.2797.6892;
    email: rnh)
Senior Development Editor: Randi Danforth (202.2797.6642; email: randi)
Managing Editor: Nadia Naqib (202.2797.6887; email: nnaqib)
Production Manager: Miriam Fahmy (202.2797.6937; email: miriam)
Associate Director of Sales and Marketing: Trevor Naylor (202.2797.5759;
    email: trevornaylor)
    Sales Manager: Tahany el-Shammaa (202.2797.6985; email: tahanys)
    Promotion Manager: Nabila Akl (202.2797.6896; email: akl)
Contracts and Rights Manager: Yasmine Gado (202.2797.6820; email: yasmine.gado)
    Assistant Publishing Manager (New York City): Tarek El-Elaimy (212.730.8800; email:
    telaimy)

International Member

Established: 1960	Admitted to AAUP: 1986
Title output 2011: 100	Title output 2012: 70
Titles currently in print: 1,500	Journals published: 2

Editorial Program

The Press is recognized as the leading English-language publisher in the Middle East, and publishes a wide range of scholarly monographs, texts and reference works, and general interest books on ancient and modern Egypt and the Middle East, as well as Arabic literature in English translation, most notably the works of Egyptian Nobel laureate Naguib Mahfouz.

Journals: *Alif: Journal of Comparative Poetics; Cairo Papers in Social Science.*

Copublishing programs: Numerous copublishing programs with US, UK, and European universities and trade publishers

Amsterdam University Press

Herengracht 221
1016 BG Amsterdam
The Netherlands

Phone: +31.20.4200050
Fax: +31.20.4203214
Email: info@aup.nl
Indiv: (user I.D.)@aup.nl

Website and Social Media:
Website: www.aup.nl
Facebook: www.facebook.com/
 AmsterdamUPress
Twitter: AmsterdamUPress

US and Canadian Sales Representative:
University of Chicago Press
Phone: 800.621.2736

UK Representative:
Manchester University Press

European Representative:
Durnell Marketing

Australia/New Zealand Rep
Footprint Books Pty Ltd

Staff

Director: Jan-Peter Wissink (email: wissink)
Finance and Administration: Judith van Jaarsveld (email: jvanJaarsveld@holding.uva.nl)
 Daniela Pinnone (email: d.pinnone); Yong Cheung (email: y.h.cheung)
Senior Acquisitions Editors: Maaike Groot (humanities) (email: m.groot); Jeroen Sondervan (humanities) (email: j.sondervan)
Acquisition Editor: Saskia Gieling (social sciences) (email: s.gieling)
Assistant Acquisition Editor: Sanne Sauer (email: s.sauer)
Electronic Publishing: Jeroen Sondervan, Publisher Digital Products (email: j.sondervan)
 Project Manager Digital Publications: Ronald Snijder (email: r.snijder)
Manuscript Editorial: Chantal Nicolaes, Chief Editor (email: c.nicolaes)
 Editors: Jaap Wagenaar (social sciences) (email: j.wagenaar); Rob Wadman (email: r.wadman)
Head of Production: Rob Wadman, Production Manager (email: r.wadman)

Production: Paul Penman (email: p.l.penman)
Head of International Sales and Marketing: Magdalena Hernas (email: m.hernas)
Head of Sales and Marketing: Jelle Bloem (email: j.bloem)
Orders: Michiel van der Drift (email: m.vander.drift)
Marketing & PR: Ebisse Rouw (email: e.rouw)
Office Managers: Atie Vogelenzang & Jacqueline Wippo (email: info@aup.nl)

International Member

Established: 1992

Admitted to AAUP: 2000

Title output 2011: 263

Title output 2012: 140

Titles currently in print: 1,078

Journals published: 10

Editorial Program

Scholarly and some trade titles (English and Dutch language) in anthropology; archaeol-ogy; art and art history; Asian studies; classical studies; cultural studies; economics; film and television studies; gender studies; history; Judaica; language and linguistics; law; literature; medieval and Renaissance studies; music; philosophy; political science; social sciences; theater and performing arts; regional titles. Textbooks for universities and higher education. AUP distributes for the University of Leiden (Leiden University Press).

Journals: *Academische Boekengids (Academic Book Review); Mens & Maatschappij (People and Society); Tijdschrift voor Muziektheorie (Dutch Journal of Music Theory); Journal of Archeology in the Low Countries (Jalc); Internationale Neerlandistiek (International Dutch Studies); Journal of Dutch Literature; Quotidian (Dutch Journal for the Study of Everyday Life); Tijdschrift voor Genderstudies (Journal for Gender Studies); Tijdschrift voor Zeegeschiedenis (Journal of Maritime History); Tijdschrift voor Sociale en Economische Geschiedenis (Journal of Social and Economic History)*

English series: American Studies; Amsterdam Archaeological Studies; Asia Studies; Care & Welfare; Changing Welfare States; European Film Studies - The Key Debates; Film Cul-ture in Transition; Islam & Society; Landscape & Heritage Research; Law, Governance and Development; MediaMatters; Studies In Language and Literature; German series: Justiz und NS-Verbrechen (A collection of postwar German trial judgments concerning Nazi crimes of a homicidal nature committed during World War II)

Imprints: AUP, AUP popular science, Vossiuspers UvA, Pallas Publications

Copublications: Princeton University Press (USA); University of California Press (USA); MIT Press (USA); Thames & Hudson (UK); Brandeis University Press (USA); Actes Sud (France); Lannoo Uitgeverij (Belgium); Uitgeverij Davidsfonds (Belgium); Mercatorfonds (Belgium)

Initiator of OAPEN (www.oapen.org): Open Access Publishing in the European Network, together with Manchester University Press (United Kingdom), Göttingen University Press (Germany), Tusculanum Press (Kopenhagen) (Denmark), Lyon University Press (France) and Florence University Press (Italy), Leiden University Press (Netherlands), Leiden University (Netherlands), University of Amsterdam (Netherlands)

The University of Arizona Press

1510 E. University, 5th Floor
P.O Box 210055
Tucson, AZ 85721-0055

Phone: 520.621.1441
Fax: 520.621.8899
Email: uapress@uapress.arizona.edu
Indiv: (user I.D.)@uapress.arizona.edu

Website and Social Media:
Website: www.uapress.arizona.edu
Facebook: www.facebook.com/AZpress
Twitter: AZpress

Orders:
Chicago Distribution Center
Phone: 800.621.2736
Email: orders@press.uchicago.edu

Canadian Representative:
University of British Columbia Press

European Representative:
Eurospan

Staff

Director: Kathryn M. Conrad (520.621.1441; email: kconrad)
  Assistant to the Director/Permissions: Julia Balestracci (520.621.3911; email: julia)
  Mellon Initiative Program Coordinator: Natasha Varner (520.626.8484; email: nvarner)
Editor-in-Chief: Allyson Carter (anthropology, archaeology, ecology, natural history, Native American studies, Latin American studies, environmental science, astronomy and space sciences, geography, regional) (520.621.3186; email: acarter)
  Acquiring Editor: Kristen Buckles (Native American literature and studies, Latin American studies, Border studies, Chicano/Latino studies and literature, environmental and western history, regional) (520.621.7921; email: kbuckles)
  Editorial Assistant: Scott DeHerrera (520.621.5919; email: scott)
Editing, Design, and Production Manager: TBA (520.621.5916)
  Production Editor: Nancy Arora (520.621.5915; email: narora)
  Production Coordinator: Miriam Fisher (520.621.7916; email: mfisher)
  Book Designer: Leigh McDonald (520.621.5824; email: lmcdonald)
Sales and Marketing Manager: Kathryn Conrad (520.621.1441; email: kconrad)
  Publicity Manager: Holly Schaffer (520.621.3920; email: hollys)
  Advertising, Direct Mail, and Electronic Marketing Manager: Abby Mogollon (520.621.8656; email: amogollon)
  Exhibits/Assistant Sales Manager : Lela Scott MacNeil (520.621.4913; email: lela)
Senior Accountant: Sarah Trotta (520.621.0064; email: trottas)
  Accounts Payable: Melissa Sotomayor (520.626.3041; email: msotomayor)
Information Systems Manager: Joshua Harrison (520.621.5815; email: josh)

Full Member

Established: 1959
Title output 2011: 60
Titles currently in print: 1,047

Admitted to AAUP: 1962
Title output 2012: 71

Editorial Program

Specialties strongly identified with the universities in the state and other significant nonfiction of regional and national interest. Especially strong fields include the American West; anthropology and archaeology; Chicano/Latino studies and literature; ecology and environmental sciences; environmental studies and literature; Latin American studies; Native American studies and literature; space sciences; western and environmental history.

The Press also distributes titles from Ironwood Press; the Arizona State Museum; Statistical Research, Inc.; SWCA, Inc.; Northern Arizona University Bilby Research Center; Center for Desert Archaeology; Center for Sustainable Environments; Crow Canyon Archaeological Center; The University of Arizona Critical Languages Program; U.S. Department of Interior Bureau of Reclamation; Grand Canyon Association; and Oregon State University Press.

Special series: Amerind Studies in Archaeology; Anthropological Papers of the University of Arizona; The Archaeology of Colonialism in Native North America; Arizona Sonora Desert Museum Studies In Natural History; Camino del Sol; Critical Issues in Indigenous Studies; First Peoples; La Frontera: People and Their Environments in the U.S.-Mexico Border; Latin American Landscapes; The Mexican American Experience; Modern American West; Native Peoples of the Americas; Society, Environment, and Place; Southwest Center Series; Space Science; Sun Tracks; Women's Western Voices

The University of Arkansas Press

McIlroy House
105 North McIlroy Avenue
Fayetteville, AR 72701-1201

Phone: 800.626.0090; 479.575.3246
Fax: 479.575.6044
Email: uapress@uark.edu
Indiv: (user I.D.)@uark.edu

Website and Social Media:
Website: www.uapress.com
Blog: uapress.blogspot.com
Facebook: www.facebook.com/UARKPRESS
Twitter: uarkpress

Customer Service/Orders:
1580 West Mitchell Street
Fayetteville, AR 72701
Phone: 800.626.0090
Fax: 479.575.5538

Canadian Representative:
Scholarly Book Services

UK/European Representative:
Eurospan

Staff
Director and Editor: Lawrence J. Malley (479.575.3096; email: lmalley)
Acquisitions Editor: Julie Watkins (479.575.7242; email: jewatki)
Manuscript Editorial, Design, and Production: Brian King, Assistant Director and Director of Editorial, Design, and Production (479.575.6780; email: brking)
  Assistant Director of Editorial, Design, and Production: David-Scott Cunningham (479.575.5767; email: dscunni)
Marketing: Melissa King, Director of Marketing and Sales (479.575.6657; email: mak001)
  Assistant Marketing Manager: Charlie Shields (479.575.7258; email: cmoss)
Business: Mike W. Bieker, Assistant Director and Business Manager (479.575.3859; email: mbieker)
  Assistant Business Manager: Sam Ridge (479.575.3459; email: sridge)
  Ordering & Customer Service: Kathleen Z. Willis (479.575.3634; email: kwillis)
UAP Distribution Services:
Distribution Services Manager: Mike Bieker (479.575.3859; email: mbieker)

Distribution Services Operations Manager: Sam Ridge (479.575.3459; email: sridge)

Full Member

Established: 1980   Admitted to AAUP: 1984
Title output 2011: 16   Title output 2012: 15
Titles currently in print: 605   Journals published: 1

Editorial Program

African American history; civil rights studies; Civil War studies; cultural studies; history; Middle East studies; regional studies; southern history; and women's studies. Submissions are not invited in general fiction, textbooks, or children's books. The Press also publishes the winner and three finalists of the Miller Williams Arkanas Poetry Prize competition.
Journal: *Philosophical Topics*
Special series: Arkansas Classics; The Carter Collection; The Civil War in the West; The Histories of Arkansas; Portraits of Conflict; Arkansas Poetry; The William Gilmore Simms Collection; World of Voices

Athabasca University Press

Peace Hills Trust Tower
1200, 10011 – 109 Street
Edmonton, AB T5J 3S8 Canada

Phone: 780.497.3412
Fax: 780.421.3298
Email: aupress@athabascau.ca

Website and Social Media:
Website: www.aupress.ca
Facebook: www.facebook.com/AUPress1
Twitter: au_press

European Distributor:
Eurospan

Canadian Orders:
University of British Columbia Press
Phone: 604.822.5959; 877.377.9378
Fax: 604.822.6083; 800.668.0821
UTP Distribution:
Phone: 800.565.9523; 416.667.7791
Fax: 800.221.9985; 416.667.7832
Email: utpbooks@utpress.utoronto.ca

US Orders:
University of Washington Press
c/o Hopkins Fulfillment Service
Phone: 800.537.5487
Fax: 410.516.6998
Email: hfscustserv@press.jhu.edu

Staff

Director: Walter Hildebrandt (780.421.2544; email: walterh@athabascau.ca)
   Coordinator: Katherine Kuzyk (780.497.3412; email: kkuzyk@athabascau.ca)
Senior Editor: Pamela Holway (780.428.7278; email: pholway@athabascau.ca)
Journals and Digital Coordinator: Kathy Killoh (780.421.2528; email: kathyk@athabascau.ca)
Digital Design Technician: Sergiy Kozakov (780.421.5846; email: sergiyk@athabascau.ca)
IT Systems Administrator/Coordinator: Shubhash Wasti (780.421.2526; email: shubhash@athabascau.ca)
Fulfillment Administrator: Linda Kadis (780.421.5062; email: lkadis@athabascau.ca)

Full Member

Established: 2007

Title output 2011: 16
Titles currently in print: 48

Admitted to AAUP: 2008 (as introductory member)
Admitted to AAUP as full member: 2011
Title output 2012: NR
Journals published: 8

Editorial Program

Our geographical focus is on Canada, the North American West, and the Circumpolar North. One of our mandates is to publish innovative and experimental works (in both fiction and non-fiction) that challenge established canons, subjects, and formats. We plan to develop series that contribute to the scholarship of established and new disciplines. As we are dedicated to making AU Press publications accessible to a broad readership through open access technologies, we cultivate the areas of open, distance, and e-learning. We promote forms such as diary, memoir, and oral history. AU Press also publishes websites (under its imprint) with content that has scholarly parameters and standards, especially grey literature on distance learning; and primary sources in labour studies, Métis and Aboriginal Studies, gender studies, and the environment.

Journals: *The Canadian Journal of Learning and Technology (CJLT)*; *Interdisciplinary Environmental Review*; *International Review of Research in Open and Distance Learning (IRRODL)*; *The Journal of Distance Education*; *Journal of Research Practice (JRP)*; *Labour/Le Travail*; *Oral History Forum d'histoire orale*; *The Trumpeter*

Web-based Publications: Aurora; Canadian Theatre Encyclopedia

Special series: Canadian Plays; Cultural Dialectics; Global Peace Studies; Historic Sites and Public Heritage; Honouring our Ancestors; Issues in Distance Education; Labour Across Borders; Mingling Voices; Our Lives: Diary, Memoir, and Letters; Print Cultures in Context, The West Unbound: Social and Cultural Studies

Baylor University Press

Street Address:
1920 South 4th Street
Waco, TX 76706 -2529

Phone: 254.710.3164
Fax: 254.710.3440
Email: (user I.D.)@baylor.edu

Website and Social Media:
Website: www.baylorpress.com
Facebook: www.facebook.com/BaylorPress
Twitter: Baylor_Press
YouTube: www.youtube.com/user/baylorpress

UK Representative:
Gazelle

Mailing Address:
One Bear Place # 97363
Waco, TX 76798-7363

Orders:
Baylor University Press
c/o Hopkins Fulfillment Service
P.O. Box 50370
Baltimore, MD 21211-4370
Phone: 800.537.5487 or 410.516.6956
Fax: 410.516.6998

Canadian Representative:
Scholarly Book Services

Staff

Director: Carey Newman (254.710.3522; email: carey_newman)
Design and Production: Diane E. Smith, Associate Director/Production Manager
 (254.710.2563; email: diane_smith)
Associate Production Manager and Electronic Publishing Manager: Jenny Hunt
 (254.710.3236; email: jenny_hunt)
Events Manager: Isla Hamilton (254.710.4880; email: isla_hamilton)
Sales and Publicity Manager: Billy Collins (254.405.3837; email: billy_collins)
Business: Karla Garrett, Finance and Operations Manager (254.710.1285;
 email: karla_garrett)

Full Member

Established: 1897
Title output 2011: 40
Titles currently in print: 320

Admitted to AAUP: 2007
Title output 2012: 40

Editorial Program

Established in 1897, Baylor University Press publishes forty new titles each year in the following academic areas: religion & public life; rhetoric & religion; religious studies & theology; religion & literature; religion & philosophy; religion & higher education. In accordance with Baylor University's mission, the Press strives to serve the academic community by producing works of excellent quality that integrate faith and understanding.

Special series: Baylor Handbook on the Greek New Testament; Baylor Handbook on the Hebrew Bible; Charles Edmondson Historical Lectures; Documents of Anglophone Christianity Series; The Making of the Christian Imagination; New Perspectives on Latina/o Religion; Provost's Series; Studies in Christianity and Literature; Studies in Religion and Higher Education; Studies in Rhetoric and Religion; World Christianity

Beacon Press

Mailing Address:
25 Beacon Street
Boston, MA 02108-2892

Phone: 617.742.2110
Fax: 617.723.3097
Marketing/Publicity/Subsidiary
Rights Fax: 617.742.2290
Email: (user I.D.)@beacon.org

Street Address:
41 Mt. Vernon Street
Boston, MA 02108

UK Representative:
Publishers Group UK

Canadian Representative:
Random House Canada

Website and Social Media:
Website: www.beacon.org
Blog: www.beaconbroadside.com
Facebook: www.facebook.com/beaconpress
Twitter: BeaconPressBks
YouTube: www.youtube.com/user/BeaconBroadside

Staff

Director: Helene Atwan (email: hatwan)
   Assistant Editor: Crystal Paul (email: cpaul)
Editorial: Gayatri Patnaik, Executive Editor (email: gpatnaik)
   Executive Editor: Amy Caldwell (email: acaldwell)
   Editor: Alexis Rizzuto (email: arizzuto)
   Associate Editor: Joanna Green (email: jgreen)
Production: Marcy Barnes, Production Director & Digital Publishing Director (email: mbarnes)
   Managing Editor: Susan Lumenello (email: slumenello)
   Creative Director: Bob Kosturko (email: bkosturko)
Marketing: Tom Hallock, Associate Publisher, Director of Sales, Marketing, and SubRights (email: thallock)
   Publicity Director: Pamela MacColl (email: pmaccoll)
   Publicist: Caitlin Meyer (email: cmeyer)
   Sales & Marketing Associate: Cailin Donoghue (email: cdonoghue)
   Rights & Permissions Associate: Ryan Mita (email: rmita)
Business: Mike Lindgren, Chief Financial Officer (email: mlindgren)
   Director of Business Operations: Greg Kanter (email: gkanter)
   Accounts Payable/Receivable: Irene Huang (email: ihuang)

Associate Member

Established: 1854
Title output 2011: 49

Admitted to AAUP: 1988
Title output 2012: 39
(64 with paperback reprints)

Titles currently in print: 895 (920)

Editorial Program

Beacon Press, the non-profit publisher affiliated with the Unitarian Universalist Association, publishes works for the general reader, specializing in African American, Native American, and Asian American studies; anthropology; current affairs; education; environmental studies; gay and lesbian studies; nature writing; personal essays; philosophy; regional books; religion; and women's studies.

Special series and joint publishing programs: The Beacon Press/Simmons College Series on Race, Education, and Democracy; The Concord Nature Library; The King Legacy; Queer Action/Queer Ideas

University of British Columbia Press

2029 West Mall
University of British Columbia
Vancouver, BC V6T 1Z2 Canada

Phone: 604.822.5959
Toll-free (in Canada): 877.377.9378
Fax: 604.822.6083
Toll-free (in Canada): 800.668.0821
Email: (user I.D.)@ubcpress.ca
Website: www.ubcpress.ca

US Orders and Returns:
University of Washington Press
C/O Hopkins Fulfillment Service
PO Box 50370
Baltimore, MD 21211-4370 USA
Phone: 800.537.5487; 410.516.6956
Email: hfscustserv@press.jhu.edu

Website and Social Media:
Website: www.ubcpress.ca
Twitter: UBCPress
Facebook: UBC Press

Canadian Orders and Returns:
University of Toronto Press
5201 Dufferin Place
Toronto, ON M3H 5T8 Canada
Phone: 416.667.7791
Fax: 416.667.7832
Email: utpbooks@utpress.utoronto.ca

UK Distributor:
Eurospan

Staff

Director: Melissa Pitts (604.822.6376; email: pitts)
   Assistant to the Publisher: Valerie Nair (604.822.4161; email: nair)
Acquisitions Editorial: Emily Andrew (Toronto) (Asian studies, communications, military history, political science and political philosophy, political and diplomatic history, sociology, transnational and multicultural studies) (416.429.0322; email: andrew); Randy Schmidt (Kelowna) (environmental studies, forestry, geography, law and society, sustainable development, urban studies and planning) (250.764.4761; email: schmidt); Darcy Cullen (Canadian history and regional history [BC and other regions], food studies, health studies, Native studies, Northern and Arctic studies, sexuality studies) (604.822.5744; email: cullen)
Production Editorial: Holly Keller, Assistant Director—Production and Editorial Services (604.822.4545; email: keller)
   Editors: Ann Macklem (604.822.0093; email: macklem); Lesley Erickson (604.822.4548; email: lerickson); Megan Brand (604.822.5885; email: brand); Anna Friedlander (email: friedlander)
Marketing: Laraine Coates, Marketing and Operations(604.822.6486; email: coates)
   Academic Sales Manager: Harmony Johnson (604.822.1978; email: johnson)
   Bibliographic Data Coordinator: Murray Tong (604.822.5790; email: tong)
   Exhibits, Reviews, and Awards Manager: Kerry Kilmartin (604.822.8244; email: kilmartin)
   Advertising Manager: Alexa Love (604.822.4546; email: love)

Special Projects Manager: Elizabeth Whitton (604.822.8226; email: whitton)
Director Emeritus/Special Projects Manager: Peter Milroy (604.822.3807; email: milroy)
Marketing Assistant: Emily Rielly (604.822.5959; email: rielly)
Finance/Distribution: Devni De Silva, Finance Manager (604.822.8938; email: desilva)
Finance Assistant: Caitlin Kopperson (604.822.5370; email: kopperson)
Inventory, Data, and Distribution Manager: Shari Martin (604.822.1221; email: martin)

Full Member

Established: 1971
Title output 2011: 71
Titles currently in print: 863

Admitted to AAUP: 1972
Title output 2012: 52

Editorial Program

Scholarly books and serious nonfiction, with special interest in First Nations culture politics and linguistics, Canadian history, environmental history and policy, resources, Canadian politics, globalization, multiculturalism, urban planning, Asian studies, and sexuality and gender studies

Special series: Asia Pacific Legal Culture and Globalization Series; Asian Religions and Society; Brenda and David McLean Canadian Series; Canada and International Relations; Canadian Democratic Audit; Canadian Yearbook of International Law; Contemporary Chinese Studies; Ethnicity and Democratic Governance Series; Equality|Security|Community; First Nations Languages; Globalization and Autonomy; Law and Society; Legal Dimensions; Nature|History|Society; Pacific Rim Archaeology; Pioneers of British Columbia; Sexuality Studies; Studies in Canadian Military History; Sustainability and the Environment; Urbanization in Asia; Women and Indigenous Studies Series

Brookings Institution Press

1775 Massachusetts Avenue, N.W.
Washington, DC 20036-2103

Phone: 202.536.3600
Email: bibooks@brookings.edu
Indiv: firstinitiallastname@brookings.edu

Website and Social Media:
Website: www.brookings.edu/press
Facebook: www.facebook.com/brookingspress
Twitter: BrookingsInst

UK Representative:
University Presses Marketing

Customer Service/Orders:
Hopkins Fulfillment Service
P.O. Box 50370
Baltimore, MD 21211-4370
Phone: 800.537.5487 or 410.516.6956
Fax: 410.516.6998

Warehouse (RETURNS ONLY):
Brookings Press—Book Returns
c/o Maple Press Distribution
704 Legionaire Drive
Fredericksburg, PA 17026

Canadian Representative:
UBC Press

Staff

Vice President & Director: Robert L. Faherty (202.536.3636)
Director of Finance and Administration: Renuka Deonarain (202.536.3637)
Electronic Media Coordinator: Steven Roman (202.536.3609

Rights Coordinator & Assistant to the VP: Kristen Harrison (202.536.3604)
Acquisitions Editor: TBA (202.536.3617)
Manuscript Editorial: Janet Walker, Managing Editor (202.536.3613)
  Editor: Eileen Hughes (202.536.3614)
Design and Production: Lawrence Converse, Production Manager (202.536.3618)
  Art Coordinator: Susan Woollen (202.536.3619)
Associate Director/Marketing Director/Senior Acquisitions Editor: Christopher Kelaher
  (202.536.3606)
  Direct Marketing Manager: Thomas Parsons (202.536.3610)
  Publicity Manager: Melissa McConnell (202.536.3611)
  Publicity Assistant: Natalie Fullenkamp (202.536.3607)
  E-Marketing Manager: Erin Celentano Wiringi (202.536.3612)
  Exhibits and Marketing Specialist: Anthony Nathe (202.536.3608)
Distribution Services Manager: Terrence Melvin (202.797.6429)
  Distribution Services Assistant: Frederick King (202.797.6311)

Full Member

Established: 1916   Admitted to AAUP: 1958
Title output 2011: 50   Title output 2012: 36
Titles currently in print: 1,230   Journals published: 2

Editorial Program

Economics, government, and international affairs, with emphasis on the implications for public policy of current and emerging issues confronting American society. The Press publishes books written by the Institution's resident and associated staff members employed or commissioned to carry out projects defined by the directors of Brookings research programs, as well as manuscripts acquired from outside authors.

The Institution also publishes Brookings Papers on Economic Activity and Economia (copublished with the Latin American and Caribbean Economic Association).

The Press distributes publications for organizations such as the American Chamber of Commerce to the European Union, the Bertelsmann Foundation, the Carnegie Endowment for International Peace, the Centre for Economic Policy Research, the Century Foundation Press, Economica, the Center for Global Development, the Institute for the Study of the Americas, the International Labor Organization, the Japan Center for International Exchange, the OECD, the Royal Institute for International Affairs, the Trilateral Commission, the United Nations University Press, and the World Trade Organization.

University of Calgary Press

2500 University Drive N.W.
Calgary, AB T2N 1N4 Canada

Phone: 403.220.7578
Fax: 403.282.0085
Email: ucpress@ucalgary.ca
Indiv: (user I.D.)@ucalgary.ca

<u>Website and Social Media:</u>
Website: www.uofcpress.com

<u>US Orders:</u>
Michigan State University Press
1405 South Harrison Road, Suite 25
Manly Miles Building
East Lansing, MI 48823-5202
Phone: 517.355.9543
Fax: 517.432.2611; 800.678.2120
Email: msupress@msu.edu

<u>Canadian Distribution & Orders:</u>
uniPRESSES
c/o Georgetown Terminal Warehouses
34 Armstrong Avenue
Georgetown, ON L7G 4R9 Canada

Phone (toll-free): 877.864.8477
Fax (toll-free): 877.864.4272
Email: orders@gtwcanada.com

<u>UK/European Distributor:</u>
Gazelle Book Services, Ltd.

Staff
Director: Donna Livingstone (403.220.3511; email: livingsd)
Operations Manager: Michelle Lipp (403.220.2606; email: mlipp)
Editorial Secretary: Karen Buttner (403.220.3979; email: kbuttner)
Senior Editor & Acquisitions: John King (403.220.4208; email: jking)
Graphic Designer: Melina Cusano (403.220.8719; email: mcusano)
Marketing Manager: Terry Rahbek-Nielsen (403.220.4343; email: ttrahbek)
Journals Manager: Judy Powell (403.220.3512; email: powell)

Full Member
Established: 1981

Title output 2011: NR
Titles currently in print: 293

Admitted to AAUP: 2002
(Affiliate member: 1992-95)

Title output 2012: NR
Journals published: 9

Editorial Program
University of Calgary Press publishes books that explore a sense of place in western Canada, the relevance of history in our lives, and our impact on the world around us.

Publishing interests include: contemporary Canadian art & architecture; African studies; energy, environment & ecology; Latin American & Caribbean studies; Western Canada; Aboriginal and Métis studies; Arctic and Northern studies; film & television; history & environment; women's studies; and public policy.

Journals: *ARIEL: A Review of International English Literature; Canadian Journal of Counseling and Psychotherapy; Canadian Journal of Latin American and Caribbean Studies; Canadian Journal of Philosophy; Canadian Journal of Program Evaluation; Canadian Journal for the Study of Adult Education; Currents: New Scholarship in the Human Services; The International Electronic Journal for Leadership in Learning; Journal of Mind-Body Regulation (in progress);*

Mousieon: Journal of the Classical Association of Canada
Special series: Africa: Missing Voices; Art in Profile; Beyond Boundaries (Canadian Defence and Strategic Studies); Canadian History and Environment; Cinemas Off Centre; Energy, Ecology, and Environment; Latin American and Caribbean Studies; Northern Lights; The West
Copublishing programs: The Arctic Institute of North America; Latin American Research Centre

University of California Press

2120 Berkeley Way
Berkeley, CA 94704-1012

Phone: 510.642.4247
Fax: 510.643.7127
Email: askucp@ucpress.edu
Indiv: firstname.lastname@ucpress.edu

Order Fulfillment:
California Princeton Fulfillment Services
1445 Lower Ferry Road
Ewing, NJ 08618-1424
Orders: 800.777.4726
Fax: 800.999.1958
Customer Service: 609.883.1759

Website and Social Media:
Website: www.ucpress.edu
Journals website: www.ucpress.edu/journals
Blog: www.ucpress.edu/blog/
Facebook: www.facebook.com/ucpress
Twitter: ucpress

UK/European Office:
John Wiley & Sons Ltd
European Distribution Centre
New Era Estate,
Oldlands Way Bognor Regis
West Sussex PO22 9NQ UK
Phone: +44 (0) 1243 843291
Fax: +44 (0) 1243 843302
Email: customer@wiley.com

Staff
Director: Alison Mudditt (510.642.5393)
Assistant to the Director: Susan Owen (510.642.2102)
Chief Financial Officer: Todor Grigorov (510.643.7993)
Chief Administrative Officer: Anna Weidman (510.642.4388)
Director Publishing Operations: Erich van Rijn (510.643.8915)
Executive Director of UC Press Foundation: May Hu (510.643.7704)
Acquisitions Editorial Director: Denise Penrose (510.642.4246)
  Publisher: Kim Robinson (regional studies) (510.643.3741)
  Executive Editors: Naomi Schneider (sociology, public anthropology, contemporary social issues, Latin American studies, global health) (510.642.6715); Niels Hooper (US History, American studies, Pacific world, western history, world history, Middle East

studies) (510.643.8331); Mary Francis (music, cinema, media studies, Mark Twain) (510.643.5558)
Sponsoring Editors: Kari Dahlgren (art history,museum copublications) (510.642.6733); Blake Edgar (ecology and evolution, environmental sciences, wine and viticulture) (510.643.4643); Reed Malcolm (anthropology, Asian studies, global studies) (510.643.1812); Kate Marshall (food studies, agriculture) (510.642.4147); Erich Schmidt (classical studies, the ancient world to late antiquity, religion) (510.643.3826); Maura Roessner (criminology, law and society, criminal justice) (510.643.9793); Peter Richardson (economics, environmental and natural resource management) (510.642.4244)
Managing Editor: Kate Warne (510.643.6858)
Project Editors: Rachel Berchten (510.642.0133); Dore Brown (510.642.4591); Mari Coates (510.643.6491); Cindy Fulton (510.642.6734); Kate Hoffman (510.643.1379); Suzanne Knott (510.642.8981); Francisco Reinking (510.643.8979); Rose Vekony (510.642.6521); Jacqueline Volin (510.642.0061)
Director of Editing, Design, and Production: Scott Norton (510.643.1335)
Production Coordinators: Pam Augspurger (510.642.5395); Sam Rosenthal (510.642.8102); Janet Villanueva (510.642.9805)
Design: Lia Tjandra (510.643.7982); Sandy Drooker (510.642.6584); Claudia Smelser (510.642.0134)
Director of Marketing & Sales: Rebekah Darksmith (510.643.0952)
Assistant Director of Marketing: Deb Nasitka (510.642.0378)
Publicity Director: Alexandra Dahne (510.643.5036)
Journals Publishing Manager: Hannah Love (510.643.1094)
Journals Production Manager: Susanna Tadlock (510.642.6221)
Business: Karla Golden, Manager (510.642.7944)
Human Resources: Doris Floyd (510.642.5338)
Administrative Services Manager: Pam Wimberly (510.642.6934)

Full Member

Established: 1893	Admitted to AAUP: 1937
Title output 2011: 254	Title output 2012: 225
Titles currently in print: 4,729	Journals published: 35

Editorial Program

Anthropology, art history, Asian studies, biology, classical studies, environmental and earth sciences, film, food studies, history, media studies, music, natural history, global health, criminology, criminal justice, economics, regional studies, religion, sociology, wine and viticulture. Submissions are not invited in original poetry or fiction.

Journals: *The American Biology Teacher; Asian Survey; The Auk; BioScience; Boom; California Management Review; Classical Antiquity; The Condor; Federal Sentencing Reporter; Film Quarterly; Gastronomica: Historical Studies in the Natural Sciences; Huntington Library Quarterly; Journal of Empirical Research on Human Research Ethics; The Journal of Musicology; Journal of Palestine Studies; Journal of the American Musicological Society; Journal of the Society of Architectural Historians; Journal of Vietnamese Studies; Law and Literature; Mexican Studies/Estudios Mexicanos; Music Perception; Music Theory Spectrum; New Criminal Law Review; Nineteenth-Century Literature; 19th-Century Music; Nova Religio; Ornithological Monographs; Pacific Historical Review; The Public Historian; Religion and American Culture; Representations; Rhetorica; Social Problems; Sociological Perspectives; Southern California Quarterly*

Special series: American Crossroads; Ancient Philosophies; Asia Pacific Modern; Asia:

Local Studies/Global Themes; California Natural History Guides; California/Milbank Books on Health and the Public; California Series in Law, Politics, and Society; California Series in Public Anthropology; California Series in Urban Development; California Studies in 19th-Century Music; California Studies in 20th-Century Music; California Studies in Critical Human Geography; California Studies in Food and Culture; California World History Library; Classics in Urban History; Encyclopedias of the Natural World; Ernest Bloch Lectures; Ethnographic Studies in Subjectivity; Experience the California Coast; Freshwater Ecology Series; From Indochina to Vietnam: Revolution and War in a Global Perspective; Global, Area, and International Archive; Hellenistic Culture and Society; Jumping Frogs: Undiscovered, Rediscovered, and Celebrated; Writings of Mark Twain; Mark Twain Library; Mark Twain Papers; Music of the African Diaspora; New California Poetry; Organisms and Environments; Origins of Human Behavior and Culture; Sather Classical Lectures; South Asia Across the Disciplines; Species and Systematics; Sport in World History; Studies in Avian Biology; The Anthropology of Christianity; The Clark Kerr Lectures On the Role of Higher Education in Society; The Collected Writings of Robert Duncan; The Huntington Library Children's Classics; The Huntington Library Classics; The Huntington Library Garden Series; The Marcus Garvey and Universal Negro Improvement Association Papers; The Middle Awash Series; The Norman and Charlotte Strouse Edition of the Writings of Thomas Carlyle; The Works of Mark Twain; The World's Finest Wines; Transformation of the Classical Heritage; Treasures from the Huntington Library; UC Publications in Anthropological Records; UC Publications in Anthropology; UC Publications in Botany; UC Publications in Catalogs and Bibliographies; UC Publications in Classical Studies; UC Publications in Entomology; UC Publications in Folklore and Mythology Studies; UC Publications in Geological Sciences; UC Publications in Ibero-Americana; UC Publications in Linguistics; UC Publications in Modern Philology; UC Publications in Zoology; Weimar and Now: German Cultural Criticism; Western Histories; Wildavsky Forum Series

Cambridge University Press

North American Branch
32 Avenue of the Americas
New York, NY 10013-4211

Phone: 212.337.5000
Fax: 212.691.3239
Email: firstinitiallastname@cambridge.org

Distribution Center (West Nyack, NY)
Phone: 845.353.7500
Fax: 845.353.4141

Website and Social Media:
Website: www.cambridge.org
Blog: www.cambridgeblog.org

Head (UK) Office:
The Edinburgh Building
Cambridge CB2 2RU UK

Staff
Chief Executive: Peter Phillips (UK)
NY Office: 212.337.5000
Managing Director, Americas and ELT: Michael Peluse (212.337.6551)
Academic Publishing:

Publishing Director, Humanities & Social Sciences: Beatrice Rehl (212.337.5096)
Editorial Director, STM: Matt Lloyd (212.337.5956)
   Academic Editors: Lewis Bateman (political science) (212.337.5965); John Berger
   (law) (212.337.5958); Ada Brunstein (computer science) (212.337.6546); Lauren
   Cowles (math, computer science) (212.337.5962); Robert Dreesen (politics, sociology)
   (212.337.5981); Deborah Gershenowitz (American and Latin American history and poli-
   tics) (212.337.5950); Diana Gillooly (mathematical sciences); Peter Gordon (engineering)
   (212.337.5944); William Hammel (Middle Eastern and African studies) (212.337.6598);
   Vince Higgs (astronomy, physics) (212.337.5081); Scott Parris (economics, business)
   (212.337.5964); Ray Ryan (literature) (212.337.5760)
Academic & Professional Production: Catherine Felgar, Production Director/Global Supply
   Chain Director (212.337.5094)
Academic Online Sales: Andrea Cernichiari, Director of Online Sales, Americas
   (212.337.5022)
Marketing: Liza Murphy, Academic and Professional Sales and Marketing Director
   (212.337.5066)
   Associate Director, of Backlist/POD Marketing: Catherine Friedl (212.337.5049)
   Associate Director, Trade Sales & Marketing: Melissanne Scheld (212.337.5988)
   Associate Director, College Sales & Marketing: Kerry Cahill (212.337.5065)
   Associate Director, Marketing & Promotions: Gary Suarez (212.337.5085)
   Library Sales & Marketing Manager: Keiko Hirano (212.337.5983)
   Exhibits Manager: James Murphy (212.337.5074)
   Rights and Permissions Manager: Marc Anderson (212.337.5048)
Journals: Jamie Hutchins, Head of Journals (212.337.5993)
   Senior Editor, STM Journals: Aaron Johnson (212.337.6595)
   Publisher, HSS Journals: Mark Zadrozny (212.337.5012)
   Journals Production Manager: Edward Carey (212.337.5985)
   Head of Marketing: Alex Engel (212.337.5967)
   Advertising Sales & Commercial Reprints: Adam Schubak (212.337.5053)
ELT Publishing
   Publishing Director: Janet Aitchison (212.337.6574)
   Associate Publishing Director: Jeff Krum (adult courses) (212.337.5005)
   Director for Adult Consumer: Sally Searby (212.337.5042)
   Global Digital Operations Manager: Jeff Chen (212.337.5971)
   Operations Manager - Production/Manufacturing: Tami Savir (212.337.5968)
   Adaptations & Versioning Unit Manager: Danielle Power (212.337.5989)
   US/Canada Sales and Marketing Director: Kenneth Clinton (212.337.5010)
   Marketing Manager: Carine Mitchell (212.337.5006)
   Associate Director, Product Marketing: Pierre Montagano (212.337.5007)
   Senior National Sales Manager: James Anderson
   Business Manager: Aniko Banfi (212.337.5030)
Information Services: David Kwederis, IT Director (212.337.5060)
HR: Judith Grace, Human Resources Director, Americas (212.337.5045)
Press Distribution Director & Director, West Nyack: Steve Miller (ext. 4339)
   Director of Accounting: Thomas Vitkowski (ext 4326)
   Credit Manager: Lydia Rodrigues (ext. 4314)
   Associate Director Customer Services: Marianne Headrick (ext. 4409)
   Inventory Operations Manager: Holly Verrill (ext. 4306)

Contract Fulfillment Manager: Alan Standish (ext. 4354)

Full Member

Established: 1534

American Branch: 1949	Admitted to AAUP: 1950
Title output 2011: over 3700	Title output 2012: over 3900
Titles currently in print: about 45,000	Journals published: 320

Editorial Program

A broad range of academic titles in the humanities; social sciences; biological and physical sciences; mathematics; medicine; psychology; law; religious studies; reference works; and English language teaching.

Journals: *Acta Numerica; Advances in Animal Biosciences; Africa: Journal of the International African Institute; African Studies Review; Ageing & Society; AI EDAM; AJS Review; American Political Science Review; Anatolian Studies; Ancient Mesoamerica; Anglo-Saxon England; animal; Animal Genetic Resources/Resources génétiques animales/Recursos genéticos animals; Animal Health Research Reviews; Annales de Limnologie - International Journal of Limnology; Annals of Actuarial Science; Annual of the British School at Athens; Annual Review of Applied Linguistics; Antarctic Science; Antiquaries Journal; ANZIAM Journal; Applied Psycholinguistics; APSIPA Transactions on Signal and Information Processing; Aquatic Living Resources; Arabic Sciences and Philosophy; Archaeological Dialogues; Archaeological Reports; arq: Architectural Research Quarterly; Asian Journal of International Law; ASTIN Bulletin; Australasian Journal of Special Education; Australian and New Zealand Journal of Organisational Psychology; Australian Educational and Developmental Psychologist; Australian Journal of Environmental Education; Australian Journal of Guidance and Counselling; Australian Journal of Indigenous Education; Australian Journal of Rehabilitation Counselling; Austrian History Yearbook; Behavioral and Brain Sciences; Behaviour Change; Behavioural and Cognitive Psychotherapy; Bilingualism: Language and Cognition; Bird Conservation International; Brain Impairment; Britannia; British Actuarial Journal; British Journal for the History of Science; British Journal of Anaesthetic & Recovery Nursing; British Journal of Music Education; British Journal of Nutrition; British Journal of Political Science; Bulletin of Entomological Research; Bulletin of the Australian Mathematical Society; Bulletin of the Hegel Society of Great Britain; Bulletin of the School of Oriental and African Studies; Business History Review; Cambridge Archaeological Journal; Cambridge Classical Journal; Cambridge Law Journal; Cambridge Opera Journal; Cambridge Quarterly of Healthcare Ethics; Canadian Entomologist; Canadian Journal of Law and Society / La Revue Canadienne Droit et Societe; Canadian Journal of Political Science/Revue canadienne de science politique; Canadian Journal on Aging / La Revue canadienne du vieillissement ; Cardiology in the Young; Central European History; Children Australia; China Quarterly; Church History; Classical Quarterly;j Classical Review; CNS Spectrums; Cognitive Behaviour Therapist; Combinatorics, Probability and Computing; Comparative Studies in Society and History; Compositio Mathematica; Contemporary European History; Continuity and Change; CORD Proceedings; Dance Research Journal; Development and Psychopathology; Dialogue: Canadian Philosophical Review/Revue canadienne de philosophie ; Diamond Light Source Proceedings; Du Bois Review: Social Science Research on Race; Early Music History; Earth and Environmental Science Transactions of The Royal Society of Edinburgh; EAS Publications Series; Ecclesiastical Law Journal; Econometric Theory; Economics & Philosophy; Edinburgh Journal of*

Botany; Eighteenth-Century Music; English Language & Linguistics; English Profile Journal; English Today; Environment and Development Economics; Environmental Conservation; Environmental Practice; Epidemiology & Infection; Epidemiology and Psychiatric Sciences; Episteme; Ergodic Theory and Dynamical Systems; ESAIM: Control, Optimisation and Calculus of Variations; ESAIM: Mathematical Modelling and Numerical Analysis; ESAIM: Probability and Statistics; Ethics & International Affairs; European Business Organization Law Review (EBOR); European Constitutional Law Review; European Journal of Applied Mathematics ; European Journal of Sociology / Archives Européennes de Sociologie ; European Physical Journal - Applied Physics; European Political Science Review; European Review; Experimental Agriculture ; Expert Reviews in Molecular Medicine; Fetal and Maternal Medicine Review; Financial History Review; Forum of Mathematics, Pi; Forum of Mathematics, Sigma; Fruits; Genetics Research; Geological Magazine; Glasgow Mathematical Journal; Global Constitutionalism; Government and Opposition; Greece & Rome ; Hague Journal on the Rule of Law; Harvard Theological Review; Health Economics, Policy and Law; Historical Journal; History in Africa; Horizons: The Journal of the College Theology Society; International & Comparative Law Quarterly; nternational Journal of Asian Studies; International Journal of Astrobiology; International Journal of Cultural Property; International Journal of Disability Management; International Journal of Law in Context; International Journal of Metrology and Quality Engineering; International Journal of Microwave and Wireless Technologies; International Journal of Middle East Studies; International Journal of Neuropsychopharmacology; International Journal of Technology Assessment in Health Care; International Journal of Tropical Insect Science; International Labor and Working-Class History; International Organization; International Psychogeriatrics; International Review of Social History; International Review of the Red Cross; International Theory Israel Law Review; Itinerario; Japanese Journal of Political Science; Journal of African History; Journal of African Law; Journal of Agricultural Science ; Journal of American Studies; Journal of Anglican Studies; Journal of Applied Animal Nutrition; Journal of Asian Studies; Journal of Biosocial Science; Journal of British Studies; Journal of Child Language; Journal of Dairy Research; Journal of Dentofacial Anomalies and Orthodontics; Journal of Developmental Origins of Health and Disease; Journal of Ecclesiastical History; Journal of Economic History; Journal of Financial and Quantitative Analysis; Journal of Fluid Mechanics; Journal of French Language Studies; Journal of Functional Programming; Journal of Germanic Linguistics; Journal of Global History; Journal of Hellenic Studies; Journal of Helminthology; Journal of Institutional Economics; Journal of Laryngology & Otology; Journal of Latin American Studies; Journal of Linguistic Geography; Journal of Linguistics; Journal of Materials Research; Journal of Mechanics; Journal of Modern African Studies; Journal of Navigation; Journal of Nutritional Science; Journal of Pacific Rim Psychology; Journal of Pension Economics & Finance; Journal of Plasma Physics; Journal of Policy History; Journal of Politics; Journal of Psychiatric Intensive Care; Journal of Public Policy; Journal of Radiotherapy in Practice; Journal of Relationships Research; Journal of Roman Studies; Journal of Smoking Cessation; Journal of Social Policy; Journal of Southeast Asian Studies; Journal of the Australian Mathematical Society; Journal of the Gilded Age and Progressive Era; Journal of the History of Economic Thought; Journal of the Institute of Mathematics of Jussieu; Journal of the International Neuropsychological Society; Journal of the International Phonetic Association; Journal of the Marine Biological Association of the United Kingdom; Journal of the Royal Asiatic Society; Journal of the Society for American Music; Journal of Tropical Ecology; Journal of Tropical Psychology; Journal of Wine Economics; Kantian Review; Knowledge Engineering Review; Language in Society; Language Teaching; Language Variation and Change; Laser and Particle Beams; Law and History Review; Legal Information Management; Legal Theory; Leiden Journal of International Law; Lichenologist; Macroeconomic Dynamics; Marine Biodiversity

Records; *Mathematical Modelling of Natural Phenomena; Mathematical Proceedings of the Cambridge Philosophical Society; Mathematical Structures in Computer Science; Mathematika; Mechanics & Industry; Medical History; Microscopy and Microanalysis; Microscopy Today ; Modern Asian Studies; Modern Intellectual History; MRS Bulletin; MRS Communications; Natural Language Engineering; Netherlands International Law Review; Netherlands Yearbook of International Law; Network Science; New Testament Studies; New Theatre Quarterly; Nineteenth-Century Music Review; Nordic Journal of Linguistics; Nutrition Research Reviews; Organised Sound; Oryx; Palliative & Supportive Care; Papers of the British School at Rome; Parasitology; Perspectives on Politics; Philosophy; Phonology; Plainsong & Medieval Music; Plant Genetic Resources; Polar Record; Political Science Research and Method; Politics & Gender; Politics and Religion; Popular Music; Powder Diffraction; Prehospital and Disaster Medicine; Primary Health Care Research & Development; Probability in the Engineering and Informational Sciences; Proceedings of the Edinburgh Mathematical Society; Proceedings of the Nutrition Society; Proceedings of the Prehistoric Society; Proceedings of the Royal Society of Edinburgh Section A: Mathematics; Proceedngs of the International Astronomical Union; PS: Political Science & Politics; Psychological Medicine; Public Health Nutrition; Publications of the Astronomical; Society of Australia; Quarterly Reviews of Biophysics; Queensland Review; Radioprotection; RAIRO - Operations Research; RAIRO - Theoretical Informatics and Applications; ReCALL; Religious Studies; Renewable Agriculture and Food Systems; Review of International Studies; Review of Politics; Review of Symbolic Logic; Reviews in Clinical Gerontology; Revista de Historia Economica - Journal of Iberian and Latin American Economic; History; Revue de Métallurgie – International Journal of Metallurgy; Robotica; Royal Historical Society Camden Fifth Series; Royal Institute of Philosophy Supplements; Rural History; Science in Context; Scottish Journal of Theology; Seed Science Research; Social Philosophy and Policy; Social Policy and Society; Spanish Journal of Psychology; Speculum; Studies in American Political Development; Studies in Second Language Acquisition; Tempo; Theatre Research International; Theatre Survey; Theory and Practice of Logic Programming; Think; TRaNS; Transactions of the Royal Historical Society; Transnational Environmental Law; twentieth-century music; Twin Research and Human Genetics; Urban History; Utilitas; Victorian Literature and Culture; Visual Neuroscience; World Politics; World Trade Review; World's Poultry Science Journal; Yearbook of International Humanitarian Law; Zygote*

Special series, joint imprints, and/or copublishing programs (partial list): Analytical Methods for Social Research; Cambridge African Studies; Cambridge Archaeological Manuals; Cambridge Astrobiology; Cambridge Astrophysics; Cambridge Companions to Philosophy; Cambridge Essential Histories; Cambridge History of China; Cambridge Latin American Studies; Cambridge Monographs on Mathematical Physics; Cambridge Opera Handbooks; Cambridge Planetary Science; Cambridge Series in Statistical and Probabilistic Mathematics; Cambridge Studies in American Literature and Culture; Cambridge Studies in Comparative Politics; Cambridge Studies in Contentious Politics; Cambridge Studies in Ecology; Cambridge Studies in Environment and History; Cambridge Studies in Medieval Life and Thought; Cambridge Studies in Public Opinion and Political Psychology; Cambridge Studies on Social Theory, Religion and Politics; Cambridge Studies on the American Constitution; Cambridge Studies on the American South; Cambridge Texts in the History of Political Thought; Cambridge Tracts in Mathematics; Cambridge World Archaeology; Case Studies in Early Civilizations; Communication, Society and Politics; Developmental and Cell Biology Series; Econometric Society Monographs; Encyclopedia of Mathematics; Hematological Oncology; Human Rights in History; Institute of Mathematical Statistics Monographs; International Hydrology Series; London Mathematical Society Lecture Note Series; Neurobiology and Psychiatry; Perspectives in Logic; Political Economy of Institutions and Decisions; Proceedings of the International Astronomical Union Symposia; Publications of the German Historical Institute; Studies in Legal History; Studies in Natural Language Processing.

Carnegie Mellon University Press

5032 Forbes Avenue
Pittsburgh, PA 15289-1021

Phone: 412.268.2861
Fax: 412.268.8706
Email:
carnegiemellonuniversitypress@gmail.com
Website: www.upne.com/distributed/dist_cmu.html

Order Fulfillment/Customer Service:
Carnegie Mellon University Press
c/o University Press of New England
1 Court Street
Lebanon, NH 03766
Phone: 800.421.1561
Fax: 603.448.9429

Website and Social Media:
Website: www.cmu.edu/universitypress
Facebook: www.facebook.com/CarnegieMellonUniversityPress
Twitter: CMUPress

Staff
Director: Gerald Costanzo (poetry editor) (email: gc3d@andrew.cmu.edu)
Senior Editor: Cynthia Lamb (nonfiction acquisitions) (email: cynthial@andrew.cmu.edu)
Managing Editor: Sara-Anne Lee (fiction acquisition)(email: saraanne@cmu.edu)
Production Manager: Connie Amoroso (email: connieamoroso@yahoo.com)
Accounts Administrator: Anna Houck (email: am2x@andrew.cmu.edu)

Full Member
Established: 1972
Title output 2011: 15
Titles currently in print: 295

Admitted to AAUP: 1991
Title output 2012: 11

Editorial Program
Carnegie Mellon University Press' particular strength lies in literary publishing: Carnegie Mellon Poetry Series, Carnegie Mellon Classic Contemporaries Series (the reissuing of significant early poetry and fiction collections by important contemporary writers), Carnegie Mellon Series in Short Fiction, Poets in Prose Series (memoir in the form of poets writing about their writing lives, poetry criticism, guidebooks and handbooks about the writing of poetry, and Carnegie Mellon Series in Translation. Additionally, the Press publishes in regional social history (titles that explore the rich history of Pittsburgh and Western Pennsylvania), art history, the performing arts (original plays and adaptations), literary analysis, education, and Carnegie Mellon University history.

The Catholic University of America Press

240 Leahy Hall
620 Michigan Avenue, N.E.
Washington, DC 20064

Phone: 202.319.5052
Fax: 202.319.4985
Email: (user I.D.)@cua.edu

Customer Service:
HFS
PO Box 50370
Baltimore, MD 21211
Phone: 800.537.5487
Fax: 410.516.6998

Website and Social Media:
Website: cuapress.cua.edu
Facebook: www.facebook.com/pages/
    The-Catholic-University-of-America-Press/232124655084
Twitter: @CUAPress

Warehouse (Returns only):
HFS
RETURNS
c/o Maple Press Co.
Lebanon Dist. Center
704 Legionaire Drive
Fredericksburg, PA 17026

UK Representative:
Eurospan

Canadian Representative:
Scholarly Book Services

Staff

Director: Trevor Lipscombe (email: lipscombe)
    Assistant to the Director: Libby Newkumet (email: newkumet)
Acquisitions Editors: James C. Kruggel (philosophy, theology) (email: kruggel);
    Trevor Lipscombe (all other fields)
Managing Editor: Theresa Walker (email: walkert)
    Editorial Assistant: Tanjam Jacobson (email: jacobsot)
Design and Production: Anne Kachergis (Kachergis Book Design, 14 Small Street North,
    Pittsboro, NC 27312)
Marketing Manager: Elizabeth Benevides (email: benevides)
    Marketing Assistant: Allison Hughes (email: hughesb)
Journals: Hubert Ngueha, Administrative Assistant (email: ngueha)

Full Member

Established: 1939
Title output 2011: 38
Titles currently in print: 610

Admitted to AAUP: 1985
Title output 2012: 38
Journals published: 4

Editorial Program

American and European history (both ecclesiastical and secular); American and European
literature; philosophy; political theory; theology. Periods covered range from late antiquity
to modern times, with special interest in late antiquity, early Christianity, and the medieval
period.
Journals: *The Catholic Historical Review; Pierre d'Angle; The Jurist: Studies in Church Law and
Ministry; and U.S. Catholic Historian*

Special series: Catholic Moral Thought; The Fathers of the Church: A New Translation; Library of Early Christianity; Medieval Texts in Translation; Patristic Monograph Series of the North American Patristics Society; Publications of the American Maritain Association (distributed); Studies in Philosophy and the History of Philosophy; Thomas Aquinas in Translation

The University of Chicago Press

1427 E. 60th Street
Chicago, IL 60637-2954

Phone: 773.702.7700
Fax: 773.702.2705 (Books Acquisitions)
  773.702.9756 (Books Marketing)
  773.834.3480 (Journals Marketing)
  773.753.4247 (Journals Production)
Email: firstinitiallastname@press.uchicago.edu

Chicago Distribution Center:
11030 South Langley Avenue
Chicago, IL 60628
Phone: 773.702.7000
Fax: 773.702.7212

Website and Social Media-Books:
Website www.press.uchicago.edu;
Chicago Blog: pressblog.uchicago.edu
Twitter: UChicagoPress
Facebook: facebook.com/UniversityofChicagoPress
Tumblr: uchicagopress.tumblr.com
Goodreads: goodreads.com/UChicagoPress
LibraryThing: www.librarything.com/profile/UChicagoPress
Website and Social Media-Journals:
Website: www.journals.uchicago.edu
Blog: pressblog.uchicago.edu
Facebook: www.facebook.com/UChicagoJournals
Twitter: ChicagoJournals

UK Representative:
University Press Marketing

Canadian Representative:
The University Press Group

Staff
Director: Garrett P. Kiely (773.702.8878)
  Deputy Director: Christopher Heiser (773.702.2998)
  Assistant to the Director and Deputy Director: Ellen M. Zalewski (773.702.8879)
  Executive Director of Information Technology: Patti O'Shea (773.702.8521)
  IT Operations Manager Information Technology Support: Derek Simmons (773.702.0510)
  Human Resources Manager: Alice Lloyd (773.702.7303)
  Digital Publishing Manager: Krista Coulson (773.702.5862)
Books Division
Acquisitions Editorial:
  Editorial Directors: Christie Henry (sciences and social sciences) (773.702.0468); Alan Thomas (humanities and social sciences) (773.702.7644)

Editors: Susan Bielstein (art, architecture, ancient archeology, classics, film studies) (773.702.7633); T. David Brent (anthropology, philosophy, psychology, psychiatry) (773.702.7642); Abby Collier (geography and cartography) (773.702.6691); Christopher Chung (life sciences evolutionary biology, ecology, and conservation biology) (773.702.3145); Robert P. Devens (American history, regional publishing) (773.702.0158); Elizabeth Branch Dyson (ethnomusicology, education, philosophy) (773.702.7637); Marta Tonegutti (music) (773.702.0427); Christie Henry (life sciences, geography, cartography) (773.702.0468); Douglas Mitchell (history, sociology, sexuality studies, rhetoric) (773.702.7639); Randolph Petilos (medieval studies, poetry in translation) (773.702.7647); Karen Darling (history, philosophy, and social studies of science) (773.702.7641); Joe Jackson (economics, business) (773.702.7638); Alan Thomas (literature, religion) (773.702.7644); John Tryneski (political science, law and society) (773.702.7648)
> Managing Editor, Phoenix Poets: Randolph Petilos (773.702.7647)
> Paperback Editor: Margaret Hivnor (773.702.7649)
> Assistant Paperback Editor: Janet Deckenbach (773.702.7034)
> Reference: Paul Schellinger, Editorial Director (773.702.2376)
> Senior Editor: David Morrow (773.702.7465)
> Senior Project Editor: Mary Laur (773.702.7326)
> Assistant Editor: Jenny Gavacs (773.702.5051)
> Contracts and Subsidiary Rights Manager: Perry Cartwright (773.702.6096)
> Foreign Rights Manager: Ines ter Horst (773.702.7741)
Manuscript Editorial: Anita Samen, Managing Editor (773.702.5081)
Design and Production: Jill Shimabukuro, Design and Production Director (773.702.7653)
Marketing Director: Carol Kasper (773.702.7733)
> Promotions Director: Levi Stahl (773.702.0289)
> Promotions Managers: Jeffrey Waxman (773.702.0279); Micah Fehrenbacher (773.702.7717); Laura Avey (773.702.0376); Melinda Kennedy (773.702.2945)
> Online Publicity Managers: Kristi McGuire (773.702.2548); Ryo Yamaguchi (773.834.8708)
> Advertising Manager: Anne Osterman (773.702.7897)
> Exhibits Coordinator: Eric DeTratto (773.834.7201)
> Exhibits Associate: Nida Masiulis (773.702.4217)
> Marketing Design Manager: Mary Shanahan (773.702.7697)
> Senior Marketing Designer: Alice Reimann (773.702.7849)
Sales: John Kessler, Associate Marketing Director/Sales Director (773.702.7248)
> Sales and Distribution Associate: Robert Hoffman (773.702.0340)
> Sales and Inventory Associate: Joseph Peterson (773.702.7723)
> Sales Representatives: Bailey Walsh (Midwest); Blake Delodder (East Coast); Gary Hart (West Coast)
> Sales Assistant: Vertelle Kanyama (773.702.7899)
> International Sales Manager: Saleem Dhamee(773.702.7898)
> International Sales Assistant: Nida Masiulis (773.702.4217)
E-commerce/Direct-to-Consumer Sales: Dean Blobaum, Electronic Marketing and E-commerce Manager (773.702.7706)

Marketing Systems Coordinator: Tom McGraw (773.702.6674)
Associate Direct Marketing Manager: Stuart Kisilinsky (773.702.8924)
Direct Mail Associate: Casimir Psujek (773.702.7887)
Reference Marketing: Ellen Gibson, Reference Marketing Manager (773.702.3233)
Reference Special Sales and Promotions Manager: Lauren Salas (773.702.0890)
Marketing Client Distribution: Carol Kasper, Director (773.702.7733)
Distributed Books Manager: Teresa Fagan (773.834.1916)
Publicity Manager: Carrie Adams (773.702.4216)

Journals Division
Journals Division Manager: Michael Magoulias (773.753.2669)
Publications Acquisitions Manager: Kari Roane (773.702.7362)
Publications Managers:Tess Mullen (773.702.7442); Gordon Rudy (773.702.2448)
Publishing Operations Manager: Ashley Towne (773.753.4241)
Manager of Electronic Publishing Technology: Michael Boudreau (773.753.3298)
Manager of Subscription Technology: Kristen Gwinn (773.753.4243)
Marketing Director: Katharine Duff (773.702.7688)
Manager of Editorial Processes: Mary E. Leas (773.702.7961)
Chief Manuscript Editor, Science Journals: Mary Nell Hoover (773.702.7679)
Chief Manuscript Editor, General Journals: Jane Jiambalvo (773.702.7689)

Chicago Distribution Center Services
President of Chicago Distribution Services: Don Linn (773.702.7020)
UHRM/Administrator: Sharon Klausner (773.702.7010)
Distribution Services Coordinator: Sue Tranchita (773.702.7014)
Customer Service Manager: Karen Hyzy (773.702.7109)
Asst. Manager, Customer Service/Instructor Trainer Title Management: Latrice Allen (773.702.7112)
Credit and Collections, A/R Manager: Nick Cole (773.702.7164)
Director of Accounting: Bob Peterson (773.702.7036)
E-Content & SRDP Manager: Mark Stewart (773.702.7238)
M.I.S. Manager: Christopher Jones (773.702.7229)
Royalty/Rights Manager: Cassandra Wisniewski (773.702.7062)
Warehouse Distribution Manager: Gail Candreva-Szwet (773.702.7080)
Warehouse Manager: Tammy Paul (773.702.7081)
Journals Warehouse Manager: Don P. Collins (773.702.7245)
Returns Manager: Jen Stone (773.834.3687)
Warehouse Asst. Mgr/Inventory Manager: Dennis Kraus (773.834.3499)

BiblioVault
BiblioVault Operations and Web Coordinator: Kate Davey (773.834.4417)

Full Member

Established: 1891	Admitted to AAUP: 1957
Title output 2011: 268	Title output 2012: 300
Titles currently in print: 4,933	Journals published: 51

Editorial Program
Sociology; anthropology; political science; business and economics; history; English; American and foreign literature; literary criticism; biological and physical sciences and mathematics; conceptual studies of science; law; philosophy; linguistics; geography and cartography; art history; classics; architecture; history of photography; education; psychiatry and psychology;

musicology. Submissions are not invited in fiction or poetry or in conventional textbooks.

Journals: *Afterall; American Art; The American Historical Review; American Journal of Education; American Journal of Sociology; The American Naturalist; American Political Thought; Art Documentation; The China Journal; Classical Philology; Comparative Education Review; Critical Inquiry; Current Anthropology; Economic Development and Cultural Change; The Elementary School Journal; Ethics; History of Religions; HOPOS; Infection Control and Hospital Epidemiology; International Journal of American Linguistics; International Journal of Plant Sciences; Isis; Journal of British Studies; Journal of Consumer Research; The Journal of Geology; Journal of Human Capital; Journal of Labor Economics; The Journal of Law and Economics; The Journal of Legal Studies; Metropolitan Museum Journal; The Journal of Modern History; Journal of Near Eastern Studies; Journal of Political Economy; The Journal of Religion; The Library Quarterly; Modern Philology; Philosophy of Science; Physiological and Biochemical Zoology; Publications of the Astronomical Society of the Pacific; The Quarterly Review of Biology; Renaissance Quarterly; Schools; Signs; Social Service Review; West 86th; Winterthur Portfolio*

Annuals: *Crime and Justice; Innovation Policy and the Economy; NBER International Seminar on Macroeconomics; NBER Macroeconomics Annual Tax Policy and the Economy; OSIRIS; Supreme Court Economic Review; The Supreme Court Review*

The Chinese University Press

The Chinese University of Hong Kong
Sha Tin
New Territories, Hong Kong

Phone: +852 2946.5300
Fax: +852 2603.7355
Email: cup@cuhk.edu.hk
Indiv: (user I.D.)@cuhk.edu.hk

Website and Social Media:
Website: www.chineseupress.com
Facebook: www.facebook.com/
    home.php#!/TheChineseUniversityPress

North American Distributor:
Columbia University Press
c/o Perseus Distribution
Phone: 800.944.8648 / 731.988.4440
Email: cup_book@columbia.edu

UK and European Distributor:
Eurospan Group
c/o Turpin Distribution
Phone: +44 (0) 1767 604972
Email: eurospan@turpin-distribution.com

Other Areas
(Customer Service and Orders)
The Chinese University Press
Phone: +852 29465300
Fax: +852 26037355
Email: cup-bus@cuhk.edu.hk

Staff
Director: Qi Gan (+852 2946.5399; email: ganqi)
Secretary to the Director: Tina Chan (+852 2946.5398; email: tinachan)
Editorial: Lin Ying, Managing Editor (+852 2946.5397; email: linying)
Production: Kingsley Ma, Manager (+852 2946.5391; email: kwaihungma)
Business/Marketing: Angelina Wong, Manager (+852 2946.5386; email: laifunwong)

International Member

Established: 1977
Title output 2011: 65
Titles currently in print: 894

Admitted to AAUP: 1981
Title output 2012: 50
Journals published: 9

<u>Editorial Program</u>

Bilingual publication of academic and general trade titles. Areas of interest include Chinese studies in literature, history, philosophy, languages, and the arts. The Press also publishes books on business, government, medicine, as well as dictionaries and general books in both the English and Chinese languages.

Journals: *Asian Anthropology; Asian Journal of English Language Teaching; The China Review; Communication & Society; Daoism: Religion, History and Society; Hong Kong Drama Review; Journal of Chinese Studies; Journal of Translation Studies, International Journal for the Study of Humanistic Buddhism*

Special series: Bibliography and Index Series; Bilingual Series on Modern Chinese Literature; Ch'ien Mu Lectures in History and Culture; Educational Studies Series; Hong Kong Taxation; Institute of Chinese Studies Monograph Series; Jintian Series of Contemporary Chinese Writing; Young Scholars Dissertation Awards, Translation Series

University Press of Colorado/Utah State University Press

<u>Colorado Address:</u>
5589 Arapahoe Avenue
Suite 206C
Boulder, CO 80303

Phone: 720.406.8849
Fax: 720.406.3443
Email: (user I.D)@upcolorado.com

<u>Utah Address:</u>
3078 Old Main Hill
Merrill-Cazier Library
Logan, UT 84322-3078

Phone: 435.797.1642
Fax: 435.797.0313

<u>Distributor:</u>
Chicago Distribution Center
11030 South Langley Ave.
Chicago, IL 60628

Phone: 800.621.2736
Fax: 800.621.8476

<u>European Representative:</u>
Gazelle Book Services

<u>Websites and Social Media:</u>
Websites: www.upcolorado.com; www.usupress.org
Facebook: www.facebook.com/pages/The-University-Press-of-Colorado/347439013387
www.facebook.com/pages/Utah-State-University-Press/164439110276267
Twitter: UPColorado

Staff

Director: Darrin Pratt (email: darrin)
Associate Director: Michael Spooner (email: michael@usupress.com)
Acquisitions Editor: Jessica d'Arbonne (email: jessica)

Managing Editor: Laura Furney (email: laura)
Production Manager: Dan Pratt (email: dan)
Marketing & Sales Manager: Beth Svinarich (email: beth)
Marketing Manager & Production (USUP): Dan Miller (email: danmiller@usupress.com)

Full Member

Established: 1965   Admitted to AAUP: 1982
Title output 2011: 29   Title output 2012: 41
Titles currently in print: 620

Editorial Program

Physical sciences; natural history; ecology; American history; Western history; anthropology; archaeology; composition studies; folklore studies; Native American studies; Western women's history; Mormon history; and regional (Mountain West) titles. Submission by invitation only in fiction and poetry for the Utah State University Press imprint.

The Press also copublishes with and distributes titles for the Denver Museum of Natural History, the Colorado Historical Society Colorado State University's Cooperative Extension, the Center for Literary Publishing, and the Institute for Mesoamerican Studies.

Special series: Atomic History & Culture; The George and Sakaye Aratani Nikkei in the Americas Series; Leonard J. Arrington Lecture Series; Life Writings of Frontier Women; May Swenson Poetry Award Series; Mesoamerican Worlds; Mining the American West; Timberline Books

Columbia University Press

61 West 62nd Street
New York, NY 10023-7015

Phone: 212.459.0600
Fax: 212.459.3677
Email: (user I.D.)@columbia.edu

Website and Social Media:
Website: www.columbia.edu/cu/cup
Blog: cupblog.org
Facebook: www.facebook.com/
  ColumbiaUniversityPress
Twitter: ColumbiaUP
YouTube: www.youtube.com/CUPvideos

Perseus Distribution Warehouse:
193 Edwards Drive
Jackson, TN 38301

Orders and Customer Service:
Phone: 800.944.8648
Fax: 800.944.1844

UK Office:
University Press Group
Southern Cross Trading Estate
Southern Cross Trading Estate
1 Oldlands Way, Bognor Regis
West Sussex PO22 9SA
Phone: +44 1243 842165
Fax: +44 1243 842167

Staff

President and Director: James D. Jordan (ext. 7118; email: jj2143)
  Assistant to the Director: Jonathan Fiedler (ext. 7142; email: jf2801)
  Chief Financial Officer: Richard G. Gehringer (ext. 7112; email: rg2665)

Director of Intellectual Property and Subsidiary Rights: Peggy Garry (ext. 7147; email: pg2371)

Manager of Subsidiary Rights: Justine Evans (ext. 7128; email: je2217)

Acquisitions Editorial: Jennifer Crewe, Associate Director and Editorial Director (Asian humanities, film studies, food studies) (ext. 7145; email: jc373)

Publisher for the Life Sciences: Patrick Fitzgerald (ext. 7136; email: pf2134)

Publisher for Finance and Economics and Columbia Business School Publishing: Myles Thompson (ext. 7161; email: mt2312)

Publisher for Philosophy and Religion: Wendy Lochner (ext. 7121; email: wl2003)

Senior Executive Editor: Jennifer Perillo (social work, criminology, psychology) (ext. 7107; email: jp3187)

Senior Editor: Anne Routon (Asian history, international relations, Middle East studies) (ext. 7116; email: akr36)

Editor: Philip Leventhal (literary studies, journalism, American history) (ext. 7159; email: pl2162)

Manuscript Editorial: Anne McCoy, Managing Editor (ext. 7111; email: aam10)

Assistant Managing Editors: Leslie Kriesel (ext. 7110; email: lrk11); Ron Harris (ext. 7155; email: rh182)

Senior Production Editor: Irene Pavitt (ext.7138; email: ip126)

Senior Manuscript Editors: Roy Thomas (ext. 7160; email: ret12); Susan Pensak (ext. 7139; email: srp4)

Electronic Manuscripts Administrator: Michael Haskell (ext. 7162; email: mh2100)

Director of Design and Production: Jennifer Jerome (ext. 7177; email: jj352)

Art Director: Julia Kushnirsky (ext. 7102; email: jk3151)

Senior Designers: Lisa Hamm (ext. 7105; email: lh400); Milenda Lee (ext. 7103; email: ml2657); Chang Jae Lee (ext. 7140; email: chl32)

Marketing: Brad Hebel, Assistant Director, Director of Marketing and Sales (ext. 7130; email: bh2106)

Assistant Marketing Director/Publicity Director: Meredith Howard (ext. 7126; email: mh2306)

Electronic Marketing Manager: Philip Leventhal (ext. 7159; email: pl2164)

Assistant Marketing Director/Direct Marketing Manager: Todd Lazarus (ext. 7152; email: tdl10)

Advertising Manager: Elena Iaffa (ext. 7124; email: ei2131)

Sales Manager and East Coast Sales Representative: Catherine Hobbs (ext. 7809; email: chobss@rlc.net)

Mid-West Sales Representative: Kevin Kurtz (ext. 7806; email: kkurtz5@earthlink.net)

West Coast Sales Representative: William Gawronski (ext. 7807; email: wgawronski@ earthlink.net)

Business: Robert Abrams, Controller (ext. 7119; email: ra2555)

Human Resources Manager: James Pakiela (ext. 7109; email: jp2483)

Accounts Payable & Royalty Manager: Frederick Stokes (ext. 7108; email: fs2445)

IT Director: Greg Lara (ext. 7132; email: gl2298)

Systems Support Specialist: Sean Chen (ext. 7106; email: sc2566)

Publishing Systems Manager: Michael Haskell (ext. 7162; email: mh2100)

Managing Editor for Reference and Electronic Publishing: Stephen Sterns (ext. 7148; email: ss724)

Full Member

Established: 1893   Admitted to AAUP: 1937
Title output 2011: 171   Title output 2012: 160
Titles currently in print: 3,240

Editorial Program

General reference works in print and electronic formats. Scholarly, general interest, and professional books, and upper-level textbooks in the humanities, social sciences, and earth and life sciences, business and social work. Subjects include animal studies; Asian Studies; botany; conservation and environmental science; criminology; ecology; evolutionary studies; film; finance and business economics; gender studies; history; international relations; journalism; literary and cultural studies; media studies; Middle East studies; philosophy; political philosophy; political science; religion; and social work. The Press publishes poetry, fiction, and drama in translation only and is the publisher of Wallflower Press titles worldwide.

Columbia University Press is the distributor in the United States, Canada, and Latin America for American Institute of Buddhist Studies, Auteur Publishing, Chinese University Press, East European Monographs, Edinburgh University Press, European Consortium for Political Research Press, Hong Kong University Press, and University of Tokyo Press. Special series, joint imprints, and/or co-publishing programs: American Academy of Religion Lectures on the History of Religions; Arts and Traditions of the Table; Asia Perspectives; Bampton Lectures in America; Biology and Resource Management; CERI Series in Comparative Politics and International Studies; Columbia Business School Publishing; Columbia Classics in Philosophy; Columbia Classics in Religion; Columbia History of Urban Life; Columbia Readings of Buddhist Literature; Columbia Series in Science and Religion; Columbia Studies in International History; Columbia Studies in Terrorism and Irregular Warfare; Columbia Themes in Philosophy, Social Criticism and the Arts; Complexity in Ecological Systems; Contemporary Asia In the World; Critical Moments in Earth History; Critical Perspectives on Animals; Cultures of History; Empowering the Powerless; End of Life Care; European Perspectives; Film and Culture; Foundations of Social Work Knowledge; Gender and Culture; Gender, Theory and Religion; Global Chinese Culture; History and Society of the Modern Middle East; Hurst Books; Initiative for Policy Dialogue at Columbia; Introduction to Asian Civilizations; Insurrections: Critical Studies in Religion, Politics, and Culture; Leonard Hastings Schoff Lectures; Modern Asian Literature; Modern Chinese Literature from Taiwan; The Neurosciences, Social Sciences, and the Arts; New Directions in Critical Theory; Political Thought/Political History; Records of Western Civilization; Religion and American Culture; Social Science Research Council Books; Translations from the Asian Classics; Weatherhead Books on Asia; Wellek Library Lectures

Cork University Press

Youngline Industrial Estate, Pouladuff Road
Cork, Ireland

Phone: +353 21 490 2980
Fax: + 353 21 431 5329
Email: corkuniversitypress@ucc.ie

<u>Website and Social Media:</u>
Website: www.corkuniversitypress.com
Blog: corkuniversitypress.org
Facebook: www.facebook.com/CorkUP

<u>UK Representative:</u>
Marston Book Services

<u>US Representative:</u>
Stylus Publishing
22883 Quicksilver Drive
Sterling, VA 20166-2012
Phone: 703.661.1504
Fax: 703.661.1501
Email: stylusmail@presswarehouse.com

<u>Irish Representative:</u>
Gill & MacMillan

Staff
Director: Mike Collins (email: mike.collins@ucc.ie)
Editorial and Production: Maria O'Donovan (email: maria.odonovan@ucc.ie)

International Member
Established: 1925
Title output 2011: 14
Titles currently in print: 200

Admitted to AAUP: 2002
Title output 2012: 20
Journals published: 1

<u>Editorial Program</u>
While the Press specializes in the broad field of Irish Culture, its subject range extends across the fields of music, art history, literary criticism and poetry. However, the focus of our list is in the areas of Irish cultural history, archaeology and landscape studies.
Journal: *Irish Review*
Special series: Field Day Monographs; Ireland into Film

Cornell University Press

Street Address:
Sage House
512 East State Street
Ithaca, NY 14850

Phone: 607.277.2338
Fax: 607.277.2374
Email: (user I.D.)@cornell.edu

Website and Social Media:
Website: www.cornellpress.cornell.edu
Blog: cornellpress.wordpress.com
Facebook: www.facebook.com/CornellUP
Twitter: CornellPress
YouTube: www.youtube.com/user/CornellPressNews

Mailing Address:
Sage House
512 East State Street
Ithaca, NY 14850

Order Fulfillment:
CUP Services
750 Cascadilla Street
Ithaca, NY 14850
Phone: 800.666.2211
Fax: 800.688.2877
Email: orderbook@cupserv.org

UK Representative:
University Presses Marketing

Canadian Representative:
Lexa Publishers' Representatives

UK/European Distributor:
NBN International

Staff

Director: John G. Ackerman (ext. 209; email: jga4)
    Assistant Director & CFO: Roger A. Hubbs (607.277.2696; email: rah9)
    Assistant to the Director: Michael Morris (ext. 210; email: mam278)
Acquisitions Editorial: Peter J. Potter, Editor-in-Chief (classics, medieval studies, literature)
    (ext. 241; email: pjp33)
    Editorial Director, ILR Press: Frances Benson (labor studies and workplace issues, health
    care, sociology, business) (ext. 222; email: fgb2)
    Executive Editor: Roger Haydon (politics, international relations, Asian studies) (ext. 225;
    email: rmh11)
    Editors: John G. Ackerman (European history, Russian/East European/Eurasian history
    and literature) (ext. 209; email: jga4); TBA (science: entomology, herpetology, natural
    history, ornithology, plant sciences); Michael J. McGandy (American history, U.S. politics,
    urban studies, New York state and regional books) (ext. 233; email: mjm475)
Manuscript Editorial: Ange Romeo-Hall, Managing Editor (ext. 243; email: asr8)
    Manuscript Editors: Karen T. Hwa (ext. 260; email: kth9); Karen Laun (ext. 236; email:
    kml35); Susan Specter (ext. 245; email: sps19)
Design and Production: Karen Kerr, Manager (ext. 235; email: kg99)
    Senior Designers: Scott Levine (ext. 263; email: sel37); Lou Robinson (email: lr11); George
    Whipple (email: gtw2)
    Designer: Richanna Patrick (ext. 240; email: rp12)

Senior Production Coordinator: Diana Silva (ext. 257; email: drs68)
Production Coordinator: Jessica A. Venezia (ext. 239; email: jav85)
Marketing: Mahinder Kingra, Marketing Director (ext. 255; email: msk55)
Sales Manager: Nathan Gemignani (ext. 251; email: ndg5)
Publicity Manager: Jonathan Hall (ext. 252; email: jlh98)
Subsidiary Rights Manager: Tonya Cook (email: cup-subrights)
Advertising Coordinator: Amelia Wise (ext. 256; email: arw45)
Publicity Coordinator: Jennifer Longley (ext. 254; email: jal225)
Exhibits/Awards Coordinator: David Mitchell (ext. 248; email: dwm23)
Copy Supervisor/Grant Writer: Susan Barnett (ext. 259; email: scb33)
Permissions Coordinator: Stephanie Munson (ext. 231; email: sm120)
Business: (607.277.2696)
Chief Financial Officer: Roger A. Hubbs (ext. 132; email: rah9)
Accounting & Operations Coordinator: Cindy Snyder (ext. 133; email: chs6)
Procurement, Disbursements & Title Accounting: Laurie McGuire (ext. 139; email: lam35)
CUP Services Distribution Center:
CUP Services Manager: Christopher Quinlan (607.277.2211, ext. 125; email: cq@cupserv.org)
Customer Service, Client Services, Accounts Receivable: Christine Jolluck (607.277.2037, ext. 126; email: cj@cupserv.org)
MIS: Patrick Garrison (607.277.2969, ext. 149; email: plg6@cupserv.org)
Warehouse and Shipping: Christopher Quinlan (607.277.2211, ext. 125; email: cq@cupserv.org)

Full Member

Established: 1869	Admitted to AAUP: 1937
Re-established in present form: 1930	
Title output 2011: 140	Title output 2012: 145
Titles currently in print: 2,514	

Editorial Program

Serious nonfiction, with particular strengths in anthropology; Asian studies; classics; German studies, history; industrial and labor relations; life science; literary criticism and theory; music; natural history; politics and international relations; race studies; Slavic studies; sociology; and women's studies. Submissions are not invited in poetry or fiction.

Cornell University Press is the distributor for Cornell University's Southeast Asia Program Publications and distributes in North America for Leuven University Press.

Special imprints: Comstock Publishing Associates; Fall Creek Books; ILR Press
Special series, joint imprints and/or copublishing programs: Agora Editions; American Institutions and Society; Ancient Commentators on Aristotle; Cornell Studies in Classical Philology/Townsend Lectures; Cornell Studies in the History of Psychiatry; Cornell Studies in Money; Cornell Studies in Political Economy; Cornell Studies in Security Affairs; The Cornell Yeats; The Culture and Politics of Health Care Work; Culture and Society after Socialism; Cushwa Center Studies of Catholicism in Twentieth-Century America; Expertise—Cultures and Technologies of Knowledge; Islandica; Religion and American Public Life; Signale—Modern German Letters, Cultures, and Thought; The United States in the World.

Duke University Press

Street Address:
905 West Main Street
Suite 18-B
Durham, NC 27701

Mailing Address:
Box 90660
Durham, NC 27708- 0660

Phone: 919.687.3600
Faxes: 919.688.4574 (general)
919.688.3524 (journals)
919.688.4391 (marketing/production-books)
Email: info@dukeupress.edu
Indiv:
firstinitiallastname@dukeupress.edu or
firstname.lastname@dukeupress.edu
(unless otherwise indicated)

Orders and Customer Service:
Phone: 888.651.0122; 919.688.5134
Fax: 888.651.0124; 919.688.2615

Warehouse:
Duke University Press
Distribution Center
120 Golden Drive
Durham, NC 27705
Phone: 919.384.0733

Website and Social Media:
Website: www.dukeupress.edu
Blog: www.dukeupress.typepad.com
Facebook: www.facebook.com/DukeUniversityPress
Twitter: DUKEpress

UK/European Representative:
Combined Academic Publishers

Canadian Representative:
Lexa Publishers' Representatives

Staff

Director: Stephen A. Cohn (919.687.3606)
  Assistant to the Director/Development Coordinator: Bonnie Perkel (919.687.3685)
  Assistant Director for Digital Publishing: Allison Belan (919.687.3683)
  Manager, Rights and Permissions: Diane Grosse (919.687.8020)
Central Administration: Robyn L. Miller, Manager (919.687.3633)
  Assistant Manager: Starr Loftis (919.687.3609)
  Logistics Coordinator: Bonnie Conner (919.687.3693)

Books [handwritten: ask who to contact - crossover staff]

Acquisitions Editorial: Ken Wissoker, Editorial Director (anthropology, cultural studies, Asian Studies, post-colonial theory, lesbian and gay studies, construction of race, gender and national identity, new media, literary criticism, film and television, popular music, science studies, visual studies) (919.687.3648; email: kwiss@duke.edu)

Senior Editor: Valerie Millholland (Latin American history, anthropology, European history and politics, U.S. history, women's history, environmental studies, Asian studies, race and ethnicity (919.687.3628; email: vmill@duke.edu)

Editor: Courtney Berger (political theory, sociology and social theory, geography, American studies, literary theory and criticism, cultural studies, gender studies, Asian American studies, Native American & indigenous studies, film and television, science and technology studies, food studies) (919.687.3652)

Associate Editor: Miriam Angress (religion, women's studies, world history, humanities, cultural studies) (919.687.3601)
Assistant Editor: Gisela Fosado (anthropology, history, Latin American studies, social movements, gender studies) (919.687.3632)
Books Editing, Design, and Production Manager: Nancy Hoagland (919.687.3629)
Art Director: Bea Jackson (919.687.3643)
Book Designers: Amy Buchanan (919.687.3651); Heather Hensley (919.687.3658)
Managing Editor: Jessica Ryan (919.687.3666)
Assistant Managing Editors: Susan Albury (919.687.3669); Elizabeth Smith (919.687.8006); Christine Dahlin (919.687.3681)
Production Manager: Patty Chase (919.687.3622)
Senior Editorial Assistant: Danielle Szulczewski (919.687.8016)
Senior Production Assistant: Tanya Davis (919.687.8019)
Marketing: Emily Young, Marketing Manager (919.687.3654)
Books Marketing Metadata and Digital Systems Manager: H. Lee Willoughby-Harris (919.687.3646)
Associate Marketing Manager and Sales Manager: Michael McCullough (919.687.3604)
Publicity and Advertising Manager: Laura Sell (919.687.3639)
Copywriter: Katie Courtland (919.687.3663)
Interim Direct Marketing Manager and Sales Associate: Julie Thomson (919.687.3603)
Exhibits Manager: Helena Knox (919.687.3647)
Journals
Editorial & Administrative Manager: Rob Dilworth (919.687.3624)
Senior Managing Editor, H&SS: Charles Brower (919.687.3688)
Senior Managing Editor, STM: Ray Lambert (919.687.3625)
Senior Managing Editor, Managing Editors' Group: Lisl Hampton (919.687.3644)
Senior Editor Journal Acquisitions: Erich Staib (919.687.3664)
Project Euclid Manager: Mira Waller (919.687.3630)
Production and Finance Manager: Michael Brondoli (919.687.3605)
Assistant Production Manager: Terri Fizer (919.687.3619)
Art Director/Journals Designer: Sue Hall (919.687.3620)
Production Technology Specialist: Bendte Fagge (919.687.3674)
Digital Content Developer: Steve Grathwohl (919.687.3634)
Marketing Manager: Cason Lynley (919.687.3631)
Assistant Marketing Manager: Jocelyn Dawson (919.687.3653)
Library Relations Manager: Kim Steinle (919.687.3655)
Library Relations Coordinator: Beth Hoskins (919.687.3627)
Academic Exhibits & Publicity Coordinator: Katie Anderson (919.687.8013)
Web & Advertising Coordinator: Kevin Woodcock (919.687.3687)
Institutional Exhibits & Direct Marketing Coordinator: Leslie Eager (919.687.8027)
Journals Marketing Projects Specialist: TBA
Business Office and Distribution: Norris Langley, Chief Financial Officer (919.687.3607)
Interim Accounting Supervisor: Carmen Marshall (919.687.8007)
Warehouse Manager: Don Griffin (919.384.1244)
Customer Service Manager: Lesley Jones (919.687.3684)
Customer Service—Journals: Alicia Matthews (919.687.8010)
Customer Service—Books: Cynthia Morgia (919.687.3617)
Information Systems: Pamela Spaulding, Manager (919.687.3641)

Assistant Manager: Sonya Johnson (919.687.3662)
Database Administrator/Advantage Programmer: Ling Mao (919.687.3665)
System Administrator: Michael Brennan (919.687.3679)
Enterprise System Integrator - Programmer: Ariel Dela Fuente (919.687.3611)
Help Desk Manager: Marcus Butts (919.687.3635)

Full Member

Established: 1921 (as Trinity College Press)
Title output 2011: 120
Titles currently in print: 2,457

Admitted to AAUP: 1937
Title output 2012: 130
Journals published: 46

Editorial Program

Scholarly books in the humanities and social sciences, with lists in art criticism and history; visual studies; cultural studies; literary theory and history; legal studies; gay and lesbian studies; gender studies; American history; African American studies; Asian American studies; Native American & indigenous studies; Latin American anthropology, history, literature, and politics; Slavic studies; European history and politics; cultural anthropology; minority politics and post colonial issues; Asian studies; South Asian studies; African studies; Middle East studies; music; film and TV; environmental studies; political science and political theory; religion; sociology and social theory; and science studies.

Journals: *American Literary Scholarship; American Literature; American Speech; boundary 2; Camera Obscura; Collected Letters of Thomas and Jane Welsh Carlyle; Common Knowledge; Comparative Literature; Comparative Studies of South Asia, Africa and the Middle East; Cultural Politics; differences; Duke Mathematical Journal; East Asian Science, Technology and Society; Eighteenth-Century Life; Ethnohistory; French Historical Studies; Genre; GLQ: A Journal of Lesbian and Gay Studies; Hispanic American Historical Review; History of Political Economy; Journal of Health Politics, Policy and Law; Journal of Medieval and Early Modern Studies; Journal of Music Theory; Kyoto Journal of Mathematics; Labor; Limnology and Oceanography: Fluids and Environments; Mediterranean Quarterly; minnesota review; Modern Language Quarterly; Nagoya Mathematical Journal; New German Critique; Nka; Notre Dame Journal of Formal Logic; Novel; Pedagogy; Philosophical Review; Poetics Today; positions; Public Culture; Radical History Review; Small Axe; Social Science History; Social Text; South Atlantic Quarterly; Theater; Tikkun*

Special series, joint imprints and/or copublishing programs: American Encounters: Global Interactions; Asia-Pacific: Culture, Politics and Society; Collected Letters of Thomas and Jane Welsh Carlyle; C. L. R. James Archives; Console-ing Passions; Body/Commodity/Text; Ecologies for the Twenty-First Century; Experimental Futures; Latin America in Translation; Latin America Otherwise: Languages, Empires, Nations; Latin America Readers; Living with the Shore; Narrating Native Histories; New Americanists; Next Wave: New Directions in Women's Studies; Objects/Histories; Perverse Modernities; Politics, Culture & History; Post-Contemporary Interventions; Public Planet; Radical Perspectives: A Radical History Review Book Series; Refiguring American Music; Science and Cultural Theory; Series Q; SIC; Sign, Storage, Transmission; World Readers

Duquesne University Press

600 Forbes Avenue
Pittsburgh, PA 15282

Phone: 412.396.6610
Fax: 412.396.5984

Website and Social Media:
Website: www.dupress.duq.edu

UK Representative:
Gazelle Book Sevices

Distribution/Orders:
CUP Services
Box 6525
750 Cascadilla Street
Ithaca, NY 14851-6525

Orders only: 800.666.2211
Fax: 607.272.6292
Customer Service: 607.277.2211

Staff

Director: Susan Wadsworth-Booth (412.396.6610; email: wadsworth@duq.edu)
Assistant to the Director/Project Coordinator: Mary Beth Yount (412.396.4863)
Production Editor: Kathy McLaughlin Meyer (412.396.1166; email: meyerk@duq.edu)
Editorial Assistant: Brock Bahler (412.396.6610)
Marketing & Business Manager: Lori R. Crosby (412.396.5732; email: crosbyl@duq.edu)
Promotions/Marketing Assistant: Tara Majdalani (412.396.4866)

Full Member

Established: 1927

Title output 2011: 9
Titles currently in print: 188

Admitted to AAUP: 1995
(Former membership: 1962-72)
Title output 2012: 10

Editorial Program

Literary studies, specifically of late medieval, Renaissance and seventeenth-century literature; ethics; philosophy; psychology; religious studies. The Press does not publish fiction, poetry, or unrevised dissertations.

Special series: Levinas Studies: An Annual Review; Medieval & Renaissance Literary Studies; Milton Studies; A Variorum Commentary on the Poems of John Milton

University Press of Florida

15 N.W. 15th Street
Gainesville, FL 32611-2079

Phone: 352.392.1351
Fax: 352.392.0590
Email: (user I.D.)@upf.com

Orders:
Phone: 800.226.3822
Fax: 352.392.7302
Toll free fax: 800.680.1955

Website and Social Media:
Website: www.upf.com
Blog: floridacurrent.wordpress.com
Facebook: www.facebook.com/pages/University-Press-of-Florida/257714960219
www.facebook.com/pages/The-Florida-Bookshelf/158260221214
Twitter: floridapress

UK Representative:
Eurospan

Canadian Representative:
Scholarly Book Services

Staff

Director: Meredith Morris Babb (ext. 204; email: mb)
  Assistant to the Director: Cindy Laukert (ext. 201; email: cl)
  Deputy Director: Dennis Lloyd (ext. 206; email: dl)
Editor-in-Chief: Amy Gorelick (Middle East, Latin American studies, literature)
  (ext. 232; email: ag)
  Senior Acquisitions Editor: Sian Hunter (919.428.8813; email: sian)
  Acquisitions Assistant: Shannon McCarthy (ext. 236; email: smccarthy)
  Rights and Permissions Manager: Sonia Dickey (ext. 234; email: sonia)
Editorial, Design & Production: Lynn Werts, Associate Director & EDP Manager
  (ext. 222; email: lw)
  Managing Editor: Michele Fiyak-Burkley (ext. 212; email: mf)
  Editorial Assistants: Marthe Walters (ext. 217; email: marthe); Jesse Arost (ext. 214; email:
  jesse); Nevil Parker (ext. 213; email: np)
  Design Manager: Larry Leshan (ext. 221; email: ll)
  Designer/Compositor: Robyn Taylor (ext. 218; email: rt)
Marketing: Teal Amthor-Shaffer, Manager (ext. 209; email: tas)
  Advertising and Direct Mail Manager: Romi Gutierrez (ext. 235; email: rg)
  Sales and Marketing Assistant: Ale Gasso (ext. 233; email: ale)
Business: Kim Lake, Associate Director for Finance (ext. 207; email: kl)
  Accounting/Order Fulfillment Manager: Sandra Dyson (ext. 210; email: sd)
  Credit Manager: Jackie Harvey (ext. 211; email: jackie)
  Order Entry: Deanna Sudbury (352.392.6867; email: ds)
  Warehouse and Shipping Manager: Charles Hall (352.392.6867; email: charles)
Information Technology: Bryan Lutz, Manager (ext. 215; email: bryan)

Full Member

Established: 1945
Title output 2011: 93
Titles currently in print: 2,717

Admitted to AAUP: 1950
Title output 2012: 86

Editorial Program

Floridiana; New World archaeology; conservation biology; Latin American studies; Caribbean studies; Middle East studies; African American studies; American history and culture; Native American studies; dance; natural history; humanities. Submissions are not invited in prose fiction or poetry.

Fordham University Press

Street Address:
Canisius Hall
2546 Belmont Avenue
Bronx, NY 10458-5172

Mailing Address:
University Box L
Bronx, NY 10458-5172

Phone: 718.817.4795
Fax: 718.817.4785
Email: (user I.D.)@fordham.edu

Website and Social Media:
Website: www.fordhampress.com
Blog: www.fordhamimpressions.com
Facebook: www.facebook.com/pages/
    Fordham-University-Press/7444504942
Twitter: FordhamPress

Orders:
Oxford University Press, Inc.
2001 Evans Road
Cary, NC 27513
Phone: 800.445.9714
Fax: 919.677.0977
Email: custserv.us@oup.com

European Representative:
Combined Academic Publishers Ltd.

Canadian Representative:
Oxford University Press, Inc.

Staff

Director: Fredric W. Nachbaur (718.817.4789; email: fnachbaur)
    Editorial Associate and Assistant to the Director: Will Cerbone (718.817.4781; email: wcerbone)
Editorial Director: Helen Tartar (718.817.4787; email: tartar)
    Assistant Editor: Thomas Lay (718.817.4790; email: tlay)
Managing Editor: Eric Newman (718.817.4784; email: ernewman)
Production Editor: Loomis Mayer (718.817.4788; email: lmayer)
Marketing Director: Kate O'Brien Nicholson (718.817.4782; email: bkaobrien)
    Assistant Marketing Manager: Kathleen A. Sweeney (718.817.4791; email: kasweeney)
Business Manager: Margaret M. Noonan (718.817.4780; email: mnoonan)
    Assistant Business Manager: Marie Hall (718.817.4783; email: mhall21)

Full Member

Established: 1907   Admitted to AAUP: 1938
Title output 2011: 73   Title output 2012: 71
Titles currently in print: 872   Journals published: 3

Editorial Program

Fordham University Press publishes primarily in the humanities and social sciences, with emphasis on the fields of philosophy, religion, theology, history, anthropology, and literature. Additionally, the Press publishes books focusing on the New York region and books of interest to the general public.

The Press distributes the publications of Creighton University Press; University of San Francisco Press; St. Joseph's University Press; Rockhurst University Press; the Institution for Advanced Study in the Theater Arts (IASTA); The Reconstructionist Press; Center for Migration Studies; and St. Bede's Publications.

Journals: *Dante Studies; Joyce Studies Annual; Traditio: Studies in Ancient and Medieval History, Thought, and Religion*

Imprints: Empire State Editions: Dedicated to publishing books about the New York Region.

Series: American Philosophy; Bordering Religions: Concepts, Conflicts, and Conversations; Catholic Practice in North America; Critical Studies in Italian America; Commonalities; Donald McGannon Research Center's Everett C. Parker Book Series; Fordham Series in Medieval Studies; Forms of Living; The Future of the Religious Past; Groundworks: Ecological Issues in Philosophy and Theology; Historicizing Dante; International Humanitarian Affairs; Just Ideas; Meaning Systems; Medieval Philosophy: Texts and Studies; The North's Civil War; Orthodox Christianity and Contemporary Thought; People and the Environment; Perspectives in Continental Philosophy; Psychoanalytic Interventions; Poets Out Loud; Reconstructing America; Transdisciplinary Theological Colloquia; Verbal Arts: Studies in Poetics; and World War II: The Global, Human, and Ethical Dimension.

Gallaudet University Press

800 Florida Avenue, N.E.
Washington, DC 20002-3695

Phone: 202.651.5488
Fax: 202.651.5489
Email: (user I.D.)@gallaudet.edu

Website and Social Media:
Website: gupress.gallaudet.edu

European Distributor:
Forest Book Services

Orders:
Gallaudet University Press
Chicago Distribution Center
11030 South Langley Avenue
Chicago, IL 60628
Phone: 800.621.2736
TTY: 888.630.9347
Fax: 800.621.8476

Staff

Executive Director: Gary Aller (202.651.5488; email: gary.aller)
Editorial: Ivey Pittle Wallace, Assistant Director and Acquisitions (202.651.5662;
  email: ivey.wallace)
Managing Editor: Deirdre Mullervy (202.651.5967; email: deirdre.mullervy)
Production: Donna Thomas, Coordinator (202.651.5488; email: donna.thomas)
Marketing: Dan Wallace, Assistant Director (202.651.5661; email: daniel.wallace)
  Marketing Assistant: Valencia Simmons (202.651.5488; email: valencia.simmons)
Business: Frances W. Clark (202.651.5455; email: frances.clark)

Full Member

Established: 1980
Title output 2011: 12
Titles currently in print: 268

Admitted to AAUP: 1983
Title output 2012: 13
Journals published: 2

Editorial Program

Scholarly books and serious nonfiction from all disciplines as they relate to the interests and
culture of people who are deaf, hard of hearing, or experiencing hearing loss. Particular areas
of emphasis include signed languages, linguistics, deaf culture, deaf history, disability studies,
biography and autobiography, parenting, and special education, as well as instructional works
and children's literature with sign language or deafness themes.
   The Press distributes select titles from Signum Verlag (Hamburg, Germany).
Journals: *American Annals of the Deaf; Sign Language Studies*
Special imprints: Kendall Green Publications; Clerc Books
Special series: Deaf Lives; Deaf Education Series; Gallaudet Classics in Deaf Studies; Interpreter Education; Sociolinguistics in Deaf Communities; Studies in Interpretation

Georgetown University Press

3240 Prospect Street NW, Suite 250
Washington, DC 20007

Phone: 202.687.5889
Fax: 202.687.6340
Email: gupress@georgetown.edu
Indiv: (user I.D.)@georgetown.edu

Website and Social Media:
Website: www.press.georgetown.edu
Blog: georgetownuniversitypress.tumblr.com
Facebook: www.facebook.com/georgetownup
News blog: georgetownup.wordpress.com
Pinterest: pinterest.com/georgetownup
Twitter: twitter.com/gupress
YouTube: www.youtube.com/user/GeorgetownUP

UK/European Distributor:
NBN International

Orders:
US: c/o Hopkins Fulfillment Service
PO Box 50370
Baltimore, MD 21211
Phone: 800.537.5487
Fax: 410.516.6998
Email: hfscustserv@press.jhu.edu

Canadian Representative:
Scholarly Book Services

Staff

Director: Richard Brown (202.687.5912; email: reb7)
  Publishing Assistant and Permissions Coordinator: Kristy Cottrell (202.687.4462;
  email: kml96)
  Assistant Director and Marketing and Sales Director: John W. Warren (202.687.9856;
  email: jww55)
Director, Georgetown Languages: Hope LeGro (202.687.4704; email: hjs6)
Acquisitions Editor, Political Science and International Affairs: Donald Jacobs
  (202.687.5218; email: dpj5)
Acquisitions Editor, Languages: David Nicholls (202.687.6263; email: dgn5)
Editorial and Production Manager: Deborah Weiner (202.687.6251; email: weinerd)
  Editorial and Production Coordinator: Nancy Driver (202.687.0159; email: njd23)
Marketing Coordinator: Maureen Mills (202.687.3671; email: mm634)
  Publicist: Jacqueline Beilhart (202.687.9298; email: jb594)
  Intellectual Property Manager: Laura Leichum (202.687.7687; email: lal75)
  Marketing Assistant: Miriam McPhie (202.687.8170; email: mhm56)
Business Manager: Ioan Suciu (202.687.5641; email: suciui)
  Accountant: Sulah Kim (202.687.8151; email: slk33)

Full Member

Established: 1964
Title output 2011: 38
Titles currently in print: 635

Admitted to AAUP: 1986
Title output 2012: 39
Journals published: 2

Editorial Program

Disciplines: bioethics; international affairs; languages and linguistics; political science, public policy, and public management; and religion and ethics.

Journals: *Al-cArabiyya: Journal of the American Association of Teachers of Arabic and Journal of the Society of Christian Ethics*

Special series: Advancing Human Rights; American Governance and Public Policy; Georgetown Classics in Arabic Language and Linguistics; Georgetown Studies in Spanish Linguistics; Georgetown University Round Table on Languages and Linguistics; Moral Traditions; Public Management and Change; Religion and Politics; South Asia in World Affairs; Working Languagess

University of Georgia Press

Main Library, Third Floor
320 S. Jackson Street
Athens, GA 30602

Phone: 706.542.4145
Fax: 706. 542.2558
Email: books@ugapress.uga.edu
Indiv: (user I.D.)@ugapress.uga.edu
(unless otherwise indicated)

Website and Social Media:
Website: www.ugapress.org
Blog: ugapress.blogspot.com
Facebook: www.facebook.com/UGAPress
Twitter: UGAPress
YouTube: UGAPress

UK Distributor:
Eurospan

Distribution Center:
University of Georgia Press
Distribution Center
4435 Atlanta Highway West Dock
Bogart, GA 30622

Orders and Customer Service:
Phone: 800.266.5842
Fax: 706.425.3061

Staff

Director: Lisa Bayer (706.542.0027; email: lbayer)
  Assistant to the Director and Development Coordinator: Sydney DuPre (706.542.1903; email: sdupre)
  Intellectual Property Manager (Contracts & Rights): Sean Garrett (706.542.7175; sgarrett)
  Director of Development: Chantel Dunham (706.542.0628; email: cdunham@uga.edu)
Acquisitions Editorial: Mick Gusinde-Duffy, Editor-in-Chief and Assistant Director
  Senior Acquisitions Editor: TBA
  Acquisitions Editor: Regan Huff (706.542.6004; email: rhuff)
  Assistant Acquisitions Editor: Beth Snead (706.542.7613; email: bsnead)
Manuscript Editorial: Jon Davies, Assistant Director for Editorial (706.542.2101; email: jdavies)
  Project Editor: John Joerschke (706.542.5137; email: johnj)

Design and Production: Kathi Dailey Morgan, Assistant Director for Design and Production
(706.542.2491; email: kdmorgan)
Production Editor: Rebecca Norton (706.542.4643; email: rnorton)
Senior Designer and Production Manager: Kaelin Broaddus (706.542.3889;
email: kbroaddus)
Senior Designer and Art Director: Erin Kirk New (email: ekirknew)
Restocking Program Manager: Melissa Bugbee Buchanan (706.542.4488;
email: mbuchanan)
Marketing and Sales: TBA, Marketing and Sales Director (706.542.9263)
Publicity Manager: Amanda Sharp (706.542.4145; email: asharp)
Electronic Information Manager: David Des Jardines (706.542.9758; email: ddesjard)
Marketing Designer: Jacqueline Baxter (706.542.4674; email: jbaxter)
Exhibits and Advertising Manager: Pat Allen (706. 542.0134; email: pallen)
Business and Order Fulfillment: Phyllis Wells, Business Manager and Assistant Director
(706.542.7250; email: pwells)
Accountant: Marena Smith (706.542.0753; email: msmith)
Accounts Payable and Permissions Coordinator: Stacey Hayes (706.542.2606;
email: shayes)
Distribution Center Manager: Jeri Headrick (706-369-6146, email: jheadrick)
Customer Service Representative: Betty Downer (706.369.6148; email: bddowner)
Shipping Clerks: Pam Bond (email: pbond); Mark Jenkins (email: mjenkins)
IT Professional Associate: Matthew Tyler (706.369.4025; email: mwtyler@uga.edu)
The New Georgia Encyclopedia Project (www.georgiaencyclopedia.org)
Editor: John Inscoe (706.542.8848; email: jinscoe@uga.edu)
Project Director & Managing Editor: Kelly Caudle (404.523.6220, ext. 18; email:
kcaudle@uga.edu)
Editor: Sarah McKee (404.523.5702; email: semckee@uga.edu)

Full Member

Established: 1938
Title output 2011: 87
Titles currently in print: 1,858

Admitted to AAUP: 1940
Title output 2012: 92

Editorial Program

Humanities and social sciences with particular interests in Atlantic world, American, and
southern history; civil rights history; legal history; environmental history; African American
studies; geography; urban studies; international relations and security studies; natural history;
environmental studies; nature writing; American and southern literature; American studies;
cinema and media studies; food studies; popular culture; and regional trade titles.
Special series and imprints: Brown Thrasher Books; Center Books on the American South;
Early American Places; Environmental History and the American South; Geographies of
Justice and Social Transformation; The New Southern Studies; Politics and Culture in the
Twentieth-Century South; Publications of the Southern Texts Society; Race in the Atlantic
World, 1700-1900; Since 1970: Histories of Contemporary America; Southern Women:
Their Lives and Times; The Spirit of the Laws; Studies in Security and International Affairs;
Studies in the Legal History of the South; UnCivil Wars; The United States and the Ameri-
cas; The Works of Tobias Smollett; A Wormsloe Foundation Nature Book; A Wormsloe

Foundation Publication
Literary competitions: Flannery O'Connor Award for Short Fiction; The Association of Writers and Writing Programs Award for Creative Nonfiction; Cave Canem Poetry Prize; National Poetry Series
Lecture series: Mercer University Lamar Memorial Lectures; George H. Shriver Lecture Series in Religion in American History

Getty Publications

1200 Getty Center Drive
Suite 500
Los Angeles, CA 90049-1682

Phone: 310.440.7365
Fax: 310.440.7758
Email: pubsinfo@getty.edu
Indiv: (user I.D.)@getty.edu

Orders:
Chicago Distribution Center
11030 South Langley Avenue
Chicago, IL 60628
Phone: 800.621.2736
Fax: 800.621.8476
Email: custserv@press.uchicago.edu

Website and Social Media:
Website: www.getty.edu/publications
Facebook: www.facebook.com/GettyPublications
Twitter: GettyPubs

UK/European Distributors:
Orca Book Services

UK/Sales Representative:
Roundhouse Group

Canada Sales Representative:
Canadian Manda Group

Staff
Publisher: Kara Kirk (310.440.6066)
Editor-in-Chief: Robert T. Flynn (310.440.6486; email: rflynn)
General Manager: Carolyn Simmons (310.440.7130; email: csimmons)
Rights Manager: Leslie Rollins (310.440.7102; email: lrollins)
Getty Research Institute: Michele Ciaccio (310.440.7453; email: mciaccio)
Getty Conservation Institute: Cynthia Godlewski (310.440.6805; email: cgodlewski
Manuscript Editorial: Ann Lucke, Managing Editor (310.440.6525; email: alucke)
Design: Deenie Yudell, Design Manager (310.440.6508; email: dyudell)
Production: Karen Schmidt, Production Manager (310.440.6504; email: kschmidt)

Associate Member
Established: 1982
Title output 2011: 51
Titles currently in print: 525

Admitted to AAUP: 1989
Title output 2012: 36

Editorial Program
Scholarly and general interest publications on the visual arts; conservation and the history of art and the humanities; and areas related to the work of the Getty Research Institute, the Getty Conservation Institute, and the collections of the J. Paul Getty Museum: antiquities, decorative arts, drawings, manuscripts, paintings, photographs, and sculpture.

Harvard University Press

79 Garden Street
Cambridge, MA 02138-1499

Phone: 617.495.2600
Faxes: 617.495.5898 (General)
617.495.2611 (Editorial)
617.495.2606 (Sales/Marketing)
Email: firstname_lastname@harvard.edu

Website and Social Media:
Website: www.hup.harvard.edu
Blog: harvardpress.typepad.com
Facebook: www.facebook.com/HarvardPress
Twitter: Harvard_Press
YouTube: www.youtube.com/user/harvardupress

European Office:
Harvard University Press
Vernon House
23 Sicilian Avenue
London WC1A 2QS United Kingdom
Email: info@harvardup.co.uk
Phone: 011.44.20.3463.2350

Customer Service/Orders:
Harvard University Press
c/o TriLiteral-LLC
100 Maple Ridge Drive
Cumberland, RI 02864-1769
Phone: 800.405.1619 (US & Canada)
401.531.2800 (all others)
Faxes: 800.406.9145 (US & Canada)
401.531.2801 (all others)

Staff

Director: William P. Sisler (617.495.2601)
Director of Intellectual Property and Subsidiary Rights: Stephanie Vyce (617.495.2603)
Assistant Director for University Relations/Executive Editor for Science and Medicine:
  Michael G. Fisher (617.495.2674)
Editor-in-Chief: Susan Wallace Boehmer (617.495.2624)
  Executive Editor for Social Sciences: Michael Aronson (617.495.1837)
  Executive Editor-at-Large: Elizabeth Knoll (617.495.0486)
  Executive Editor-at-Large: John Kulka (203.227.4706)
  Executive Editor-at-Large (Europe): Ian Malcolm (44 7843 301 029)
  Executive Editor for History: Kathleen McDermott (617.495.4703)
  Senior Executive Editor for History and Contemporary Affairs: Joyce Seltzer
  (212.337.0280)
  Executive Editor-at-Large: Sharmila Sen (617.495.8122)
  Executive Editor for the Humanities: Lindsay Waters (617.495.2835)
  Editor for Digital Publications Development: Emily Arkin (617.496.4690)
  Managing Editor: Mary Ann Lane (617.495.1846)
  Editorial Manager: David Foss (617.496.8170)
Director of Design and Production: Tim Jones (617.495.2669)
  Assistant Production Director: Abigail Mumford (617.496.9421)

Assistant Director/Sales and Marketing Director: Susan Donnelly (617.495.2606)
  Sales Manager/Digital Content Manager: Vanessa Vinarub (617.495.2650)
  Publicity Manager: Phoebe Kosman (617.495.0303)
  Senior Publicist: Lisa LaPoint (617.495.1284)
  Web Marketing Manager: Gregory Kornbluh (617.496.3281)
  Promotion Manager: Sheila Barrett (617.495.2618)
  Special Sales: Briana Ross (617.384.7515)
  Exhibits Manager: Val Hunt (617.495.2607)
  Sales Manager (Europe): Richard Howells (011.44.20.3463.2350)
  Marketing Manager (Europe): Rebekah White (011.44.20.3463.2350)
CFO/COO: TBA

Full Member

Established: 1913

Title output 2011: 277

Titles currently in print: 5,010

Admitted to AAUP: 1937

Title output 2012: 267

Editorial Program

Scholarly books and serious works of general interest in the humanities, the social and behavioral sciences, the natural sciences, and medicine. The Press does not normally publish poetry, fiction, festschriften, memoirs, symposia, or unrevised doctoral dissertations.

The Press distributes publications for a number of Harvard University departments and affiliates: Archaeological Exploration of Sardis, Center for Hellenic Studies, Center for the Study of World Religions, David Rockefeller Center for Latin American Studies, Department of Celtic Languages and Literatures, Department of the Classics, Department of Comparative Literature, Department of English, Department of Music, Department of Near Eastern Languages and Civilizations, Department of Sanskrit and Indian Studies, Derek Bok Center, Dumbarton Oaks Research Library and Collection, FXB Center for Health and Human Rights, Harvard Center for Middle Eastern Studies, Harvard College Library, Harvard Divinity School, Harvard Global Equity Initiative, Harvard University Asia Center, Harvard University Center for Jewish Studies, Harvard University Graduate School of Design, Houghton Library of the Harvard College Library, Ilex Foundation, Islamic Legal Studies Program, Harvard Law School, Peabody Museum Press, School of Public Health, the Ukrainian Research Institute of Harvard University, and Villa I Tatti.

Special imprints: The Belknap Press

Special series, joint imprints, and/or copublishing programs: The Adams Papers; Bernard Berenson Lectures; Carl Newell Jackson Lectures; Charles Eliot Norton Lectures; Dumbarton Oaks Medieval Library; Edwin O. Reischauer Lectures; Godkin Lectures; Harvard Historical Studies and Monographs; Harvard Studies in Business History; I Tatti Renaissance Library; I Tatti Renaissance Monographs; John Harvard Library; Loeb Classical Library; Loeb Classical Monographs; Nathan I. Huggins Lectures; Oliver Wendell Holmes Lectures; Revealing Antiquity; Tanner Lectures; W.E.B. Du Bois Lectures; William E. Massey Sr. Lectures

University of Hawai'i Press

2840 Kolowalu Street
Honolulu, HI 96822-1888

Phone: 808.956.8257
Fax: 808.988.6052
Email: (user I.D.)@hawaii.edu

Orders:
Phone: 888.UHPRESS; 808.956.8255
Fax: 800.650.7811; 808.988.5203

Website and Social Media:
Website: www.uhpress.hawaii.edu
Blog: uhpress.wordpress.com
Facebook: www.facebook.com/pages/University-of-Hawaii-Press/200519105362
Twitter: UHPRESSNEWS

European Distributor:
Eurospan

Staff

Director: TBA (808.956.8257)
  Secretary to the Director: Cheryl Reyes (808.956.8257; email: cherylre)
Acquisitions Editorial: Patricia Crosby, Executive Editor (808.956.6209; email: pcrosby)
  Editors: Pamela Kelley (808.956.6207; email: pkelley); Nadine Little (808.956.6208;
  email: nlittle); Masako Ikeda (808.956.8696; email: masakoi)
Manuscript Editorial: Cheri Dunn, Managing Editor (808.956.6210; email: cheri)
  Managing Editor: Ann Ludeman (808.956.8695; email: aludeman)
Design and Production: Santos Barbasa, Manager (808.956.8877; email: barbasa)
  Production Editors: Julie Matsuo-Chun (808.956.8276; email: jsmatsuo); Mardee Melton
  (808.956.2858; email: mmelton); Lucille Aono (808.956.6328; email: lucille)
  Fiscal Support Specialist: Terri Miyasato (808.956.8275; email: terrimiy)
Marketing and Sales: Colins Kawai, Manager (808.956.6417; email: ckawai)
  Sales Manager: Royden Muranaka (808.956.6214; email: royden)
  Direct Mail Manager/Copywriter: Stephanie Chun (808.956.6426; email: chuns)
  Product Manager: Steven Hirashima (808.956.8698; email: stevehir)
  Promotion Manager: Carol Abe (808.956.8697; email: abec)
Journals: Joel Bradshaw, Manager (808.956.6790; email: bradshaw)
  Production Editor: Cindy Chun (808.956.8834; email: cindychu)
  Administrative Assistant: Norman Kaneshiro (808.956.8833; email: uhpjourn)
East-West Export Books: Royden Muranaka, International Sales Manager (808.956.6214;
  email: royden)
  Assistant: Kiera Nishimoto (808.956.8830; email: eweb)
Business: Joel Cosseboom, Manager (808.956.6292; email: cosseboo)
  Credit Manager: Kari Hirata (808.956.6228; email: karis)
  Order Processing: Cindy Yen (808.956.8256; email: cyen); Danny Li (808.956.6279;
  email: wingon)
  Warehouse: Kyle Nakata, Clifford Newalu (808.956.3357; email: uhpwhse)
Information Systems: Claudia Butcher, Computer Operations Manager (808.956.6227;
  email: mc2011)

Full Member

Established: 1947
Title output 2011: 77
Titles currently in print: 1,591

Admitted to AAUP: 1951
Title output 2012: 74
Journals published: 20

Editorial Program

Asian, Pacific, and Asian American studies in history; art; anthropology; architecture; economics; sociology; philosophy and religion; languages and linguistics; law; literature; performing arts; political science; physical and natural sciences; regional studies.

Journals: *Archives of Asian Art; Asian Perspectives; Asian Theatre Journal; Azalea; Biography; Buddhist-Christian Studies; China Review International; The Contemporary Pacific; Cross-Currents; Journal of Korean Religions; Journal of World History; Korean Studies; Language Documentation and Conservation; Manoa; Oceanic Linguistics; Pacific Science; Philosophy East and West; Review of Japanese Culture and Society; U.S.-Japan Women's Journal; Yearbook of the Association of Pacific Coast Geographers*

Special series, joint imprints, and/or copublishing programs: ABC Chinese Dictionary; ASAA (Asian Studies Association of Australia) Southeast Asia Publications; Asian Interactions and Comparisons (Association for Asian Studies); Biography Monographs; Center for Southeast Asian Studies (Kyoto University); Classics in East Asian Buddhism (Kuroda Institute); Critical Interventions; Dimensions of Asian Spirituality; Extraordinary Lives: The Experience of Hawai'i Nisei; Fiction From Modern China; Hawai'i Studies on Korea (Korean Studies); Insects of Hawaii; Intersections: Asian and Pacific American Transcultural Studies; KLEAR Textbooks in Korean Language (Korean Language Education and Research Center/Korea Foundation); Kuroda Institute Studies in East Asian Buddhism; Modern Korean Fiction, Nanzan Library for Asian Religion and Culture; National Foreign Language Resource Center Monographs; Oceanic Linguistics Special Publications; PALI Language Texts; Pacific Islands Monographs; Perspectives on the Global Past; Pure Land Buddhist Studies; Social Process in Hawaii Monographs; Society for Asian and Comparative Philosophy; Southeast Asia: Politics, Meaning, and Memory; Spatial Habitus; Studies in East Asian Buddhism; Studies in the Buddhist Traditions; Studies of the Weatherhead East Asian Institute (Columbia University); Talanoa: Contemporary Pacific Literature; Topics in Contemporary Buddhism; The World of East Asia; Writing Past Colonialism

Hong Kong University Press

The University of Hong Kong
14/F Hing Wai Centre
7 Tin Wan Praya Road
Aberdeen, Hong Kong

Phone: +852 25502703
Fax: +852 28750734
E-mail: hkupress@hku.hk
Indiv: (user I.D.)@hku.hk

North American Distributors:
(As of February 1, 2012)
Columbia University Press
61 West 62nd Street
New York, NY 10023
Phone: 212.459.0600
Fax: 212.459.3678

Website and Social Media:
Website: www.hkupress.org

UK/European Distributor:
Eurospan

Staff
Publisher: Michael Duckworth (+852 25502670; email: duckwort)
Administration: Maria Yim (+852 25502670; email: hkupress)
Acquisitions: Christopher Munn, Acquisitions Editor (+852 25502791; email: cmunn)
Editorial: Dennis Cheung, Managing Editor (+852 25521344; email: dwcheung)
  Assistant Managing Editor: Clara Ho (+852 25502791; email: cscho)
Production: Jennifer Flint, Production Manager (+852 25507871; email: jbflint)
Business/Marketing: Winnie Chau, Sales & Marketing Manager (+852 25524789; email: wywchau)
  Accounting & Fulfillment Executive: Connie Yip (+852 25502703; email: uporders)
Rights: Christy Leung, Assistant Editor & Rights Manager (+852 25502670; email: leungsyc)

International Member
Established: 1956
Title output 2011: 65
Titles currently in print:-870+

Admitted to AAUP: 2009
Title output 2012: NR

Editorial Program
English and Chinese scholarly books in humanities, art, social sciences, law, medicine, education, science, architecture/urban planning; particular strengths in Asian film and cultural studies, China studies, gender studies, linguistics and language training, as well as Asian law, history, politics, economics, photography, natural history, and Hong Kong/Macau studies.
Special series: Asian Englishes Today; Global Connections; Echoes: Classics of Hong Kong Culture and History; Education in China: Reform and Diversity; HKU Press Law Series; The New Hong Kong Cinema; Hong Kong Culture and Society; Hong Kong Teacher Education; Queer Asia; Royal Asiatic Society Hong Kong Studies Series; Studying Multicultural Discourses; Traces: A Multilingual Series of Cultural Theory and Translation; TransAsia: Screen Cultures; Understanding China: New Viewpoints on History and Culture

University of Illinois Press

1325 S. Oak Street
Champaign, IL 61820-6903

Phone: 217.333.0950
Fax: 217.244.8082
Email: uipress@uillinois.edu
Journals: journals@uillinois.edu
Indiv: (user I.D.)@uillinois.edu

Website and Social Media:
Website: www.press.uillinois.edu
Blog: www.press.uillinois.edu/wordpress
Facebook: www.facebook.com/UniversityofIllinoisPress
Twitter:@IllinoisPress

Warehouse Address and Orders:
University of Illinois Press
c/o Chicago Distribution Center
11030 South Langley Avenue
Chicago, IL 60628

Orders:
Books: 800.621.2736
Email: orders@press.uchicago.edu
Journals: 866.244.0626

UK/European Representative:
Combined Academic Publishers

Canadian Representative:
Scholarly Book Services

Staff

Director: Willis G. Regier (217.244.0728; email: wregier)
  Assistant to the Director: Kathy O'Neill (217.244.4691; email: oneill2)
  Rights, Permissions, and Awards Manager: Kathleen Kornell (217.244.0820; email: uip-rights, kkornell)
Acquisitions Editors: Laurie Matheson, Editor-in-Chief (American history, Appalachian studies, labor studies, music, folklore) (217.244.4685; email: lmatheso); Willis G. Regier (ancient religion, literature, translations, sports history, Lincoln studies, Nietzsche studies, classics) (217.244.0728; email: wregier); Larin McLaughlin (African American studies, women's studies, American studies, religion) (217.244.8978; email: larinmc); Daniel Nasset (communication studies, anthropology, film studies, military history) (217.244.5182; email: dnassset)
  Assistant Editors: Vijay Shah (Asian American studies)(217.333.6088; email: vishah); Dawn Durante (217.265.8491; email: durante9)
Electronic Publisher: Paul Arroyo (217.244.7147; email: parroyo)
Editorial, Design, and Production Manager: Jennifer Reichlin (217.244.3279; email: reichlin)
  Assistant Managing Editor: Jennifer Clark (217.244.8041; email: jsclark1)
  Copyeditor: Tad Ringo (217.265.0238; email: tringo)
  Production: Kristine Ding, Production Manager (217.244.4701; email: kding)
  Assistant Production Manager: TBA
  Production Coordinator: Tamara Shidlauski (217.265.0940; email: shidlaus)
  Art Director: Dustin Hubbart (217.333.9227; email dhubbart)
  Designer: Kelly Gray (email: kellyg)
Marketing: Michael Roux, Marketing Manager (217.244.4683; email: mroux)
  Publicity Manager: TBA (217.244.4689)
  Sales Manager: Lynda Schuh (217.333.9071; email: lschuh)

Exhibits Manager: Margo Chaney (217.244.6491; email: mechaney)
Direct Marketing & Advertising Manager: Denise Peeler (217.244.4690; email: dpeeler)
Catalog & Copywriting Coordinator: Joe Peeples (217.244.4687; email: jpeeples)
Journals: Clydette Wantland, Journals Manager (217.244.6496; email: cwantlan)
  Associate Journals Manager: Jeff McArdle (217.244.0381; email: jmcardle)
  Journals Production Editors: Heather Munson (217.244.6488; email: hmunson); Stephanie Turza (217.244.8870; email: sturza2); Rohn Koester (217.244.9179; email: rkoester)
  Journals Circulation Manager: Cheryl Jestis (866.244.0626; email: jestis)
  Journals Marketing and Advertising Manager: Jeff McArdle (217.244.0381; email: jmcardle)
Chief Financial Officer: Alice Ennis (217.244.0091; email: atennis)
  Network Administrator: Louis W. Mesker (217.244.8025; email: lmesker)

Full Member

Established: 1918

Admitted to AAUP: 1937

Title output 2011: 110

Title output 2012: 93

Titles currently in print: 2053

Journals published: 32

Editorial Program
Scholarly books and serious nonfiction, with special interests in American history; American literature (especially twentieth century); critical theory; American music; African American history and literature; sport history; religious studies; cultural studies; communications; cinema studies; law and society; regional photography and art; philosophy; architectural history; environmental studies; sociology; western history; women's studies; working-class history

Journals: *American Journal of Psychology; American Journal of Theology & Philosophy; American Literary Realism; American Music; American Philosophical Quarterly; Black Music Research Journal; Bulletin of the Council for Research in Music Education; Ethnomusicology; Feminist Teacher; History of Philosophy Quarterly; History of the Present; Illinois Classical Studies; Journal of the Abraham Lincoln Association; Journal of Aesthetic Education; Journal of American Ethnic History; Journal of American Folklore; Journal of Animal Ethics; Journal for the Anthropological Study of Human Movement; Journal of Education Finance; Journal of English and Germanic Philology; Journal of Film & Video; Journal of the Illinois State Historical Society; Music and Moving Image; Perspectives on Work; The Pluralist; Polish American Studies; The Polish Review; Public Affairs Quarterly; Scandinavian Studies; Visual Arts Research; Women, Gender and Families of Color; World History Connected*

Special series, joint imprints, and/or copublishing programs: African American Music in Global Perspective; American Composers; The Asian American Experience; Bach Perspectives; The Beauvoir Series; Beethoven Sketchbook Series; Contemporary Film Directors; Critical Public Policy Issues; Democracy, Free Enterprise, and the Role of Law; Dissident Feminisms; Feminist Media Studies; The History of Communication; The History of Emotions; Interpretations of Culture in the New Millennium; The Knox College Lincoln Studies Center; Latinos in Chicago and the Midwest; Modern Masters of Science Fiction; Music in American Life; The New Black Studies Series; New Perspectives on Gender in Music; Popular Culture and Politics In Asia Pacific; Race and Gender In Science Studies; Sport and Society; Studies in the History of Music Theory and Literature; Studies in Sensory History; Studies of World Migrations; Topics in the Digital Humanities; Traditions; Women in

American History; Working Class in American History; Women Composers; Women and Film History International; Women, Gender and Technology

IMF Publications (International Monetary Fund)

Street Address:
700 19th Street, NW
Washington, DC 20431

Mailing Address:
Publications Services
P.O. Box 92780
Washington, DC 20090

Phone: 202.623.7430
Fax: 202.623.7201
Email: publications@imf.org

Orders:
202.623.7430
202.623.7201
Online: www.imfbookstore.org

Website and Social Media:
Websites: www.imfbookstore.org; www.elibrary.imf.org
Twitter: IMFNews
Blog: blog-iMFdirect.imf.org

Canadian Representative:
Renouf Publishing Co. Ltd.

UK/European Representative:
Eurospan Group

Staff

Publisher: Jeremy Clift (202.623.9464; email: jclift@imf.org)
Associate Publisher: Sean M. Culhane (202.623.9730; email: sculhane@imf.org)
Rights Manager/Acquisitions Editor/Conference Manager: Patricia Loo (202.623.8296;
    email: ploo@imf.org)
  Administrative Assistant: Suzanne Alavi (202.623.5348; email: salavi@imf.org)
  Staff Assistant: Phoebe Kieti (202.623.5694; email: pkieti@imf.org)
Electronic Publishing Officer: Jim Beardow (202.623.7899; email: jbeardow@imf.org)
Web Publishing Officer: Lynnette Simpson (202.623.8797; email: lsimpson@imf.org)
Digital Publishing Officer: S.M. Hassan Zaidi (202.623.8102; email: szaidi@imf.org)
Senior Editor: Linda Kean (202.623.4124; email: lkean@imf.org)
Editors: Joanne Blake (202.623.8807; email: jblake@imf.org); Michael Harrup
    (202.623.7504; email: mharrup@imf.org); Joseph Procopio (202.623.9258; email: jpro-
    copio@imf.org); Cathy Gagnet (202.623.6037; email: cgagnet@imf.org)
Marketing Manager: Cathy Willis (202.623.7426; email: cwillis@imf.org)
Licensing and Contracts Agent: Alexa Smith (952.944.5729; email: asmith2@imf.org)
Finance Administrator: Cristina Pagan (202.623.4824; email: cpagan@imf.org)
Process Management Consultant: John Brenneman (202.623.7092;
    email: jbrenneman@imf.org)

Associate Member

Established: 1948
Title output 2011: 25
Titles currently in print: 682

Admitted to AAUP: 2011
Title output 2012: 31
Journals published: 2

Editorial Program

The International Monetary Fund publishes a wide variety of books, periodicals, and electronic products covering economics, international finance, monetary issues, statistics, and exchange rates.

Journals: *Finance & Development; IMF Economic Review*

Special series: Departmental Papers; Occasional Papers; Staff Discussion Notes; Technical Notes and Manuals; World Economic and Financial Surveys (includes World Economic Outlook, Fiscal Monitor, Global Financial Stability Report, and Regional Economic Outlooks); Working Papers

Joint imprints and copublishing programs: Select titles copublished with John Wiley & Sons, MIT Press, Oxford University Press, Palgrave Macmillan, and Routledge.

Indiana University Press

601 North Morton Street
Bloomington, IN 47404-3797

After April 1, 2013
Herman B Wells Library 350
1320 E. 10th Street
Bloomington, IN 47405

Phone: 812.855.8817
Fax: 812.855.8507
Email: iupress@indiana.edu
Indiv: (user I.D.)@indiana.edu

Website and Social Media:
Website: iupress.indiana.edu
Blog: iupress.typepad.com/blog
Facebook: www.facebook.com/iupress
Twitter: iupress
Google+: plus.google.com/115444288032700584669
YouTube: www.youtube.com/iupress

Warehouse Address:
802 E. 13th Street
Bloomington, IN 47408-2101
Phone: 812.855.4362
Orders:
Phone: 800.842.6796
Fax: 812.855.7931
Email: iuporder@indiana.edu

UK/European Representative:
Combined Academic Publishers

Canadian Representative:
Lexa Publishers' Representative

Staff

Director: Janet Rabinowitch (812.855.4773; email: jrabinow) (Russian, East European, and Jewish and Holocaust studies)
  Rights and Permissions Manager and Assistant to the Director: Peter Froehlich (812.855.6314; email: pfroehli)
Acquisitions Editorial: Robert Sloan, Editorial Director (African American and African Diaspora studies, bioethics, American history, military, paleontology, philanthropy) (812.855.7561; email: rjsloan)
  Senior Sponsoring Editor: Dee Mortensen (Africa, philosophy, religion) (812.855.0268; email: mortense)

Sponsoring Editors: Raina Polivka (music, film/media/cultural studies) (812.855.5261; email: rpolivka); Linda Oblack (regional, Quarry books, railroads) (812.855.2175; email: loblack); Rebecca Tolen (anthropology, Asia, Middle East, international studies) (812.855.2756; email: retolen)

Assistant Sponsoring Editors: Sarah Jacobi (assistant to Dee Mortensen, Linda Oblack, and Rebecca Tolen) (812.855.5262; email: sajacobi); Jenna Whittaker (assistant to Raina Polivka and Robert Sloan) (812.856.5810; email: jewhitta)

Manuscript Editorial: Angela Burton, Managing Editor (812.855.9686; email: burtonan)

Project Managers: June Silay (812.856.4645; email: jsilay); Nancy Lightfoot (812.855.1744; email: nlightfo); Marvin Keenan (812.855.5064; email: mwkeenan); Chandra Mevis (812.855.5428; email: cnmevis); Darja Malcolm-Clarke (812.855.5428; dmalcolm)

Production and Design: Bernadette Zoss, Production Director (812.855.5563; email: bzoss)

Senior Artists and Book Designers: Pam Rude (812.855.0264; email: psrude); Jamison Cockerham (812.855.9640; email: jrc9); Mary Blizzard (812.855.8778; email: mblizzar)

Production Coordinator: Dan Pyle (812.856.5233; email: dapyle)

Publishing Services Coordinator: Tony Brewer (812.855.9444; email: tbrewer)

Production Assistant: Laura Hohman (812.855.6777; email: lhohman)

Marketing and Sales: Dave Hulsey, Marketing and Sales Director (812.855.6553; email: hulseyd)

Trade Marketing and Publicity Manager: Mandy Clarke (812.855.5429; email: mlclarke)

Electronic Marketing Manager: Laura Baich (812.855.8287; email: lbaich)

Advertising and Exhibit Manager: Mollie Ables (812.855.5429; email: mables)

Publicity Coordinator: Theresa Halter (812.855.8054; email: thalter)

Marketing Designer: Jennifer Witzke (812.855.4415; email: jwitzke)

Sales: Mary Beth Haas, Sales Manager (812.855.9440; email: mbhaas)

Assistant Sales Manager: Kate Matthen (812.855.5366; email: kmatthen)

Sales and Marketing Assistant: Rhonda Van Der Dussen (812.855.6657; email: rdussen)

Journals, Electronic, and Serials Publishing: Kathryn Caras, Director of Electronic and Serials Publishing (812.855.3830; email: kcaras)

Electronic and Serials Manager: Joy Andreakis (812.856.5218; email: jandreak)

Journals Marketing Manager: Linda Bannister (812.855.9449; email: llbannis)

Journals Production Manager: Judith Caldwell (812.856.0582; email: jucaldwe)

Business and Operations: Dan Nichols, Director of Operations (812.855.4901; email: nichodan)

Senior Accounting Coordinator: Kathy Stout (812.855.2726; email: kwhaley)

Assistant Business Manager for Network Systems and Order Processing: Janie Pearson (812.855.1588; email: cjfender)

Assistant Business Manager for Accounts Receivable & Customer Service: Kim Childers (812.855.4134; email: kchilder)

Senior Customer Service Representative: Mary Lou Shelly (812.855.8818; email: mlshelly)

Customer Service Representatives: Jessica Murphy (812.855.1519; email: thompsjr); Jennifer Coyle (812.855.0263; jjauxier)

Warehouse Manager: Steve Carter (812.855.4362; email: stmcarte)

Information Technology: Ted Boardman, Technology Director for Publishing Operations (812.855.6468; email: tboardma)

IT Manager: Rich Pierce (812.856.0210; email: ripierce)

Full Member
Established: 1950
Title output 2011: 140
Titles currently in print: 2,000

Admitted to AAUP: 1952
Title output 2012: 133
Journals published: 29

Editorial Program
African studies; African American and African Diaspora studies; anthropology; Asian and South Asian studies; bioethics; cultural studies; ethnomusicology; film and media studies; folklore; history; international studies; Jewish and Holocaust studies; Latin American studies; Middle East studies; military history; music; paleontology; philanthropy; philosophy; railroad history; religion; Russian and East European studies; state and regional studies; women's and gender studies.

Journals: *Africa Today; ACPR: African Conflict and Peacebuilding Review; Aleph: Historical Studies in Science & Judaism; Black Camera; e-Service Journal; Ethics & the Environment; Film History; The Global South; History & Memory; Indiana Journal of Global Legal Studies; IJFAB: International Journal of Feminist Approaches to Bioethics; Israel Studies; Jewish Social Studies; Journal of Feminist Studies in Religion; JFR: Journal of Folklore Research; JMEWS: Journal of Middle East Women's Studies; Journal of Modern Literature; Meridians: feminism, race, transnationalism; Nashim: A Journal of Jewish Women's & Gender Issues; PMER: Philosophy of Music Education Review; Prooftexts: A Journal of Jewish Literary History; Race/Ethnicity; Research in African Literatures; Spectrum: The Journal of Black Men; Teaching and Learning Inquiry; Textual Cultures; Transactions of the Charles S. Peirce Society: A Quarterly Journal in American Philosophy; Transition; Victorian Studies*

Special series: 21st Century Studies; African Epic; African Expressive Cultures; African Systems of Thought; American Philosophy; Bioethics and the Humanities; Blacks in the Diaspora; Chinese in Context Language Learning Series; Cinematheque Ontario Monographs; Counterpoints: Music and Education; Digital Game Studies; Ethnomusicology Multimedia; Excavations at Ancient Halieis; Excavations at Franchthi Cave, Greece; Global African Voices; The Helen and Martin Schwartz Lectures in Jewish Studies; A History of the Trans-Appalachian Frontier; Indiana Natural Science; Indiana Repertoire Guides; Indiana Series in Middle East Studies; Indiana Series in the Philosophy of Religion; Indiana Series in Sephardi and Mizrahi Studies; Indiana Studies in Biblical Literature; Indiana-Michigan Series in Russian and East European Studies; Jewish Literature and Culture; KINtop Studies in Early Cinema; Library of Indiana Classics; Life of the Past; The Modern Jewish Experience; Music and the Early Modern Imagination; Musical Meaning and Interpretation; New Anthropologies of Europe; New Directions in National Cinema; Philanthropic and Nonprofit Studies; Polis Center Series on Religion and Urban Culture; Profiles in Popular Music; Public Cultures of the Middle East and North Africa; Publications of the Early Music Institute; Railroads Past and Present; Readings in African Studies; Religion in North America; Russian Music Studies; Scholarship of Teaching and Learning; Selections from the Writing of Charles S. Peirce; South Asian Cinema; Spatial Humanities; Special Publications of the Folklore Institute, Indiana University; Studies in Continental Thought; Textual Cultures; Tracking Globalization; Twentieth-Century Battles; United Nations Intellectual History Project; The Variorum Edition of the Poetry of John Donne; World Philosophies; The Year's Work: Studies in Fan Culture and Cultural Theory

University of Iowa Press

Editorial Office:
119 West Park Road
100 Kuhl House
Iowa City, IA 52242-1000

Phone: 319.335.2000
Fax: 319.335.2055
Email: (user I.D.)@uiowa.edu

Website and Social Media:
Website: www.uiowapress.org
Blog: buroakblog.blogspot.com/
Facebook: www.facebook.com/UIowaPress

Order Fulfillment:
University of Iowa Press
c/o Chicago Distribution Center
11030 South Langley Avenue
Chicago, IL 60628
Phone: 800.621.2736
Fax: 800.621.8476

UK/European Representative:
Eurospan

Staff

Director: Jim McCoy (319.335.2013; email: james-mccoy)
  Assistant to the Director: Faye Schillig (319.335.3424; email: faye-schillig)
  Rights and Permissions: Lydia Crowe (319.384.2008; email: lydia-crowe)
Editorial:
  Acquisitions Editors: Elisabeth Chretien (literary criticism, poetics, creative nonfiction, humanities) (319.335.2015; email: elisabeth-chretien); Catherine Cocks (natural history, regional history, anthropology/archaeology, fan studies, food studies, performance studies) (319.384.1910; email: cath-campbell); Jim McCoy (poetry, short fiction, general trade) (319.335.2013; email: james-mccoy)
Managing Editor: Charlotte Wright (319.335.2011; email: charlotte-wright)
Design and Production: Karen Copp, Associate Director and Design and Production Manager (319.335.2014; email: karen-copp)
Marketing: Allison Thomas Means, Marketing Manager (319.335.3440; email: allison-means)

Full Member

Established: 1969
Title output 2011: 45
Titles currently in print: 850

Admitted to AAUP: 1982
Title output 2012: 39

Editorial Program

American literary criticism and history, particularly children's literature, biography, and women's studies, contemporary American literature; memoirs; short fiction (award winners only); poetry (single-author titles and anthologies); creative nonfiction; regional studies; regional natural history; archaeology/anthropology; theatre history; American studies; food studies; fan studies; public humanities.

Special series: American Land and Life Series; Bur Oak Books and Bur Oak Guides; Contemporary North American Poetry; Iowa Poetry Prize; Iowa Short Fiction Award and John Simmons Short Fiction Award; Iowa and the Midwest Experience; Iowa Whitman Series; Kuhl House Poets; Muse Books; New American Canon; Sightline Books: The Iowa Series in Literary Nonfiction; Studies in Theatre History and Culture; Writers in Their Own Time

Island Press

Editorial/Administration:
2000 M St NW, Suite 650
Washington, DC 20036

Phone: 202.232.7933
Fax: 202.234.1328
Email: firstinitiallastname@islandpress.org

Order Fulfillment:
Chicago Distribution Center
11030 South Langley Avenue
Chicago, IL 60628
Phone: 800.621.2736
Fax: 800.621.8476

Website and Social Media:
Website: www.islandpress.org
Blog: blog.islandpress.org
Facebook: www.facebook.com/IslandPress
Twitter: IslandPress

UK/European Representative:
Oxford Publicity Partners

Canadian Representative:
University of British Columbia Press

Staff
President: Charles C. Savitt
Assistant to the President: Caryn Cabaniss (ext. 27)
Senior VP & Publisher: David Miller (ext.14)
VP & Chief Financial Officer: Ken Hartzell (301.576.6221)
VP for Strategic Advancement: Denise Schlener (ext. 25)
Permissions: Amy Bridges (ext. 10)
Acquisitions/Editorial: Barbara Dean, Executive Editor (ecosystems, natural environment) (ext. 19); Heather Boyer, Executive Editor (built environment) (303.641.5344); Emily Davis, Editor (health, freshwater and marine environments) (323.522.3281)
Design and Production: Maureen Gately, Director of Production and Design (ext. 49)
Marketing/Sales/Advertising/Publicity: Julie Marshall, VP of Marketing and Sales (ext. 32)
IT: Craig Elie, IT Manager (ext. 45)

Associate Member
Established: 1984
Title output 2011: 46
Titles currently in print: 821

Admitted to AAUP: 1999
Title output 2012: 42

Editorial Program
Scholarly and professional titles in environmental studies and natural resource management; nonfiction trade titles on nature and the environment; electronic publishing on environmental topics and news. Subject areas include ecosystems management, sustainable communities, protection of biodiversity and human health, environmentally responsible land use planning, sustainable design, marine science and policy, climate and energy, and economics and policy. The Press's full name is Island Press—Center for Resource Economics.
Special series, joint imprints, and/or copublishing programs: Case Studies in Land and Community Design (with the Landscape Architecture Foundation); Ecoregions of the World: A Conservation Assessment (with The World Wildlife Fund); Foundations of Contemporary Environmental Studies; The Millennium Ecosystem Assessment; The Science and Practice of

Ecological Restoration (with the Society for Ecological Restoration International); State of the Wild (with Wildlife Conservation Society); The World's Water (with The Pacific Institute for Studies in Development, Environment, and Security); International Assessment of Agricultural Knowledge, Science and Technology for Development; State of the World and Vital Signs (with the Worldwatch Institute), Metropolitan Planning + Design Series (with the University of Utah).

The Johns Hopkins University Press

2715 N. Charles Street
Baltimore, MD 21218-4363

Phone: 410.516.6900
Fax: 410.516.6998/6968
Email: (user I.D.)@press.jhu.edu

Website and Social Media:
Website: www.press.jhu.edu, hfs.jhu.edu
muse.jhu.edu
Facebook: www.facebook.com/JohnsHopkinsUniversityPress
Twitter: JHUPress

UK Representative:
Yale Representation, Ltd.

Distribution Center:
C/O Maple Logistics Solutions
Lebanon Distribution Center
704 Legionaire Drive
Fredericksburg, PA 17026

Orders and Customer Service:
Phone: 800.537.5487

Staff

Director: Kathleen Keane (410.516.6971; email: kk)
  Assistant to the Director: Jane Barchichat (410.516.6971; email: jeb)
  Rights and Permissions Manager: Kelly Rogers (410.516.6063; email: klr)
  Office and Facilities Coordinator: Nora Reedy (410.516.7035; email: ncr)
  Director, Finance and Administration: Erik Smist (410.516.6941; email: eas)
  Chief Information Officer: Timothy Fuller (410.516.3844; email: tdf)
Acquisitions Editorial: Gregory M. Britton, Editorial Director (410.516.6919; email: gb)
  Executive Editors: Vincent J. Burke (science & math) (410.516.6999; email: vjb); Jacqueline C. Wehmueller (consumer health, history of medicine, psychology and psychiatry) (410.516.6904; email: jcw)
  Senior Editor: Robert J. Brugger (American history) (410.516.6909; email: rjb)
  Editors: Matt McAdam (humanities and classics) (410.516.6903; email: mxm); Kelley Squazzo (public health) (410.516.6997; email: kas)
  Associate Editor: Suzanne Flinchbaugh (political science, international relations, public policy, and WWCP) (410.516.6917; email: skf)
  Assistant Editor: Greg Nicholl (poetry and fiction, American studies, Anabaptist studies, and regional books)(410.516.6906; email: gan)
Project MUSE: Dean J. Smith, Director (410.516.6981; email: djs)
  Financial Manager: Nicole Kendzejeski (410.516.6969; email: nak)
  Director, Marketing and Sales: Melanie B. Schaffner (410.516.3846; email: mbs)
  Manager, International Sales: Ann Snoeyenbos (410.516.6992; email: aps)

Customer Service Coordinator: Lora Czarnowsky (410.516.2890; email: llc)
Associate Director, Publishing Technology: Wendy Queen (410.516.3845; email: wjq)
Associate Director, Content Development: Teresa A. Ehling (410.516.6966; email tae)
Manager, Content Development: Elizabeth W. Brown (410.516.6834; email: ewb)
Indexing Coordinator/Chief Metadata Librarian: William Kulp (410.516.8968; email: wak)
MUSE Production Manager: Elizabeth R. Windsor (410.516.6510; email: brw)
Manuscript Editorial: Juliana M. McCarthy, Managing Editor (410.516.6912; email: jmm)
Assistant Managing Editor: Linda E. Forlifer (410.516.6911; email: lef)
Senior Manuscript Editors: Michele Callaghan (410.516.6910; email: mtc); Anne M. Whitmore (410.516.6916; email: amw)
Senior Production Editors: Andre M. Barnett (410.516.6995; email: amb); Courtney Bond (410.516.6905; email: cmb); Debby Bors (410.516.6914; email: dlb); Kimberly F. Johnson (410.516.6915; email: kfj); Mary Lou Kenney (410.516.6897; email: mk)
Assistant Manuscript Editor: Hilary Jacqmin (410.516.6901; email: hsj)
Design and Production: John Cronin, Design & Production Manager (410.516.6922; email: jgc)
Art Director: Martha Sewall (410.516.6921; email: mds)
Senior Book Designers: Glen Burris (410.516.6924; email: gmb); Wilma Rosenberger (410.516.6925; email: wer)
Production Controller, Electronic Repress: Robert Schreur (410.516.3855; email: rjs)
Production Controller, Electronic Media: Carol Eckhart (410.516.3862; email: cle)
Production Coordinator, Print Production: Linda West (410.516.6920; email: lmw)
Production Coordinator, Digital Archive: Patricia Bolgiano (410.516.7872; email: prb)
Marketing: Becky Brasington Clark, Director Marketing and Online Book Publishing (410.516.6931; email: rbc)
Sales Director: Tom Lovett (410.516.6936; email: tjl)
Promotion Manager: Karen Willmes (410.516.6932; email: klw)
Publicity Manager: Kathy Alexander (410.516.4162; email: ka)
Exhibits & Awards Manager: Brendan Coyne (410.516.6937; email: bcc)
Electronic Books: Claire McCabe Tamberino, Electronic Promotion Manager (410.516.6935; email: cmt)
Digital Production Manager: Michael B. Carroll (410.516.3841; email: mbc)
Journals: William M. Breichner, Publisher (410.516.6985; email: wmb)
Journals Fulfillment Systems Project Manager: Matt Brook (410.516.6899; email: mb)
Journals Marketing Manager: Lisa Klose (410.516.6689; email: llk)
Journals Production Manager: Carol Hamblen (410.516.6986; email: crh)
Journals Subscription Manager: Alta Anthony (410.516.6938; email: aha)
Journals Publicist: Brian Shea (410.516.7096; email: bjs)
Business: Tony Jacobson, Accounting Manager (410.516.6974; email: tlj)
Fulfillment: Davida G. Breier, Manager, Fulfillment Operations (410.516.6961; email: dgb)
Fulfillment: Melinda Kelly, Assistant Manager, Fulfillment Operations (410.516.4449; email: mrk)

Credit & Collections: Keith Brock, Accounts Receivable Coordinator (410.516.3854; email: klb)

Information Systems: Stacey L. Armstead Sr., IT Manager (410.516.6979; email: sla)

Full Member

Established: 1878

Title output 2011: 156

Titles currently in print: 2489

Admitted to AAUP: 1937

Title output 2012: 175

Journals published: 70

Editorial Program

History (American, ancient, history of science, technology, and medicine); humanities (literary and cultural studies, classics); medicine and health (consumer health, public health, psychology and psychiatry); science (biology, physics, and natural history); mathematics; political science; higher education; reference books; and regional books.

The Press is copublisher with the Woodrow Wilson Center Press.

The Press through Hopkins Fulfillment Service (HFS) handles book order processing and distribution for: Baylor University Press, Brookings Institution Press, Catholic University of America Press, Center for Talented Youth, Georgetown University Press, Johns Hopkins University Press, University of Kentucky Press, Maryland Historical Society, University of Massachusetts Press, University of Pennsylvania Press, University of Pennsylvania Museum Publications, University of Washington Press, and Urban Institute Press.

The Press, in cooperation with the Johns Hopkins University's Milton S. Eisenhower Library and the participating publishers, manages Project MUSE®://muse.jhu.edu). Project MUSE provides electronic subscription access to full-text, current periodical content from some 500 titles published by more than 125 not-for-profit publishers in the humanities and the social sciences. UPCC e-book collections on Project MUSE, fully integrated with the existing journal collections, launched in January 2012 with more than 14,000 scholarly books from 66 publishers. Other online publishing initiatives include electronic versions of *The Early Republic*; *The Johns Hopkins Guide to Literary Theory and Criticism*; *The Papers of Dwight David Eisenhower*; *the Encyclopedia of American Studies*; and *the World Shakespeare Bibliography*

Journals: *American Imago*; *American Jewish History*; *American Journal of Mathematics*; *American Journal of Philology*; *American Quarterly*; *Arethusa*; *Book History*; *Bookbird*; *The Bulletin of the Center for Children's Books*; *Bulletin of the History of Medicine*; *Callaloo*; *Children's Literature*; *Children's Literature Association Quarterly*; *Configurations*; *diacritics*; *Eighteenth-Century Studies*; *Encyclopedia of American Studies*; *The Emily Dickinson Journal*; *ELH: English Literary History*; *Feminist Formations*; *German Studies Review*; *The Henry James Review*; *Historically Speaking: The Bulletin of Historical Society*; *The Hopkins Review*; *Human Rights Quarterly*; *Journal of Asian American Studies*; *Journal of College Student Development*; *Journal of Colonialism and Colonial History*; *Journal of Democracy*; *Journal of Early Christian Studies*; *Journal of Health Care for the Poor and Underserved*; *Journal of Late Antiquity Journal of Modern Greek Studies*; *Journal of the History of Childhood and Youth*; *Journal of the History of Philosophy*; *Journal of Women's History*; *Kennedy Institute of Ethics Journal*; *Late Imperial China*; *L'Esprit Créateur*; *Library Trends*; *The Lion and the Unicorn*; *Literature and Medicine*; *MLN*; *Modern Fiction Studies*; *Modernism/Modernity*; *Narrative Inquiry in Bioethics and Digital Philology*; *New Literary History*; *Partial Answers: Journal of Literature and the History of Ideas*; *Perspectives in Biology & Medicine*; *Philosophy and Literature*; *Philosophy, Psychiatry, and Psychology*; *portal: Libraries and the Academy*; *Postmodern Culture*; *Reviews in American History*; *Progress In Community Health Partnerships: Research, Education, and Action*; *Reviews in Higher Educa-*

tion; *SAIS Review*; *Sewanee Review*; *Shakespeare Bulletin*; *Shakespeare Quarterly*; *Sirena*; *South Central Review*; *Spiritus: A Journal of Christian Spirituality*; *SEL: Studies in English Literature*; *Studies in American Fiction*; *Technology & Culture*; *Theatre Journal*; *Theatre Topics*; *Theory and Event*; *The Wallace Stevens Journal*; *Transactions of the American Philological Association*; *Victorian Periodical Review*; *World Shakespeare Bibliography Online*

Online-only journals: *Journal of Colonialism and Colonial History*; *Postmodern Culture*; *Theory and Event*

The Press also handles subscription fulfillment for *Imagine*, a publication of the Center for Talented Youth of The Johns Hopkins University and *Better: Evidence–Based Education* for The Johns Hopkins University School of Education.

Special series, joint imprints, and/or copublishing programs: The Complete Poetry of Percy Bysshe Shelley; Documentary History of the First Federal Congress; Johns Hopkins: Poetry and Fiction; The Johns Hopkins Studies in the History of Technology; The Johns Hopkins University Studies in History and Political Science; The Papers of Dwight David Eisenhower; The Papers of George Catlett Marshall; The Papers of Frederick Law Olmsted; The Papers of Thomas A. Edison; New Series in NASA History

University Press of Kansas

2502 Westbrooke Circle
Lawrence, KS 66045-4444

Phone: 785.864.4154
Fax: 785.864.4586
Email: upress@ku.edu
Indiv: (user I.D.)@ku.edu

Website and Social Media:
Website: www.kansaspress.ku.edu
Facebook: www.facebook.com/kansaspress

Warehouse Address:
2445 Westbrooke Circle
Lawrence, KS 66045-4440
Phone: 785.864.4156

Orders:
Phone: 785.864.4155
Email: upkorders@ku.edu

UK / European Representative:
Eurospan

Canadian Representative:
Scholarly Book Services

Staff
Director: Fred Woodward (785.864.4667; email: fwoodward)
    Assistant Director: TBA (785.864.9165; email: TBA)
    Assistant to the Director: Sara Henderson White (785.864.9125; email: shwhite)
Editorial: Michael Briggs, Editor-in-Chief (political science, military history, law)
    (785.864.9162; email: mbriggs)
    Acquisitions Editors: TBA (American history, American studies, Native American studies, women's studies) (785.864.9160); Fred Woodward (political science, presidential studies, US political history, American political thought, regional studies) (785.864.4667)
Manuscript Editorial, Design and Production:
    Production Editors: Larisa Martin (785.864.9169; email: lmartin); Kelly Chrisman Jacques (785.864.9186; email: kjchrism)

Marketing: TBA, Assistant Director and Marketing Manager (785.864.9165)
  Publicity Manager: Rebecca Murray Schuler (785.864.9170; email: rmschuler)
  Direct Mail & Exhibits Manager: Debra Diehl (785.864.9166; email: ddiehl)
  Art Director & Advertising Manager: Karl Janssen (785.864.9164; email: kjanssen)
  Marketing Assistant: Suzanne Galle (785.864.9167; email: sgalle)
Business: Conrad Roberts, Business Manager (785.864.9158; email: ceroberts)
  Accounting Manager: Britt DeTienne (785.864.9159; email: bdetienne)

Full Member

Established: 1946
Title output 2011: 53
Titles currently in print: 1022

Admitted to AAUP: 1946
Title output 2012: 57

Editorial Program

American history; military and intelligence studies; Western history and Native American studies; American government and public policy; presidential studies; constitutional and legal studies; environmental studies; American studies and popular culture; women's studies; Kansas, the Great Plains, and the Midwest. The Press does not consider fiction, poetry, or festschriften for publication.

Special series, joint imprints, and/or copublishing programs: American Political Thought; American Presidential Elections; American Presidency; Constitutional Thinking; CultureAmerica; Kansas Nature Guides; Landmark Law Cases and American Society; Modern First Ladies; Modern War Studies; Studies in Government and Public Policy; US Army War College Guides to Civil War Battles.

The Kent State University Press

Street Address:
1118 University Library
1125 Risman Drive
Kent, OH 44242-0001

Mailing Address:
1118 University Library
PO Box 5190
Kent, OH 44242-0001

Phone: 330.672.7913
Fax: 330.672.3104
Email: (user I.D.)@kent.edu

Orders:
Phone: 419.281.1802
Fax: 419.281.6883

Website and Social Media:
Website: www.kentstateuniversitypress.com
Facebook: www.facebook.com/kentstateuniversitypress
Twitter: KentStateUPress

UK/European Representative:
Eurospan

Canadian Representative:
Scholarly Book Services

Staff

Director: Will Underwood (330.672.8094; email: wunderwo)
Acquisitions: Joyce Harrison, Acquiring Editor (330.672.8099; email: jharri18)
Editorial: Mary D. Young, Managing Editor (330.672.8101; email: mdyoung)
Design and Production: Christine A. Brooks, Manager (330.672.8092; email: cbrooks)

Assistant Design and Production Manager: Darryl M. Crosby (330.672.8091; email: dcrosby)
Marketing: Susan L. Cash, Manager (330.672.8097; email: scash)
Journals Circulation/Administrative Assistant: Carol Heller (330.672.8090; email: cheller1)
Bookkeeper: Norma E. Hubbell (330.672.8096; email: nhubbell)

Full Member

Established: 1966
Title output 2011: 35
Titles currently in print: 632

Admitted to AAUP: 1970
Title output 2012: 35
Journals published: 2

Editorial Program
History: American Civil War era; US military, cultural/social, diplomatic, true crime; Ohio/Midwestern studies; fashion/costume; material culture. Literature: US (to ca. 1970); regional/Midwestern; British (Inklings). Ethnomusicology. Regional literary nonfiction; poetry only through Wick Poetry Center; no fiction.
Journals: *Civil War History*; *Ohio History*
Special series: American Abolitionism and Antislavery; Civil War in the North; Civil War Soldiers and Strategies; Cleveland Theater; Interpreting American History; Literature and Medicine; New Studies in US Foreign Relations; Reading Hemingway; Sacred Landmarks; Symposia on Democracy; Teaching Hemingway; Translation Studies; True Crime History; Violence Prevention, Intervention, and Policy; Wick Poetry.

The University Press of Kentucky

663 South Limestone Street
Lexington, KY 40508-4008

Warehouse Address:
Maple Press Lebanon Distribution Center
704 Legionaire Drive
Fredericksburg, PA 17026

Phone: 859.257.8400
Fax: 859.257.7975
Email: (user I.D.)@uky.edu

Orders:
c/o Hopkins Fulfillment Services
PO Box 50370
Baltimore, MD 21211
Phone: 800.537.5487 or 410.516.6956
Fax: 410.516.6998
Email: hfscustserv@ press.jhu.edu

Website and Social Media:
Website: www.kentuckypress.com
Blog: kentuckypress.wordpress.com
Facebook: www.facebook.com/KentuckyPress
Twitter: KentuckyPress
YouTube: YouTube.com/univpressofky

UK/European Representative:
Eurospan

Canadian Representative:
Scholarly Book Services

Staff

Director: Stephen M. Wrinn (859.257.8432; email: smwrin2)
  Executive Assistant to the Director: Allison Webster (email: allison.webster2)
Acquisitions Editors: Stephen M. Wrinn (American history, American studies, world history, Civil War, military history, political science, political theory, public policy, international studies, African American studies); Anne Dean Watkins (film studies, popular culture, American and southern history) (859.257.8434; email: annedean.watkins); Ashley Runyon (Kentuckiana, regional studies, Appalachian studies, folklore) (859.257.8150; email: ashley.runyon)
  Editorial Assistant: Bailey Johnson (859.257.9492; email: bailey.johnson)
Editing, Design and Production: David Cobb, Director of Editing, Design and Production (859.257.4252; email: dlcobb2)
  Production Manager: Pat Gonzales (859.257.4669; email: pagonz0)
  Senior Supervising Editor: Ila McEntire (859.257.8433; email: ila.mcentire)
  Editorial Assistant: Iris Law (859.257.8438; email: iala224)
Marketing: Amy Harris, Director of Marketing and Sales (859.257.4249; email: ae.harris)
  Publicity and Exhibits Manager: Mack McCormick (859.257.5200; email: permissions)
  Publicity and Direct Promotions Manager: Cameron Ludwick (859.257.2817; email: cameron.ludwick)
Assistant Director/Director of Finance & Administration: Craig R. Wilkie (859.257.8436; email: crwilk00)
  Database Administrator and Technology Support: Tim Elam (859.257.8761; email: taelam2)
  Assistant Director of Finance and Administration: Teresa W. Collins (859.257.8405; email: twell1)
  Administrative Assistant: Robert Brandon (859.257.8400, 800.839.6855; email: rbrandon)

Full Member

Established: 1943
Title output 2011: 71
Titles currently in print: 1,301

Admitted to AAUP: 1947
Title output 2012: 82

Editorial Program

Scholarly books in the fields of American history; military history; film studies; political science; international studies; folklore and material culture; African American studies; serious nonfiction of general interest. Regionally, the Press maintains an interest in Kentucky and the Ohio Valley, Appalachia, and the upper South. Submissions are not invited in fiction, drama, or poetry.

Special series: American Warriors; Asia in the New Millennium; Battles and Campaigns; Civil Rights and the Struggle for Black Equality in the Twentieth Century; Culture of the Land: A Series in the New Agrarianism; Essential Readers in Contemporary Media; Foreign Military Studies: Kentucky Remembered: An Oral History Series; Kentucky Voices; Material Worlds; New Books for New Readers; New Directions in Southern History; The Ohio River Valley; The Philosophy of Popular Culture; Place Matters: New Directions in Appalachian and Regional Studies; Political Companions to Great American Authors; Provocations: Political Thought and Contemporary Issues; Public Papers of the Governors of Kentucky; Religion in the South; Screen Classics; Studies in Conflict, Diplomacy, and Peace; Thomas D. Clark Studies in Education, Public Policy, and Social Change; Topics in Kentucky History; Virginia at War

Leuven University Press/Universitaire Pers Leuven

Minderbroedersstraat 4 - bus 5602
B-3000 Leuven
Belgium

Phone: +32 16 32 53 45
Fax: +32 16 32 53 52
Email: info@upers.kuleuven.be
Indiv. (user I.D.)@upers.kuleuven.be

US Representative:
Cornell University Press Services
P.O. Box 6525
750 Cascadilla Street
Ithaca, NY 14851-6525 USA
Phone: 607.277.2211
Email: orderbook@cupserv.org

Website and Social Media:
Website: www.lup.be
Facebook: www.facebook.com/pages/Leuven-University-Press/130250583714129

UK and European Sales Representative:
University Presses Marketing

UK and European Orders:
NBN International

Staff
Director and Acquisitions Editorial: Marike Schipper (+32 16 32 53 47; email:
   marike.schipper)
Acquisitions Editorial: Veerle De Laet (+32 16 32 81 26; email: veerle.delaet)
Manuscript Editorial: Beatrice Van Eeghem (+32 16 32 53 40; email: beatrice.vaneeghem)
Production: Patricia di Costanzo (+32 16 32 53 53; email: patricia.dicostanzo)
Marketing: Annemie Vandezande (+32 16 32 53 51; email: annemie.vandezande)
Customer Service and Order Processing: Margreet Meijer (+32 16 32 53 50; email:
   margreet.meijer)

International Member
Established: 1971
Title output 2011: 45
Titles currently in print: 900

Admitted to AAUP: 2005
Title output 2012: NR
Journals published: 1

Editorial Program
Scholarly publications with emphasis on music, art & theory, text & literature, history &
archaeology, philosophy & religion and society, law & economics
Journal: *Humanistica Lovaniensia: A Journal of Neo-Latin Studies*
Special series: Alfred Cauchie Series; Ancient and Medieval Philosophy Series 1; Ancient
and Medieval Philosophy Series 2: Henrici de Gandavo Opera Omnia; Ancient and Medi-
eval Philosophy - Series 3 Francisci de Marchia Opera Philosophica et Theologica; Avisos de
Flandes; Collected Writings of the Orpheus Institute; Corpus Latinum Commentariorum in
Aristotelem Graecorum; Dynamics of Religious Reform; Egyptian Prehistory Monographs;
Figures of the Unconscious; Humanistica Lovaniensia: journal of Neo-Latin Studies; ICAG
Studies; Jean François Lyotard Writings on Contemporary Art and Artists; Kadoc-Artes;
Kadoc-Studies on Religion, Culture and Society; Lieven Gevaert Series; Mediaevalia Lovani-
ensia - Series 1/ Studia; Plutarchea Hypomnemata; Sagalassos; Society, Crime & Criminal
Justice; Sociology Today; Studia Anthropologica; Studia Paedagogica; Studies in Archaeologi-
cal Sciences; Studies in Musical Form; Studies in Social and Economic History; Subseries
Orpheus Research Centre in Music; Supplementa Humanistica Lovaniensia.

Lincoln Institute Land Policy

113 Brattle Street
Cambridge, MA 02138

Phone: 617.661.3016
Fax: 617.661.7235
Email: help@lincolninst.edu

Orders:
Publishers Storage and Shipping Company
(PSSC)
Phone: 978.345.2121 ext. 282;
877.526.3257
Email: ewilson@pssc.com
Website: www.pssc.com

Website and Social Media:
Website: www.lincolninst.edu
Facebook: www.facebook.com/lincolninstituteoflandpolicy
Twitter: landpolicy
YouTube: www.youtube.com/user/LincolnLandPolicy
Blog: www.lincolninst.edu/news-events/at-lincoln-house-blog

Staff

Director of Publications and Senior Editor: TBA
Managing Editor: Emily McKeigue (617.503.2115; email: emckeigue@lincolninst.edu)
Publications Coordinator: Susan Pace (617.503.2177; email: space@lincolninst.edu)
Marketing Consultant: Marissa Benson (617.309.9792; email: mbenson@lincolninst.edu)

Introductory Member

Established: 1974
Title output 2010: 11
Titles currently in print: 129

Admitted to AAUP: 2011
Title output 2012: 15
Journals published: 1

Editorial Program

The Lincoln Institute of Land Policy's publishing mission is to improve the quality of information, debate, and decisions in the areas of land policy and land-related taxation. Lincoln publishes books, eBooks, Policy Focus Reports; Working Papers; and Multimedia Resources (CDs and DVDs; short online videos).

Topics include land valuation; property taxation; urban and regional planning; urban economics; legal land use issues; housing and urban development; smart growth; land conservation; climate change; planning, architecture, and urban design; and international land policy focusing on Latin America and China.

Journal: *Land Lines*

Louisiana State University Press

3990 W. Lakeshore Drive
Baton Rouge, LA 70808

Phone: 225.578.6294
Indiv: (user I.D.)@lsu.edu

Website and Social Media:
Website: www.lsupress.org
Blog: lsupress.typepad.com/lsu_press_blog
Facebook: www.facebook.com/pages/LSU-Press/38236386996
Twitter: lsupress

Canadian Distributor:
Scholarly Book Services

Warehouse, Orders and Cust. Service:
Longleaf Services
PO Box 8895
Chapel Hill, NC 27515-8895
Phone: 800.848.6224
Fax: 800.272.6817
Email: longleaf@unc.edu

Staff
Director: MaryKatherine Callaway (225.578.6144; email: mkc)
    Assistant to the Director, Subrights and Permissions: Erica Bossier (email: ebossie)
Acquisitions Editorial: Rand Dotson (southern history, music studies) (225.578.6412; email: pdotso1); Margaret Lovecraft (trade) (225.578.6319; email: lovecraft); Alisa Plant (European history, media studies, environmental studies, foodways) (225.578.6433; email: aplant)
Manuscript Editorial: Lee Sioles, Managing Editor (225.578.6467; email: lsioles)
    Senior Editor: Catherine Kadair (email: clkadair)
Design and Production: Laura Gleason, Assistant Director and Production Manager (225.578.6469; email: lgleasn)
    Assistant Production Manager: Amanda Scallan (email: amandas)
Marketing: Erin Rolfs, Manager (225.578.8282; email: erolfs)
    Digital Initiatives and Database Manager: Robert Keane (email: rkeane)
    Assistant Marketing Manager Exhibits and Advertising Coordinator: Kate Barton (email: kbart04)
Financial Operations Manager: Rebekah Brown (225.578.6415; email: rbrown1)
Subsidiary Rights: McIntosh & Otis, Inc., 353 Lexington Ave., New York, NY 10016 (212.687.7400)
The Southern Review
    Fiction and Nonfiction Editor: Cara Blue Adams (225.578.5159; email: carablue)
    Poetry Editor: Jessica Faust (225.578.0896; email: jfaust1)

Full Member
Established: 1935
Title output 2011: 74
Titles currently in print: 1,984

Admitted to AAUP: unknown
Title output 2012: 71

Editorial Program
Humanities and social sciences, with special emphasis on Southern history and literature; regional studies; European history in the Atlantic world; environmental studies; poetry; and Louisiana roots music.

Special series, joint imprints and/or copublishing programs: Antislavery, Abolition, and the Atlantic World; Conflicting Worlds; Making the Modern South; Media and Public Affairs; Papers of Jefferson Davis; Southern Biography Southern Literary Studies; Southern Messenger Poets; W.L. Fleming Lectures in Southern History; Walt Whitman Award of the Academy of American Poets; Yellow Shoe Fiction

The Press also distributes the Lena-Miles Weaver Todd Poetry Series.

The University of Manitoba Press

Street Address:
301 St. John's College
University of Manitoba
Winnipeg Manitoba R3T 2M5
Canada

Phone: 204.474.9495
Fax: 204.474.7556
Email: uofmpress@umanitoba.ca

Website and Social Media:
Website: uofmpress.ca
Blog: uofmpress.ca/blog
Facebook: www.facebook.com/UofMPress

Canadian Orders:
University of Toronto Press
Phone: 800.565.9523
Email: utpbooks@utpress.utoronto.ca

US Orders:
Michigan State University Press
Phone: 800.678.2120

Canadian Representative:
Ampersand and Company

Staff
Director: David Carr (204.474.9242; email: carr@cc.umanitoba.ca)
Senior Acquisitions Editor: Jean L. Wilson (email: jeanl.Wilson@shaw.ca)
Managing Editor: Glenn Bergen (204.474.7338; email: glenn_bergen@umanitoba.ca)
Marketing: Cheryl Miki, Sales and Marketing Supervisor (204.474.9998; email: miki@cc.umanitoba.ca)
Promotion/Editorial Assistant: Ariel Gordon (204.474.8048; email: gordojd@cc.umanitoba.ca)

Full Member
Established: 1967
Title output 2011: 8
Titles currently in print: 130

Admitted to AAUP: 2011
Title output 2012: 9

Editorial Program
Native studies; Native history; Canadian history; the Arctic and the North; ethnic studies; Aboriginal languages; Canadian literary studies, especially Aboriginal literature; political studies; regional trade titles.
Special series: Contemporary Studies on the North; Critical Studies in Aboriginal History (formerly Manitoba Studies in Native History); Publications of the Algonquian Text Society; Studies in Immigration and Culture

Marquette University Press

1415 West Wisconsin Avenue
Box 3141
Milwaukee, WI 53201-3141

Phone: 414.288.1564
Fax: 414.288.7813
Email: (user I.D.)@marquette.edu

Website and Social Media:
Website: marquette.edu/mupress

UK/European Distributor:
Eurospan

Warehouse Address:
30 Amberwood Parkway, PO Box 388
Ashland, OH 44805

Orders and Customer Service:
Phone: 800.247.6553; 419.281.1802
Fax: 419.281.6883

Canadian Representative:
Scholarly Book Services

Staff

Director: Andrew Tallon (414.288.1564; email: andrew.tallon)
Editorial, Marketing, Design and Production: Andrew Tallon
Business: Maureen Kondrick (414.288.1564; email: maureen.kondrick)
Journals: Andrew Tallon
Journals Marketing: Pamela K. Swope (800.444.2419 ext. 1; email: pkswope@pdcnet.org)

Full Member

Established: 1916
Title output 2011: 16
Titles currently in print: 400

Admitted to AAUP: 1998
Title output 2012: 17
Journals published: 1

Editorial Program

Philosophy; theology; history; urban studies; journalism; education; regional studies; and mediæval history.

Journal: *Philosophy & Theology*

Philosophy series: Aquinas Lecture; Marquette Studies in Philosophy; Mediæval Philosophical Texts in Translation

Theology series: Marquette Studies in Theology; Père Marquette Lecture; Reformation Texts with Translation: Series 1, Biblical Studies; Series 2, Women in the Reformation; Series 3, Late Reformation

History series: Klement Lecture (Civil War); Marquette Studies in History (Modern); Urban Studies Series

Communication series: Diederich Studies in Media and Communication

University of Massachusetts Press

East Experiment Station
671 North Pleasant Street
Amherst, MA 01003

Phone: 413.545.2217
Fax: 413.545.1226
Email: (user I.D.)@umpress.umass.edu
(unless otherwise indicated)

<u>Website and Social Media:</u>
Website: www.umass.edu/umpress
Facebook: www.facebook.com/umasspress

<u>Canadian Representative:</u>
Scholarly Book Services

Boston Office:
Brian Halley
Provost Office, Quinn Building
UMass Boston
100 Morrissey Boulevard
Boston, MA 02125

<u>Orders:</u>
c/o Hopkins Fulfillment Services
PO Box 50370
Baltimore, MD 21211
Phone: 800.537.5487
Fax: 410.516.6998
Email: hfscustserv@press.jhu.edu

<u>UK/European Distributor:</u>
Eurospan

Staff

Director: Bruce Wilcox (413.545.4990; email: wilcox)
Acquisitions Editorial: Clark Dougan, Senior Editor (413.545.4989; email: cdougan)
 Boston Editor: Brian Halley (617.287.5610; email: brian.halley@umb.edu)
Manuscript Editorial: Carol Betsch, Managing Editor (413.545.4991; email: betsch)
Design and Production: Jack Harrison, Manager (413.545.4998; email: harrison)
 Designer & Associate Production Manager: Sally Nichols (413.545.4997; email: snichols)
Business and Marketing: Yvonne Crevier, Business Manager (413.545.4994; email: ycrevier)
 Promotion Manager: Karen Fisk (413.545.2217; email: kfisk)

Full Member

Established: 1963
Title output 2011: 40
Titles currently in print: 1,000

Admitted to AAUP: 1966
Title output 2012: 39

Editorial Program

Scholarly books and serious nonfiction, with special interests in African American studies;
American history; American studies; architecture and landscape design; disability studies;
environmental studies; gender studies; history of the book; journalism and media studies;
literary and cultural studies; Native American studies; science and technology studies; urban
studies; and books of regional interest.

Special series, joint imprints and/or copublishing programs: American Popular Music;
AWP Award Series in Short Fiction (Grace Paley Prize); Culture, Politics, and the Cold War;
Environmental History of the Northeast; Juniper Prizes (poetry and fiction); Library of
American Landscape History (Critical Perspectives in the History of Environmental Design;
Designing the American Park); Massachusetts Studies in Early Modern Culture; Native
Americans of the Northeast; Public History in Historical Perspective; Science/Technology/
Culture; Studies in Print Culture and the History of the Book

The MIT Press

55 Hayward Street
Cambridge, MA 02142-1315
Phone: 617.253.5646 (main)
Fax: 617.258.6779
Email: (user I.D.)@mit.edu

Journals:
Phone: 617.253.2864 (main)
Fax: 617.258.6779

Website and Social Media:
Website: mitpress.mit.edu
Journals Website: www.mitpressjournals.org
Blog: mitpress.typepad.com/mitpresslog/
Facebook: www.facebook.com/mitpress
Twitter: mitpress

Book Orders/Customer Service:
Phone: 800.405.1619 (US/Can);
401.531.2800 (International)
Fax: 800.406.9145 (US/Can);
401.531.2801 (International)
Email: mitpress-orders@mit.edu

London Office:
The MIT Press, Ltd.
Fitzroy House
11 Chenies Street
London WC1E 7EY
United Kingdom
Phone: +44 (20) 7306 0603
Fax: +44 (20) 7306 0604
Email: info@hup-mitpress.co.uk

Staff

Director: Ellen Faran (617.253.4078; email: ewfaran)
  Assistant to the Director: Nia Lewis (617.253.5255; email: niav)
Associate Director and Director of Finance & Operations: Rebecca Schrader (617.253.5250;
  email: recs)
Director of Technology: Bill Trippe (617.452.3747; email: trippe)
Acquisitions Editorial: Gita Manaktala, Editorial Director (617.253.3172; email: manak)
  Editors: Marguerite Avery (science, technology & society (STS), information science
  & communication) (617.253.1653; email: mavery); James DeWolf (computer science, linguistics) (617.253.1588; email: jdewolf); Roger Conover (art, architecture,
  visual culture) (617.253.1677; email: conover); John S. Covell (economics, business,
  finance) (617.253.3757; email: jcovell); Philip Laughlin (cognitive science, philosophy) (617.252.1636; email: laughlin); Jane Macdonald (economics, business, finance)
  (617.253.1605; email: janem); Clay Morgan (environmental studies, bioethics, political science) (617.253.4113; email: claym); Robert Prior (life sciences, neuroscience,
  biology) (617.253.1584; email: prior); Doug Sery (new media, game studies, design)
  (617.253.5187; email: dsery)
Manuscript Editorial: Michael Sims, Managing Editor (617.253.2080; email: msims)
Digital Publishing Manager: Jake Furbush (617.258.0583; email: jfurbush)
Design: Yasuyo Iguchi, Design Manager (617.253.8034; email: iguchi)
Production: Janet Rossi, Production Manager (617.253.2882; email: janett)
Marketing and Promotions: Marketing Director: Katie Hope (617.258.0603; email: khope)
  Advertising Manager: Anar Badalov (617.258.7821; email: badalov)
  Exhibits Manager: John Costello (617.258.5764; email: jcostell)
  Promotions Manager & Direct Mail Manager: Astrid Baehrecke (617.253.7297; email:
  baehreck)
  Publicity Manager: Colleen Lanick (617.253.2874; email: colleenl)
  Subsidiary Rights Manager: Cristina Sanmartín (617.253.0629; email: csan)
  Permissions Manager: Pamela Quick (617.253.0080; email: quik)

Textbook Manager: Michelle Pullano (617.253.3620; email: mpullano)
Sales: Anne Bunn, Sales Director (617.253.8838; email: annebunn)
  Sales Manager: Erika Valenti (617.258.0582; email: erikav)
Journals: Nick Lindsay, Journals Director (617.258.0594; email: nlindsay)
  Journals Business Manager: June McCaull (617.258.0593; email: jmccaull)
  Journals and Digital Products Customer Service Manager: Abbie Hiscox (617.452.3765;
  email: hiscox)
  Journals Editorial & Production Manager: Rachel Besen (617.258.0585; email: rbesen)
  Journals Subsidiary Rights Manager: Pam Quick (617.253.0080; email: quik)
Warehouse: Robert O'Handley, Director of Operations (email: bob.ohandley@triliteral.org)
  Customer Service Manager: Cathy Morrone (401.531.2800; email:
  cathy.morrone@triliteral.org)

Full Member

Established: 1961

Title output 2011: 238

Titles currently in print: 3,850

Admitted to AAUP: 1961

Title output 2012: 224

Journals published: 30

Editorial Program

Architecture; artificial intelligence; bioethics; biology; business; cognitive sciences; communication; computer science; contemporary art; design; earth sciences; economics; environmental studies; finance; game studies; information sciences; life sciences; linguistics; natural history; nature; new media studies; neuroscience; philosophy; photography; political science; psychology; regional/MIT titles; science, technology, and society (STS); security studies.

Co-publishing and distribution programs: Afterall Books; Alphabet City; Boston Review Books; Perspecta; Semiotext(e); Whitechapel Documents of Contemporary Art; Zone Books.

Journals: *African Arts; Artificial Life; ARTMargins; Asian Economic Papers; The Baffler; Computational Linguistics; Computer Music Journal; Daedalus; Design Issues; Education Finance and Policy; Evolutionary Computation; Global Environmental Politics; Grey Room; Innovations; International Journal of Learning & Media, International Security; Journal of Cognitive Neuroscience; Journal of Cold War Studies; Journal of Interdisciplinary History; Leonardo; Leonardo Music Journal; Linguistic Inquiry; Neural Computation; The New England Quarterly; October; PAJ: A Journal of Performance and Art; Perspectives on Science; Presence: Teleoperators and Virtual Environments; The Review of Economics and Statistics; TDR: The Drama Review*

Special series: Acting with Technology; Adaptive Computation and Machine Learning; Afterall: One Work; Alphabet City; Alvin Hansen Symposium Series on Public Policy; American Academy Studies in Global Security; American and Comparative Environmental Policy; Annotating Art's Histories; Arne Ryde Memorial Lectures; Basic Bioethics; BCSIA Studies in International Security; Boston Review Books; Bradford Books; Cairoli Lectures; Cellular and Molecular Neuroscience; Centre for European Policy Studies (CEPS); CESifo Book; CESifo Seminar; Cognitive Neuroscience; Computational Molecular Biology; Computational Neuroscience; Cooperative Information Systems; Current Studies in Linguistics; Dahlem Workshop Reports; Design Thinking, Design Theory Developmental Cognitive Neuroscience; Dibner Institute Studies in the History of Science and Technology; Digital Communication; Digital Libraries & Electronic Publishing; Documentary Sources in Contemporary Art; Documents Books; Documents of Contemporary Art; Earth System Governance; Economic Learning and Social Evolution; Electronic Culture; Engineering Studies; Engineering Systems; Essential Knowledge; Eurasian Population & Family History; Explorations in Cognitive Science; Food, Health, and the Environment; Gaston Eyskens Lectures; George

Santayana: Definitive Works; Global Environmental Accord: Strategies for Sustainability and Institutional Innovation; History and Foundation of Information Science; History of Computing; Information Revolution and Global Politics; The Information Society Series; Infrastructures; Inside Technology; Intelligent Robotics and Autonomous Agents; International Security Readers; Irving Singer Library; Issues in Clinical and Cognitive Neuropsychology; Issues in the Biology of Language & Cognition; Jean Nicod Series; John D. & Catherine T. MacArthur Foundation Reports on Digital Media and Learning; John D. & Catherine T. MacArthur Foundation Series on Digital Media and Learning; Lemelson Center Studies in Invention and Innovation; Leonardo Books; Life and Mind; Linguistic Inquiry Monographs; Lionel Robbins Lectures; Media in Transition; Mediawork pamphlet series; MIT Readers in Contemporary Philosophy; Munich Lectures; Neural Information Processing; October Books; October Files; Ohlin Lectures;; Oppositions Books; Perspecta: The Yale Architecture Journal; Philosophical Psychopathology: Disorders in Mind; Platform Studies; Politics, Science, and the Environment; Publications of the Burndy Library; Representation and Mind; Scientific and Engineering Computation; Semiotext(e); Short Circuits; Simplicity: Design, Technology, Business, Life; Social Neuroscience; Software Studies; Special Issues of Physica D; Structural Mechanics; Strüngmann Forum Reports; Studies in Contemporary German Social Thought; Studies in Neuropsychology & Neurolinguistics; Sustainable Metropolitan Communities Books; Tax Policy and the Economy; Technologies of Lived Abstraction; Topics in Contemporary Philosophy; Transformations: Studies in the History of Science and Technology; Urban and Industrial Environments; Vienna Series in Theoretical Biology; Walras-Pareto Lectures; Wicksell Lectures; Work Books; Writing Architecture; Writing Art; Yrjo Jahnsson Lectures Series; Zeuthen Lecture Series.

McGill-Queen's University Press

Montreal Office:
1010 Sherbrooke Street West
Suite 1720
Montreal, QC H3A 2R7
Canada

Phone: 514.398.3750
Fax: 514.398.4333
Email: mqup@mcgill.ca
Indiv: (user I.D.)@mcgill.ca

Website and Social Media:
Website: www.mqup.mcgill.ca
Blog: www.mqup.typepad.com
Facebook: www.facebook.com/McGillQueens
Twitter: scholarmqup

Canadian Distributor:
Georgetown Terminal Warehouses
34 Armstrong Avenue
Georgetown, ON L7G 4R9
Canada
Phone: 877.864.8477
Fax: 877.864.4272
Email: orders@gtwcanada.com

Kingston Office:
Queen's University
144 Barrie Street
Kingston, ON K7L 3J9
Canada

Phone: 613.533.2155
Fax: 613.533.6822
Email: mqup@queensu.ca

US Distributor:
CUP Services
PO Box 6525
750 Cascadilla Street
Ithaca, NY 14851-6525
Phone: 800.666.2211
Fax: 800.688.2877
Email: orderbook@cupserv.org

UK/European Distributor:
Marston Book Services Ltd

Staff

Executive Director: Philip J. Cercone (Montreal, 514.398.3750; email: philip.cercone)
   Business Manager: TBA
   Rights and Special Projects Manager: Adrian Galwin (514.398.2121; email: adrian.galwin)
   Systems Administrator: David Ilacqua (514.398.4419; email: david.ilacqua)
   Senior Administrative Coordinator: TBA
   Accounts Payable: Carmie Vacca (514.398.2056; email: carmie.vacca)
   Accounts Receivable/Receptionist: Morgan Bell (514.398.3750; email: morgan.bell)
Montreal Office Editors: John Zucchi (514.398.3750; email: john.zucchi); Mark Abley (514.398.6652; email: mark.abley); Jonathan Crago (514.398.7480; email: jonathan.crago); Kyla Madden (514.398.2056; email: kyla.madden); Jacqueline Mason (514.398.2250; email: jacqueline.mason)
   Editorial Assistants: Joanne Pisano (514.398.2068; email: joanne.pisano); Jessica Howarth (514.398.3279; email: jessica.howarth)
Managing Editor: Ryan Van Huijstee (514.398.3922; email: ryan.vanhuijstee)
Production Manager: Elena Goranescu (514.398.7395; email: elena.goranescu)
   Assistant Production Manager: Rob Mackie (514.398.1342; email: robert.mackie)

Production Assistant: Andrew Pinchefsky (514.398.6996; email: andrew.pinchefsky)
Marketing Manager: Susan McIntosh (514.398.6306; email: susan.mcintosh)
Sales Manager: Jack Hannan (514.398.5165; email: jack.hannan)
Educational Sales Administrator: Roy Ward (514.398.7177; email: roy.ward)
Direct Mail & Exhibits Coordinator: Filomena Falocco (514.398.2912; email: filomena.falocco)
Web Marketing Data Administrator: Louise Sa (514.398.6166; email: louise.sa)
Marketing Assistant: Katie Heffring (514.398.2914; email: marketing.mqup)
Publicist: Jacqueline Davis (514.398.2555; email: jacqueline.davis)

Full Member
Established: 1969 as a joint press
Admitted to AAUP: 1963 (as McGill University Press)
Title output 2011: 136   Title output 2012: 124
Titles currently in print: c. 2,800

Editorial Program
Scholarly books and well-researched studies of general interest in the humanities and social sciences, including anthropology, especially North American native peoples; architecture; Arctic and northern studies; art history; biography; Canadian studies; Canadian literature; classics; communication and media studies; cultural studies; demography; economics; education; environmental studies; ethnic studies; European studies; film studies; folklore and material culture; gender studies; geography; health and society; history; history of medicine; history of science; Irish and Gaelic studies; law; linguistics; literary criticism; medieval and renaissance studies; military studies; music history and theory; native studies; philosophy; poetry; photography; political economy; political science; public administration; public affairs; public health; Quebec studies; religious studies; Slavic and Eastern European studies; sociology; theatre; urban studies; and women's studies.
Special series: Art of Living; The Art of the State; Arts Insights; CHORA, Intervals in the Philosophy of Architecture; Canada Among Nations; Canada: The State of the Federation; Canadian Association of Geographers Series in Canadian Geography; Canadian Public Administration; Carleton Library; Central Problems of Philosophy; Central Works of Philosophy; Centre for Editing Early Canadian Texts; Comparative Charting of Social Change; Continental European Philosophy; Critical Perspectives on Public Affairs; Culture of Cities; Fontanus Monograph; Footprints; Foreign Policy, Security and Strategic Studies; Fundamentals of Philosophy; Global Dialogue on Federalism; Global Dialogue on Federalism Booklet; Governance and Public Management; Harbinger Poetry; Heretics; How Ottawa Spends; Hugh MacLennan Poetry; Innovation, Science, Environment; International Social Survey Programme; John Deutsch Institute; Key Concepts; Library of Political Leadership; McGill-Queen's Native and Northern; McGill-Queen's Studies in Ethnic History; McGill-Queen's Studies in the History of Ideas; McGill-Queen's Studies in the History of Religion; McGill-Queen's/Associated Medical Services Studies in the History of Medicine, Health, and Society; McGill/Queen's/Beaverbrook Canadian Foundation Studies in Art History; Migration and Diversity: Comparative Issues and International Comparisons; Nordic Voices; Philosophy Now; Philosophy and Science; Public Policy; Queen's Policy Studies; Rupert's Land Record

Society; Social Union; Studies in Nationalism and Ethnic Conflict; Studies on the History of Quebec/Études d'histoire du Québec; Thematic Issues in Federalism; Understanding Movements in Modern Thought; War and European Society.

Medieval Institute Publications

Street Address:
100 E Walwood Hall
Western Michigan University
Kalamazoo, MI 49008-5432

Mailing Address:
Western Michigan University
1903 W. Michigan Ave.
Kalamazoo, MI 49008-5432

Phone: 269.387.8754
Fax: 269.387.8750

Website and Social Media:
Website: www.wmich.edu/
     medievalpublications/

Orders:
Phone: 269.387.8755

Staff

Managing Editor: Patricia Hollahan (email: patricia.hollahan@wmich.edu)
Editor and Exhibits Manager: Theresa M. Whitaker (email: theresa.m.whitaker@wmich.edu)
Production Editor: Thomas P. Krol (email: thomas.p.krol@wmich.edu)
Order Fulfillment Manager: Cynthia Seedorff (email: cynthia.seerdorff@wmich.edu)

Introductory Member

Established: 1978
Title output 2011: 9
Titles currently in print: 203

Admitted to AAUP: 2011
Title output 2012: 9
Journals published: 2

Editorial Program

Publications in archeology, art history, dance, drama, history, literature, music, philosophy, and theology of the European Middle Ages and early modern period, with very occasional publications on the history of science and technology.
Special series: Studies in Medieval Culture; Early Drama, Art, and Music; Publications of the Richard Rawlinson Center
Journals: *Medieval Prosopography; Studies in Iconography*

Mercer University Press

1400 Coleman Avenue
Macon, GA 31207

Phone: 478.301.2880
Fax: 478.301.2585
Email: (user I.D.)@mercer.edu

Orders:
Phone: 866.895.1472
Email: mupressorders@mercer.edu

Website and Social Media:
Website: www.mupress.org
Blog: merceruniversitypress.wordpress.com/
Facebook: www.facebook.com/MercerUniversityPress
Twitter: mupress

Staff
Director and Acquisitions: Marc A. Jolley (email: jolley_ma)
  Production: Marsha Luttrell, Publishing Assistant (email: luttrell_mm)
Marketing: Mary Beth Kosowski, Director of Marketing and Sales (email: kosowski_mb)
  Business: Regenia (Jenny) Toole, Business Office (email: toole_rw)
  Customer Service: Candice Morris (email: morris_ce)

Full Member
Established: 1979
Title output 2011: 37
Titles currently in print: 650+

Admitted to AAUP: 2000
Title output 2012: 36

Editorial Program
Regional trade titles and serious works of nonfiction in history, particularly in the history of the United States (with an emphasis on the American South), the history of religion, and the history of literature; Southern regional studies; literature and literary criticism; Southern literary fiction; poetry; African American studies; political science; natural history.
Special series: Baptists; Civil War Georgia; the International Kierkegaard Commentary; Mercer Classics in Biblical Studies; the Mercer Commentary on the Bible; the Melungeons; Mercer Paul Tillich Series; Mercer Flannery O'Connor Series; Music and the American South; Sports and Religion; Voices of the African Diaspora.

The University of Michigan Press

839 Greene Street
Ann Arbor, MI 48104-3209

Phone: 734.764.4388
Fax: 734.615.1540
Email: um.press@umich.edu
Indiv: (user I.D.)@umich.edu

<u>Website and Social Media:</u>
Website: www.press.umich.edu
Blog: blog.press.umich.edu
Facebook: www.facebook.com/pages/University-of-Michigan-Press/37383103953
Twitter: UofMPress
YouTube: youtube.com/umichpress

<u>UK and European Representative:</u>
Eurospan

<u>Orders:</u>
University of Michigan Press
c/o Perseus Distribution
 210 American Drive
Jackson, TN 38301
Phone: 800.343.4499, ext. 1154
ESL Helpline: 877.364.2942
Fax: 877.364.7062
International Customers Fax: 731.935.7731

Staff

Director: John Wilkin (734.764.8016; email: jpwilkin)
  Assistant to the Director/Permissions: Debra Shafer (734.615.6478; email: dshafer)
Acquisitions Editorial:
  Editors: Ellen Bauerle, Executive Editor (music, writing, classical studies, German studies, early modern history) (734.615.6479; email: bauerle); Tom Dwyer, Editor-in-Chief (media studies, cultural studies) (734.936.4922; email: thdwyer); LeAnn Fields (class studies, theater and performance studies) (734.647.2463; email: lfields); Melody Herr (political science, law, American history) (734.763.6419; email: mrherr); Scott Ham (regional) (734.764.4387; email: scottom); Chris Hebert, Editor-at-Large (popular music and jazz) (email: hebertc); Kelly Sippell (ESL, applied linguistics) (734.764.4447; email: ksippell)
  Editorial Assistants: Susan Cronin (734.936.2841; email: sjcronin); Christopher Dreyer (734.647.2463; email: mikage); Alexa Ducsay (734.936.8932; email: ducsaya)
English as a Second Language: Kelly Sippell, Assistant Director and ESL Director (734.764.4447; email: ksippell)
  Assistant Marketing Manager: Jason Contrucci (734.936.0459; email: contrucc)
  ELT Market Analyst: Claudia Leo (734.936.0459; email: cvleo)
Digital Publishing Production: Kevin Hawkins, Head (734.763.6860; email: kshawkin)
Manuscript Editorial: Christina Milton, Managing Editor (734.764.4390; email: cmilton)
  Senior Copyediting Coordinators: Mary Hashman (734.936.0461; email: mhashman); Marcia LaBrenz (734.647.4480; email: mlabrenz); Andrea Olson (734.936.0394; email: ajolson); Kevin Rennells (734.763.1526; email: rennells)
  Assistant Editor: Rosemary Bush (734.763.0170; email: rabush)
Design and Production: John Grucelski, Production Manager (734.764.4391; email: jgrucel)
  Senior Production Coordinators: Mary Sexton (734.763.1525; email: sextonm); Jillian Downey (734.615.8114; email: jilliand); Paula Newcomb (734.763.6417; email: newcombp)

Designer: Heidi Dailey (734.764.4128; email: hdailey)
Digital Production Assistant, Editorial Assistant: Alix Keener (734.615.9335;
email: alixkee)
Digital Publishing Project Manager: Jonathan McGlone (734.763.4260; email: jmcglone)
Digital Publishing Assistant: Kelly Witchen (734.763.6860; email: kwitchen)
Marketing and Sales: Michael Kehoe, Assistant Director and Marketing and Sales Director
(734.936.0388; email: mkehoe)
  Marketing Manager: Emily Westlake (734.615.6477; email: ewestlak)
  Marketing Manager: Shaun Manning (734.763.0163; email: shaunman)
Publishing Technology Group: Jeremy Morse, Head (734.615.5739; email: jgmorse)
  Web Designer: Melissa Baker-Young (734.764.6802; email: mbakeryo)
  Programmer: Seth Johnson (734.764.3417; email: sethajoh)
  Applications Programmer/Analyst: Bryan Smith (734.730.1847; email: besmit)
  Systems Administrator: James Vanderwill (734.936.3636; email: jvanderw)
Business: Gabriela Beres, Business Manager (734.936.2227; email: gsberes)
  Accountant: Karyn McIntire (734.763.0146; email: klydic)
  Accounts Payable: Linda Rowley (734.647.9083; email: lrowley)
  Facilities: Larry Gable (734.764.2468; email: lgable)
  Mail: Will Lovick (email: willski)

Full Member
Established: 1930
Title output 2011: 125
Titles currently in print: 3,200

Admitted to AAUP: 1963
Title output 2012: 124

Editorial Program
Scholarly and trade works in African American studies; American studies; American history; cultural studies; disability studies; English as a second language; environmental studies; gay and lesbian studies; German studies; law; literature; media studies and film; Michigan and Great Lakes; music; Native American studies; political science; theater and performance; women and gender studies; - sports.

The Press distributes works of the Center for Chinese Studies and the Center for South and Southeast Asian Studies, the American Academy in Rome.

Special series: Analytical Perspectives on Politics; The CAWP Series in Gender and American Politics; the Bard Graduate Center Cultural Histories of the Material World; Class: Culture; Contemporary Political and Social Issues; Corporealities: Discourses of Disability; Critical Performances; Culture of Knowledge In the Early Modern World; Editorial Theory and Literary Criticism; English for Academic & Professional Purposes; Great Lakes Environment; Intensive Course in English; International Series on the Research of Learning and Instruction of Writing; Jazz Perspectives; Kelsey Museum Studies; Landmark Video Games; Law and Society in the Ancient World; Law, Meaning, and Violence; The Memoirs of the American Academy in Rome; The Michigan American Music Series; Michigan Series in English for Academic and Professional Purposes; The Michigan Series on Teaching Multilingual Writers; Michigan Studies in International Political Economy; Michigan Studies in Political Analysis; New Comparative Politics; The New Media World; The Papers and Monographs of the American Academy in Rome; Perspectives on Contemporary Korea; Poets on Poetry; The Politics of Race and Ethnicity; Social History, Popular Culture, and Politics in Germany; Societas: Historical Studies In Classical Culture; Studies in Literature and Science; Technologies of the Imagination: New Media in Everyday Life; Theater: Theory/Text/Performance; Thomas Spencer Jerome Lectures; Tracking Pop; Triangulations: Lesbian/Gay/Queer/Theater/Drama/Performance; Under Discussion; Writers on Writing

Michigan State University Press

1405 South Harrison Road, Suite 25
East Lansing, MI 48823-5245

Phone: 517.355.9543
Director's Office Fax: 517.432.2611
Email: msupress@msu.edu
Indiv: (user I.D.)@msu.edu

Website and Social Media:
Website: msupress.org
Facebook: facebook.com/MSUPress
Twitter: msupress

Orders:
Chicago Distribution Center
11030 S. Langley Ave.
Chicago, IL 60628
Phone: 800.621.2736; 773.702.7000
Fax: 800.621.8476; 773.702.7212

UK/European Distributor:
Eurospan

Canadian Distributor:
Chicago Distribution Center

Staff

Director: Gabriel Dotto (517.884.6900; email: dotto)
Editorial: Julie L. Loehr, Editor-in-Chief/Assistant Director (517.884.6905; email: loehr)
   Acquisitions Editor: TBA
Managing Editor: Kristine Blakeslee (517.884.6912; email: blakes17)
   Digital Production Specialist: Annette Tanner, Manager (517.884.6910; email: tanneran)
   Editorial Assistant: Elise Jajunga (517.884.6913; email: jajugael)
Marketing & Sales: Julie Reaume, Manager (517.884.6920; email: reaumej)
   Marketing Assistant: Travis E. Kimbel (517.884.6918; email: kimbel)
   Website Coordinator: Dawn Martin (517.884.6919; email: marti778)
Journals:
   Production Editor: Natalie Eidenier (517.884.6915; email: eidenie1)
Finance/Business Officer: Julie Wrzesinski (517.884.6922; email: wrzesin2)
   Logistics: Brett Robinson (517.884.6909)
Information Systems: Jesse Howard, Manager (517.884.6908; email: howard10)

Full Member

Established: 1947

Admitted to AAUP: 1992
(Previous membership, 1951-1972)

Title output 2011: 37
Titles currently in print: 838

Title output 2012: 38
Journals published: 9

Editorial Program

Scholarly books and general nonfiction with areas of special interest in African studies; African American studies; Agricultural Science; American studies; American Indian studies; creative nonfiction; environmental science and natural history; Great Lakes studies; immigration studies; Latino/a studies; politics and the global economy; mimetic theory; poetry; US history; urban studies; women's studies.

The Press distributes publications for University of Calgary Press; University of Manitoba Press; the Michigan State University Museum

Journals: *Contagion: Journal of Violence, Mimesis, and Culture*; *CR: The New Centennial Review*; *Fourth Genre: Explorations In Nonfiction*; *French Colonial History*; *Journal for the Study of Radicalism*; *Northeast African Studies*; *Real Analysis Exchange*; *Red Cedar Review*; *Rhetoric & Public Affairs*

Special series: American Indian Studies Series; The Animal Turn Series; Breakthroughs in Mimetic Theory Series; Courageous Conversations Series; Environmental Research Series; Discovering the Peoples of Michigan Series; Latinos in the United States Series; Makwa Enewed Series; Rhetoric and Public Affairs Series; Rhetorical History of the United States Series; Ruth Simms Hamilton African Diaspora Series; Studies in Violence, Mimesis, and Culture Series; Transformations in Higher Education Series

Minnesota Historical Society Press

345 Kellogg Blvd. West
Saint Paul, MN 55102

Orders:
Chicago Distribution Center
11030 South Langley Ave.
Chicago, IL 60628
Phone: 800.621.2736; 773.568.1550
Fax: 800.621.8476; 773.660.2235

Phone: 651.259.3200
Fax: 651.297.1345
Email: (user I.D.)@mnhs.org

Website and Social Media:
Website: www.mhspress.org
Blog: discussions.mnhs.org/10000books/
Facebook: www.facebook.com/home.php?#!/
pages/Minnesota-Historical-Society-Press-and-Borealis-Books/44328618980
Twitter: @mhspress

UK/European Distributor:
Gazelle Book Services

Canadian Distributor:
Scholarly Book Service

Staff

Director: Pamela McClanahan (651.259.3210; email: pamela.mcclanahan; Twitter: @mcclan)

Acquisitions: Pamela McClanahan, Ann Regan, Shannon Pennefeather

Editor-in-Chief, Rights and Permissions: Ann Regan (651.259.3206; email: ann.regan)

Manuscript Editorial: Shannon Pennefeather (651.259.3212; email: shannon.pennefeather)

Design and Production: Dan Leary (651.259.3209; email: daniel.leary)

Digital Production: Robin Moir (651.259.3211; email: robin.moir)

Publicity and Promotions: Alison Aten (651.259.3203; email: alison.aten)

Sales and Marketing: Mary Poggione (651.259.3204; email: mary.poggione)

Journals: Anne Kaplan (651.259.3207; email: anne.kaplan)

MNopedia (online Minnesota encyclopedia) Editor: Molly Huber (651.259.3216; email: molly.huber)

Associate Member

Established: 1859

Title output 2011: 20

Titles currently in print: 433

Admitted to AAUP: 2001

Title output 2012: 21

Journals published: 1

Editorial Program

The Minnesota Historical Society Press publishes books and digital products on the history and culture of the Upper Midwest. Specific list strengths include history, regional studies, Native American studies, nature and conservation, travel and tourism, food and cookery, the immigration experience, Scandinavian studies, regional children's picture books, and teaching Minnesota history.

Journal: *Minnesota History*

Special series: Minnesota Byways; Native Voices; People of Minnesota; the Northern Plate

Imprints: MHS Press; Borealis Books

University of Minnesota Press

111 Third Avenue South
Suite 290
Minneapolis, MN 55401-2552

Phone: 612.627.1970
Fax: 612.627.1980
Email: (user I.D.)@umn.edu

Orders:
University of Minnesota Press
Chicago Distribution Center
11030 South Langley Avenue
Chicago, IL 60628
Phone: 800.621.2736; 773.568.1550
Fax: 800.621.8476; 773.660.2235

Website and Social Media:
Website: www.upress.umn.edu
Blog: www.uminnpressblog.com
Facebook: www.facebook.com/pages/Minneapolis-MN/
University-of-Minnesota-Press/40070783448
Twitter: UMinnPress

UK Distributor:
NBN Plymbridge

UK Representative:
University Presses Marketing

Staff
Director: Douglas Armato (612.627.1972; email: armat001)
  Associate Director and Test Division Manager: Beverly Kaemmer (612.627.1963;
  email: kaemm002)
  Rights and Permissions: Jeff Moen (612.627.1978; email: moenx017)
Acquisitions Editorial: Richard Morrison, Editorial Director (literary and cultural studies, art
  and visual studies, anthropology) (612.627.1974; email: morri094)
  Senior Editor: Todd Orjala (regional) (612.627.1973; email: t-orja)
  Editors: Pieter Martin (architecture, political science, urban studies) (612.627.1976;
  email: marti190); Jason Weidemann (geography, sociology) (612.627.1975; email:
  weide007)
  Associate Editor: Danielle Kasprzak (cinema, media) (612.627.0122; email: kasp0079)
Managing Editor: Laura Westlund (612.627.1985; email: westl003)
  Assistant Managing Editor: Michael Stoffel (612.627.1977; email: stoff004)
Design and Production: Daniel Ochsner, Manager (612.627.1981; email: ochsn013)
  Assistant Design and Production Manager: Rachel Moeller (612.627.1984; email:
  moel0067)
Marketing: Emily Hamilton, Director (612.627.1936; email: eph)
  Sales Manager: Erik Anderson (612.627.0124; email: and00900)
  Publicist: Heather Skinner (612.627.1932; email: skinn077)
  Advertising and Promotions Coordinator: Anne Klingbeil (612.627.1938; email: klin0207)
  Direct Marketing Coordinator: Maggie Sattler (612.627.1934; email: sattl014)
Business: Susan Doerr, Manager (612.627.1967; email: doer0012)
Journals: Susan Doerr, Business; Jason Weidemann, Acquisitions
IT Systems: John Henderson (612.627.1944; email: hende291)

Full Member
Established: 1925
Title output 2011: 131
Titles currently in print: 2,941

Admitted to AAUP: 1937
Title output 2012: 120
Journals published: 9

Editorial Program
Literary and cultural studies; social and political theory; cinema and media studies; art and
visual studies; digital culture; feminist studies; gay and lesbian studies; anthropology; architecture; geography; international relations; Native American studies; personality assessment,
clinical psychology and psychiatry; philosophy; and Upper Midwest studies.
Journals: *Buildings & Landscapes; Cultural Critique; Culture/Clinic: Applied Lacanian Psy-
choanalysis; Future Anterior; Kalfou; Mechademia; The Moving Image; Native and Indigenous
Studies Journal; Wicazo Sa Review*
Special series, joint imprints, and/or copublishing programs: Borderlines; Contradic-
tions; Critical American Studies; Cultural Studies of the Americas; difference incorporated;
Electronic Mediations; Fesler-Lampert Minnesota Heritage Book Series; First Peoples: New
Directions in Indigenous Studies; Globalization and Community; Indigenous Americas;
Minnesota Studies in the Philosophy of Science; MMPI-2 Monographs; MMPI-A Mono-
graphs; Posthumanities; Public Worlds; Quadrant Program; Social Movements, Protest, and
Contention; Theory and History of Literature; Visible Evidence

University Press of Mississippi

3825 Ridgewood Road
Jackson, MS 39211-6492

Phone: 601.432.6205
Fax: 601.432.6217
Email: press@mississippi.edu
Indiv: (user I.D)@mississippi.edu

Website and Social Media:
Website: www.upress.state.ms.us
Blog: upmississippi.blogspot.com
Facebook: www.facebook.com/UPMiss
Twitter: UPMiss

Canadian Representative:
Scholarly Book Services

Warehouse Address:
Maple -Vail Book Mfg. Group
Lebanon Distribution Center
704 Legionaire Drive
Fredericksburg, PA 17026

Orders:
Phone: 800.737.7788; 601.432.6205

UK Representative:
Roundhouse Publishing

Staff

Director: Leila W. Salisbury (601.432.6275; email: lsalisbury) (film studies, popular culture, regional trade)

Administrative Assistant/Rights and Permissions Manager: Cynthia Foster (601.432.6205; email: cfoster)

Development Assistant: Tracey Curtis (601.432.6205; email: bookfriends)

Acquisitions Editorial: Craig Gill, Assistant Director/Editor-in-Chief (601.432.6371; email: cgill) (history, music, folklore, ethnomusicology, regional trade)

Acquisitions Editor: Walter Biggins (601.432.6102; email: wbiggins) (literature, Caribbean studies, American studies, African American studies, comics studies)

Electronic Publishing: Steve Yates, Assistant Director /Marketing Director (601.432.6695; email: syates)

Electronic Projects Manager: Todd Lape (601.432.6274; email: tlape)

Manuscript Editorial: Anne Stascavage, Managing Editor (601.432.6249; email: astascavage)

Editorial Associate: Valerie Jones (601.432.6272; email: vjones)

Editorial Assistant: Katie Keene (601.432.6206; email: kkeene)

Design and Production: John A. Langston, Assistant Director/Art Director (601.432.6554; email: jlangston)

Assistant Production Manager/Designer/Electronic Projects Manager: Todd Lape (601.432.6274; email: tlape)

Senior Production Editor: Shane Gong Stewart (601.432.6795; email: sgong)

Designer: Pete Halverson (601.432.6274; email: phalverson)

Marketing and Sales: Steve Yates, Assistant Director/Marketing Director (601.432.6695; email: syates)

Advertising and Marketing Services Manager: Kathy Burgess (601.432.6105; email: kburgess)

Publicist: Clint Kimberling (601.432.6424; email: ckimberling)

Electronic and Direct-to-Consumer Marketing Specialist: Kristin Kirkpatrick

(601.432.6459; email: kkirkpatrick)
Marketing Assistant: Courtney McCreary (601.432.6516; email: cmccreary)
Business: Isabel Metz, Assistant Director/Business Manager (601.432-6551;
    email: imetz)
Customer Service and Order Supervisor: Sandy Alexander (601/432-6704;
    email: salexander)

Full Member

Established: 1970
Title output 2011: 140
Titles currently in print: 1,109

Admitted to AAUP: 1976
Title output 2012: 144

Editorial Program

Scholarly and trade titles in African American studies; African Diaspora studies; American studies, literature, history, and culture; art and architecture; Caribbean studies; children's literature studies, comic studies; ethnic studies; folklore; film studies; media studies; music; ethnomusicology; natural sciences; photography; popular culture; regional studies; serious nonfiction of general interest; Southern studies; women's studies; other liberal arts.

Special series: African American Material Culture; American Made Music; Caribbean Studies; Chancellor Porter L. Fortune Symposium in Southern History; Children's Literature Association Series; Conversations with Comics Artists; Conversations with Filmmakers; Faulkner and Yoknapatawpha; Folklore Studies in a Multicultural World; Great Comic Artists; Hollywood Legends; Literary Conversations; Margaret Walker Alexander Series in African American Studies; Race, Rhetoric, and Media; Television Conversations Series; Willie Morris Books in Memoir and Biography

University of Missouri Press

2910 LeMone Boulevard
Columbia, MO 65201

Phone: 573.882.7641
Fax: 573.884.4498
Email: upress@missouri.edu
Indiv: (user ID)@missouri.edu

Website and Social Media:
Website: press.umsystem.edu
Facebook: www.facebook.com/pages/
    University-of-Missouri-Press/177293766515
Twitter: umissouripress

Orders:
University of Missouri Press
c/o Chicago Distribution Center
11030 South Langley Avenue
Chicago, IL 60628-3830
Phone: 800.621.2736; 773.702.7000
Fax: 800.621.8476
Email: orders@press.uchicago.edu

UK Representative:
Eurospan

Canadian Representative:
Scholarly Book Services

Staff

Director: Jane Lago, Consulting Director (573.882.9478; email: lagoj)

Acquisitions: Clair Willcox, Associate Director and Editor-in-Chief (573.882.9997; email: willcoxc)

   Acquisitions Editor: TBA (573.884.1277)

Editorial: Sara Davis, Managing Editor (573.882.8714; email: davissd)

Production: Nikki Waltz, Assistant Production Manager (573.882.0184; email: waltzn)

Marketing: TBA, Marketing and Sales Manager (573.882.9672)

   Publicity Manager: Jennifer Gravley (573.882.8735; email: gravleyj)

   Publicity and Sales Assistant: Lyn Smith (573.882.3000; email: smithls)

Business: Tracy Tritschler, Business Manager (573.882.9459; email: tritschlert)

Full Member

Established: 1958

Title output 2011: 31

Title currently in print: 1,092

Admitted to AAUP: 1960

Title output 2012: 29

Editorial Program

American and European history, including intellectual history and biography; African American studies; women's studies; American and British literary criticism; journalism; political science, including foreign relations; political philosophy and ethics; regional studies of Missouri, and the Midwest; and creative non-fiction.

Special series: American Military Experience; Give 'Em Hell Harry; Mark Twain and His Circle; Missouri Biography; Missouri Heritage Readers; Shades of Blue and Gray; Sports and American Culture

Modern Language Association of America

26 Broadway, 3rd floor
New York, NY 10004-1789

Phone: 646.576.5000
Fax: 646.458.0030
Email: info@mla.org
Indiv: firstinitiallastname@mla.org

Book Orders:
Phone: 646.576.5161
Fax: 646.576.5160
Email: bookorders@mla.org

Website and Social Media:
Website: www.mla.org
Twitter: MLAnews

Staff

Executive Director: Rosemary G. Feal (646.576-5102)

Director of Scholarly Communication: Kathleen Fitzpatrick (646.576.5110)

   Associate Director of Scholarly Communication: Anna Chang (646.576.5029)

   Senior Acquisitions Editor: Margit Longbrake (646.576.5022)

   Acquisitions Editor: James E. Hatch (646.576.5044)

   Permissions and Contracts Manager: Marcia E. Henry (646.576.5042)

Manuscript Editorial (includes journals): Judy Goulding, Associate Executive Director and Director of Publishing Operations: (646.576.5015)

Associate Managing Editor, Book Publications: Angela Gibson (646.576.5016)
Director of Print and Electronic Production: Judith Altreuter (646.576.5010)
Marketing and Sales Director: Kathleen Hansen (646.576.5018)
Member and Customer Services Manager: Leonard J. Moreton (646.576.5146)
Information Technology Center Manager: Kinglen Wang (646.576.5200)

Associate Member

Established: 1883	Admitted to AAUP: 1992
Title output 2011: 15	Title output 2012: 12
Titles currently in print: 291	Journals published: 6

Editorial Program
Scholarly, pedagogical, and professional books on language and literature.
Journals: *ADE and ADFL Bulletins; MLA International Bibliography; MLA Newsletter; PMLA; Profession*
Book series: Approaches to Teaching World Literature; New Variorum Edition of Shakespeare; Options for Teaching; Teaching Languages, Literatures, and Cultures; Texts and Translations; World Literatures Reimagined

The Museum of Modern Art

11 West 53rd Street
New York, NY 10019

Orders:
Individuals: 800.447.6662
www.momastore.org
Trade: 212.627.9484 / www.artbook.com

Phone: 212.708.9443
Fax: 212.333.6575 or 212.708.9779
Email: moma_publications@moma.org
Indiv: firstname_lastname@moma.org

Website and Social Media:
Website: www.moma.org
Blog: www.moma.org/insideout
Facebook: www.facebook.com/MuseumofModernArt
Twitter: MuseumModernArt
YouTube: www.youtube.com/MoMAvideos
Flickr: www.flickr.com/themuseumofmodernart

UK Representative:
Thames & Hudson

Canadian Representative:
ARTBOOK | D.A.P.

Staff
Publisher: Christopher Hudson (212.708.9445)
Associate Publisher: Charles Kim (212.708.9456)
Assistant to the Publisher: Makiko Wholey (212.708.9512)
Editorial Director: David Frankel (212.708.9448)

Editors: Libby Hruska (212.708.9418); Emily Hall (212.708.9511)
Associate Editor: Rebecca Roberts (212.708.9883)
Production Director: Marc Sapir (212.708.9745)
Production Manager: Matthew Pimm (212.708.9742)
Senior Designer: Amanda Washburn (212.708.6572)
Marketing and Book Coordinator: Hannah Kim (212.708.9449)
Assistant Business Manager: Bryan Stauss (212.708.9743)

Associate Member
Established: 1929
Title output 2011: 17
Titles currently in print: 257

Admitted to AAUP: 2008
Title output 2012: 17

Editorial Program
Modern and contemporary art, including painting, sculpture, drawings, prints and illustrated books, photography, film, media, architecture and design
Special series: MoMA Artist Series, MoMA Design Series, MoMA Primary Documents, Studies in Modern Art

The National Academies Press

500 Fifth Street, N.W.
Washington, DC 20001

Bookstore phone: 202.334.2612
Fax: 202.334.2793
Email: (user I.D.)@nas.edu

Website and Social Media:
Website: www.nap.edu
Facebook: www.facebook.com/NationalAcademiesPress
Twitter: NAPress

Orders (US and Canada):
Phone: 800.624.6242; 202.334.3313
Fax: 202.334.2451
Email: zjones@nas.edu

UK Distributor:
Marston Book Services

Staff
Executive Director: Barbara Kline Pope (202.334.3328; email: bkline)
Executive Assistant to the Director: Shelly Wolfe (202.334.3038; email: sewolfe)
Director of Operations: Sandy Adams (202.334.3157; email: sadams)
Executive Editor: Stephen M. Mautner (202.334.3336; email: smautner)
Production Manager: Dorothy Lewis (202.334.2409; email: dlewis)
Director, Composition, Graphics and Design: Jim Gormley (202.334.3325; email: jgormley)
Director, Marketing and Technology: Alphonse MacDonald (202.334.3625; email: amacdonald)
Sales and Marketing Manager: Virginia Bryant (202.334.3037; email: vbryant)
Permissions Editor: Barbara Murphy (202.334.1902; email: bmurphy)
Business Manager: Rachel Levy (202.334.3329; email: rlevy)
Customer Service Manager: Zina Jones (202.334.3116; email: zjones)

Associate Member

Established: 1864
Title output 2011: 200
Titles currently in print: 3,853

Admitted to AAUP: 1988
Title output 2012: 150
Titles currently in print: 3,943

Editorial Program

Primarily professional-level, policy-oriented titles in agricultural sciences; behavioral and social sciences; biology; chemistry; computer sciences; earth sciences; economics; education; energy; engineering; environmental issues; industry; international issues; materials science; medicine; natural resources; nutrition; physical sciences; public policy issues; statistics; transportation; and urban and rural development.

National Gallery of Art

Street Address:
Sixth Street and Constitution Avenue NW
Washington, DC

Mailing Address:
2000B South Club Drive
Landover, MD 20785

Phone: 202.842.6200
Fax: 202.408.8530
Email: (initial-last name)@nga.gov

Online shop:
shop.nga.gov
Customer Service / Order Fulfillment:
800.697.9350

Website and Social Media:
Website: www.nga.gov
Facebook: www.facebook.com/NationalGalleryofArt
Twitter: ngadc

Staff

Deputy Director: Franklin Kelly
Editor in Chief: Judy Metro (202.842.6205; email: j-metro)
Deputy Publisher and Production Manager: Chris Vogel (202.842.6209; email: c-vogel)
    Senior Editor and Manager of Systematic Catalogues: TBA
    Senior Editors: Tam Bryfogle (202.842.6498; email: t-bryfogle); Julie Warnement (202.842.6136; email: j-warnement); Ulrike Mills (202.842.6613; email: u-mills)
    Assistant Editor: Caroline Weaver (202.842.6032; email: c-weaver)
Managing Editor of CASVA Publications: Cynthia Ware (202.842.6204; email: c-ware)
Design Manager: Wendy Schleicher (202.789.4601; email: w-schleicher)
    Designers: Brad Ireland (202.789.3082; b-ireland); Rio DeNaro (202.842.6697; email: r-denaro)
    Assistant Production Manager: John Long (202.842.6423; email: j-long)
    Production Assistant: Mariah Shay (202.842.6758; email: m-shay)
Permissions Coordinator: Sara Sanders-Buell (202.842.6719; email: s-sanders-buell)
Rothko Resarch Associates: Laili Nasr (202.842.6779; email: l-nasr); Mary Lee Corlett (202.842.6603; email: m-corlett)
Program Assistant: Mari Pappas (202.842.6200; email: m-pappas)

Associate Member

Established: 1941

Title output 2011: 10

Titles currently in print: 160

Admitted to AAUP: 1992

Title output 2012: 9

Editorial Program

The National Gallery publishes exhibition catalogues on all subjects and permanent collection catalogues (including Western art of the early Renaissance through the contemporary era); a symposium series; Studies in the History of Art, in conjunction with the Center for Advanced Study in the Visual Arts; educational online programs and catalogues; exhibition brochures and wall texts; online features and apps for permanent collection and special exhibitions; scholarly and popular publications based on objects in the museum's collections; scholarly publications on conservation; educational materials and guides for use by the public and by teachers and schools; and the calendar of events, film and music programs, bulletins, and all Gallery ephemera. Unsolicited manuscripts are not invited.

stion catalogues (including Western art of the early Renaissance through the contemporary era); a symposium series; Studies in the History of Art, in conjunction with the Center for Advanced Study in the Visual Arts; educational online programs and catalogues; exhibition brochures and wall texts; online features and apps for permanent collection and special exhibitions; scholarly and popular publications based on objects in the museum's collections; scholarly publications on conservation; educational materials and guides for use by the public and by teachers and schools; and the calendar of events, film and music programs, bulletins, and all Gallery ephemera. Unsolicited manuscripts are not invited.

Naval Institute Press

291 Wood Road
Annapolis MD 21402-5034

Phone: 410.268.6110
Fax: 410.295.1084/5
Email: firstinitiallastname@usni.org

Website and Social Media:
Website: www.nip.org
Facebook: www.facebook.com/NavalInstitute
Twitter: USNIBooks

UK/European Representatives
Eurospan Group (as of October 1, 2012)

Orders:
Phone: 800.233.8764

Canadian Representatives
Scholarly Book Service

Staff

Director: Richard A. Russell (410.295.1031)
   Business Manager: Prospero Hernandez (410.295.1046)
   Editorial Production Manager: Carol Parkinson (410.295.1030)
Senior Acquisitions Editor/Director, Professional Publishing: Thomas J. Cutler (410.295.1038)
   Senior Acquisitions Editor/Subsidiary Rights/Imports: Susan Todd Brook (410.295.1037)
   Senior Acquisitions Editor/Electronic Publications Manager: Adam Kane (410.295.1080)

Assistant Editors: Taylor Skord (410.295.1030); Adam Nettina (410.295.1089)
Managing Editor: Susan Corrado (410.295.1032)
   Production Editors: Emily Bakely (410.295.1020); Marlena Montagna (410.295.1040)
Director of Sales and Marketing: George Keating (410.295.1025)
   Marketing Manager: Claire Noble (410.295.1039)
   Publicist: Judy Heise (410.295.1028)
   Exhibits and Special Sales Manager: Brian Walker (410.295.1082)
Journals, U.S. Naval Institute:
   Proceedings, Editor-in-Chief: Paul Merzlak (410.295.1072)
   Naval History, Editor-in-Chief: Richard Latture (410.295.1076)
   Publisher, U.S. Naval Institute: William M. Miller (410.295.1068)
   Chief Financial Officer, U.S. Naval Institute: Robert Johnson (410.295.1707)

Full Member

Established: 1898   Admitted to AAUP: 1949
Title output 2011: 80   Title output 2012: 76
Titles currently in print: 700   Journals published: 2

Editorial Program
Joint and general military subjects; military biography; naval history and literature; naval and military reference; oceanography; navigation; military law; naval science textbooks; sea power; shipbuilding; professional guides; nautical arts and lore; technical guides; fiction.
Journals: *Naval History*; *Proceedings*
Special series: Anatomy of the Ship Series; Bluejacket Books (paperback series); Blue and Gold Professional Library; Illustrated Design Histories; Leatherneck Classics; New Perspectives on Maritime History and Nautical Archaeology; Scarlet & Gold Professional Library

University of Nebraska Press

1111 Lincoln Mall
Lincoln, NE 68588-0630

Phone: 402.472.3581
Fax 402.472.6214
Email: (user I.D.)@unl.edu

Website and Social Media:
Website: www.nebraskapress.unl.edu;
bisonbooks.com
Blog: nebraskapress.typepad.com
Facebook: www.facebook.com/NebraskaPress

UK Distributor:
Combined Academic Publishers

Orders:
University of Nebraska Press
Longleaf Services
116 S. Boundary Street
Chapel Hill, NC 27514-3808

Phone: 800.848.6224
Fax: 800.272.6817
Email:
customerservice@longleafservices.org

Canadian Distributor:
Codasat Canada Ltd.

Staff
Director: Donna A. Shear (402.472.2861; email: dshear2)

Assistant Director for Business/CFO: Tera Beermann (402.472.0011; email: tbeermann2)
  Rights and Permissions: Leif Milliken (402.472.7702; email: lmilliken2)
Acquisitions Editorial: Derek Krissoff, Editor-in-Chief (402.472.4311; email: dkrissoff2)
  Sports History Editor: Rob Taylor (402.472.0325; email: rtaylor6)
  Indigenous Studies Editor: Matthew Bokovoy (402.472.4452; email: mbokovoy2)
  History Editor: Bridget Barry (402.472.0645; email: bbarry2)
  Humanities Editor: Kristen Elias Rowley (402.472.5949; email: keliasrowley2)
  Bison Books Manager: Tom Swanson (402.472.5945; email: tswanson3)
  Bison Books Editor: Alicia Christensen (402.472.0317; email achristensen6)
Editorial, Design, and Production: Ann Baker, Manager, EDP (402.472.0095; email: abaker2)
  Project Editors: Joeth Zucco (402.472.0199; email: jzucco2); Sara Springsteen (402.472.4008; email: sspringsteen1); Sabrina Stellricht (402.472.7712; email: sstellrecht2); Kyle Simonsen (402.472.5333; email: ksimonsen2)
  Assistant Production Manager: Alison Rold (402.472.7706; email: arold1)
  Book Production Associate: Terry Boldan (402.472.0890; email: tboldan2)
  Compositor: Laura Wellington (402.472.7716; email: lwellington2)
  Designers: Andrea Shahan (402.472.7718; email: ashahan1); Roger Buchholz (402.472.7713; email: rbuchholz1); Nathan Putens (402.472.5943; email: nputens2)
Marketing and Sales: Rob Buchanan, Sales Coordinator (402.472.0160; email: rbuchanan1)
  Publicity Manager: Acacia Gentrup (402.472.5938; email: agentrup3)
  Publicist: Rosemary Vestal (402.472.9658; email: rvestal2)
  Direct Mail Manager: Tish Fobben (402.472.4627; email: pfobben2)
  Author Events and Exhibits Coordinator: Emily Giller (402.472.2759; email: egiller2)
  Design Coordinator: Kim Mahrt (402.472.5514; email: kmahrt2)
  Electronic Marketing Coordinator: Erica Corwin (402.472.9313; email: ecorwin1)
Accelerated Publishing and Management: Manjit Kaur, Manager (402.472.7703; email: mkaur2)
  Project Supervisor: Terence Smyre (402.472.2292; email: tsmyre2)
  Marketing and Fulfillment Manager: Joyce Gettman (402.472.8330; email: jgettman2)
  Fulfillment Coordinator: Odessa Anderson (402.472.8536; email: oanderson2)
  Project Coordinator: Joel Puchalla (402.472.3572; email: jpuchalla2)
  Desktop Compositor: Shirley Thornton (402.472.5028; email: sthorton3)
Business Services: Deborah Kohl, Senior Accountant & Analyst, Royalty Accountant (email: dkohl2)
  Accounts Payable: Claire Schwinck (402.472.7711; email: cschwinck2)
Digital Assets and IT: Jana Faust, Manager, Digital Assets and IT (402.472.0171; email: jfaust2)
  Coordinator: Amy Lage (402.472.3663; email: alage2)

Full Member

Established: 1941	Admitted to AAUP: Unknown
Title output 2011: 131	Title output 2012: 150
Titles currently in print: 3,120	Journals published: 19

Editorial Program

African American studies; American literature; American studies; the American West; anthropology and ethnology; geography; civil rights; creative nonfiction; history; food history and culture; French colonial history; the Great Plains; Jewish studies and Judaica; memoir;

Mexico; military history; Native Americans and First Nations; Nebraskiana; race and ethnicity; regional fiction; science fiction; sports history; translations; women's studies. Submissions are not invited in original poetry.

The Press distributes for the Buros Institute of Mental Measurement, Caxton Press, Open Letter, the Society for American Baseball Research, and Whale & Star Press.

Journals: *American Indian Quarterly; Anthropological Linguistics; Collaborative Anthropologies; French Forum; Frontiers: A Journal of Women's Studies; Histories of Anthropology Annual; Journal of Sports Media; Legacy: A Journal of American Women Writers; Native South; NINE: A Journal of Baseball History & Culture; Nineteenth-Century French Studies; Nouvelles Etudes Francophones; Qui Parle: Critical Humanities and Social Sciences; Storyworlds: A Journal of Narrative Studies; Studies in American Indian Literatures; Studies in American Naturalism; symploke: A Journal for the Intermingling of Literary, Cultural, and Theoretical Scholarship; Women and Music: A Journal of Gender and Culture; Women in German Yearbook: Feminist Studies in German Literature and Culture*

Imprints: Bison Books; JPS (The Jewish Publication Society)

Book series: American Lives; American Indian Lives; At Table; Beyond Armageddon; Bison Frontiers of Imagination; Cather Studies; Complete Letters of Henry James; Critical Studies in the History of Anthropology; Engendering Latin America; European Women Writers; Extraordinary Worlds; France Overseas; Frontiers of Narrative; Great Campaigns of the Civil War; History of the American West; Indians of the Southeast; Indigenous Education; Iroquoians and Their World; Journals of the Lewis and Clark Expedition; Key Issues of the Civil War Era; Latin American Women Writers; Law in the American West; North American Indian Prose Award; Our Sustainable Future; Politics and Governments of the American States; Post-Western Horizons; Sources of American Indian Oral Literature; Stages; Studies in Jewish Civilization (for Creighton University Press); Studies in the Anthropology of North American Indians; Studies in the Native Languages of the Americas; Studies in War, Society, and the Military; Texts and Contexts; This Hallowed Ground: Guides to Civil War Battlefields; Willa Cather Scholarly Edition; Women in German Yearbook; Women in the West

University of Nevada Press

Morrill Hall, Mail Stop 0166
Reno, NV 89557-0166

Phone: 775.784.6573
Fax: 775.784.6200
Email: (user I.D.)@unpress.nevada.edu

Order Fulfillment:
Chicago Distribution Center
11030 South Langley Ave.
Chicago, IL 60628
Phone: 800.621.2736
Fax: 800.621.8476

Website and Social Media:
Website: www.unpress.nevada.edu
Facebook: www.facebook.com/pages/University-of-Nevada-Press/138820916192937

Canadian Representative:
Scholarly Book Services

UK Representative:
Eurospan

Staff

Director: Joanne O'Hare (775.682.7389; email: johare)
Acquisitions Editors: Matt Becker (775.882.7390; email: mbecker); Joanne O'Hare
Marketing & Sales Manager: Michael O. Campbell (775.682.7395; email: mcampbell)
   Marketing and Editorial Associate: Mayanne Coyne (775.682.7394; email: mcoyne)
Design & Production Manager: Kathleen Szawiola (775.682.7391; email: kszawiola)
Business Manager: JoAnne Banducci (775.682.7387; email: jbanducci)

Full Member

Established: 1961
Title output 2011: 21
Titles currently in print: 401

Admitted to AAUP: 1982
Title output 2012: 16

Editorial Program

Scholarly and general interest books about the history, literature, anthropology, archaeology, and natural history of the American West, Nevada, and the Great Basin. Additional interests include books dealing with the Basque peoples of Europe and the Americas; Native American Studies; mining; environmental studies; and gaming and gambling.
Special series: Basque Studies; Gambling Studies; The Urban West; Western Literature; West Word Fiction; Wilbur S. Shepperson Series in Nevada History

University Press of New England

1 Court Street, Suite 250
Lebanon, NH 03766-1358

Phone: 603.448.1533
Fax: 603.448.7006
Email: university.press@dartmouth.edu
Indiv: firstname.lastname@dartmouth.edu

Website and Social Media:
Website: www.upne.com
Facebook: www.facebook.com/
   UniversityPressOfNewEngland

Canadian Representative:
University of British Columbia Press

Customer Service/Order Fulfillment:
Phone: 800.421.1561
Fax: 603.448.9429

Warehouse:
UPNE Fulfillment Center
c/o Maple Press Company
Lebanon Distribution Center
704 Legionaire Drive
Fredricksburg, PA 17026

European Representative:
Eurospan

Staff

Director: Michael Burton (ext. 241)
   Assistant to the Director, Permissions Manager: Deborah J. Gray (ext. 201)
   Associate Director, Operations: Thomas Johnson (ext. 251)
   Systems Administrator/Webmaster: David Bellows (ext. 257)
Editor-in-Chief: Phyllis Deutsch (603.448.1533, ext. 222)
   Acquisitions Editors: Stephen P. Hull (781.736.4605); Richard Pult (ext. 226)
   Editorial Assistant: Lori Miller (ext. 221)
Manuscript Editorial: TBA, Managing Editor (ext. 243)

Production Editors: TBA (ext. 244); Amanda Dupuis (ext. 235)
Production Assistant: Sara Rutan (ext. 217)
Design and Production: Eric M. Brooks, Assistant Director of Design and Production (ext. 211)
Designer: Mindy B. Hill (ext. 246)
Production Coordinator: Douglas Tifft (ext. 245)
Marketing: David Corey, Assistant Director Marketing & Sales (ext. 234)
Sales & Trade Exhibits Manager: Sherri Strickland (ext. 238)
Publicity and Subsidiary Rights Manager: Barbara Briggs (ext. 233)
Web Producer & New Media Marketing Coordinator: Loretta A. (Lori) Stammer (ext. 232)
Publicity/Subsidiary Rights Assistant: Catherine A. (Katy) Grabill (ext. 237)
Business: Thomas Johnson, Associate Director, Operations (ext. 251)
Accounting Supervisor: Donna Youngman (ext. 252)
Accounting Associate: Timothy Semple (ext. 253)
Order Fulfillment Supervisor: Barbara Benson (ext. 255)
Senior Customer Service Clerk: Barbara McBeth (ext. 256)

Full Member

Established: 1970   Admitted to AAUP: 1975
Title output 2011: 55   Title output 2012: 65
Titles currently in print: 898
Publishes books under the consortium member imprints of Brandeis University Press, Dartmouth College Press, University of New Hampshire Press, Northeastern University Press, and University Press of New England.

Editorial Program

General trade, scholarly, instructional, and reference works for scholars, teachers, students, and the public. The Press concentrates in American studies, literature, history, religion, and cultural studies; art, architecture, photography, and material culture; ethics; ethnic studies (including African American, Jewish, Native American, and Shaker studies); interdisciplinary studies; folklore, music, and popular culture; languages; nature and the environment; natural sciences; marine ecology; maritime culture; New England studies; social issues/social sciences; and Trans-Atlantic and cross-cultural studies. Special series feature such topics as criminology, modernism, visual culture, and sustainability.

The Press, through UPNE Book Partners handles book order processing and distribution for: Acdemia Press; Cavankerry Press; Chaucer Press Books; Chipstone Foundation; Four Way Books; Gordian Knot Books; Tagus Press; International Polar Institute Press; Nightboat Books; Saturnalia Books; Sheep Meadow Press; and Wesleyan University Press.
Special series: Becoming Modern: New Nineteenth-Century Studies; Brandeis Series in American Jewish History, Culture and Life; HBI Series on Gender, Culture, Religion, and Law; HBI Series on Jewish Women; Civil Society: Historical and Contemporary Perspectives; Collected Writings of Rousseau; Interfaces: Studies in Visual Culture; Menahem Stern Jerusalem Lectures: Brandeis University/Historical Society of Israel; The Northeastern Library of Black Literature; The Northeastern Series on Gender, Crime, and Law; Revisiting New England: The New Regionalism; Re-Mapping the Transnational: A Dartmouth Series in American Studies; Tauber Institute for the Study of European Jewry Series.

University of New Mexico Press

Mailing Address:
MSCO5 3185
1 University of New Mexico
Albuquerque NM 87131-0001

Phone: 505.277.3495
Fax: 505.277.3343
Email: unmpress@unm.edu
Indiv: (user I.D.)@unm.edu
(unless otherwised indicated)

Website and Social Media:
Website: www.unmpress.com
Facebook: www.facebook.com/pages
   /University-of-New-Mexico-Press/109620976711
Twitter: UNMPress

Street Address:
1717 Roma NE
NE Albuquerque NM 87106-4509

Business and Order Fulfillment:
1312 Basehart Road SE
Albuquerque NM 87106-4363

Orders:
Phone: (800) 249.7737; (505) 272.7777
Fax: (505) 272.7778

UK/European Representative:
Eurospan

Canadian Representative:
CODASAT

Staff

Director: John Byram (505.277.3280; email: jbyram; Twitter: @jwbyram) (anthropology, archaeology, linguistics, sciences)

Rights and Permissions: Briony Jones (505.277.3495; email: briony)

Editor-in-Chief: Clark Whitehorn (505.277.2293; email: clarkw) (Chicano/a studies, history, Latin American studies, Native studies, natural history)

Senior Acquisitions Editor: Elise McHugh (505.277.3327; email: elisemc) (American literature and criticism, poetry, fiction, art, photography)

Production Manager: Maya Allen-Gallegos (505.277.3324; email: mayag)

Production Editor: Amanda Piell (505.277.3436; email: apiell)

Production Coordinator: Lila Sanchez (505.277.3333; email: lilamar)

Designer: Catherine Leonardo (505.277.3299; email: davinci@unm.edu)

Marketing Manager: Katherine MacGilvray (505.277.3291; email: katm)

Advertising, Exhibits and Events: Nadya Guerrero-Pezzano (505.277.3289; email: nadyagp)

Sales Manager and Digital Publishing Coordinator: Katherine White (505.277.3294; email: kwhite03)

Sales Representatives: Kay Marcotte (505.272.7544; email: kaym); Sheri Hozier (email: sherih)

Associate Director for Business Operations: Richard Schuetz (505.277.3284; email: rschuetz)

Business Services: Ernest Earick (505.925.9512; email: earick)

Fiscal Services: Lyudmila Markova (505.272.7774; email: milam)

Accounts Receivable/Payable: Yolanda Green (505.272.7775; email: ygreen)

Customer Service and Credit Manager: Stewart Marshall (505.925.9506; email: stewartm)

Customer Service Associate: Susan Hoffman (505.925.9508; email: soozjh)

Warehouse Manager: Susan Coatney (505.272.7770; email: susanc)

IT Support: Darrell Banward (505.277.0978; email: dbanward)

Full Member

Established: 1929   Admitted to AAUP: 1937
Title output 2011: 57   Title output 2012: 68
Titles currently in print: 1,090

Editorial Program

Scholarly books, fiction, poetry, and literary nonfiction, with special interests in social and cultural anthropology; archaeology of the Americas; art and photography; Chicano/a studies; frontier history; legal studies, especially water issues; Western American literature; Latin American studies; Native studies; and books that deal with important aspects of Southwest or Rocky Mountain states, including natural history and land grant studies

Special series, joint imprints and/or copublishing programs: Barbara Guth Worlds of Wonder Science Series for Young Readers; Diálogos Series; Histories of the American Frontier; Mary Burritt Christiansen Poetry Series; Pasó por Aquí Series on the Nuevomexicano Literary Heritage; Recencies Series on Twentieth-Century American Poetics; Archaeologies of Landscapes in the Americas Series; Cambio Series on Business, Economics, and Society in Latin America

New York University Press

838 Broadway, 3rd Floor
New York, NY 10003-4812

Phone: 212.998.2575
Fax: 212. 995.3833
Email: orders@nyupress.edu
Indiv: firstname.lastname@nyu.edu

Website and Social Media:
Website: www.nyupress.org
Blog: www.fromthesquare.org
Facebook: www.facebook.com/fromthesquare
Twitter: NYUpress

UK/European Representative:
Combined Academic Publishers

Orders and Customer Service:
Phone: 800.996.6987
Fax: 212.995.4798

Warehouse:
The Maple Press
Lebanon Distribution Center
704 Legionnaire Drive
Fredricksburg, PA 17026

Staff

Director: Steve Maikowski (212.998.2573)
   Assistant to the Director/Subsidiary Rights Administrator: Margie Guerra (212.998.2540)
Acquisitions Editorial: Eric Zinner, Assistant Director and Editor-in-Chief (cultural and media studies, literary studies, American studies, twentieth-century American history) (212.998.2544)
   Executive Editor: Ilene Kalish (sociology, criminology, politics) (212.998.2556)
   Editor: Clara Platter (American history, military history, law) (212.998.2570)

Senior Editor: Jennifer Hammer (religion, Jewish studies, psychology, anthropology) (212.998.2491)

Managing Editor, Library of Arabic Literature: Chip Rossetti (212.998.2433)

Assistant Editors: Alicia Nadkarni (film and media studies) (212.998.2426); Caelyn Cobb (212.992.9013)

Editorial Assistant: Constance Grady (212.998.4252)

Program Officer for Digital Scholarly Publishing: Monica McCormick (212.998.2528)

Manuscript Editorial/Design and Production: Despina P. Gimbel, Managing Editor (212.998.2572)

Production Manager: Charles Hames (212.998.2628)

Assistant Production Manager: Adam Bohanan (212.998.2578)

Production Editor: Alexia Traganas (212.992.9998)

Editing and Production Specialist: Edith Alston (212.992.7303)

Marketing and Sales: Mary Beth Jarrad, Marketing and Sales Director (212.998.2588)

Advertising and Direct Mail Specialist: Patricia Palao (212.998.2558)

Senior Publicist: Betsy Steve (212.992.9991)

Exhibits Coordinator: Bernadette Blanco (212.998.2547)

E-marketing Coordinator: Jodi Narde (212.998.2591)

Business: Tom Helleberg, Business and Budget Manager (212.998.2569)

Accounts Receivable Supervisor: Lakisha Williams (212.992.9987)

Accounts Payable and Royalties Coordinator: Susan Hamilton (212.998.2524)

Customer Service and Print on Demand Coordinator: Kevin Cooper (212.998.2546)

Computer and Information Systems: Miguel Sandoval, Information Systems Manager (212.998.2536)

Full Member

Established: 1916

Title output 2011: 114

Titles currently in print: 2,699

Admitted to AAUP: 1937

Title output 2012: 125

Editorial Program

American history; law; sociology; Asian American studies; African American studies; Latino/a studies, political science; criminology; psychology; gender studies; cultural and literary studies; media, film, and communications; urban studies; Jewish studies; anthropology; religion; American business and finance; New York regional interest.

NYU Press is the exclusive North American distributor for Monthly Review Press.

Special series: Alternative Criminology; America and the Long Nineteenth Century; American History and Culture; Biopolitics; American Literatures Initiative; Children and Youth in America; Citizenship and Migration in the Americas; Clay Sanskrit Library; Critical Cultural Communications; Cultural Front; Culture, Labor, History; Early American Places; Families, Law, and Society; Gender and Political Violence; The History of Disability; Intersections: Transdisciplinary Perspectives on Genders and Sexualities; Library of Arabic Literature; Modern and Contemporary Catholicism; Nation of Newcomers; New and Alternative Religions; New Perspectives on Crime, Deviance, and Law; NOMOS; North American Religions; NYU Series in Social & Cultural Analysis; Possible Futures; Postmillenial Pop; Psychology and Crime; Psychology of Law; Qualitative Studies in Psychology; Religion and Social Transformation; Religion, Race, and Ethnicity; Re-imagining North American Religions; Qualitative Studies in Psychology; Qualitative Studies in Religion; Sexual Cultures; Warfare and Culture

The University of North Carolina Press

116 South Boundary Street
Chapel Hill, NC 27514-3808

Phone: 919.966.3561
Fax: 919.966.3829
Email: uncpress@unc.edu
Indiv: first name_last name@unc.edu

Website and Social Media:
Website: www.uncpress.unc.edu
Blog: uncpressblog.com
Facebook: www.facebook.com/UNCPress
Twitter: uncpressblog

UK/European Representative:
Eurospan

Warehouse:
Maple Press Company
Lebanon Distribution Center
704 Legionnaire Drive
Fredericksburg, PA 17026

Orders:
Longleaf Services
Phone: (800) 848.6224
Fax: (800) 272.6817
Email: customerservice@longleafservices.org

Canadian Representative:
Scholarly Book Services

Staff

Director: John Sherer (919.962.3748)
   Assistant to the Director and Advancement Coordinator: Laura Gribbin (919.962.0358)
   Director of Development: Joanna Ruth Marsland (919.962.0924)
Acquisitions Editorial: Mark Simpson Vos, Editorial Director (American studies, African American studies, gender and sexuality, Native American and Indigenous studies, nature and environmental studies, regional trade) (919.962.0535)
   Associate Editor and Assistant to the Editorial Director: Zachary Read (919.962.0536)
   Assistant Director and Editor-in-Chief: David Perry (regional trade, Civil War, military history, Southern studies) (919.962.0482)
   Assistant Director and Senior Editor: Charles Grench (history, craft studies) (919.962.0481)
   Senior Executive Editor: Elaine Maisner (religious studies, Latin American and Caribbean studies, cooking and foodways, regional trade) (919.962.0810)
   Senior Editor: Joe Parsons (politics, public policy, sociology, geography, social medicine, business and entrepreneurship) (919.962.0690)
   Assistant Editors: Caitlyn Bell-Butterfield (919.962.0538); Sara Cohen (919.962.0390)
Manuscript Editorial: Ron Maner, Assistant Director and Managing Editor (919.962.0540)
   Associate Managing Editor: Paula Wald (919.962.0544)
   Assistant Managing Editor: Paul Betz (919.962.0530)
   Manuscript Editors: Mary Caviness (919.962.0545); Stephanie Wenzel (919.962.0366); Jay Mazzocchi (919.962.0546)
   Assistant Editor: Ian Oakes (919.962.0549)
Design and Production: Heidi Perov, Assistant Director and Design and Production Manager (919.962.0572)
   Design Director and Assistant Production Manager: Kim Bryant (919.962.0571)

Reprints Controller & Designer: Jackie Johnson (919.962.0569)
Senior Book Designer & Compositor: Rebecca Evans (919.962.0575)
Journals Production Manager/Composition Controller: Michelle Coppedge
(919.962.0577)
Production Assistant: Sally Fry (919.962.0690)
Marketing: Dino Battista, Assistant Director and Senior Director of Marketing and Digital
Business Development (919.962.0579)
Sales Director: Michael Donatelli (919.962.0475)
Sales Assistant: Susan Garrett (919.843.7897)
Director of Publicity: Gina Mahalek (919.962.0581)
Publicist: Jennifer Hergenroeder (919.962.0585)
Director of Electronic Marketing: Ellen Bush (919.962.0582)
Direct Mail Manager & Copywriter: Beth Lassiter (919.962.0583)
Exhibits Manager and Awards Coordinator: Ivis Bohlen (919.962.0594)
Marketing Designer: Joanne Thomas (919.962.0590)
Journals: Suzi Waters, Journals Manager (919.962.4201)
Business: Robbie Dircks, Associate Director & CFO (919.962.1400)
Office Manager: Laura Gribbin (919.962-0358)
Director of Contracts and Subsidiary Rights: Vicky Wells (919.962.0369)
Assistant to the Director of Contracts and Subsidiary Rights: Kathryn Thornton
(919.962.4200)
Accounting Manager: Jami Clay (919.962.4203)
Accounts Payable Manager and Accounting Assistant: Deborah Strickland (919.962.4204)
Operations Manager for Longleaf Services: BJ Smith (919.962.1230)
Customer Service Manager: Teresa Thomas (919.962.1231)
Credit Manager: Terry Miles (919.962.1263)
Information Systems: Tom Franklin, Information Technology Manager (919.962.4196)
Network Support Specialist: Juancarlos Aponte (919.962.0486)
Network Manager: Jim Dawson (919.962.0331)
Digital Assets Coordinator: Marjorie Fowler (919.962.0471)
Digital Production Specialist: Thomas Elrod (919.843.8644)

Full Member

Established: 1922

Admitted to AAUP: 1937

Title output 2011: 115

Title output 2012: 102

Titles currently in print: 3,049

Journals published: 9

<u>**Editorial Program**</u>

African American studies; American and European history; American literature; American
studies; ancient history and classics; business and entrepreneurship; cooking and foodways;
craft and craft history; diplomatic history; geography; Latin American studies; legal history;
military history; Native American and Indigenous studies; nature and environmental studies; politics; popular culture; public policy; regional trade and North Caroliniana; religious
studies; sexuality and gender studies; social medicine; sociology; Southern studies; Women's
studies. Submissions are not invited in fiction, poetry, or drama.

Journals: *Appalachian Heritage; The Comparatist; Early American Literature; The High School
Journal; Journal of the Civil War Era; Southern Cultures; Southern Literary Journal; Studies in
Philology; Southeastern Geographer*

Special series: Civil War America; Documentary Arts and Culture; Envisioning Cuba; Gender and American Culture; Islamic Civilization and Muslim Networks; The John Hope Franklin Series in African American History and Culture; Justice, Power, and Politics; Latin America in Translation/en Traducción/em Traducão;The Luther H. Hodges, Jr. and Luther H. Hodges, Sr. Series in Business and Entrepreneurship; The New Cold War History; New Directions in Southern Studies; Richard Hampton Jenrette Series in Architecture and the Decorative Arts; The Steven and Janice Brose Lectures in the Civil War Era; Studies in Social Medicine; Studies in the History of Greece and Rome; Studies in the Romance Languages and Literatures
Joint imprints: Omohundro Institute of Early American History and Culture, sponsored by Colonial Williamsburg and the College of William and Mary

University of North Texas Press

1155 Union Circle #311336
Denton, TX 76203

Orders:
Phone: 800.826.8911

Phone: 940.565.2142
Fax: 940.565.4590
Email: firstname.lastname@unt.edu

UK Representative:
Eurospan

Canadian Representative:
Scholarly Book Services

Website and Social Media:
Website: untpress.unt.edu
Facebook: www.facebook.com/pages/University-of-North-Texas-Press/
  365891204624

Staff
Director: Ronald Chrisman
  Assistant to the Director: Lori Belew
Assistant Director/Managing Editor: Karen DeVinney
Marketing Manager: Paula Oates

Full Member
Established: 1988
Title output 2011: 23
Titles currently in print: 427

Admitted to AAUP: 2003
Title output 2012: 21
Journals published: 2

Editorial Program
Humanities and social sciences, with special emphasis on Texas history and culture, military history, western history, music, criminal justice, folklore, multicultural topics, nature writing, natural and environmental history, culinary history, and women's studies. Submissions in poetry and fiction are invited only through the Vassar Miller and Katherine Anne Porter Prize competition.
Journals: *Theoria*; *Journal of Schenkerian Studies*
Special series: A. C. Greene; Al Filo: Mexican American Studies; Evelyn Oppenheimer; Frances B. Vick; Great American Cooking; Katherine Anne Porter Prize in Short Fiction;

North Texas Crime and Criminal Justice; North Texas Lives of Musicians; North Texas Military Biography and Memoir; Philosophy and the Environment; Practical Guide; Publications of the Texas Folklore Society; Southwestern Nature Writing Series; Temple Big Thicket; Texas Poets; Texas Writers; Vassar Miller Prize in Poetry; War and the Southwest; Western Life

Northern Illinois University Press

2280 Bethany Road
DeKalb, IL 60115

Phone: 815.753.1075
Fax: 815.753.1845
Email: (user I.D.)@niu.edu

Orders:
Chicago Distribution Center
11030 S. Langley Ave.
Chicago, IL 60628
Phone: 800.621.2736
Fax: 800.621.8476
Email: orders@press.uchicago.edu

Website and Social Media:
Website: www.niupress.niu.edu/
www.switchgrass.niu.edu
Facebook: www.facebook.com/pages/Northern-Illinois-University-Press/21437572447
www.facebook.com/pages/Switchgrass-Books/95919201436

UK Distributor:
John Wiley Distribution Center

Staff
Director: TBA
Assistant to the Director: Pat Yenerich (815.753.1075; email: pyenerich)
Editor-in-Chief: Mark Heineke (815.753.9906; email: mheineke) (US History, regional studies, fiction)
Acquisitions Editor: Amy Farranto (815.753.9946; email: afarranto) (Russian studies, European history, religion, history of religion, and philosophy)
Manuscript Editorial: Susan Bean, Managing Editor (815.753.9908; email: sbean)
Design and Production: Shaun Allshouse, Manager (815.753.0387; email: sallshou)
Business: Cara Carlson, Business Manager (815.753.1826; email: ccarlso2)

Full Member
Established: 1964
Title output 2011: 33
Titles currently in print: 481

Admitted to AAUP: 1972
Title output 2012: 33

Editorial Program
US history; US Civil War; European history; Russian history and culture; history of religion; Southeast Asian studies; urban studies; women's studies; studies on alcohol and substance abuse, regional studies on Chicago and the Midwest; Midwest literary novels.
Special series: Drugs and Alcohol: Contested Histories; Orthodox Christian Studies; Railroads in America; Russian Studies
Imprint: Switchgrass Books

Northwestern University Press

629 Noyes Street
Evanston, IL 60208-4210

Phone: 847.491.2046
Fax: 847.491.8150
Email: nupress@northwestern.edu
Indiv: (user I.D.)@northwestern.edu

Orders:
Northwestern University Press
Chicago Distribution Center
11030 South Langley Avenue
Chicago, IL 60628
Phone: 800.621.2736; 773.568.1550
Fax: 800.621.8476; 773.660.2235

Website and Social Media:
Website: www.nupress.northwestern.edu
Facebook: www.facebook.com/pages/Northwestern-University-Press/116644703843
Twitter: NorthwesternUP

UK Distributor:
Eurospan

Canadian Distributor:
Scholarly Book Service

Staff

Director: Jane Bunker (847.491.8111; email: j-bunker)
Assistant Director, Foreign Rights Manager, and Senior Editor: Henry Carrigan
   (847.491.8112; email: h-carrigan)
Acquisitions Editor: Mike Levine (847.491.7384; email: mike-levine)
   Assistant Acquisitions Editor: Peter Raccuglia (847.467.1279; email: p-raccuglia)
Managing Editor and Manager of Design and Production: Anne Gendler (847.491.3844;
   email: a-gendler)
Senior Project Editor: TBA
Art Director: Marianne Jankowski (847.467.5368; email: ma-jankowski)
Production Manager: A. C. Racette (847.491.8113; email: a-racette)
   Production Coordinator: Morris (Dino) Robinson (847.467.3392; email: morris-robinson)
Sales and Subsidiary Rights Manager: Parneshia Jones (847.491.7420; email: p-jones3)
   Marketing and Publicity Manager: Rudy Faust (847.467.0319; email: r-faust)
   Sales and Marketing Coordinator: Greta Bennion (847.491.5315; email g-bennion)
   Sales Representatives: Blake Delodder (301.322.4509; email: bdelodder@press.uchi-
   cago.edu); Gary Hart (323.663.3529; email: ghart@press.uchicago.edu); Bailey Walsh
   (608.218.1669; email: bwalsh@press.uchicago.edu); George Carroll (425.922.1045; email:
   george@redsides.com); Don Morrison, Barbara Arendall, Amy Willis (336.775.0226;
   email: msgbooks@aol.com)
Business Manager: Kirstie Felland (847.491.8310; email: kfelland)
   Administrative Assistant: Liz Hamilton (847.491.2458; email: emhamilton)

Full Member

Established: 1959
Title output 2011: 60
Titles currently in print: 1,216

Admitted to AAUP: 1988
Title output 2012: 60
Journals published: 2

Editorial Program
The Press publishes in drama/performance studies; Chicago region; fiction; German studies; poetry; Latino fiction and biography; literary criticism; literature in translation; law; philosophy; Slavic studies.

Distributed presses: Lake Forest College Press; Tia Chucha Press; Third World Press
Imprints: Curbstone; The Marlboro Press; TriQuarterly Books
Journals: *Islamic Africa*; *Renaissance Drama*
Special series: Comparative and Continental Philosophy; Cultural Expressions of World War II; Flashpoints; IDIOM; Jewish Lives; Medill School of Journalism's Visions of the American Press; Northwestern World Classics; the Northwestern-Newberry Edition of the Writings of Herman Melville; Rereading Ancient Philosophy; Rethinking the Early Modern; Studies in Phenomenology and Existential Philosophy; Studies in Russian Literature and Theory; Topics in Historical Philosophy

University of Notre Dame Press

310 Flanner Hall
Notre Dame, IN 46556

Phone: 574.631.6346
Fax: 574.631.8148
Email: undpress.1@nd.edu
Indiv: (user I.D.)@nd.edu

Orders:
University of Notre Dame Press
Chicago Distribution Center
11030 South Langley Avenue
Chicago, IL 60628
Phone: 800.621.2736
Fax: 800.621.8476

Website and Social Media:
Website: www.undpress.nd.edu
Facebook: www.facebook.com/pages/
    University-of-Notre-Dame-Press/296947140331384
Twitter: UNDPress
YouTube: www.youtube.com/user/UofNotreDamePress?feature=watch

UK/European Representative:
Eurospan

Staff
Interim Managing Director: Harv Humphrey (574.631.3265; email: hjhumphrey.undpress)
Senior Acquisitions Editor: Charles Van Hof (574.631.4912; email: cvanhof)
    Acquisitions Editor: Stephen Little (574.631.4906; email: slittle2)
    Acquisitions Coordinator: Robyn Karkiewicz (574.631.4913; email: karkiewicz.2)
Manuscript Editorial: Rebecca DeBoer, Managing Editor (574.631.4908; email: rdeboer)
    Manuscript Editor: Matthew Dowd (574.631.4914; email: mdowd1)
    Assistant Editor: Elizabeth Sain (574.631.4911; email: sain.6)
Design and Production: Wendy McMillen, Manager (574.631.4907; email: mcmillen.3)
    Assistant Production Manager: Jennifer Bernal (574.631.3266; email: bernal.7)
Marketing: Kathryn Pitts, Manager (574.631.3267; email: pitts.5)
    Electronic Marketing Manager: Emily McKnight (574.631.4909; email: mcknight.3)
    Assistant Manager: Ann Bromley (574.631.4910; email: bromley.1)
    Exhibits Coordinator: Susan Berger (574.631.4905; email: susan.m.berger)

Business: Diane Schaut, Manager (574.631.4904; email: schaut.1)
  Coordinator of Office Services: Gina Bixler (574.631.6346; email: bixler.1)
IT: Stephen Little, IT Consultant (574.631.4906; email: slittle2)

Full Member

Established: 1949   Admitted to AAUP: 1959
Title output 2011: 47   Title output 2012: 51
Titles currently in print: 1,000

Editorial Program
Religion; theology; philosophy; ethics; political science; medieval and early modern studies; classics; Catholic studies; business ethics; American history; European history; European Studies, Latin American studies; religion and literature; Irish studies; history and philosophy of science; international relations; literary criticism; peace studies; patristics; political science, political theory. Submissions are not invited in the hard sciences, mathematics, psychology, or novel-length fiction.
Special series, joint imprints, and/or copublishing programs: African American Intellectual Heritage; Andrés Montoya Poetry Prize; The Catholic Social Tradition; Christianity and Judaism in Antiquity; The Collected Works of Cardinal Newman; The Collected Works of Jacques Maritain; Contemporary European Politics and Society; Conway Lectures; Ernest Sandeen Prize in Poetry; The Notre Dame Review Prize; Faith and Reason; History, Languages, and Cultures of the Spanish and Portuguese Worlds; The Irish in America; Kellogg Institute for International Studies; Latino Perspectives; Notre Dame Studies in Ethics and Culture; Notre Dame Studies in Medical Ethics; Notre Dame Texts in Medieval Culture; Poetics of Orality and Literacy; Richard Sullivan Prize in Short Fiction; Studies in Spirituality and Theology; ReFormations: Medieval and Early Modern; Ward-Phillips Lectures in English Language and Literature; William and Katherine Devers Series in Dante and Medieval Italian Literature.

Ohio University Press

19 Circle Drive, The Ridges
Athens, OH 45701-2979

Phone: 740.593.1155
Fax: 740.593.4536
Email: (user I.D.)@ohio.edu

Website and Social Media:
Website: www.ohioswallow.com
Facebook: www.facebook.com/pages/Ohio-University-Press-Swallow-Press/317964522187

UK/European Representative:
Eurospan

Orders:
Ohio University Press
Chicago Distribution Center
11030 South Langley Avenue
Chicago, IL 60628
Phone: 800.621.2736
Fax: 800.621.8476

Staff

Interim Executive Editor: Kevin Haworth (740.593.1157; email: haworth)
Editorial Director: Gillian Berchowitz (740.593.1159; email: berchowi)
Managing Editor: Nancy Basmajian (740.593.1161; email: basmajia)
Production Manager: Beth Pratt (740.593.1162; email: prattb)
Marketing and Sales: Sarah Welsch, Sales and Marketing Director (740.593.1160; email: welsch)
  Publicity Manager: Jeff Kallet (740.593.1158; email: kallet)
  Marketing Designer: Sebastian Biot (740.597.2998; email: biot)
Business Manager: Kristi Goldsberry (740.593.1156; email: goldsbek)
  Customer Service and Permissions Specialist: Sally Welch (740.593.1154; email: welchs)

Full Member

Established: 1964

Admitted to AAUP: 1966

Title output 2011: 37

Title output 2012: 43

Titles currently in print: 1,042

Editorial Program

Imprints: Swallow Press

Special series, joint imprints, and/or copublishing programs: Africa in World History; Cambridge Centre of African Studies Series; The Civil War in the Great Interior; The Collected Letters of George Gissing; The Collected Works of William Howard Taft; The Complete Works of Robert Browning; Hollis Summers Poetry Prize; Law, Society, and Politics in the Midwest; Modern African Writing; Ohio Bicentennial; Ohio Quilt Series; Ohio Short Histories of Africa; Perspectives on the History of Congress and Perspectives on the Art and Architecture of the United States Capitol (for the US Capitol Historical Society); Perspectives on Global Health; Polish and Polish-American Studies Series; Research in International Studies: Southeast Asia, Africa, Latin America, and Global and Comparative Studies Series; Series in Race, Ethnicity and Gender in Appalachia; Series in Continental Thought; Series in Ecology and History; War and Society in the Midwest; White Coat Pocket Guide

University of Oklahoma Press

2800 Venture Drive
Norman, OK 73069

Orders:
Phone: 800.627.7377
Fax: 405.364.5798; 800.735.0476

Phone: 405.325.2000
Faxes: 405.325.4000 (director/rights/acquisitions/marketing);
405.307.9048 (manuscript editing/production/finance)
Email: (user I.D.)@ou.edu

Website and Social Media:
Website: www.oupress.com
Blog: www.oupressblog.com
Facebook: www.facebook.com/oupress
Twitter: OUPress

UK Representative:
Bay Foreign Language Books

Canadian Representative:
Hargreaves, Fuller & Co.

Staff

Director: B. Byron Price (405.325.5666; email: b_byron_price)

Editorial: Charles E. Rankin, Associate Director and Editor-in-Chief; Publisher, Arthur H. Clark imprint (405.325.2873; email: cerankin)

Acquisitions Editors: Jay Dew (contemporary American West, Texas history, political science, regional studies, natural history) (405.325.7991; email: jaydew); Alessandra Jacobi Tamulevich (native studies: North, Central, and South America, classical studies) (817.538.9802; email: jacobi); Kathleen Kelly (women's history, literature)(405.325.1216; email: kathleenkelly); Charles E. (Chuck) Rankin (American West, military history, Mormon studies, Borderlands) (405.325.2873; email: cerankin)

Manuscript Editing: Steven Baker, Managing Editor (405.325.1325; email: steven.b.baker) Assistant Managing Editor and Special Projects Editor: Alice Stanton (405.325.4922; email: astanton)

Production: Emmy Ezzell, Assistant Director/Production Manager (405.325.3186; email: eezzell) Production Editor: Susan Garrett (405.325.2408; email: sgarrett)

Marketing and Sales: Dale Bennie, Associate Director/Sales and Marketing Manager (405.325.3207; email: dbennie) Electronic Publishing Manager: Brent Greyson (405.325.3202; email: bgreyson) Publicity Manager: Sandy See (405.325.3200; email: ssee) Designer: Tony Roberts (405.325.4283; email: tonyroberts)

Business: Diane Cotts, Assistant Director/Chief Financial Officer (405.325.3276; email: dcotts) Customer Service: Kathy Benson (405.325.2287; email: presscs) Operations & Accounts Receivable: Diane Cannon (405.325.2326; email: pressdist)

Full Member

Established: 1928

Title output 2011: 84

Titles currently in print: 1,664

Admitted to AAUP: 1937

Title output 2012: 77

Editorial Program

Scholarly books, general nonfiction, and some fiction with special interests in the American West, Military History, Classical Studies, Native Studies (North, Central, and South America), Natural History, Political Science, and Regional Studies.

Special series: After Gold (A.H. Clark); American Exploration and Travel; American Indian Law and Policy; American Indian Literature and Critical Studies; Animal Natural History; Campaigns and Commanders; Charles M. Russell Center Series on Art and Photography of the American West; Chicana & Chicano Visions of the Américas; Chinese Literature Today; The Civilization of the American Indian; Congressional Studies; Early California Commentaries (A.H. Clark); Gilcrease-Oklahoma Series on Western Art and Artists; International and Security Affairs; Julian J. Rothbaum Distinguished Lecture Series; Kingdom in the West - The Mormons and the American Frontier (A. H. Clark); Latin American and Caribbean Arts and Culture - Mellon Initiative; Motoring West (A. H. Clark); New Directions in Native American Studies; Oklahoma Series in Classical Culture; The Oklahoma Western Biographies; Race and Culture in the American West; Recovering Languages and Literacies In the Americas - Mellon Initiative; Sam Noble Oklahoma Museum of Natural History Publications; Variorum Chaucer; Western Frontier Library; The Western Legacies

Oregon State University Press

121 The Valley Library
Corvallis, OR 97331-4501

Phone: 541.737.3166
Fax: 541.737.3170
Email: osu.press@oregonstate.edu
Indiv: (user I.D.)@oregonstate.edu

Order Fulfillment & Distribution:
Chicago Distribution Center
11030 S. Langley Ave.
Chicago, IL 60628
Phone: 800.621.2736
Fax: 800.621.8476

Website and Social Media:
Website: osupress.oregonstate.edu
Facebook: www.facebook.com/OregonStateUniversityPress
Twitter: osupress

Canadian Distributor:
University of British Columbia Press

Staff
Director: Faye A. Chadwell (541.737.8528; email: faye.chadwell)
Associate Director: Tom Booth (503.796.0547; fax 503.796.0549; email: thomas.booth)
Acquisitions Editor: Mary Elizabeth Braun (541.737.3873; email: mary.braun)
Managing Editor & Production Manager: Jo Alexander (541.737.3864; email: jo.alexander)
Marketing Manager: Micki Reaman (541.737.4620; email: micki.reaman)
Editorial & Production Assistant: Judy Radovsky (541.737.3302; email: judy.radovsky)

Full Member
Established: 1961
Title output 2011: 20
Titles currently in print: 258

Admitted to AAUP: 1991
Title output 2012: 18

Editorial Program
The Oregon State University Press publishes scholarly and general interest books in the environmental humanities; forestry; natural resource management; environmental and natural history; Native American and Indigenous studies; and the history, culture, and arts of the Pacific Northwest.

University of Ottawa Press/Les Presses de l'Université d'Ottawa

542 King Edward Avenue
Ottawa, ON K1N 6N5 Canada

Phone: 613.562.5246
Fax: 613.562.5247
Email: puo-uop@uottawa.ca

<u>Website and Social Media:</u>
Website: www.press.uottawa.ca
Facebook: www.facebook.com/uOttawaPress
Twitter: www.twitter.com/uOttawaPress

<u>US Orders (English titles):</u>
University of Toronto Press
2250 Military Road
Tonawanda NY 14150 USA
Phone: 800.565.9523
Fax: 800.221.9985
Email: utpbooks@utpress.utoronto.ca

<u>US Orders (French titles):</u>
Exportlivre
Phone: 450.671.3888
Fax: 450.671.2121
Email: order@exportlivre.com

<u>Canadian Orders (English titles):</u>
University of Toronto Press
5201 Dufferin Street
North York ON M3H 5T8 Canada
Phone: 800.565.9523; 416.667.7791
Fax: 800.221.9985; 416.667.7832
Email: utpbooks@utpress.utoronto.ca

<u>Canadian Orders (French titles):</u>
Prologue Inc.
1650 Lionel-Bertrand Boulevard
Boisbriand, Quebec J7H 1N7 Canada
Phone: 800.363.2864; 450.434.0306
Fax: 800.361.8088; 450.434.4135
Email: prologue@prologue.ca

<u>UK and European Orders (English titles):</u>
Marston Book Services

Staff

Director: Lara Mainville (613.562.5663; email: lara.mainville@uottawa.ca)
Digital Content Manager: Rebecca Ross (613.562.5800 ext. 2854;
 email: rebecca.ross@uottawa.ca)
Managing Editor: Marie Clausén (613.562.5800 ext. 3064; email: msec@uottawa.ca)
Production Manager: Sylvie Dugas (613.562.5800 ext. 2853;
 email: sylvie.dugas@uottawa.ca)

Full Member

Established: 1936
Title output 2011: 23
Titles currently in print: 442

Admitted to AAUP: 2005
Title output 2012: 21
Journals published: 3

Editorial Program

Translation, Canadian literature, education, French America, international development and globalization, philosophy, law, Canadian archeology and ethnography, health and society
Journals: *Cahiers Charlevoix; Francophonies d'Amérique; Journal of Prisoners on Prisons*
Special series: Amérique française; Archives des lettres canadiennes; Canadian Literature Collection, Critical Issues in Risk Management; Law, Technology and Society; Studies in International Development and Globalization; Governance; Mercury Series; Perspectives

on Translation; Philosophica; Reappraisals: Canadian Writers; Health and Society; Literary Translation; Cultural Transfers; Visual Arts;
Imprints: Harvest House

Oxford University Press, Inc.

Editorial Offices:
198 Madison AvenueG
New York, NY 10016
Phone: 212.726.6000
Fax: 212.726.6440
Email: firstname.lastname@oup.com

Website and Social Media:
Website: www.oup.com
Blog: blog.oup.com

Customer Service:
Orders/Prices: 800.451.7556
Inquiries: 800.445-9714
ELT: 800.441-5445
Journals: 800.852.7323
Music Retail: 800.292.0639
Fax: 919.677.1303

Oxford University Press (UK):
Great Clarendon Street
Oxford OX2 6DP
United Kingdom
Phone: +44 1865 556767
Fax: +44 1865 556646

Distribution Center &
Journals Marketing Office:
2001 Evans Road
Cary, NC 27513
Phone: 919.677.0977
Dist. Fax: 919.677.8877
Journals Fax: 919.677.1714

American English Language Teaching (AMELT):
Phone: 212.726.6300
Fax: 212.726.6388

Staff

President: Niko Pfund
   Assistant to the President: Henry Singleton
   Senior Vice President Administration and CFO, Finance Distribution, Accounting: Scot Kuehm
   Vice President, Legal, and General Counsel: Barbara Cohen
   Vice President and Publisher, Higher Education Group: John Challice
   Publisher, Reference and Online: Damon Zucca
   Publisher, Trade, Academic and Journals: Niko Pfund
   Vice President, Global Business Development and Rights, Academic & US Divisions: Nancy Roberson
   Vice President, Global Marketing and US Sales: Colleen Scollans
   Vice President, Human Resources: Marilyn Okrent
   Vice President, Operations: Tom Shannon
   Vice President and Director, Content Operations: Catherine Pearce
   AMELT General Manager: Laura Pearson

Trade and Academic
Publisher: Niko Pfund
  Editorial: Terry Vaughn (economics and finance); Tim Bent (trade, history and politics);
  James Cook (sociology, criminology); Susan Ferber (history); Nancy Toff (history); Jeremy
  Lewis (chemistry); Brendan O'Neill (literature and film); Peter Ohlin (philosophy and lin-
  guistics; Cynthia Read (religion); Theo Calderara (religion); Suzanne Ryan (music); Norm
  Hirschy (music), Todd Waldman (music); Stefan Vranka (classics and ancient history);
  David McBride (politics, law); Angela Chnapko (politics); Donald Kraus (Bibles); Phyllis
  Cohen (math, physics)
Law
Publisher: Peter Berkery
  Editorial: Matt Gallaway (intellectual property, media & communications law)
Medical
Editorial Director, GAB: Catherine Barnes
  VP/Editorial Director: Joan Bossert (neuropsychology, cognitive psychology)
  Associate Editorial Director: Craig Panner (neurology, clinical neuroscience)
  Senior Editors: Dana Bliss (social work); Andrea Seils (Oxford American handbooks, pain
  medicine, anesthesia, critical care, palliative care & oncology, radiology)
  Editors: Abby Gross (social psychology, positive psychology, industrial & organizational
  psychology, educational psychology); Sarah Harrington (clinical psychology, developmental
  psychology, forensic psychology); Chad Zimmerman (public health/epidemiology, clinical
  genetics); Chris Reid (medicine journals, psychiatry)
  Associate Editor: David D'Addona (psychiatry); Nicholas Liu: digital development editor,
  medical editorial
Reference and Online
Publisher: Damon Zucca
  Reference Editorial: Alixandra Gould (Content Development); Tanya Laplante (online);
  Anna-Lise Santella (Oxford/Grove Music); Jennifer Bantz (Oxford/Grove Art); Robert Re-
  pino (African American Studies); David Pervin (Economics, Business); Eric Crahan (Politi-
  cal Science); Julia Kostova (Humanities); Adina Berk (History, Classics); Max Sinsheimer
  (Trade Reference); Katherine Martin (US Dictionaries)
  Digital Publishing Management: Scott Beebe
Higher Education
Publisher: John Challice
  Editorial: Robert Miller (philosophy & religion); Carrie Brandon (English & Linguistics);
  Fred Speers (English & linguistics); Richard Carlin (art & music); Jennifer Carpenter (poli-
  tics); Sherith Pankratz (sociology, anthropology, & archaeology); Sarah Calabi (criminology
  & criminal justice); Jane Potter (psychology); Jason Noe (life sciences & chemistry); Patrick
  Lynch (economics, finance, & business, engineering & computer science); Dan Kaveney
  (earth and environmental sciences); Brian Wheel (history of the Americas); Charles Cava-
  liere (world history and classics)
  Marketing: Frank Mortimer
  Sales: Bill Marting
Content Operations
Head of Content Operations: Deborah Shor

Production Managers: Kate Hind, Diem Bloom, David Ford
Demand Planning Manager: Nancy Wu
Creative Director: Linda Secondari

Business Development and Rights

Director, Global Business Development and Rights: Nancy Roberson
Business Development Manager, Americas: Peter da Silva Vint
Business Development Operations Manager: Andi Bailey
Business Development Coordinator: Cassie Kull
Assistant to Vice President: Meredith Keller

Sales and Marketing

Vice President, Global Marketing and US Sales: Colleen Scollans
Marketing Directors: Kim Craven (OUP USA); Sarah Ultsch (Digital); Frank Mortimer (Higher Education);Charlotte Capanni (Journals)
Publicity Director: C. Purdy
Marketing Director of Medicine and Law Publishing: Greg Bussy
Director of Retail and Wholesale Sales: Larisa Elt
Director of Library Sales: Rebecca Seger
Director of Direct Response Marketing: Rose Pintaudi-Jones
Director of Distribution Client Management: Kurt Hettler
Manager of E-Book Sales: Margaret Harrison
International Sales: Ray McFadden

Operations

Operations: Tom Shannon
Human Resources: Marilyn Okrent
Office Services: Terese Dickerson

Finance

Senior Vice President and Chief Financial Officer: Scot Kuehm
Finance Director: Tina Pace

American English Language Teaching (AMELT) Group

General Manager: Laura Pearson
US Publisher: Stephanie Karras
US Sales Director: Myndee Males
US Marketing Director: Karen Horton
ADP Director: Susan Sanguily
Executive Publishing Manager, AMELT International Adult: Erik Gundersen
Executive Publishing Manager, AMELT International Primary: Shelagh Speers

Journals (North Carolina)

US Editor-in-Chief: Alison Denby
US Customer Services Manager: Carolyn Wilson
Senior Marketing Manager: Tricia Hudson
US Production Director: Cindy Brown
US Director, Corporate Sales: Amy Luchsinger

Distribution Center (North Carolina)

Inventory Planning / Control: Kenneth Guerin
Credit and Collection: Banks Honeycutt
Customer Service: Cheryl Ammons-Longtin
Warehouse Operations: Todd Hayes
Accounting Services: Dottie Warlick

Cary Facilities: Chris Vidourek
Technology
 Director of Business Technology: Erik Diaz

Full Member

Established: 1895

Title output 2011: 1,320

Titles currently in print: 21,000

Admitted to AAUP: 1950

Title output 2012: 1400

Journals published (US only): 64

Editorial Program

Scholarly monographs; general nonfiction; Bibles; college textbooks; medical books; music; reference books; journals; children's books; English language teaching. Submissions are not invited in the area of fiction.

Journals published in the US: *American Historical Review; American Journal of Agricultural Economics, American Journal of Epidemiology; American Journal of Hypertension; American Literary History; Applied Economic Perspectives and Policy; Archives in Clinical Neuropsychology; Cerebral Cortex, Children and Schools, Christian Bioethics, Clinical Infectious Diseases; Early Music; Enterprise & Society: The International Journal of Business History; Environmental History; Epidemiologic Reviews; The Gerontologist; Health Education Research; Health Promotion International; Health & Social Work; Holocaust and Genocide Studies; ILAR Journal Interdisciplinary Studies in Literature and Environment; Journal of American History; Journal of Analytical Toxicology; Journal of Chromatographic Science; Journal of Church and State, Journal of Deaf Studies and Deaf Education; The Journal of Gerontology, Series A: Biological Sciences and Medical Sciences; The Journals of Gerontology Series B: Psychological Sciences and Social Sciences; Journal of Infectious Diseases; Journal of Islamic Studies; Journal of Pediatric Psychology; Journal of Medicine and Philosophy; Journal of the Pediatric Infectious Diseases Society; Journal of Public Administration Research and Theory; Journal of Social History; Journal of the American Academy of Religion; Journal of the History of Medicine and Allied Sciences; Journal of Theological Studies; JNCI: Journal of the National Cancer Institute; Literary Imagination; Melus; Modern Judaism; Music and Letters; The Musical Quarterly; Nicotine and Tobacco Research; OAH Magazine of History; The Opera Quarterly; Political Analysis; Public Opinion Quarterly; Publius: The Journal of Federalism; Quarterly Journal of Economics; Review of Asset Pricing; Review of Environmental Economics and Policy; The Review of Financial Studies; Schizophrenia Bulletin; Social Forces; Social Politics; Social Work; Social Work Research; Sociology of Religion; Toxicological Sciences; The World Bank Economic Review; The World Bank Research Observer*

University of Pennsylvania Press

3905 Spruce Street
Philadelphia, PA 19104-4112

Phone: 215.898.6261
Fax: 215.898.0404
Email: (user I.D.)@upenn.edu

Website and Social Media:
Website: www.pennpress.org
Blog: pennpress.typepad.com
Facebook: www.facebook.com/PennPress
Twitter: PennPress

Warehouse & Returns:
Maple Press Company
Lebanon Distribution Center
704 Legionaire Drive
Fredericksburg, PA 17026

Order Department:
PO Box 50370
Baltimore, MD 21211-4370
Phone: 800.537.5487
Fax: 410.516.6998
Email (inquiries only):
custserv@pobox.upenn.edu

UK/European Distributor:
Marston Book Services

Canadian Representative:
Scholarly Book Services

Staff

Director: Eric Halpern (215.898.1672; email: ehalpern)
  Assistant to the Director and Rights Administrator: Jaime Estrada (215.898.6263; email: estradaj)
Acquisitions: Peter Agree, Editor-in-Chief (human rights, policy and politics, anthropology) (215.573.3816; email: agree)
  Senior Editors: Jerome E. Singerman (literary criticism and cultural studies; ancient, medieval, and Renaissance studies; landscape architecture; Jewish studies) (215.898.1681; email: singerma); Robert Lockhart (American history, regional books) (215.898.1677; email: rlockhar)
  Acquiring Editors: TBA (business, economics) (215.746.5421); Bill Finan (peace and conflict studies, international relations) (215.573.7129; email: wfinan)
  Consulting Editor, UK: Deborah Blake (ancient studies) (44-7867-540881; email: dcblake. pennpress@virginmedia.com)
  Assistant Editor: Caroline Winschel (215.898.3252; email: winschel)
  Acquisitions Assistant: Rachel Taube (215.898.6262; email: rtaube)
Manuscript Editing and Production: Elizabeth Glover, Editing & Production Manager (215.898.1675; email: gloverel)
  Assistant Production Manager: William Boehm (215.573.4059; email: boehmwj)
  Managing Editor: Alison Anderson (215.898.1678; email: anderaa)
  Associate Managing Editor: Erica Ginsburg (215.898.1679; email: eginsbur)
  Production Editor: Noreen O'Connor (215.898.1709; email: nmoconno)
  Production Coordinator: Susan Staggs (215.898.1676; email: sstaggs)
  Art Director: John Hubbard (215.573.6118; email: wmj)
Marketing: Laura Waldron, Marketing Director (215.898.1673; email: lwaldron)
  Publicity & Public Relations Manager: Saunders Robinson (215.898.1674; email: jorobin)
  Electronic Promotion Coordinator: Stephanie Brown (215.898.8678; email: browns2)

Direct Mail & Advertising Manager: Sara Davis (215.898.9184; email: saradav)
Marketing Assistant: Melissa Marshall (215.898.6264; email: memar)
Journals: Paul Chase (circulation) (215.573.1295; email: paulbc); Dave Lievens (editing and production) (215.898.7588; email: lievens)
Business: Joseph Guttman, Business Manager (215.898.1670; email: josephgg)
Financial Coordinator: Kathy Ranalli (215.898.1682; email: ranalli)
Customer Service Representative: Marlene DeBella (215.898.1671; email: custserv@pobox. upenn.edu)

Full Member

Established: 1890	Admitted to AAUP: 1967
Title output 2011: 135	Title output 2012: 145
Titles currently in print: 1,650	Journals published: 13

Editorial Program

Scholarly and semipopular nonfiction, with special interests in American history and culture; ancient, medieval, and Renaissance studies; human rights; urban studies, political science; Jewish studies; anthropology; landscape architecture; corporate governance and business ethics; economics of poverty; and Pennsylvania regional studies.

Journals: *Change Over Time; Dissent; Early American Studies; The Eighteenth-Century: Theory and Interpretation; Hispanic Review; Humanity; Jewish Quarterly Review; Journal for Early Modern Cultural Studies; J19: The Journal of Nineteenth-Century Americanists; Magic, Ritual, and Witchcraft; Journal of the Early Republic; Journal of the History of Ideas; Revista Hispanica Moderna*

Special series: American Business, Politics, and Society; American Governance; Arts and Intellectual Life in Modern America; Contemporary Ethnography; City in the 21st Century; Democracy, Citizenship, and Constitutionalism; Divinations; Early American Studies; Early Modern Americas; Empire and After; Encounters with Asia; Ethnography of Political Violence; Jewish Culture and Contexts; Material Texts; Metropolitan Portraits; The Middle Ages; National and Ethnic Conflict in the 21st Century; Penn Studies in Landscape Architecture; Pennsylvania Studies in Human Rights; Personal Takes; Politics and Culture in Modern America

Copublishing programs: Ceramics Handbooks, International Food Policy Research Institute

Imprint: Pine Street Books, University of Pennsylvania Museum of Archaeology and Anthropology

Pennsylvania State University Press

820 North University Drive
USB-1, Suite C
University Park, PA 16802-1003

Phone: 814.865.1327
Fax: 814.863.1408
Email: (user I.D.)@psu.edu

Orders:
Phone: 800.326.9180
Fax: 877.778.2665

Website and Social Media:
Website: www.psupress.org
Twitter: PSUPress
Facebook: www.facebook.com/psupress

UK Representative:
Eurospan
Manchester University Press (art & art history)

Canadian Distributor:
University of Toronto Press

Staff

Director: Patrick H. Alexander (814.867.2209; email: pha3)
 Assistant to the Director: Teresa Craig (814.865.1327; email: tac6)
Acquisitions Editorial: Kendra Boileau, Editor-in-Chief (814.867.2220; email: klb60)
 Executive Editor, Art History and Humanities: Eleanor Goodman (814.867.2212; email: ehg11)
 Acquisitions Editor: Kathryn Yahner (814.865.1327; email: kby3)
 Editorial Assistants: Charlee Redman (814.865.1592; email: cmr5291); Robert Turchick (814.865.1328; email: rst5043)
Managing Editor: Laura Reed-Morrisson (814.865.1606; email: lxr168)
 Manuscript Editors: John Morris (email: jpm42); Julie Schoelles (814.867.2214; email: jls1001)
Design and Production: Jennifer Norton, Associate Director/Design and Production Manager (814.863.8061; email: jsn4)
 Chief Designer: Steven Kress (814.867.2215; email: srk5)
 Book Production Coordinator: Patty Mitchell (814.867.2216; email: pam18)
 Production Assistant: Jon Gottshall (814.867.2213; email: jeg31)
Sales/Marketing: Tony Sanfilippo, Assistant Director/Marketing and Sales Director (814.863.5994; email: ajs23)
 Advertising Manager: Brian Beer (814.867.2210; email: bxb110)
 Publicity Manager: Daniel Bellet (814.865.1329; email: djb49)
 Sales Manager: Kathleen Scholz-Jaffe (814.867.2224; email: kxs56)
Business Manager: Tina Laychur (814.863.5993; email: txs17)
 Assistant Business Manager: Kathy Vaughn (814.863.6771; email: kmv1)
 Shipping Clerk: Dave Buchan (814.863.5496; email: deb11)
Journals Manager: Diana Pesek (814.867.2223; email: dlp28)
 Production Coordinator: Julie Shippee (814.863.5992; email: jas1035)
 Marketing Manager: Heather Smith (814.863.0524; email: hms7)
 Managing Editor: Astrid Meyer (814.863.3830; email: aum38)

Information Systems Manager: Ed Spicer (814.867.2219; email: res122)
Rights and Permissions Manager: Sheila S. Sager (814.867.2831; email: sss2)

Full Member

Established: 1956	Admitted to AAUP: 1960
Title output 2011: 87	Title output 2012: 157 (includes new in paper)
Titles currently in print: 1,469	Journals published (for 2012): 21

Editorial Program

Scholarly books in the humanities and social sciences, with current emphasis on animal studies; architecture; art history; American, European, and Latin American history; communication studies and rhetoric; medieval studies; philosophy; religion. Submissions are not invited in fiction, poetry, or drama.

Journals: *Chaucer Review; Comparative Literature Studies; Eugene O'Neill Review; The Good Society; Interdisciplinary Literature Studies; Journal of Assessment and Institutional Effectiveness Journal of General Education; Journal of Medieval Religious Cultures; Journal of Modern Periodical Studies; Journal of Moravian History Journal of Nietzsche Studies; Journal of Speculative Philosophy; Mediterranean Studies; Pennsylvania History; Philosophy and Rhetoric; Preternature; Soundings; SHAW: The Annual of Bernard Shaw Studies; Studies in American Jewish Literature; Transportation Journal; Utopian Studies*

Special series: Animalibus: Of Animals and Cultures; Buildings, Landscapes, and Societies; Edinburgh Edition of Thomas Reid; Graphic Medicine; Interdisciplinary Perspectives on Jewish Experience and Culture Latin American Originals; Magic in History; Max Kade Institute German-American Research Series; Penn State Series in the History of the Book; Pietist, Moravian, and Anabaptist Studies; Refiguring Modernism; Religion Around; Re-Reading the Canon; Rhetoric and Democratic Deliberation; Rome Perspectives; The Stone Art Theory Institutes; Signifying on Scriptures

Special imprints: Keystone Books®

PISA University Press

Lungarno Pacinotti, 43/44
56126 Pisa Italy

Phone: +39 050 2212056
Fax: + 39 050 2212945
Email: press@unipi.it

<u>Website and Social Media:</u>
Website: www.pisauniversitypress.It

<u>Orders:</u>
Phone: +39 050 2212055
Fax: +39 050 2212945

<u>UK/North American Representatives:</u>
Libro Co. Italia
Herder Editrice e Libreria, Casalini Libri

Board of Directors
President Scientific Committee: Ada Carlesi
Chief Executive: Riccardo Grasso

Staff
Marketing Manager and Acquisitions Editorial: Claudia Napolitano (+39 050 2212053; email: napolitano.press@unipi.it, press@unipi.it)
Central Administration/Order Processing: Ambra Seymons (+39 050 2212055; email: seymons.press@unipi.it, press@unipi.It)

International Member
Established: 2000
Title output 2011: 40
Titles currently in print: 767

Admitted to AAUP: 2005
Title output 2012: 43
Journals published: 14

Editorial Program
Pisa University Press supports the academic mission of Pisa University by publishing scholarly books and journals for a diverse, worldwide readership. These publications, written by authors representing a broad range of intellectual perspectives, reflect the academic and institutional strengths of the university. Pisa University Press publishes handbooks and peer-reviewed works of academic distinction, of very good editorial and production quality, in many subjects. These publications primarily service the scholarly community, and many also reach the general reading public.

Journals: *Agogè; Agricoltura Mediterranea; Agrochimica; Archives Italiennes de Biologie; Atti della Società Toscana di Scienze Naturali A and B; Atti e Sipari; Cultura e Diritti; Egitto e Vicino Oriente; Frustula Entomologica; Paleontographia Italica; Polittico; Studi Classici e orientali; Rivista d Igiene*

Special series: Conversations at the "Sapienza"; Eco-history Notebooks; History and Sociology of Modernity; Greek, Arabic, Latin: Roads to Knowledge; Methexis Project; Peace Studies; Pisan Linguistics Studies; Russian Literature; Studies and Sources for the History of Sculpture; Teaching in a University Context

University of Pittsburgh Press

Fifth Floor Eureka Building
3400 Forbes Avenue
Pittsburgh, PA 15260
Phone: 412.383.2456
Fax: 412.383.2466
Email: (user I.D.)@pitt.edu

Order Fulfillment:
University of Pittsburgh Press
Chicago Distribution Center
11030 South Langley Avenue
Chicago, IL 60628
Phone: 773.568.1550; 800.621.2736
Fax: 773.660.2235

Website and Social Media:
Website: www.upress.pitt.edu
Facebook: www.facebook.com/pages/Pitt-Poetry-Series/123300654375394?
Twitter: UPittPress

UK Representative:
Eurospan

Canadian Representative:
Scholarly Book Services

Staff
Director: Cynthia Miller (email: cymiller)
   Assistant to the Director: Kelley Johovic (email: khj4)
Editorial Director: Peter Kracht (email: pek6)
   Acquisitions Editor: Joshua Shanholtzer (email: jos85)
   Subsidiary Rights Manager: Margie Bachman (email: mkbachma)
   Editorial Assistant: Amberle Sherman (email: uppacq)
Production Director: F. Ann Walston (email: awalston)
   Managing Editor: Alex Wolfe (email: apw20)
   Production Assistant: Joel Coggins (email: jwc38)
Marketing Director: Lowell Britson (email: lbritson)
   Direct Mail/Advertising Manager: David Bauman (email: ddb13)
   Publicist: Maria Sticco (email: mes5)
Business Manager: Cindy Wessels (email: caw1)

Full Member
Established: 1936
Title output 2011: 44
Titles currently in print: 1,032

Admitted to AAUP: 1937
Title output 2012: 50

Editorial Program
History; Russian and East European studies; Central Eurasian studies; Latin American studies; composition and literacy studies; poetry; history and philosophy of science; history of architecture; urban studies; environmental history; Pittsburgh and western Pennsylvania. The Press does not invite submissions in the hard sciences, original fiction (except DHLP), festschriften, memoirs, symposia, or unrevised doctoral dissertations.

   The Press distributes and copublishes selected titles with the Carnegie Museum of Art, the Carnegie Museum of Natural History, the Frick Art and Historical Center, the Historical Society of Western Pennsylvania, the Mattress Factory, and the Westmoreland Museum of American Art.

Special series: Agnes Lynch Starrett Poetry Prize; Ayn Rand Society Philosophical Studies; Central Eurasia In Context; Cuban Studies; Culture, Politics, and the Built Environment;

Drue Heinz Literature Prize; History of the Urban Environment; Illuminations: Cultural Formations of the Americas; Pitt Latin American Series; Pitt Poetry Series; Pitt Series in Russian and East European Studies; Pittsburgh Series in Composition, Literacy, and Culture; Pittsburgh/Konstanz Series in Philosophy and History of Science

Princeton University Press

Executive Offices:
41 William Street
Princeton, NJ 08540-5237

Phone: 609.258.4900
Fax: 609.258.6305
Email:
firstname_lastname@press.princeton.edu

Website and Social Media:
Website: press.princeton.edu
Blog: press.princeton.edu/blog
Facebook: www.facebook.com/PrincetonUniversityPress
Twitter: PrincetonUPress

European Editorial Office:
6 Oxford St.
Woodstock, Oxfordshire OX20 1TW
United Kingdom
Phone: +44 1993 814500
Fax: +44 1993 814504
Email: firstinitiallastname@pupress.co.uk

Order Fulfillment (US and Canada):
California/Princeton Fulfillment Services
1445 Lower Ferry Road
Ewing, NJ 08618
Phone: 800.777.4726; 609.883.1759
Fax: 800.999.1958; 609.883.7413

UK/European Sales Representation:
Univ. Presses of California,
Columbia, & Princeton, Ltd
1 Oldlands Way, Bognor Regis
West Sussex PO22 9SA
United Kingdom
Phone: +44 1243 842165
Fax: +44 1243 842167

Staff

Director: Peter J. Dougherty (609.258.6778)
   Assistant to the Director: Martha Camp (609.258.4953)
   Associate Director and Controller: Patrick Carroll (609.258.2486)
   Human Resources Generalist: Carol Swoboda (609.258.7737)
   Contracts, Copyrights, and Permissions Supervisor: Mike Schwartz (609.258.1611)
Acquisitions Editorial (see also European Office): Brigitta van Rheinberg, Assistant Director, Editor-in-Chief and Executive Editor (history) (609.258.4935)
   Behavioral & Life Sciences: Seth Ditchik, Group Publisher and Executive Editor (finance, economics) (609.258.9428); Alison Kalett, Senior Editor (biology, earth science) (609.258.9232); Eric Schwartz, Editor (cognitive science & sociology) (609.258.4908)
   Humanities: Rob Tempio, Group Publisher and Executive Editor (philosophy, ancient world, political theory) (609.258.0843); Beth Clevenger, Associate Editor (609.258.2336); Alison MacKeen, Senior Editor (art, literature) (609.258.4569); Anne Savarese, Executive Editor and Reference & Backlist Editor (reference) (609.258.4937)
   Mathematics & Science: Robert Kirk, Group Publisher and Executive Editor and Publisher, (field guides and natural history) (609.258.4884); Ingrid Gnerlich, Executive Editor

(physical sciences) (609.258.5775); Samantha Hasey, Associate Editor (609.258.2938);
Vickie Kearn, Senior Editor (mathematics) (609.258.2321)
Social Sciences: Charles Myers, Group Publisher and Executive Editor (political science)
(609.258.4922); Fred Appel, Senior Editor (anthropology, religion) (609.258.2484); Peter
Dougherty, Director (economic history & education) (609.258.6778)
Editorial Administrator: Linny Schenck (609.258.0183)
Manuscript Editorial: Neil Litt, Director of Editing, Design, and Production (609.258.5066)
Managing Editor: Elizabeth Byrd (609.258.2589)
Managing Editor, Digital Publications: Ken Reed (609.258.2485)
Art Director: Maria Lindenfeldar (609.258.7557)
Electronic Manuscripts Manager: Eileen Reilly (609.258.2719)
Production Manager: Betsy Litz (609.258.1253)
Marketing: Adam Fortgang, Assistant Press/Marketing Director (609.258.4896)
Sales Director: Tim Wilkins (609.258.4898)
Advertising Manager: Donna Liese (609.258.4924)
Associate Marketing Director: Leslie Nangle (609.258.5881)
Digital Sales Director: Priscilla Treadwell (609.258.9387)
Digital Information Manager: Avi Paradise (609.258.5745)
Domestic Subsidiary Rights Manager: Shaquona Crews (609.258.5799)
Exhibits Manager: Melissa Burton (609.258.4915)
Senior Text Promotion Manager: Julie Haenisch (609.258.6856)
Publicity Director: Andrew DeSio (609.258.5165)
Web and Data Supervisor: Ann Ambrose (609.258.7749)
Business: Patrick Carroll, Associate Director and Controller (609.258.2486)
Associate Controller: Debbie Greco (609.882.0550)
Information Systems: Patrick Carroll, Acting Director of Information Technology
(609.258.2486)
European Office:
European Publishing Director: Al Bertrand (humanities) (+44 1993 814501)
Editors: Ben Tate (humanities) (+44 1993 814502); Kimberley Williams (translations)
(+44 1993 814509)
International Rights Manager: Kimberley Williams (+44 1993 814509)
European Director of Publicity: Caroline Priday (+44 1993 814503)

Full Member

Established: 1905 — Admitted to AAUP: 1937
Title output 2011: 327 — Title output 2012: 322
Titles currently in print: 7,075

Editorial Program
Humanities: American, European, World, Asian, Slavic, and Jewish history; ancient world;
classics; art history; philosophy; political theory; literature; religion
Reference: humanities; social sciences; and science
Science: astrophysics; biology; earth sciences; mathematics; natural history; ornithology;
physics
Social science: anthropology; cognitive science; economics; finance; law; political science;

sociology. The Press does not publish drama or fiction.

Special imprints: The Bollingen Series, established in 1941 by the Bollingen Foundation, has been published by Princeton University Press since 1967. The Press is not accepting further contributions to the series.

Special monograph series: 20/21; Advances in Financial Engineering; America in the World; A.W. Mellon Lectures in the Fine Arts; Annals of Mathematics Studies; The Bard Music Festival; Buddhism; Carl G. Hempel Lecture Series; CREI Lectures in Macroeconomics; The Econometric and Tingergen Institutes Lectures; Frontiers of Biology; Frontiers of Economic Research; The Gorman Lectures in Economics; Great Battles: History, Culture, and Memory; Human Rights and Crimes against Humanity; In a Nutshell; In-Formation; The Isaac Newton Institute Lectures; James Madison Library in American Politics; Jews, Christians, and Muslims from the Ancient to the Modern World; Jung Seminars; The Kauffman Foundation Series on Innovation and Entrepreneurship; The Lawrence Stone Lectures; Lives of Great Religious Books; London Mathematical Society Monographs; Magie Classical Publications; Martin Classical Lectures; Mathematical Notes; Miriam S. Balmuth Lectures in Ancient History and Archaeology; Monographs in Behavior and Ecology; Monographs in Population Biology; Mythos; National Gallery of Art Systematic Catalogues; New Forum Books; Oddly Modern Fairy Tales; POINT: Essays on Architecture; Politics and Society in Twentieth-Century America; Porter Lectures; Portland Press; Primers in Complex Systems; Princeton-China Series; Princeton Classic Editions; Princeton Computer Science Notes; Princeton Economic History of the Western World; Princeton Environmental Institute Series; Princeton Essays in Literature; Princeton Field Guides; Princeton Field Guides to Art; Princeton Foundations of Contemporary Philosophy; The Princeton Frontiers of Biology Lecture Series; Princeton Frontiers in Physics; Princeton Illustrated Checklists; Princeton Landmarks in Biology; Princeton Landmarks in Mathematics and Physics; Princeton Lectures in Finance; Princeton Library of Asian Translations; Princeton Lectures In Politics and Public Affairs; Princeton Mathematical Series; Princeton Monographs in Philosophy; Princeton Pocket Guides; Princeton Primers in Climate; Princeton Readings in Religion; Princeton Science Library; Princeton Series in Applied Mathematics; Princeton Series in Astrophysics; Princeton Series in Computer Science; Princeton Series in Evolutionary Biology; Princeton Series in Finance; Princeton Series in International Economics; Princeton Series in Physics; Princeton Series in Theoretical and Computational Biology; Princeton Studies in American Politics; Princeton Studies in Business and Technology; Princeton Studies in Complexity; Princeton Studies in Cultural Sociology; Princeton Studies in International History and Politics; Princeton Studies in Modern Observational Astronomy; Princeton Studies in Muslim Politics; Princeton Texts in Math; The Public Square; Richard Ullman Lectures; The Roundtable Series in Behavioral Economics; The Russian Archives Project; Science Essentials; Studies in Church and State; Soochow University Lectures in Philosophy; The Toni Morrison Lecture Series; The Toulouse Lectures in Economics; Translation/Transnation; The University Center for Human Values Series; W. H. Auden: Critical Editions; Where to Watch Birds; Writers on Writers

Poetry series: Facing Pages; The Lockert Library of Poetry in Translation; Princeton Series of Contemporary Poets

Original source series: The Collected Papers of Albert Einstein; Collected Works of Spinoza; The Complete Works of W. H. Auden; Kierkegaard's Writings; Kierkegaard's Journals and Notebooks; The Papers of Thomas Jefferson (also Second Series; Retirement Series); The Papers of Woodrow Wilson; The Philosophical, Political and Literary Works of David Hume; Selected Writings of Wilhelm Dilthey; The Writings of Henry D. Thoreau

University of Puerto Rico Press

Street Address:
Edificio Editorial/Diálogo
Jardín Botánico Área Norte
Carretera No. 1, KM 12.0
Río Piedras, San Juan, PR 00931
Phone: 787.250.0435
Fax: 787.753.9116, 751.8785

Mailing Address:
PO Box 23322
U.P.R. Station
San Juan, PR 00931-3322

Website and Social Media:
Website: www.laeditorialupr.com

Staff
Executive Director: José Ortiz Valladares (email: jose.ortiz3@upr.edu)
Editor: Rosa V. Otero
Sales: José Burgos (email: jburgos@upr.edu)
Marketing and Promotion: Ruth Morales (email: ruth.morales2@upr.edu)
Exhibits and Special Projects: José Burgos (email: jburgos@upr.edu), Ruth Morales (email: ruth.morales2@upr.edu)
Shipping, Receiving and Inventory: Ernesto Pancorbo (email: ernesto.pancorbo@upr.edu)
Warehouse: Ángel Ortiz
Journals: *Revista La Torre*
Journals Marketing: Ruth Morales

Full Member
Established:1943
Title output 2011: NR
Titles currently in print: 989

Admitted to AAUP: 1971
Title output 2012: NR
Journals published: 1

Editorial Program
Scholarly studies on Puerto Rico, the Caribbean and Latin America; philosophy; history; architecture; law; social sciences; health; women's studies; economics; literary theory and criticism; creative poetry and prose; literary anthologies; nature studies; flora; fauna; ecosystems; children's books; reference; other general interest publications.
Journals: *Revista La Torre* (the humanities). In distribution: *Revista de Estudios Hispánicos* (Spanish language studies); and *Historia y Sociedad* (Puerto Rican and Caribbean history); *Diálogos* (philosophy)
Special series: literary anthologies; philosophy; creative literature; scholarly nonfiction; nature
Special imprints: Antología Personal (Selections by renowned hispanic writers); Clásicos no tan clásicos (Faithful re-edition of works written between 1890 and 1930 with annotations by 21st century scholars); Books on Puerto Rican Cooking; Colección Eugenio María de Hostos (complete works); San Pedrito (children's books); Colección Nueve Pececitos (young readers); Cuentos de un mundo perdido (middle school readers)

Purdue University Press

Stewart Center, Room 370
504 West State Street
West Lafayette, IN 47907-2058

Phone: 765.494.2038
Fax: 765.496.2442
Email: pupress@purdue.edu
Indiv: (user I.D.)@purdue.edu

Website and Social Media:
Website: www.thepress.purdue.edu
Facebook: www.facebook.com/purduepress
Twitter: publishpurdue

European Distributor:
Eurospan

Orders:
Purdue University Press
PO Box 388
Ashland, OH 44805
Phone: 800.247.6553
Fax: 419.281.6883
Email: order@bookmasters.com

Canadian Distributor:
Bookmasters

Staff
Director: Charles Watkinson (765.494.8251; email: cwatkinson)
Production & Marketing Manager: Bryan Shaffer (765.494.8428; email: bshaffer)
Lead Production Editor: Katherine Purple (765.494.6259; email: kpurple)
Production Editors: Kelley Kimm (765.494.8024; email: kkimm); Dianna Gilroy
  (765.494.2035; email: dianna)
Administrative Assistant: Becki Corbin (765.494.8144; email: rlcorbin)
Editorial Assistant: Jennifer Lynch (email: lynch23)

Full Member
Established: 1960
Title output 2011: 25
Titles currently in print: 470

Admitted to AAUP: 1993
Title output 2012: 26
Journals published: 14

Editorial Program
Dedicated to the dissemination of scholarly and professional information, the Press provides quality resources in several key subject areas including business, technology, health, veterinary medicine, and other selected disciplines in the humanities and sciences.

Journals: *CLCWeb: Comparative Literature and Culture*; *Data Curation Profiles Directory*; *Education and Culture: The Journal of the John Dewey Society*; *First Opinions—Second Reactions*; *Global Business Languages*; *The Interdisciplinary Journal of Problem Based Learning*; *The Jewish Role in American Life: An Annual Review*; *Journal of Aviation Technology and Engineering*; *Journal of Human Performance in Extreme Environments*; *Journal of Pre-College Engineering Education Research*; *Journal of Problem Solving*; *Phillip Roth Studies*; *Shofar: An Interdisciplinary Journal of Jewish Studies*; *Studies in Jewish Civilization*

Special series: Central European Studies; Comparative Cultural Studies; New Directions in the Human-Animal Bond; Purdue Studies in Romance Literatures; Shofar Supplements in Jewish Studies; Purdue Information Literacy Handbooks; Charleston Insights in Library, Archival, and Information Sciences

RAND Corporation

Street Address:
1776 Main Street
Santa Monica, CA 90407

Mailing Address:
PO Box 2138
Santa Monica, CA 90407-2138

Phone: 310.393.0411
Fax: 310.451.7026

Customer Service:
Phone: 877.584.8642
Fax: 412.802.4981
Email: order@rand.org

Website and Social Media:
Website: www.rand.org/publications
Facebook: www.facebook.com/RANDCorporation
Twitter: RANDCorporation

US Distributor:
National Book Network
Phone: 800.462.6420 or 717.794.3800
Fax: 800.338.4550

UK/European Distributor:
NBN International

Staff
Director: Jane Ryan (ext. 7260; email: ryan@rand.org)
Manager, Production, Printing, and Distribution: Paul Murphy (ext. 7806;
  email: murphy@rand.org)
Business Manager: Russell Nakamura (ext. 6722; email: nakamura@rand.org)
Managing Editor: Steve Kistler (ext. 6318; email: skistler@rand.org)
Computing Manager: Edward Finkelstein (ext. 7417; email: edwardf@rand.org)

Associate Member
Established: 1948
Title output 2011: 172
Titles currently in print: 19,672

Admitted to AAUP: 2000
Title output 2012: 175
Journals published: 2

Editorial Program
For more than 65 years, decision-makers in the public and private sectors have turned to the RAND Corporation for objective analysis and effective solutions that address the challenges facing the nation and the world. Publication topics include policy issues such as education; environment and energy; health care; immigration, labor, and population; international affairs; national security; public safety and justice; science and technology; and terrorism and homeland security. Unsolicited manuscripts are not accepted.
Journal: *RAND Health Quarterly; RAND Journal of Economics*

RIT Cary Graphic Arts Press/RIT Press

90 Lomb Memorial Drive
Rochester, NY 14623-5604

Orders:
Phone: 585.475.6766

Phone: 585.475.6766
Fax: 585.475.4090
Email: mqcwml@rit.edu, mdwml@rit.edu

Website and Social Media:
Website: carypress.rit.edu
Facebook: www.facebook.com/pages/RIT-Cary-Graphic-Arts-Press/172326337130

Staff
Director: David Pankow (585.475.2408; email: dppwml@rit.edu)
Managing Editor: Molly Q. Cort (585.475.4088; email: mqcwml@rit.edu)
Business Manager: Laura DiPonzio Heise (585.475.5819; email: lmdwml@rit.edu)
Design & Marketing Specialist: Marnie Soom (585.475.4089; email: mxswml@rit.edu)

Introductory Member
Established: 2001
Title output: 2011: 8
Titles currently in print: 60

Admitted to AAUP: 2009
Title output: 2012: NR

Editorial Program
The RIT Cary Graphic Arts Press initially focused on publishing titles that documented graphic communication processes, printing history, and bookmaking. As the Press's editorial policies have evolved, we have broadened our reach to include content that supports the academic disciplines offered at Rochester Institute of Technology, our host institution, including–but not limited to—business, computer science, applied science and technology, graphic arts, deaf studies, and liberal arts. In 2007, a new imprint, RIT Press, was established for all titles that are not related to graphic arts.

Our objective is to develop a well-rounded university press that maintains a strong commitment to scholarship, while maintaining a high standard of content and design. We utilize traditional as well as innovative digital technologies to reach niche academic markets in the most economical and efficient way possible.

Special series: Comics Monograph Series; Digital Innovation Series; First Person Corporate History; Graphic Design Archives Chapbook; Philosophy and Ethics; Printing Industry Center Series

The University of Rochester Press

668 Mount Hope Avenue
Rochester NY 14620-2731

Phone: 585.275.0419
Fax: 585.271.8778

Orders:
Phone: 585.275.0419
Email: boydell@boydellusa.net

Website and Social Media:
Website: www.urpress.com
Facebook: www.facebook.com/boydellandbrewerfans
Twitter: boydellbrewer

UK Representative:
Boydell & Brewer, Ltd.

Canadian Representative:
Scholarly Book Services

Staff

Editorial Director: Sonia Kane (585.273.5778; email: sonia.kane@rochester.edu)
Managing Editor/Manuscript Editorial: Ryan Peterson (585.273.4429; email: peterson@boydellusa.net)
Production Manager: Sue Smith (585.273.2817; email: smith@boydellusa.net)
Production Editor: Tracey Engel (585.273.2818; email: engel@boydellusa.net)
Sales and Marketing: Kristin Stine (585.273.5779; email: stine@boydellusa.net)
Web Manager: Joan Simpson (585.273.5709; email: simpson@boydellusa.net)
Customer Service: Jennifer Shannon (585.273.2959; email: shannon@boydellusa.net)
Accounts Manager: Eloise Puls (585.273.5777; email: puls@boydellusa.net)

Full Member

Established: 1989

Admitted to AAUP: 2008 (as introductory member)
Admitted to AAUP as full member: 2011

Title output 2011: 22
Titles currently in print: 555

Title output 2012: 26

Editorial Program

Musicology and music theory; ethnomusicology; African and diaspora studies with an emphasis on political and economic history; the history of medicine in the US and internationally; early modern European history; Central and Eastern European studies; gender and race in nineteenth and twentieth century America; political theory and philosophy; regional trade titles emphasizing the history of Western New York State.

Special series: Changing Perspectives on Early Modern Europe; Eastman Studies in Music; Eastman/Rochester Studies in Ethnomusicology; North American Kant Society Publications; Race and Gender in American History; Rochester Studies in African History and the Diaspora; Rochester Studies in Central Europe; Rochester Studies in Medical History

The Rockefeller University Press

1114 First Avenue, 3rd Floor
New York, NY 10065-8325

Phone: 212.327.7938
Fax: 212.327.8587
Email: (user I.D.)@rockefeller.edu

Website and Social Media:
Websites: www.rupress.org, jcb.rupress.org, jem.rupress.org, jgp.rupress.org
Blogs: news.rupress.org, jcb-biowrites.rupress.org
Facebook: www.facebook.com/JCellBiol, www.facebook.com/JExpMed, www.facebook.com/JGenPhysiol
Twitter: JCellBiol, JExpMed, JGenPhysiol

Staff

Executive Director: Mike Rossner (212.327.8881; email: rossner)
  Assistant to the Executive Director: JoAnn Greene (212.327.8025; email: greenej)
Manuscript Editorial: Liz Williams, Executive Editor, *The Journal of Cell Biology* (212.327.8011; email: lwilliams); Marlowe Tessmer, Senior Editor, The Journal of Experimental Medicine (212.327.8393; email: mtessmer); Liz Adler, Executive Editor, *The Journal of General Physiology* (212.327.8651; email: eadler)
Advertising: Lorna Petersen, Sales Director (212.327.8880; email: petersl)
Journals: Robert O'Donnell, Electronic Publishing and Production Director (212.327.8545; email: odonner)
Business: Raymond T. Fastiggi, Finance Director (212.327.8567; email: fastigg)
  Business Development Director: Gregory Malar (212.327.7948; email: malarg)

Full Member

Established: 1958
Title output 2011: 0
Titles currently in print: 40

Admitted to AAUP: 1982
Title output 2012: 1
Journals published: 3

Editorial Program

The Rockefeller University Press publishes three biomedical research journals. *The Journal of Cell Biology* provides a rigorous forum for publication of topics across the complete spectrum of cell biology. *The Journal of Experimental Medicine* publishes seminal work in all areas of experimental medicine, with a current emphasis on immunological, stem cell, and disease research. Articles in *The Journal of General Physiology* elucidate important biological, chemical, or physical mechanisms of broad physiological significance.

Russell Sage Foundation

112 East 64th Street
New York, NY 10065

Phone: 212.750.6000
Fax: 212.371.4761
Email: pubs@rsage.org
Indiv: firstname@rsage.org

Website and Social Media:
Website: www.russellsage.org
Facebook: www.facebook.com/pages/New-York-NY/Russell-Sage-Foundation/63515091250
Twitter: RussellSageFdn

UK/European Representative:
University Presses Marketing

Orders:
Russell Sage Foundation
CUP Services
750 Cascadilla St.
PO Box 6525
Ithaca, NY 14851
Phone: 800.666.2211; 607.277.2211
Fax: 800.688.2877; 607.277.6292

Staff
Director of Publications: Suzanne Nichols (212.750.6026)
Publications Assistant: Parvoneh Shirgir (212.750.6038)
Production Editor: April Rondeau (212.750.6034)
Director of Public Relations: David A. Haproff (212.750.6037)
Book Marketing Manager: Stephen Sachs (212.750.6021)
Exhibits/Permissions: Parvoneh Shirgir (212.750.6038)
Foundation President: Eric Wanner

Associate Member
Established: 1907
Title output 2011: 24
Titles currently in print: 700

Admitted to AAUP: 1989
Title output 2012: 33

Editorial Program
Scholarly books on current research and policy issues in the social sciences. Recent research programs sponsored by the Russell Sage Foundation include the future of work, sustainable employment, current US immigration, the analysis of the 2010 US Census, the social psychology of cultural contact, the role of trust in shaping social relations, the social dimensions of inequality, carework, and behavioral economics.
Copublishing programs: limited joint publications with Princeton University Press

Rutgers University Press

106 Somerset Street, 3rd Floor
New Brunswick, NJ 08901

Phone: 848.445.7762
Fax: 732.445.7039
Email: (user I.D.)@rutgers.edu

Warehouse, Fulfillment, & Cust. Service:
c/o Longleaf Services, Inc.
PO Box 8895
Chapel Hill, NC 27515-8895
Phone: 800.848.6224
Fax: 800.272.6817
Email: longleaf@unc.edu

Website and Social Media:
Website: rutgerspress.rutgers.edu
Facebook: www.facebook.com/pages/Rutgers-University-Press/212072346925

UK/European Representative:
Eurospan

Canadian Representative:
Scholarly Book Services

Staff

Director: Marlie Wasserman (848.445.7784; email: marlie)
  Assistant to the Director/Permissions and Subsidiary Rights Manager/E-book Coordinator: Allyson Fields (848.445.7785; email: amfields)
Acquisitions Editorial: Leslie Mitchner, Associate Director and Editor-in-Chief (humanities, American studies, Latino studies, and film) (848.445.7787; email: lmitch)
  Editors: Marlie Wasserman (anthropology and human rights) (848.445.7784; email: marlie); Peter Mickulas (health, sociology, environment, and criminology) (848.445.7752; email: mickulas)
  Editorial Associate: Katie Keeran (Asian American studies, higher education, literary studies) (848.445.7786; email: ckeeran)
  Editorial Assistant: Lisa Boyajian (848.445.7791; email: lboyajian@rutgerspress.rutgers.edu)
Manuscript Editorial and Production: Marilyn Campbell, PrePress Director (848.445.7756; email: marilync)
  Production Manager: Anne Hegeman (848.445.7761; email: hegeman)
  Production Coordinator: Bryce Schimanski (848.445.7764; email: brycesch)
  Reprints Manager: Suzanne Kellam (848.445.7755; email: skellam)
Marketing: Elizabeth Scarpelli, Associate Director and Sales and Marketing Director (848.445.7781; email: escarpel)
  Advertising and Direct Marketing Manager: Jeanne Ambrosio (848.445.7782; email: ja604)
  Webmaster and E-Marketing Manager: Brice Hammack (848.445.7765; email: bhammack)
  Marketing and Publicity Director: Lisa Fortunato (848.445.7775; email: lisafort)
Business: David Flum, Manager (848.445.7763; email: dflum)
  Customer Service Liaison: Penny Burke (848.445.7788; email: pborden)

Full Member

Established: 1936
Title output 2011: 90
Titles currently in print: 2,300

Admitted to AAUP: 1937
Title output 2012: 88

Editorial Program

American Literatures Initiative; American studies; anthropology; Asian American studies; African American studies and literature; environmental studies; film and media; history of science/technology; human rights; Jewish studies; public policy; regional studies; sociology; women's studies; Latino Studies.

Special series: Comics Culture; Critical Issues in Crime and Society; Critical Issues in Health and Medicine; Critical Issues in Sport and Society; Families in Focus; Genocide, Political Violence, Human Rights; Jewish Cultures of the World; Key Words in Jewish Studies; New Directions in International Studies; Latinidad: Transnational Cultures in the United States; Rivergate Regionals; Rutgers Series in Childhood Studies; Techniques of the Moving Image

Saint Joseph's University Press

5600 City Avenue
Philadelphia, PA 19131-1395

Phone: 610.660.3402
Fax: 610.660.3412
Email: sjupress@sju.edu
Indiv.: (user I.D.)@sju.edu

Orders:
Phone: 610.660.3402
Email: orders@sjupress

Website and Social Media:
Website: www.sjupress.com

Staff

Director: Carmen Robert Croce (610.660.3402; email: ccroce)
Editorial Director: Joseph F. Chorpenning (610.660.1214; email: jchorpen)

Introductory Member

Established: 1997
Title output 2011: 5
Titles currently in print: 55

Admitted to AAUP: 2011
Title output 2012: 5

Editorial Program

Jesuit studies (with an emphasis on history and the visual arts), regional studies (Philadelphia and environs)
Special series: Early Modern Catholicism and the Visual Arts (1500-French Revolution)

Society of Biblical Literature

The Luce Center
825 Houston Mill Road, Suite 350
Atlanta, GA 30329

Phone: 404.727.3100
Fax: 404.727.3101
Email: sblexec@sbl-site.org
Indiv: firstname.lastname@sbl-site.org

Orders:
Phone: 877.725.3334
Fax: 802.864.7626

Journal Subscriptions and Membership:
Phone: 866.727.9955
Fax: 404.727.2419

Website and Social Media:
Website: www.sbl-site.org
Facebook: www.facebook.com/group.php?gid=49602519254

Staff

Executive Director: John F. Kutsko (404.727.3038)
Editorial Director: Bob Buller (970.669.9900)
Managing Editor: Leigh Andersen (404.727.2327)
Acquisitions Editor: Billie Jean Collins (404.727.0807)
Publishing Marketing Manager: Kathie Klein (404.727.2325)
Director of Finance and Administration: Susan Madara (404.727.3103)
Director of Administrative and Technology Services: Missy Colee (404.727.3124)
Manager of Technology: Chris O'Connor (404.727.2187)
Manager of Web Communications: Sharon Johnson (404.727.3102)
Development Officer: Sandra Stewart-Kruger (404.727.9484)
Manager of Programs: Charles Haws (404.727.3095)
Director of Global Conferences: Trista Krock (404.727.3137)
Manager of Membership & Subscriptions: Navar Steed (404.727.9494)
Public Initiatives Coordinator: Moira Bucciarelli (404.727.9484)

Associate Member

Established: 1880
Title output 2011: 32
Titles currently in print: 752

Admitted to AAUP: 2003
Title output 2012: 30
Journals published: 2

Editorial Program

The SBL publishes works in biblical and religious studies. Monographic publications include major reference works; commentaries; text editions and translations; collections of essays; doctoral dissertations; and tools for teaching and research fields; archaeological, sociological, and historical studies; volumes that use archaeological and historical data to illuminate Israelite religion or the culture of biblical peoples; scholarly works on the history, culture, and literature of early Judaism; scholarly works on various aspects of the Masorah; scholarly congress proceedings; critical texts of the Greek Fathers including evaluations of data; philological tools; studies employing the methods and perspectives of linguistics, folklore studies, literary criticism, structuralism, social anthropology, and postmodern studies; studies of the Septuagint including textual criticism, manuscript witnesses and other versions, as well as its literature, historical milieu, and thought; studies related to the Jewish apocrypha and pseudepigrapha of the Hellenistic period, and the subsequent development of this literature in

Judaism and early Christianity; studies in biblical literature and/or its cultural environment; text-critical works related to Hebrew Bible/Old Testament and New Testament including investigations of methodology, studies of individual manuscripts, critical texts of a selected book or passage, or examination of more general textual themes; translations of ancient Near Eastern texts; translations of ancient texts from the Greco.Roman world.

SBL is the exclusive North American distributor for Sheffield Phoenix Press (UK), and the sole producer and distributor of volumes in the Brown Judaic Studies series (Brown University). SBL also distributes the Manuscripts of the Greek New Testament Series by Reuben Swanson.

Journals: *Journal of Biblical Literature; Review of Biblical Literature*

Special series: Ancient Israel and Its Literature; Archaeology and Biblical Studies; Biblical Encyclopedia Translations; Biblical Scholarship in North America; Commentary on the Septuagint; Early Christianity and Its Literature; Early Judaism and Its Literature; Global Perspectives on Biblical Scholarship; History of Biblical Studies; Masoretic Studies; The New Testament in the Greek Fathers; Resources for Biblical Study; Semeia Studies; Septuagint and Cognate Studies; Studia Philonica Annual and Monographs; Text-Critical Studies; Wisdom Literature from the Ancient World; Writings from the Ancient World; Writings from the Ancient World Supplements; Writings from the Greco-Roman World; Writings from the Greco-Roman World Supplements

Joint imprints and co-publishing programs: SBL Handbook of Style for Ancient Near Eastern, Biblical, and Early Christian Studies with Hendrickson Publishers; HarperCollins Study Bible (NRSV), HarperCollins Bible Dictionary, Revised Edition, HarperCollins Bible Commentary, Revised Edition, and Harper's Bible Pronunciation Guide with HarperCollins; Hardback editions with Brill Academic Publishers of Leiden, The Netherlands; The Greek New Testament: SBL Edition with Logos Bible Software.

Online books: SBL, along with six participating partners, provides PDF files of academic books for free download to individuals and libraries in underresourced areas of the globe. Through software that recognizes the IP address of the web visitor, persons from countries whose GDP is considerably less than the average GDP of the US and the EU are given access to the files. The program, as of late 2012, includes almost 350 titles.

EBooks: SBL has entered the e-book market and partners with Bibliovault to make titles available in multiple formats.

The University of South Carolina Press

1600 Hampton Street
5th Floor
Columbia, SC 29208-3400

Phone: 803.777.5243
Fax: 803.777.0160
Email: (user I.D.)@sc.edu

Website and Social Media:
Website: www.sc.edu/uscpress
Facebook: www.facebook.com/USC.Press

Business Office and Warehouse:
718 Devine Street
Columbia, SC 29208-0001
Phone: 800.768.2500
Fax: 800.868.0740
Email: (user I.D.)@sc.edu

UK/European Distributor:
Eurospan

Canadian Distributor:
Scholarly Book Services

Staff

Director: Jonathan Haupt (803.777.2243; email: jhaupt)
  Assistant Director for Operations: Linda Haines Fogle (803.777.4848; email: lfogle)
  Assistant to the Director: Vicki Bates (803.777.5245; email: batesvc)
Acquisitions Editors: Linda Haines Fogle (regional, trade) (803.777.4848; email: lfogle);
  Alexander Moore (African American studies, history, Southern studies) (803.777.8070;
  email: alexm); Jim Denton (literature, religious studies, rhetoric/communication, social
  work) (803.777.4859; email: denton)
Manuscript Editorial: Bill Adams, Managing Editor (803.777.5075; email: adamswb)
  Editor: Karen Rood (803.777.5877; email: roodk)
  Editorial Assistant: Elizabeth Jones (803.777.9055; email: jonesem6)
Design and Production: Pat Callahan, Design and Production Manager (803.777.2449;
  email: mpcallah)
  Book Designer: Brandi Lariscy-Avant (803.777.9056; email: lariscyb)
  Design and Production Assistant: Ashley Mathias (803.777.2238; email: samathi)
Marketing: TBA, Director
  Promotions Manager: Carolyn Martin (803.777.5029; email: clmartin)
  Advertising and Direct Mail Manager: Lynne Parker (803.777.5231; email: parkerll)
Business/Warehouse: Vicki Sewell, Acting Business Manager and Permissions (803.777.7754;
  email: sewellv)
  Customer Service Representative: Libby Mack (803.777.1774; email: lmack)
  Warehouse Assistant: Eddie Hill (803.777.0184; email: jehill)

Full Member

Established: 1944
Title output 2011: 70
Titles currently in print: 1,050

Admitted to AAUP: 1948
Title output 2012: 62

Editorial Program

Scholarly works, mainly in the humanities and social sciences, and general interest titles,
particularly those of importance to the state and region. Subjects include African American
studies; history, especially American history, military history, maritime history, and South-

ern history; literature and literary studies; religious studies, including comparative religion; Southern studies; rhetoric/communication; and social work.

Special series, joint imprints, and/or copublishing programs: AccessAble Books; The Belle W. Baruch Library in Marine Science; The Carolina Lowcountry and the Atlantic World; Chief Justiceships of the United States Supreme Court; Historians in Conversation; Joseph M. Bruccoli Great War Series; The Papers of John C. Calhoun; The Papers of Henry Laurens; The Papers of Howard Thurman; Social Problems and Social Issues; South Carolina Encyclopedia Guides; South Carolina Poetry Initiative Book Prize; Southern Classics; Southern Revivals; Studies in Comparative Religion; Studies in Maritime History; Studies in Rhetoric / Communication; Studies on Personalities of the New Testament; Studies on Personalities of the Old Testament; Understanding Contemporary American Literature; Understanding Contemporary British Literature; Understanding Modern European and Latin American Literature; Women's Diaries and Letters of the South; Young Palmetto Books

Southern Illinois University Press

1915 University Press Drive
SIUC Mail Code 6806
Carbondale, IL 62901-6806

Phone: 618.453.2281
Fax: 618.453.1221
Email: (user I.D.)@siu.edu

Website and Social Media:
Website: www.siupress.com
Facebook: www.facebook.com/siupress
Twitter: SIUPress

Orders:
Southern Illinois University Press
c/o Chicago Distribution Center
11030 South Langley Avenue
Chicago, IL 60628-3830
Phone: 800.621.2736
Fax: 800.621.8476
Email: custserv@press.uchicago.edu
EDI; PUBNET at 202-5280

UK/European Distributor:
Eurospan

Canadian Representative:
Scholarly Book Services

Staff

Interim Director: Barb Martin (618.453.6614; email: bbmartin)

Rights and Permissions: Angela Moore-Swafford (618.453.6617; email: angmoore) (Rights email: rights)

Acquisitions Editorial: Karl Kageff, Editor-in-Chief (Beat studies, regional studies, rhetoric and composition) (618.453.6629; email: kageff)

  Executive Editor: Sylvia Frank Rodrigue (Civil War, Reconstruction) (508.297.2162; email: sylvia@sylverlining.com)

  Acquisitions Editor: Kristine Priddy (composition, theater and film) (618.453.6631; email: mkpriddy)

Editorial, Design, and Production: Barb Martin, EDP Manager (618.453.6614; email: bbmartin)

  Project Editor: Wayne Larsen (618.453.6628; email: wlarsen)

Book Designer: Mary Rohrer (618.453.6612; email: mrohrer)
Production Assistant: Lola Starck (618.453.6635; email: lolas)
IT Specialist: Matt MacCrimmon (618.453.6615; email: macc)
Marketing and Sales Manager: Amy Etcheson (618.453.6623; email: aetcheson)
Marketing Associates: Bridget Brown (618.453.6633; email: bcbrown); Hannah New (618.453.6634; email: hknew)
Accounts Payable: Dawn Vagner (618.453.3786; email: dvagner)

Full Member
Established: 1956
Title output 2011: 33
Titles currently in print: 1,200

Admitted to AAUP: 1980
Title output 2012: 36

Editorial Program
Scholarly books, primarily in the humanities and social sciences. Particular strengths are film studies; theatre and stagecraft; regional and Civil War history, rhetoric, and composition; Beat studies; philosophy; aviation; contemporary poetry. Submissions in fiction and festschriften are not invited.

Special series: Aviation Management; Civil War Campaigns in the Heartland; The Collected Works of John Dewey; The Concise Lincoln Library; The Crab Orchard Series in Poetry; The Holmes-Johnson Series in Criminology; The Illustrated Flora of Illinois; Landmarks in Rhetoric and Public Address; The Papers of Ulysses S. Grant; Shawnee Classics; Shawnee Books; Studies in Rhetorics and Feminisms; Studies in Writing and Rhetoric; Theater in the Americas

Southern Methodist University Press

Street Address:
314 Fondren Library West
6404 Hilltop Lane
Dallas, TX 75275-0415

Mailing Address:
PO Box 750415
Dallas, TX 75275-0415

Phone: 214.768.1432
Fax: 214.768.1428

Orders:
Phone: 800.826.8911

Website and Social Media:
Website: www.tamu.edu/upress/smu/smugen.html

Staff
TBA

Full Member
Established: 1937
Titles currently in print: 226

Admitted to AAUP: 1946

Editorial Program
Creative nonfiction; literary fiction; medical humanities; Southwestern studies; and sport. The press is not currently acquiring new books.

Special series: Medical Humanities; Sport in American Life

Stanford University Press

1450 Page Mill Road
Palo Alto, CA 94304-1124

Phone: 650.723.9434
Fax: 650.725.3457
Email: (user I.D.)@stanford.edu

Orders:
Chicago Distribution Center
11030 South Langley Avenue
Chicago, IL 60628
Phone: 800.621.2736; 773.702.7000
Fax: (800) 621-8476; 773.702.7212
Orders@press.uchicago.edu

Website and Social Media:
Website: www.sup.org
Blog: www.sup.org/blog
Facebook: www.sup.org/facebook
Twitter: stanfordpress

European Representative:
Eurospan

Canadian Representative:
Lexa Publishers' Representatives

Staff

Director: Alan Harvey (650.723.6375; email: aharvey)

Rights, Permissions, and Contracts: Ariane de Pree-Kajfez, Senior Rights Manager (650.725.0815; email: arianep)

Acquisitions: Kate Wahl, Publishing Director and Editor-in-Chief (sociology, Middle East studies) (650.723.3077; email: kwahl)

Executive Editor: Geoffrey Burn (security studies, international relations, politics) (650.736.1942; email: grhburn)

Director of Scholarly Publishing: Norris Pope (history, Jewish studies, Latin American studies) (650.725.0827; email: npope)

Senior Editors: Emily-Jane Cohen, (literature, philosophy, religion) (650.725.7717; email: beatrice); Margo Beth Fleming (economics, organizational studies) (650.724.7079; email: mbfleming)

Acquisitions Editors: Stacy Wagner (Asian studies, political science) (650.725.0845; email: swagner); Michelle Lipinski (anthropology, Asian studies, law) (650.736.4641; email: mlipinsk)

Editorial Assistants: Jessica Walsh (650.736.0924; email: jawalsh); Emma Harper (650.721.5616; email: esharper); Frances Malcolm (650.724.7080; email: fmalcolm)

Editorial, Design, and Production: Patricia Myers, EDP Director (650.724.5365; email: pmyers)

Senior Production Editor: Judith Hibbard (650.736.0719; email: jhibbard)

Production Editors: Mariana Raykov (650.725.0835; email: mraykov); John Feneron (650.725.0828; email: johnf); Emily Smith (650.736.0686; email: emilys); Carolyn Brown (650.724.9990; email: carolynb)

Art Director: Rob Ehle (650.723.1132; email: ehle)
Designer: Bruce Lundquist (650.723.6808; email: brucel)
Production Manager: Harold Moorehead (650.725.0836; email: hmoorehead)
Production Coordinator: Mike Sagara (650.725.0839; email: msagara)
Sales and Marketing: David Jackson, Sales and Marketing Director (650.736.1782; email: david.jackson)
Publicity: Mary Kate Maco, Publicity Manager (650.724.4211; email: mmaco)
Advertising and Direct Mail Coordinator: Ysabel Moran (650.725.0823; email: ysabelm)
Exhibits Manager: Christie Cochrell (650.725.0820; email: cochrell)
Marketing Assistant: Sarah Pilat (650.736.1781; email: spilat)
Business: Jean Kim, Director of Finance and Operations (650.725.0838; email: jean.h.kim)
Royalties/Accounts Receivable: Su-Mei Lee (650.725.0837; email: sumeilee)
Accounts Payable: Aurelia Hernandez (650.724.8697; email: aureliah)
Systems: Chris Cosner, IT Manager (650.724.7276; email: ccosner)
Desktop Support Administrator: Meide Guo (650.723.9598; email: meideguo)

Full Member

Established: 1925

Admitted to AAUP: 1937

Title output 2011: 159

Title output 2012: 156

Titles currently in print: 2,800

Editorial Program

Scholarly titles and textbooks in philosophy, history, literature, religion, sociology, anthropology, and political science; and on Asia, Latin America, and the Western United States. Scholarly titles, textbooks, and professional titles in business, economics, security studies, law, policy, and education.

Special series: The Amherst Series in Law, Jurisprudence, and Social Thought; Asian America; Asian Security; Cold War International History Project; Comparative Studies in History, Institutions, and Public Policy; The Complete Works of Friedrich Nietzsche; Contemporary Issues in Asia and the Pacific; Critical Perspectives on Crime and Law; The Cultural Lives of Law; Cultural Memory in the Present; Cultural Sitings; Global Competition Law and Economics; High Reliability and Crisis Management; Innovation and Technology in the World Economy; Jurists: Profiles in Legal Theory; Law, Politics, and the Media; Law, Society, and Culture in China; Meridian: Crossing Aesthetics; Post*45; Social Science History; Stanford Business Classics; Stanford Nuclear Age Series; Stanford Series in Comparative race and Ethnicity; Stanford Studies in Human Rights; Stanford Studies in Jewish History and Culture; Stanford Studies in Middle Eastern and Islamic Societies and Cultures; Studies in Asian Security; Studies in Social Inequality; Studies in the Modern Presidency; Studies of the East Asian Institute; Studies of the Walter H. Shorenstein Asia-Pacific Research Center; Verbal Art: Studies in Poetics

Special imprints: Stanford Briefs; Stanford Business Books; Stanford Law Books, Stanford Politics and Policy; Stanford Social Sciences; Stanford Economics and Finance; Stanford Security Studies; Stanford General Books

Copublishing arrangements: The Woodrow Wilson Center; and the East-West Center

State University of New York Press

22 Corporate Woods Boulevard, 3rd Floor
Albany, NY 12211-2504

Phone: 518.472.5000
Fax: 518.472.5038
E-mail: info@sunypress.edu
Indiv: firstname.lastname@sunypress.edu

Website and Social Media:
Website: www.sunypress.edu
Facebook: www.facebook.com/pages/
   SUNY-Press/112308762113504

UK Representative:
Andrew Gilman
University Presses Marketing

Canadian Representative:
Lexa Publishers' Representatives

Customer Service:
SUNY Press
PO Box 960
Herndon, VA 20172-0960
Phone: 703.661.1575
Toll free: 877.204.6073 (US only)
Fax: 703.996.1010
Toll free: 877.204.6074 (US only)
Email: suny@presswarehouse.com

UK/European Distributor:
NBN International

Staff
Co-Directors: Donna Dixon (518.641.0651); James Peltz (518.641.0668)
   Assistant to the Co-Directors: Janice Vunk (518.641.0674)
   Receptionist: Diana Altobello (518.472.5000)
Acquisitions Editorial:
   Co-Director: James Peltz (518.641.0668) (Excelsior Editions, film studies, Italian Ameri-
   can studies, Jewish studies)
   Senior Acquisitions Editors: Nancy Ellegate (518.641.0679) (Asian studies, religious stud-
   ies, transpersonal psychology); Michael Rinella (518.641.0664) (African American studies,
   environmental studies, political science)
   Acquisitions Editors: Beth Bouloukos (518.641.0666) (education, Hispanic studies,
   women's and gender studies); Andrew Kenyon (518.641.0661) (philosophy)
   Assistant Acquisitions Editor: Amanda Lanne (518.641.0662) (New York State studies,
   native and indigenous studies)
   Editorial Assistants: Rafael Chaiken (518.641-0681); Jen Stelling (518.641.0647)
Production:
   Co-Director: Donna Dixon (518.641.0651) (journals)
   Senior Production Editors: Diane Ganeles (518.641.0678); Laurie Searl (518.641.0671);
   Eileen Nizer (518.641.0665)
   Senior Journals and Accelerated Publishing Editor: Ryan Morris (518.641.0667)
   Production Assistant: Emily Keneston (518.641.0669)
Marketing and Publicity:
   Director of Marketing and Publicity: Fran Keneston (518.641.0660)
   Executive Promotions Manager: Anne Valentine (518.641.0673)
   Senior Promotions Manager: Michael Campochiaro (518.641.0680)
   Exhibits and Awards Manager: Michelle Alamillo (518.641.0677)

Promotions Manager: Kate McDonnell (518.641.0663)
Revenue and Business Operations:
  Associate Director-Revenue and Business Operations: Dan Flynn (518.641.0676)
  Accounting Manager: Sharla Clute (518.641.0653)
  Sales Assistant: Renee Jones (518.641.0659)
  Network Administrator: Bob Sajeski (518.641.0670)
  Digital Programs Manager: Greg Smith (518.641.0672)

Full Member

Established: 1966

Title output 2011: 135

Titles currently in print: 5,135

Admitted to AAUP: 1970

Title output 2012: 143

Journals published: 7

Editorial Program

Scholarly titles and serious works of general interest in many areas of the humanities and the social sciences, with special interest in African American studies; Asian studies; education; gender studies; Hispanic studies; native and indigenous studies; philosophy; political science; psychology; queer studies; religious studies; transpersonal psychology; and women's and gender studies.

  SUNY Press distributes books from the Albany Institute of History and Art, Codhill Press, Global Academic Publishing, Hudson River Valley National Heritage Area, Mount Ida Press, Muswell Hill Press, New Netherland Institute, Parks & Trails New York, Rockefeller Institute Press, Samuel Dorsky Museum and the Uncrowned Queens Institute.

Journals: *AUDEM*; *Binghamton Journal of Philosophy*; *The Evolutionary Review*; *International Journal of Servant-Leadership*; *Mediaevalia*; *Palimpsest*; *philoSOPHIA*

Imprints: Excelsior Editions

Syracuse University Press

621 Skytop Road, Suite 110
Syracuse, NY 13244-5290

Phone: 315.443.5534
Fax: 315.443.5545
Email: (user I.D.)@syr.edu

Website and Social Media:
Website: syracuseuniversitypress.syr.edu
Blog: syracusepress.wordpress.com/
Facebook: www.facebook.com/pages/
  Syracuse-University-Press/224301261901
Twitter: twitter.com/supress

Warehouse:
Maple Press Company
Lebanon Distribution Center
704 Legionnaire Drive
Fredericksburg, PA 17026

Orders:
Longleaf Services
Phone: 800.848.6224
Fax: 800.272.6817

Canadian Distributor:
Scholarly Book Services, Inc.

UK Distributor:
Eurospan

Staff

Director: Alice R. Pfeiffer (315.443.5535; email: arpfeiff)
  Office Coordinator: Erica Sheftic (315.443.5541; email: esheftic)

Acquisitions Editorial: Suzanne E. Guiod, Editor-in-Chief (315.443.5539; email: seguiod)
  Acquisitions Editors: Jennika Baines (315.443.5647; email: jsbaines); Deanna McCay (315.443.5543; email dhmccay)
  Editorial Assistant: Kelly Balenske (315.443.5541; email: klbalens)
Editorial and Production Manager: Kay Steinmetz (315.443.9155; email: kasteinm)
  Senior Designers: Victoria Lane (315.443.5540; email: vmlane); Fred Wellner (315.443.5540; email: fawellne)
  Editorial & Production Assistant: Marcia Hough (315.443.5542; email: mshough)
Marketing: Mona Hamlin, Marketing Analyst (315.443.5547; email: mhamlin)
  Design Specialist: Lynn Hoppel (315.443.1975; email: lphoppel)
  Marketing Coordinator: Lisa Kuerbis (315.443.5546; email: lkuerbis)
Business: Karen Lockwood, Senior Business Manager (315.443.5536; email: kflockwo)
  Customer Service Liaison: Lori Lazipone (315.443.5538; email: ljlazipo)

Full Member

Established: 1943
Title output 2011: 43
Titles currently in print: 1,576

Admitted to AAUP: 1946
Title output 2012: 47

Editorial Program

Scholarly books and works of general interest in the areas of Middle East, Irish, Jewish, New York State, women's, Native American, ethnic, and disability studies; religion; television; popular culture; sports history; journalism; human and urban geography; politics; peace and conflict resolution; and selected fiction.

The Press distributes books bearing the imprints of Adirondack Museum; Moshe Dayan Center for Middle Eastern and African Studies (Tel-Aviv University); New Netherlands Project; Jusoor; National Library of Ireland; Arlen House; Dedalus Press; Blackhall Publishing; NUI Galway, Women's Studies Centre; Litteraria Pragensia; Ethnic Heritage Studies Center of Utica College; New City Community Press; Syracuse University In Florence; Graduate School Press; Syracuse University; Point of Contact; Syracuse University; and the Pucker Gallery, Boston.

Special series, joint imprints, and/or copublishing programs: The Adirondack Museum; The Albert Schweitzer Library; America in the Twentieth Century; Arab-American Writing; Contemporary Issues in the Middle East; Critical Perspectives on Disability; Gender, Culture, and Politics in the Middle East; Gender and Globalization; Irish Studies; Iroquois and Their Neighbors; Judaic Traditions in Literature, Music, and Art; Library of Modern Jewish Literature; The Martin Buber Library; Medieval Studies; Middle East Beyond Dominant Paradigms; Middle East Literature in Translation; Modern Intellectual and Political History of the Middle East; Modern Jewish History; Mohamad El-Hindi Books on Arab Culture and Islamic Civilization; New York State Studies; Religion and Politics; Religion, Theology and the Holocaust; Space, Place, and Society; Sports and Entertainment; Syracuse Studies in Peace and Conflict Resolution; Television and Popular Culture; Women in Religion; Writing American Women

Teachers College Press

1234 Amsterdam Avenue
New York, NY 10027-6696

Phone: 212.678.3929
Fax: 212.678.4149
Email: (user I.D.)@tc.edu
(unless otherwise indicated)

Orders:
Teachers College Press
PO Box 20
Williston, VT 05495-0020
Phone: 800.575.6560
Fax: 802.864.7626

Website and Social Media:
Website: www.tcpress.com
Facebook: www.facebook.com/TCPress
Twitter: TCPress

European Representative:
Eurospan

Canadian Representative:
University of Toronto Press

Staff

Director: Carole Pogrebin Saltz (212.678.3927; email: saltz)
  Assistant to the Director: Emily Renwick (212.678.3965; email: ballengee)
  Rights and Permissions Manager/Special Sales Coordinator: Libby Powell (212.678.3827; email: lpowell)
Acquisitions Editorial: Brian Ellerbeck, Executive Acquisitions Editor (administration, school change, leadership, policy, special and gifted education, multicultural education, teacher research, curriculum studies) (212.678.3908; email: ellerbeck)
  Senior Acquisitions Editor: Marie Ellen Larcada (early childhood education, sociology, educational research, school reform, higher education) (212.678.3928; email: larcada)
  Acquisitions Editor: Emily Spangler (language and literacy, technology and education) (212.678.3909; email: spangler)
  Consulting Senior Acquisitions Editor: Jean Ward (curriculum, professional development, literacy) (847.224.02785; email: ward)
  Assistant Acquisitions Editor: Meg Hartmann (212.678.3905; email: hartmann)
Production: Michael Weinstein, Production Manager (212.678.3926; email: weinstein)
  Senior Production Editor: Karl Nyberg (212.678.3806; email: nyberg)
  Production Editors: Aureliano Vazquez (212.678.3945; email: vasquez); Lori Tate (212.678.3907; email: tate); John Bylander (212.678.3914; email: bylander); Jennifer Baker (212.678.3902; email: baker)
  Production Assistants: Debra Jackson-Whyte (212.678.3926; email: jackson-whyte)
Marketing: Leyli Shayegan, Director, Sales and Marketing and Assistant Director (212.678.3475; email: shayegan)
  Marketing Manager: Nancy Power (212.678.3915; email: power)
  Graphic Arts Manager: David Strauss (212.678.3982; email: strauss)
  Publicity Coordinator: Beverly Rivero (212.678.3963; email: rivero)
  Outreach Coordinator: Michael McGann (212.678.3919; email: mcgann)
Business: TBA, Financial Controller (212.678.3913)
  Secretary/Receptionist: Marcia Ruiz (212.678.3929; email: myr3@columbia.edu)

Full Member

Established: 1904   Admitted to AAUP: 1971
Title output 2011: 66   Title output 2012: 66
Titles currently in print: 700

Editorial Program

Scholarly, professional, text, and trade books on education, education-related areas, and parenting. Multimedia instructional materials, tests, and evaluation materials for classroom use at all levels of education.

Specific areas of interest in education are: curriculum; early childhood; school administration and educational policy; counseling; mathematics; philosophy; psychology; language and literacy; multicultural education; science; sociology; special education; social justice; social studies; teacher education; cultural studies; technology and education; women and higher education.

Special series: Advances in Contemporary Educational Thought; Between Teacher & Text; Counseling and Development; Critical Issues in Educational Leadership; Disability, Culture, and Equity; Early Childhood Education; Education and Psychology of the Gifted; International Perspectives on Education Reform; John Dewey Lecture; Language and Literacy; Multicultural Education; Practitioner Inquiry; Professional Ethics in Education; Reflective History; The Series on School Reform; Teaching for Social Justice; Technology, Education—Connections (TEC); Ways of Knowing in Science and Mathematics

Temple University Press

Mailing Address: Street Address:
TASB   TASB
1852 N. 10th Street   2450 West Hunting Park Avenue
Philadelphia, PA 19122   Philadelphia, PA 19129

Phone: 215.926.2140   Orders:
Fax: 215.926.2141   Chicago Distribution Center
Email: firstname.lastname@temple.edu   11030 South Langley Avenue
                                               Chicago, IL 60628
Website and Social Media: Phone: 800.621.2736
Website: www.temple.edu/tempress   Fax: 800.621.8471
Blog: templepress.wordpress.com
Facebook: www.facebook.com/pages/
   Temple-University-Press/21638877349
Twitter: TempleUnivPress

UK Distributor: Canadian Distributor:
Combined Academic Publishers   Lexa Publishers' Representatives

Staff

Director: Alex Holzman (215.926.2145)
Rights and Permissions: Amanda Steele (215.926.2159)

Electronic Publishing Manager: Barry Adams (215.926.2150)
Acquisitions: Janet M. Francendese, Assistant Director and Editor-in-Chief (215.926.2144)
  Senior Editors: Micah Kleit (215.926.2157)
  Assistant Editor: Amanda Steele (215.926.2159)
Production: Charles H. E. Ault, Assistant Director and Director of Production and
  Electronic Publishing (215.926.2142)
  Senior Production Editor: Joan Vidal (215.926.2148)
  Production Coordinator/Designer: Kate Nichols (215.926.2167)
Marketing: Ann-Marie Anderson, Assistant Director and Director of Marketing
  (215.926.2143)
  Advertising and Promotion Manager: Irene Imperio (215.926.2153)
  Publicity Manager: Gary Kramer (215.926.2154)
Business: Barry Adams, Assistant Director and Financial Manager (215.926.2150)
  Customer Service/Operations Manager: Karen Baker (215.926.2156)

Full Member

Established: 1969
Title output 2011: 59
Titles currently in print: 1,360

Admitted to AAUP: 1972
Title output 2012: 57

Editorial Program

African American studies; American studies; anthropology; Asian studies; Asian American studies; cinema and media studies; communication; criminology; disability studies; education; ethnicity and race; gay and lesbian studies; gender studies; geography; health; labor studies; Latin American studies; law and society; Philadelphia regional studies; political science and public policy; religion; sociology; sports; urban studies; US and European history; women's studies.

Temple University Press distributes books for the Asian American Writers' Workshop.

Special series: America in Transition: Radical Perspectives; American Subjects; Animals, Culture, and Society; Asian American History and Culture; Critical Perspectives on the Past; Emerging Media; Gender, Family, and the Law; Labor in Crisis; Mapping Racisms; The New Academy; Place, Culture, and Politics; Politics, History, and Social Change; Queer Politics, Queer Theories; Rhetoric, Culture, and Public Address; Sound Matters; Studies in Latin American and Caribbean Music; Teaching/Learning Social Justice; Voices of Latin American Life; Wide Angle Books

University of Tennessee Press

Mailing Address:
110 Conference Center
Knoxville, TN 37996-4108

Shipping Address:
600 Henley Street
Suite 110 Conference Center
Knoxville, TN 37902-2911

Phone: 865.974.3321
Fax: 865.974.3724
Email: custserv@utpress.org
Indiv: (user I.D.)@utk.edu

Orders:
Chicago Distribution Center
11030 South Langley Ave.
Chicago, IL 60628
Phone: 800.621.2736
Fax: 773.702.7212

Website and Social Media:
Website: utpress.org
Blog: utpress.org/utpressblog
Facebook page: www.facebook.com/pages/
    University-of-Tennessee-Press/80814711590?ref=ts
Twitter: utennpress

Staff

Director: Scot Danforth (email: danforth)
Acquisitions Editorial: Kerry Webb (email: webbke)
Manuscript Editorial: TBA, Managing Editor
   Manuscript Editor: Gene Adair (email: gadair)
   Editorial Assistant: Thomas Wells (email: twells)
Design and Production: Barbara Karwhite, Manager (email: bkarwhit)
   Book Designer: Chad Pelton (email: cpelton)
   Production Coordinator: Stephanie Thompson (email: sthomp20)
Marketing: Cheryl Carson, Manager (email: ccarson3)
   Exhibits/Publicity Manager: Tom Post (email: tpost)
Business: Lisa Davis, Manager (email: ldavis49)
   Receptionist/Bookkeeper: Linsey Sims (email: lsims9)
IT Manager: Jake Sumner (email: jsumner2)

Full Member

Established: 1940
Title output 2011: 36
Titles currently in print: 825

Admitted to AAUP: 1964
Title output 2012: 33

Editorial Program

American studies; Appalachian studies; African American studies; history; religion; folklore; vernacular architecture; historical archaeology; material culture; literature; and literary fiction. Submissions in poetry, textbooks, and translations are not invited.
Special series, joint imprints, and/or copublishing programs: Appalachian Echoes; Charles K. Wolfe American Music Series; Correspondence of James K. Polk; Legacies of War; Outdoor Tennessee; The Papers of Andrew Jackson; Sport and Popular Culture; Tennessee Studies in Literature; Vernacular Architecture Studies; Voices of the Civil War; and The Western Theater in the Civil War

University of Texas Press

Street Address:
2100 Comal Street
STOP E4800
Austin, TX 78712-1303

Mailing Address:
PO Box 7819
Austin, TX 78713-7819

Phone: 512.471.7233
Fax: 512.232.7178
Email: info@utpress.utexas.edu
Indiv: firstinitiallastname@utpress.utexas.edu

Orders:
Phone: 800.252.3206
Fax: 800.687.6046

Website and Social Media:
Website: www.utexaspress.com
Blog: utpressnews.blogspot.com/
Facebook: www.facebook.com/utexaspress
Twitter: UTexasPress

Staff

Director: David Hamrick (512.232.7604)
  Assistant to the Director: Allison Faust (512.232.7603)
  Special Projects and Development Officer: John McLeod (512.232.7605)
  Information Technology Manager: William Bishel (512.232.7609)
Rights and Permissions Manager: Laura Young Bost (512.232.7625)
  Rights and Permissions Assistant: Peggy Gough (512.232.7624)
Assistant Director and Editor-in-Chief: Theresa May (social sciences, Latin American
  studies, art) (512.232.7612)
  Senior Editor: Jim Burr (humanities) (512.232.7610);
  Acquisitions Editor: Casey Kittrell (Texana, music, natural history, environmental studies,
  food culture) (512.232.7616)
  Editorial Assistant: Brian Contine (512.232.7608)
Managing Editor: Leslie Tingle (512.232.7614)
  Manuscript Editors: Lynne Chapman (512.232.7607); Victoria Davis (512.232.7613)
  Assistant Manuscript Editor: Molly Frisinger (512.475.9187)
  Editorial Department Fellow: Sandra Spicher (512.232.7613)
Design & Production Manager: Ellen McKie (512.232.7640)
  Designers: Derek George (512.232.7642); Lindsay Starr (512.232.7641)
  Production Editor: Regina Fuentes (512.232.7639)
  Production Coordinator: Kaila Wyllys (512.232.7637)
  Production Assistant: Andy Sieverman (512.232.7638)
Marketing and Communications Manager: Brady Dyer (512.232.7627)
  Assistant Marketing Manager: Nancy Bryan (512.232.7628)
  Website and Direct Mail Manager: Meg Askey (512.471.1728)
  Digital Publishing Manager: Sharon Casteel (512.232.7631)
  Publicist: Colleen Devine Ellis (512.232.7634)
  Advertising and Exhibits Manager: Christopher Farmer (512.232.7630)
  Marketing Assistant: Bailey Morrison (512.232.7633)

Sales Manager: Gianna LaMorte (512.832.9111)
  Sales Representative: Chris Hoyt (512.232.7632)
Journals Manager: Sue Hausmann (512.232.7620)
  Journals Production Coordinators: Karen Broyles (512.232.7622); Stacey Salling (512.232.7622)
  Journals Marketing Coordinator: TBA
  Journals Circulation and Rights and Permissions Manager: Rebecca Frazier (512.232.7621)
  Journals Accounting Clerk: Janet Fan (512.232.7617)
Assistant Director and Financial Officer: Joyce Lewandowski (512.232.7646)
  Accounts Receivable: TBA
  Royalties Accountant: Kristin Duvall (512.232.7648)
  Accounts Payable Manager: Linda Ramirez (512.232.7649)
  Office Manager: Andrea Prestridge (512.232.7647)
  Customer Service Supervisor: Brenda Jo Hoggatt (512.232.7650)
  Customer Service Assistant: Dawn Bishop (512.232.7652)
Warehouse (512.471.3634)
  Warehouse Supervisor: George Mill (512.232.7656)
  Warehouse Staff: Rogelio Rocha Jr. (512.232.7658); Rey Renteria (512.232.7655); Paul Guerra (512.232.7657)

Full Member

Established: 1950   Admitted to AAUP: 1954
Title output 2011: 95   Title output 2012: 95
Titles currently in print: 2,000   Journals published: 11

Editorial Program

American music, American studies, anthropology, applied language, architecture, art, Chicano/a studies, classics and the ancient world, conservation, cookbooks and gardening, Egyptology, environmental studies, film and media studies, fine art and documentary photography, food studies, Jewish studies, Latin American and pre-Columbian studies, Latina/o studies, literary modernism, Middle Eastern studies and translations of Middle Eastern literature, natural history, New and Old World archaeology, ornithology, Texas and the Southwest, and women's studies. Original fiction, poetry, and children's books are not invited.

The Press distributes publications for the Jack S. Blanton Museum of Art; Center for Mexican American Studies; Center for Middle Eastern Studies; Dolph Briscoe Center for American History; Harry Ransom Center; and Teresa Lozano Long Institute of Latin American Studies.

Journals: *Archaeoastronomy; Asian Music; Cinema Journal; The Journal of Individual Psychology; Journal of Latin American Geography for the Conference of Latin Americanist Geographers; The Journal of the History of Sexuality; Latin American Music Review; Studies in Latin American Popular Culture; Information and Culture; Texas Studies in Literature and Language; The Velvet Light Trap*

Special series, joint imprints, and/or copublishing programs: American Music; Center for Mexican American Studies History, Culture, and Society; Center for Middle Eastern Studies

(CMES) Binah Yitzrit Foundation Series in Israel Studies; CMES Emerging Voices from the Middle East; CMES Modern Literatures in Translation; CMES Modern Middle East; Chicana Matters; Cognitive Approaches to Literature and Culture; Discovering America; Focus on American History; Handbook of Latin American Studies; Harry Ransom Humanities Research Center (HRC) Imprint; HRC Photography; Inter-America; Literary Modernism; Teresa Lozano Long Institute of Latin American Studies (LLILAS) New Interpretations of Latin America; LLILAS Translations from Latin America; Oratory of Classical Greece; Schusterman Center for Jewish Studies; Southwestern Writers Collection; Texas Field Guides; Texas Archaeology and Ethnohistory; Texas Film and Media Studies; Wittliff Gallery Series of Southwestern and Mexican Photography

Endowed book series: Ashley and Peter Larkin Series in Greek and Roman Culture; Bill and Alice Wright Photography Series; Brad and Michele Moore Roots Music Series; Bridwell Texas History Series; Charles N. Prothro Texana Series; Clifton and Shirley Caldwell Texas Heritage Series; The Corrie Herring Hooks Series; Ellen and Edward Randall Series; Jack and Doris Smothers Series in Texas History, Life, and Culture; Jamal and Rania Daniel Series in Contemporary History, Politics, Culture, and Religion of the Levant; Jess and Betty Jo Hay Series; Jewish History, Life, and Culture; Joe R. and Teresa Lozano Long Series in Latin American and Latino Art and Culture; Linda Schele Series in Maya and Pre-Columbian Studies; Louann Atkins Temple Women and Culture Series; M. Georgia Hegarty Dunkerley Contemporary Art Series; Mildred Wyatt-Wold Series in Ornithology; Peter T. Flawn Series in Natural Resources; Roger Fullington Series in Architecture; Terry and Jan Todd Series on Physical Culture and Sports; William and Bettye Nowlin Series in Art, History, and Culture of the Western Hemisphere

Texas A&M University Press

Street Address:
John H. Lindsey Building, Lewis Street
College Station, TX 77843

Mailing Address:
4354 TAMU
College Station, TX 77843-4354

Phone: 979.845.1436
Fax: 979.847.8752
Email: upress@tamu.edu
Indiv: (user I.D.)@tamu.edu

Orders:
Phone: 800.826.8911
Fax: 888.617.2421
Email: bookorders@tamu.edu

Website and Social Media:
Website: www.tamupress.com
Blog: tamupress.blogspot.com/
Facebook: www.facebook.com/tamupress
Twitter: TAMUPress
YouTube: www.youtube.com/user/TAMUPressConsortium

European Representative:
Eurospan

Staff
Press Director: Charles Backus (979.458.3980; email: charles.backus)
Acquisitions Editorial: Mary Lenn Dixon, Editor-in-Chief (Texas and Western history,

military history, borderland studies, presidential studies, anthropology, archaeology)
(979.845.0759; email: mary-dixon)
Louise Lindsey Merrick Editor for the Natural Environment: Shannon Davies (natural history & natural sciences; agriculture; gardening & horticulture; conservation & the environment) (979.458.3976; email: sdavies)
    Acquisitions Assistant: Katie Cowart (979.458.3975; email: katie.cowart)
Manuscript Editorial: Thom Lemmons, Managing Editor (Texas music) (979.845.0758;
email: thom.lemmons)
    Assistant Editor: Patricia Clabaugh (979.458.3979; email: pclabaugh)
Design/Production: Mary Ann Jacob, Design & Production Manager (979.845.3694;
email: m-jacob)
    Pre-press and Electronic Publishing Manager: Kevin Grossman (979.458.3995; email:
k.grossman)
Marketing: Gayla Christiansen, Marketing Manager (979.845.0148; email: gayla-c)
    Publicity and Advertising Manager: Holli Estridge (979.458.3982; email: holli.estridge)
    Marketing Graphics/Web Manager/Database Liaison: Kyle Littlefield (979.458.3983;
email: k-littlefield)
    Exhibits and Electronic Publications Manager: Caitlin Churchill (979.458.3984; email:
caitlin.churchill)
    Sales Manager: David Neel (979.458.3981; email: d-neel)
Financial Manager: Dianna Sells (979.845.0146; email: d-sells)
    Business Operations Manager: Sharon Pavlas-Mills (979.458.3994; email: sharon-mills)
    Accounts Receivable Manager: Wynona McCormick (979.458.3989; email: wynona)
    Order Fulfillment Supervisor: Christin Wuensche (979.458.3991;
email: christin.wuensche)
Warehouse Manager: Mike Martin (979.458.3986; email: mike.martin)
    Assistant Warehouse Manager: Cliff O'Connell (979.458.3987; email: c-oconnell)

Full Member
Established: 1974   Admitted to AAUP: 1977
Title output 2011: 51   Title output 2012: 64
Titles currently in print: 1,185

Editorial Program
American and Western history; natural history; the environment; agriculture; natural re-
source science; nautical archaeology; women's studies; military history; economics; business;
architecture; art; veterinary medicine; presidential studies; borderland studies; Texas and the
Southwest. Submissions are not invited in poetry or fiction.
Special series: AgriLife Research and Extension; Brannen Series in Military Studies;
Canseco-Keck History; Centennial of Flight Series; Centennial Series of the Association of
Former Students; Dickson Series in Texas Music; Fay Series in Analytical Psychology; Foreign
Relations and the Presidency; Environmental History; Fronteras; Gulf Coast Books; Harte
Research Institute for Gulf of Mexico Studies; Hughes Presidency and Leadership Studies;
Landmark Speeches on American Politics; Library of Presidential Rhetoric; Lindsey Series
in the Arts and Humanities; Meadows Center for Water & the Environment; Moore Texas
Art; Merrick Natural Environment; Montague Business and Oil History; Moody Natural

History; Peoples and Cultures of Texas; Perspectives on South Texas; Presidential Rhetoric; Prothro Texas Photography; Rachal Foundation Series in Nautical Archaeology; Red River Valley Books; Rio Grande/Rio Bravo; Sam Rayburn Rural Life; Spencer Series in the West and Southwest; Studies in Architecture and Culture; Tarleton State University Southwestern Studies in the Humanities; Texas A&M Agriculture; Texas A&M Economics; Texas A&M University Anthropology; University of Houston Mexican American Studies; Wardlaw Books; West Texas A&M University; Williams-Ford Series in Military History; Williams Texas Life

TCU Press

Mailing Address:
Box 298300
Fort Worth, TX 76129

Street Address:
3000 Sandage
Fort Worth, TX 76109

Phone: 817.257.7822
Fax: 817.257.5075

Orders:
Phone: 800.826.8911

Website and Social Media:
Website: www.prs.tcu.edu
Facebook: www.facebook.com/pages/
   Fort-Worth-TX/TCU-PRESS/291943790611

Staff
Director Dan Williams (email: d.e.williamms@tcu.edu)
Editor: Susan Petty (email: s.petty@tcu.edu)
Production Manager: Melinda Esco (email: m.esco@tcu.edu)

Full Member
Established: 1966
Title output 2011: 21
Titles currently in print: 376

Admitted to AAUP: 1982
Title output 2012: NR

Editorial Program
Humanities and social sciences, with special emphasis on Texas and Southwestern history and literature; American studies; fiction; and women's studies.
Special series: Chaparral Books for Young Readers; The Chisholm Trail Series; Literary Cities; The Texas Tradition Series; The Texas Biography Series; TCU Texas Poets Laureate; Texas Small Books

Texas Tech University Press

Street Address:
Media and Communication Building
9th Floor
3003 15th Street
Lubbock, TX 79409-1037

Mailing Address:
Box 41037
Lubbock, TX 79409-1037

Phone: 806.742.2982
Fax: 806.742.2979
Email: firstname.lastname@ttu.edu

Website and Social Media:
Website: www.ttupress.org
Facebook: www.facebook.com/pages/
   Lubbock-TX/Texas-Tech-University-Press/
   46737328830
Twitter: TTUPress

Orders:
Chicago Distribution Center
11030 South Langley Ave.
Chicago, IL 60628
Phone: 800.621.2736; 773.702.7010;
International 773. 702.7000
Fax: 800.621.8476; International
773.702.7212

UK and European Distributor
Eurospan

Staff
Director: Robert Mandel
   Assistant to the Director: Jada Rankin
Acquisitions: Judith Keeling, Assistant Director and Editor-in-Chief
Managing Editor: Joanna Conrad
Design and Production Manager: Kasey McBeath
Marketing Manager: Barbara Brannon
Exhibits and Publicity Manager: John Brock
Office Manager: Isabel Williams
   Customer Service: LaTisha Roberts

Full Member
Established: 1971
Title output 2011: 30
Titles currently in print: 415

Admitted to AAUP: 1987
Title output 2012: 29
Journals published: 4

Editorial Program
American liberty and justice; costume and textile studies; history and culture of Texas and
the West, the Great Plains, and modern Southeast Asia during and after the Vietnam War;
Jewish studies and literature; Latin American and Latino fiction; natural history and natural
science; poetry (by invitation only); fiction and nonfiction for young readers; and sport in
the American West.
Journals: *Conradiana*; *Helios*; *Intertexts*; *The William Carlos Williams Review*
Special series: American Liberty and Justice; The Americas; Costume Society of America;
Grover E. Murray Studies in the American Southwest; Modern Jewish History; Modern
Jewish Literature and Culture; Modern Southeast Asia; Modern Southeast Asian Literature;
Plains Histories; Sport in the American West; Walt McDonald First-Book Series in Poetry;
Voice in the American West; Women, Gender, and the West

University of Tokyo Press

7-3-1 Hongo, Bunkyo-ku
Tokyo 113-8654, Japan

US Representative:
Columbia University Press

Phone: +81-3-3811-0964, +81-3-3811-8814
Fax: +81-3-3814-9458, +81-3-3812-6958
Email: info@utp.or.jp

Staff
President: Junichi Hamada
Chairman of the Board: Hiroshi Watanabe
Managing Director: Masami Yamaguchi (email: ajup@utp.or.jp)
Associate Director: Hidetoshi Takenaka
Associate Director & Marketing Director: Takuya Kuroda
Editorial Director: Mika Komatsu
Editor-in-Chief & International Liaisons Executive: Kensuke Goto
Production Director: Hiroshi Takagi

International Member
Established: 1951
Title output 2011: 132
Titles currently in print: 4,450

Admitted to AAUP: 1970
Title output 2012: NR

Editorial Program
Titles published in Japanese reflect the research carried out at the university in the humanities, social sciences, and natural sciences. Continuing series are published in biology, earth sciences, sociology, economics, philosophy, and Japanese art and historical studies. Special projects include publication of textbooks and reprinting of historical source materials.

English-language publishing began in 1960; special strengths include Japanese and Asian studies (including art, history, economics, law, and sociology). English-language publications also include translations of historical and important literary works and diaries.

University of Toronto Press

Scholarly Publishing Division:
10 St. Mary Street, Suite 700
Toronto, ON M4Y 2W8 Canada
Phone: 416.978.2239
Fax: 416.978.4738
Email: publishing@utpress.utoronto.ca

Higher Education Division:
199 Woolwich Street, 2nd Floor
Guelph, ON N1H 3V4 Canada
Phone: 519.837.1403
Fax: 519.767.1643
Email: requests@highereducation.com

P-Shift:
10 St Mary Street, Suite 700
Toronto, ON M4Y 2W8 Canada
Phone: 416.978.2239

Websites and Social Media:
Publishing: www.utppublishing.com
Blog: utpblog.utpress.utoronto.ca/
Journals: www.utpjournals.com
P-Shift: www.utpshift.com
Facebook: www.facebook.com/utpress; www.facebook.com/utpjournals
Twitter: utpress; utpjournals

Journals Division:
5201 Dufferin Street
North York, ON M3H 5T8 Canada
Phone: 416.667.7810
Fax: 416.667.7881; 800.221.9985
Email: journals@utpress.utoronto.ca

UTP Distribution Centre:
5201 Dufferin Street
North York, ON M3H 5T8 Canada
Phone: 416.667.7791; 800.565.9523
Fax: 416.667.7832; 800.221.9985
Email: utpbooks@utpress.utoronto.ca

UK Representative:
Oxford Publicity Partnership Ltd.
gary.hall@oppuk.co.uk

UK/Europe Distribution:
NBN International

US Warehouse:
2250 Military Road
Tonawanda, NY 14150
Phone: 716.693.2768

Staff
Administration
Indiv. email: firstinitiallastname@utpress.utoronto.ca
President, Publisher and CEO: John Yates (ext. 222)
Senior Vice President, HR & Administration: Kathryn Bennett (ext. 224)
Vice President, Finance: Shawn O'Grady (416.667.7765)
Scholarly Publishing
Indiv. email: firstinitiallastname@utpress.utoronto.ca
Vice President, Scholarly Publishing: Lynn Fisher (ext. 243)
Publishing Coordinator: Charley LaRose (ext. 237)
Permissions & Rights Coordinator: Lisa Jemison (ext. 226)

Acquisitions Editorial

Senior Acquisitions Editor: Suzanne Rancourt (classics, medieval and renaissance studies, ext. 239)

Acquisitions Editors: Len Husband (Cdn history, native studies, philosophy, ext. 238); Siobhan McMenemy (film, Cdn literature, cultural studies, book history, communications, ext. 231); Ron Schoeffel (Erasmus, Lonergan studies, Italian studies, ext. 241); Richard Ratzlaff (history, literature, semiotics, ext. 233); Daniel Quinlan (political science & law, ext. 254); Jennifer DiDomenico (business & economics, ext. 259); Doug Hildebrand (anthropology, education, geography, sociology, urban studies, ext. 251); Eric Carlson (social work, medicine & health, ext 230)

Manuscript Editorial & Production

Managing Editor: Anne Laughlin (ext. 236)

Production Manager: Ani Deyirmenjian (ext. 227)

Electronic Publishing

Electronic Publishing Coordinator: Barry Miekle (ext. 232)

Sales & Marketing

Sales and Marketing Manager: Brian MacDonald (ext. 253)

Publicist: Chris Reed (ext. 248)

Advertising, Journal Review Coordinator: Deepshikha Dutta (ext. 247)

Sales & Electronic Marketing Coordinator: Taylor Berry (ext. 250)

Catalogue & Copy Coordinator: Shoshana Wasser (ext. 257)

Exhibits & Examination Copies Coordinator: Elizabeth Glenn (ext. 260)

Data & Web Coordinator: Bob Currer (ext. 249)

Journals (5201 Dufferin St.)

Indiv. email: firstinitiallastname@utpress.utoronto.ca

Vice-President, Journals: Anne Marie Corrigan (416.667.7838)

Editorial Manager, Journals: Sylvia Hunter (416.667.7777 ext. 7806)

Supervisor, Circulation & Distribution: Adele D'Ambrosio (416.667.7777 ext. 7781)

Permissions Coordinator, Journals: Siobhan Juniku (416.667.7777 ext. 7849)

Advertising and Marketing Coordinator: Audrey Greenwood (416.667.7777 ext. 7766)

Higher Education

Indiv. email: @utpress.utoronto.ca

Vice President: Michael Harrison (519.837.1403 ext. 222; email: mharrison)

Acquisitions: Anne Brackenbury, Executive Editor (anthropology; sociology; social work; education; development studies; environmental studies; women's studies; indigenous studies; Latin American studies & Canadian & North American studies) (416.537.0847; email: brackenbury)

Editor: Natalie Fingerhut (history, Medieval & Renaissance studies; religious studies; international political science) (416.922.2171; email: fingerhut)

Assistant Editor: Megan Pickard (519.837.1403 ext. 227; email: mpickard)

Sales & Marketing:

Marketing Manager: Anna Del Col (519.837.1403 ext. 224; email: adelcol)

Sales Manager: Michelle Lobokowicz (519.837.1403 ext. 231; email: mlobkowicz)

Senior Publisher's Representative: Mat Buntin (519.837.1403 ext. 223; email: mbuntin)

Production & Editorial: Beate Schwirtlich, Production Editor (519.837.1403 ext. 228; email: bschwirtlich)

P-Shift

Using Word files, P-Shift generates XML code within your manuscript that marks key information, validates and crosschecks references, and properly formats your document to give you an active, user-friendly file. It is then all easily stored and accessed in our data asset management system.

Indiv. email: firstinitiallastname@utpress.utoronto.ca
President, Publisher & CEO: John Yates (416.978.2239 ext. 222)

UTP Distribution Centre

Indiv email: firstinitiallastname@utpress.utoronto.ca
Vice President, Distribution & MIS: Hamish Cameron (416.667.7773)
  Manager, Client Publisher Services: Carol Trainor (416.667.7845)
  Credit Manager: Clive Williams (416.667.7774)

Full Member

Established: 1901	Admitted to AAUP: 1937
Title output 2011: 160	Title output 2012: 175
Titles currently in print: 3,800	Journals published: 32

Editorial Program

Scholarly books, serious non-fiction, course books and books for business professionals with a particular focus on: Business & economics; classical studies; medieval studies; renaissance studies; Slavic studies; environmental studies; Erasmian studies; Victorian studies; english literature; Canadian studies; North American Studies; Canadian literature; cultural studies; literary theory and criticism; modern languages and literatures; philosophy; political science; law and criminology; religion and theology; education; Canadian and international history; history of science and medicine; sociology; anthropology; gender studies; Native studies; social work; geography; urban studies; and women's studies. Submissions are not invited in poetry or fiction.

Journals: *ArsMedica; Canadian Historical Review; Canadian Journal of Criminology and Criminal Justice; Canadian Journal of Information and Library Sciences; Canadian Journal of Linguistics; Canadian Journal of Law and Society; Canadian Journal of Mathematics; Canadian Journal of Women and the Law; Canadian Mathematical Bulletin; Canadian Modern Language Review; Canadian Public Policy; Canadian Review of American Studies; Canadian Theatre Review; Cartographica; Diaspora: A Journal of Transnational Studies; Eighteenth Century Fiction; Histoire Sociale; INFOR Information Systems and Operational Research; Journal of Canadian Studies; Journal of Scholarly Publishing; Journal of Veterinary Medical Education; Lexicons of Early Modern English; Modern Drama; Seminar; Simile: Studies in Media and Information Literacy Education; The Tocqueville Review; Ultimate Reality and Meaning; University of Toronto Law Journal; University of Toronto Quarterly; Yearbook of Comparative and General Literature*
Special series, joint imprints and/or copublishing programs: Rotman-UTP Publishing Imprint. New series include: Asian Canadian Studies, Business & Sustainability Series, The Kenneth Michael Tanenbaum Series in Jewish Studies, and Toronto Iberic. Ongoing series include: Anthropological Horizons; Benjamin Disraeli Letters; Canadian Cinema; Canadian Social History Series;l Collected Works of Bernard Lonergan; Collected Works of Erasmus; Collected Works of Northrop Frye; Cultural Spaces; Dictionary of Canadian Biography; Digital Futures; Erasmus Studies; European Union Studies; Frye Studies; IPAC Series in

Public Management and Governance; Japan and Global Society; Joanne Goodman Lectures; Lonergan Studies; Lorenzo DaPonte Italian Library; Medieval Academy Books; Medieval Academy Reprints for Teaching; New Studies in Phenomenology and Hermeneutics; Osgoode Society for Canadian Legal History; Phoenix Supplementary Volumes; Renaissance Society of America Reprint Texts; Robson Classical Lectures; Selected Correspondence of Bernard Shaw; Studies in Book and Print Culture; Studies in Comparative Political Economy and Public Policy; Studies in Gender and History; Themes in Canadian History; Toronto Anglo Saxon Series; Toronto Italian Studies; Toronto Old Norse-Icelandic Series; Toronto Studies in Medieval Law; Toronto Studies in Philosophy; Toronto Studies in Semiotics and Communication; UCLA Clark Memorial Library Series; University of Toronto Romance Series.

United Nations University Press

53-70, Jingumae 5-chome
Shibuya-ku, Tokyo 150-8925
Japan

Phone: +81-3-5467-1212
Fax: +81-3-3406-7345
Email: press@unu.edu
Indiv: (user I.D.)@unu.edu

<u>Website and Social Media:</u>
Website: www.unu.edu/unupress
Facebook: www.facebook.com/UNUPress

<u>US Distributor:</u>
Brookings Institution Press

<u>Orders:</u>
Fax: +81-3-3406-7345
Email: sales@unu.edu

<u>UK Distributor:</u>
UPM (through Brookings)

Staff
Head: Vesselin Popovski, Senior Academic Programme Officer (ext. 1299; email: popovski)
Acquisitions and Manuscript Editorial: Kae Sugawara, Editor (ext. 1280; email: sugawara)
Design and Production: Yoko Kojima, Senior Publications Coordinator (ext. 1316; email: kojima)
Marketing and Sales: Marc Benger, Senior Marketing and Sales Coordinator (ext. 1310; email: benger)

International Member
Established: 1990
Title output 2011: 14
Titles currently in print: 251

Admitted to AAUP: 1997
Title output 2012: 9

Editorial Program
United Nations University Press is the publishing arm of the United Nations University, which was established as a subsidiary organ of the United Nations by General Assembly Resolution 2951 (XXVII) in 1972. UNU Press publishes scholarly and policy-oriented books and periodicals on the issues facing the United Nations and its peoples and member states, with particular emphasis on international, regional and trans-boundary policies.

United States Institute of Peace Press

2301 Constitution Avenue, NW
Washington, DC 20037

Phone: 202.457.1700
Fax: 202.223.9320
Email: (user I.D)@usip.org

<u>Website and Social Media:</u>
Website: bookstore.usip.org
Facebook: United States Institute of Peace
Twitter: U.S. Inst. of Peace

<u>UK/European Representative:</u>
University Presses Marketing

<u>Orders:</u>
PO Box 605
Herndon, VA 20172
Phone: 800.868.8064; 703.661.1590
Fax: 703.661.1501
Email:
usipmail@presswarehouse.com

<u>Canadian Representative:</u>
Renouf Books

Staff
Director of Publications: Valerie Norville (202.429.4147; email: vnorville)
Managing Editor: Michelle Slavin (202.429.3821; email: mslavin)
Production Manager: Marie Marr (202.429.3815; email: mmarr)
Sales and Marketing Manager: Kay Hechler (202.429.3816; email: khechler)

Associate Member
Established: 1991
Title output 2011: 11
Titles currently in print: 175

Admitted to AAUP: 1993
Title output 2012: 5

Editorial Program
The Press publishes books that are based on work supported by the Institute. Created by Congress in 1984, the Institute is an independent, nonpartisan institution that works to prevent, mitigate, and resolve violent international conflicts. The Institute's publications range across the spectrum of international relations, including conflict prevention, management, and resolution; diplomacy and negotiation; human rights; mediation and facilitation; foreign policy; gender; ethnopolitics; political science; and religion and ethics.
Special series: Academy Guides; Cross-Cultural Negotiation Series; Peacemaker's Toolkits

W. E. Upjohn Institute for Employment Research

300 South Westnedge Avenue
Kalamazoo, MI 49007-4686

Phone: 269.343.4330
Fax: 269.343.7310
Email: publications@upjohn.org
Indiv: lastname@upjohn.org

Orders:
Phone: 888.227.8569

Website and Social Media:
Website: www.upjohn.org

Staff

Director of Publications: Kevin Hollenbeck (269.343.5541)
  Assistant to the Director: Claire Black (269.343.5541)
Manager of Publications and Marketing: Richard Wyrwa (269.343.5541)
Editor: Ben Jones (269.343.5541)
Production Coordinator: Erika Jackson (269.343.5541)

Associate Member

Established: 1945
Title output 2011: 7
Titles currently in print: 218

Admitted to AAUP: 1997
Title output 2012: 7

Editorial Program

Scholarly works on employment-related issues; labor economics; current issues in the social sciences, with an emphasis on public policy. Books are authored by resident research staff and other scholars in the academic and professional communities. The Institute also publishes working papers, policy papers, and technical reports authored by the resident research staff and grantees; a quarterly journal on the West Michigan economy, Business Outlook for West Michigan, and a quarterly newsletter, *Employment Research*.

University of Utah Press

295 South 1500 East, Suite 5400
Salt Lake City, UT 84112-0860

Phone: 801.581.6771
Fax: 801.581.3365
Indiv: (user I.D.)@utah.edu

Orders:
Chicago Distribution Center
11030 South Langley Ave.
Chicago, IL 60628
Phone: 800.621.2736
Fax: 800.621.8476

Website and Social Media:
Website: www.UofUpress.com
Facebook: www.facebook.com/uofupress
Twitter: UofUPress

UK/European Representative:
Eurospan University Press Group

Staff
Director: Glenda Cotter (801.585.0083; email: glenda.cotter)
Acquisitions Editors: Peter DeLafosse (American History; American West, trade)
  (801.585.0086; email: peter.delafosse); Reba Rauch (anthropology and archaeology)
  (801.585.0081; email: reba.rauch)
  Assistant Editor: Stephanie Warnick (email: stephanie.warnick)
Managing Editor: Glenda Cotter (email: glenda.cotter)
Production Manager: Jessica Booth (email: jessica.booth)
Marketing Manager: Linda Manning (801.585.9786; email: linda.manning)
Business Manager, Rights and Permissions: Sharon Day (email: sharon.day)

Full Member
Established: 1949
Title output 2011: 36
Titles currently in print: 450

Admitted to AAUP: 1979
Title output 2012: NR

Editorial Program
Anthropology and archaeology, linguistics, Mesoamerica, America Indian studies, history of
the North American West, environmental history, Utah and Mormon studies, Middle East
studies, natural history, nature writing, regional guidebooks, and general titles of regional
interest.
Special series: Agha Shahid Ali Prize in Poetry; Foundations of Archaeological Inquiry; Don
D. and Catherine S. Fowler Prize (Anthropology & Archaeology); The Juanita Brooks Prize
in Mormon Studies; Tanner Lectures on Human Values; Utah Series in Middle East Studies;
University of Utah Anthropological Papers; The Wallace Stegner Prize in Environmental and
American Western History

Vanderbilt University Press

Street Address:
2014 Broadway
Suite 320
Nashville, TN 37203

Phone: 615.322.3585
Fax: 615.343.8823
Email: vupress@vanderbilt.edu
Indiv: firstname.lastname@vanderbilt.edu

Website and Social Media:
Website: www.vanderbiltuniversitypress.com

Canadian Distributor:
Scholarly Book Services

Mailing Address:
VU Station B 351813
Nashville, TN 37235

Customer Service/Order Fulfillment:
OU Press Book Distribution Center
2800 Venture Drive
Norman, OK 73069
Phone: 800.627.7377
Fax: 800.735.0476

UK/European Distributor:
Eurospan

Staff
Director: Michael Ames
Acquisitions Editor: Eli J. Bortz
Managing Editor: Joell Smith-Borne
Editing, Design, and Production Manager: Dariel Mayer
Marketing Manager: Sue Havlish
Marketing and New Media Associate: Betsy Phillips
Business Manager: Bethany Graham

Full Member

Established: 1940
Title output 2011: 24
Titles currently in print: 285

Admitted to AAUP: 1993
Title output 2012: 24

Editorial Program
Scholarly books and serious nonfiction in most areas of the humanities, the social sciences, health care, and higher education. Special interests include health care and social issues; caregiving and family policy; studies of race, class, gender, and sexuality; human rights and social justice; public policy; Hispanic and Latin American studies; African American studies; sociology and anthropology; and regional books.
Copublishing program: Country Music Foundation

The University of Virginia Press

Street Address:
Bemiss House
210 Sprigg Lane
Charlottesville, VA 22903-0608

Mailing Address:
PO Box 400318
Charlottesville, VA 22904-4318

Phone: 434.924.3468
Fax: 434.982.2655
Email: vapress@virginia.edu
Indiv: (user I.D.)@virginia.edu

Warehouse Address:
500 Edgemont Road
Charlottesville, VA 22903-0608
Phone: 434.924.6305
Fax: 434.982.2655

Website and Social Media:
Website: www.upress.virginia.edu
Facebook: www.facebook.com/uvapress
Twitter: uvapress

UK/European Representative:
Eurospan

Canadian Representative:
Scholarly Book Services

Staff
Interim Director: Mark H. Saunders (434.924.6064; email: msaunders)
    Assistant Editor and Rights/Permissions Manager: Angie Hogan (434.924.3361; email: arh2h)

Acquisitions Editorial: Cathie Brettschneider (humanities) (434.982.3033; email: cib8b); Richard K. Holway (history and social sciences) (434.924.7301; email: rkh2a); Boyd Zenner (architecture, environmental studies, ecocriticism, and regional) (434.924.1373; email: bz2v)
  Editorial Assistant: Raennah Mitchell (434.924.4725; email: rm3xa)
Electronic Imprint: Mark H. Saunders, Manager (434.924.6064; email: mhs5u)
  Editorial and Technical Manager: David Sewell (434.924.9973; email: dsewell)
  Project Editor and Technical Specialist: Markus Flatscher (434.982.2310; email: markus. flatscher)
  Programmer/Analyst: Shannon Shiflett (434.924.4544; email: shiflett)
Manuscript Editorial: Ellen Satrom, Managing Editor (434.924.6065; email: egs6s)
  Assistant Managing Editor: Mark Mones (434.924.6066; email: emm4t)
  Project Editor: Morgan Myers (434.924.6067; email: jm3yg)
Design and Production: Martha Farlow, Design/Production Manager (434.924.3585; email: mfarlow)
  Assistant Design/Production Manager: Chris Harrison (434.924.6069; email: crh4w)
  Design/Production Assistant: Lindsey Saxby (434.982.2704, les4yg@virginia.edu)
Marketing: Mark H. Saunders, Assistant Director and Director of Marketing (434.924.6064; email: msaunders)
  Marketing and Publicity Manager: Emily Grandstaff (434.982.2932; email: egrandstaff)
  Advertising and Exhibits Associate: Stephanie Lovegrove (434.924.6070; email: stephanie. lovegrove)
  Marketing and Promotions Manager: Jason Coleman (434.924.4150; email: jcoleman)
Chief Accountant: Duncan Pickett (434.924.6068; email: fdp7e)
  Customer Service Manager: Brenda Fitzgerald (434.924.3469; email: bwf)
  Customer Service Assistant: Kati Runkle (434.924.3468; email: kar9x)
  Warehouse Manager: Johnny Tyler (434.924.6305; email: jrt3u)
  Warehouse Assistant: Willie Clark (434.924.3712; email: wec8e)

Full Member

Established: 1963   Admitted to AAUP: 1964
Title output 2011: 59   Title output 2012: 67
Titles currently in print: 1,048

Editorial Program

Scholarly publications in humanities and social sciences, with concentrations in American history; African American studies; Southern studies; political science; literary and cultural studies, with particular strengths in African and Caribbean studies; Victorian studies; religious studies; architecture and landscape studies; environmental studies; animal studies; regional trade; Virginiana.

The Press also publishes digital publications, primarily critical and documentary editions, and an architectural dictionary, through Rotunda. Documentary editions (ongoing): The Dolly Madison Digital Edition; The Papers of George Washington; The Papers of James Madison; The Papers of Abraham Lincoln; The Eleanor Roosevelt Papers; Selected Papers of John Jay; The Diaries of Gouverneur Morris.
Special series: The American Literatures Initiative; The American South; Buildings of the

United States; CARAF Books (Caribbean and African Literature translated from the French); The Carter G. Woodson Institute Series in Black Studies; Constitutionalism and Democracy; Cultural Frames, Framing Culture; Early American Histories; Jeffersonian America; The Modern Language Initiative; A Nation Divided: Studies in the Civil War Era; New World Studies; The Page-Barbour and Richard Lecture Series; Race, Ethnicity, and Politics; Reconsiderations in Southern African History; Studies in Early Modern German History; Studies in Pure Sociology; Studies in Religion and Culture; Under the Sign of Nature: Explorations in Ecocriticism; Victorian Literature and Culture; Walker Cowen Memorial Prize in Eighteenth-Century Studies

University of Washington Press

Street Address:
4333 Brooklyn Avenue NE
Seattle, WA 98195

Mailing Address:
PO Box 50096
Seattle, WA 98145-5096

Phone: 206.543.4050
Fax: 206.543.3932
Email: (user I.D.)@u.washington.edu

Orders:
Hopkins Fulfillment Services
Phone: 410.516.6956
Fax: 410.516.6998

Website and Social Media:
Website: www.washington.edu/uwpress
Facebook: www.facebook.com/pages/
   University of Washington Press
Twitter: UWAPress
YouTube: YouTube.com/uwashingtonpress
Pinterest: pinterest.com/uwapress/

UK Representative:
Combined Academic Publishers

Canadian Sales Group:
University of British Columbia Press

Staff
Administration:
   Director: Nicole Mitchell (206.685.9373; email: nfmm)
   Assistant to Director and Permissions Manager: Denise Clark (206.543.4057;
   email: ddclark)
   Associate Director and General Manager: Mary Anderson (206.221.5892;
   email: maryande)
   Advancement Officer and Grants Manager: Beth Fuget (206.616.0818; email: bfuget)
Acquisitions: Lorri Hagman, Executive Editor (206.221.4989; email: lhagman)
   Senior Acquisitions Editors: Ranjit Arab (206.221.4984; email: rarab); Marianne Kedding-
   ton-Lang (206.450.5383; email: mkedlang)
   Assistant Acquisitions Editor: Tim Zimmermann (206.221.4940; email: tjz)
Editorial: TBA, Managing Editor
   Assistant Managing Editor: Mary Ribesky (206.685.9165; email: ribesky)
   Editor and Website Manager: Kathleen Pike Jones (206.221.4986; email: kpike)
Production and Design: Pamela Canell, Production Manager (206.221.4993; email: pcanell)
   Production Coordinator: Diane Murphy (206.221.4992; email: kdm)

Senior Designer: Tom Eykemans (206.685.9877; email: eykemans)
Designer: Dustin Kilgore (206.685.9877; email: mrdustin)
Marketing and Sales: TBA,-Director
  Sales and Publicity Manager: Rachael Levay (617.871.0295; email: remann)
  Assistant Marketing Manager: Phoebe Daniels (206.221.4996; email: phoebea)
Business:
  Accounts Receivable: Linda Tom (206.543.4722; email: lindatom)
  Accounts Payable: Heidi Olson (206.543.2858; email: hoatar)

Full Member

Established: 1915   Admitted to AAUP: 1937
Title output 2011: 44   Title output 2012: 56
Titles currently in print: 2,300

Editorial Program

Art history, architecture and sustainable design, Asian studies, Asian American studies, Native American studies, Scandinavian studies, anthropology, Western and environmental history, natural history, environmental studies, and regional history and culture of the Pacific Northwest.

Special series and imprints: Art History Publication Initiative (AHPI); Capell Family Books; Center for Korea Studies Publications; China Program Books; Classics of Chinese Thought; Classics of Tlingit Oral Literature; Critical Dialogues in Southeast Asian Studies; Culture, Place, and Nature: Studies in Anthropology and Environment; Donald R. Ellegood Publications in International Studies; Emil and Kathleen Sick Lecture-Book Series in Western History and Biography; Franklin D. Murphy Lecture Series; Gandharan Buddhist Texts; Global Re-Visions; A History of East Central Europe; In Vivo: The Cultural Mediations of Biomedical Science; Jackson School Publications in International Studies; Jacob Lawrence Series on American Artists; Korean Studies of the Henry M. Jackson School of International Studies; Literary Conjugations; McLellan Books in the Humanities; Modern Language Initiative (MLI); Naomi B. Pascal Books; New Directions in Scandinavian Studies; Pacific Northwest Poetry Series; Weinstein Series in Post-Holocaust Studies; Robert B. Heilman Books; Samuel and Althea Stroum Lectures in Jewish Studies; Samuel and Althea Stroum Books; Scott and Lauri Oki Series in Asian American Studies; Studies on Ethnic Groups in China; Studies in Modernity and National Identity; Sustainable Design Solutions from the Pacific Northwest; Thomas Burke Memorial Washington State Museum Monographs; V Ethel Willis White Books; Weinstein Series in Post-Holocaust Studies; Weyerhaeuser Environmental Books

Publishing partners (sales rights in parentheses): Canadian Museum of Civilization (US); Fowler Museum at UCLA (world); Hearst Museum of Anthropology (world); International Sculpture Center (world); Museum for African Art (world); National Gallery of Australia (North America); Power Publications (North America); Silkworm Books (world outside Southeast Asia); UCLA Chicano Studies Research Center (CSRC) Press(world); University of British Columbia Press (US)

Washington State University Press

Cooper Publications Building
Grimes Way
PO Box 645910
Pullman, WA 99164-5910

Orders:
Phone: 800.354.7360; 509.335.7880

Phone: 509.335.3518
Fax: 509.335.8568
Email: wsupress@wsu.edu
Indiv: (user I.D.)@wsu.edu

Canadian Representatives:
Ingram Book Company
Baker & Taylor Books

Website and Social Media:
Website: wsupress.wsu.edu
Facebook: www.facebook.com/pages/
   Washington-State-University-Press/121327661093

Staff
Director: Mary Read (509.335.3518; email: read)
Permissions: Marc Lindsey (509.335.3518; email: lindseym)
Editor-in-Chief: Robert Clark (509.335.3518; email: robert.clark)
Production Editor: Nancy Grunewald (509.335.3518; email: grunewan)
Marketing Manager: Caryn Lawton (509.335.3518; email: lawton)
Order Fulfillment Coordinator: TBA (509.335.7880; email: wsupress)

Full Member
Established: 1927
Title output 2011: 2
Titles currently in print: 122

Admitted to AAUP: 1987
Title output 2012: 3
Journals published: 1

Editorial Program
Pacific Northwest; natural history; history, science, politics, and culture relating to the region; Western American history; ethnic studies; Native American studies; women's studies; and environmental issues. The Press distributes publications for the Hutton Settlement, Oregon Writers Colony, Pacific Institute, Tornado Creek Publications, Wenatchee Valley Museum and Cultural Center, WSU Center to Bridge the Digital Divide, WSU Museum of Art, WSU Thomas S. Foley Institute, and Washington State Historical Society.
Journal: *Northwest Science*

Wayne State University Press

The Leonard N. Simons Bldg.
4809 Woodward Avenue
Detroit, MI 48201.1309

Orders:
Phone: 800.WSU.READ (978.7323)

Phone: 313.577.6126
Fax: 313.577.6131
Email: (user I.D.)@wayne.edu

Website and Social Media:
Website: wsupress.wayne.edu
Facebook: www.facebook.com/pages/Wayne.State.University.Press/108867051009
Twitter: WSUPress

Canadian Distributor:
Scholarly Book Services

UK/European Distributor:
Eurospan

Staff

Director: Jane Hoehner (313.577.4220; email: jane.hoehner)

Community Engagement and Development: Gabe Gloden (313.577.6130; email: ggloden)

Acquisitions Editorial: Kathryn Wildfong, Editor-in-Chief (313.577.6070; email: k.wildfong) (Great Lakes, Judaica, citizenship studies)

Editor: Annie Martin (313.577.8335; email: annie.martin) (film, fairy tale studies, Africana, speech language pathology)

Assistant Editor, Rights and Permissions: Kristina Stonehill (313.577.6127; email: as8399) (television)

Editorial, Design, and Production: Kristin Harpster, EDP Manager (313.577.4604; email: khlawrence)

Assistant Editorial Manager and Reprints Manager: Carrie Downes Teefey (313.577.6123; email: carrie.downes)

Assistant Design and Production Manager: Maya Whelan (313.577.4600; email: m.whelan)

Marketing/Sales: Emily Nowak, Marketing and Sales Manager (313.577.6128; email: aj3076)

Promotion and Direct Mail Manager: Sarah Murphy (313.577.6077; email: murphysa)

Advertising and Exhibits Manager: Jamie Jones (313.577.6054; email: eh3495)

Journals: Alicia Vonderharr, Journals Manager (313.577.4607; email: aliciav)

Journals Marketing and Sales Coordinator: Lauren Crocker (313.577.4603; email lauren.crocker)

Business: Andrew Kaufman, Business Manager (313.577.3671; email ae4245)

Fulfillment Manager: Theresa Martinelli (313.577.6126; email: theresa.martinelli)

Customer Service: Colleen Stone (313.577.6120; email: colleen.stone)

Accounts Receivable: DeLisa Fields (313.577.6257; email: ak2081)

Warehouse Manager: Todd Richards (313.577.4619; email: aa5624)

Shipping: John Twomey (313.577.4609; email: ai7331)

Technical Project Manager: Bonnie Russell (313.577.1283; email: dt2877)

Full Member

Established: 1941

Title output 2011: 30

Titles currently in print: 914

Admitted to AAUP: 1956

Title output 2012: 34

Journals published: 7

Editorial Program

Scholarly books and serious nonfiction, with special interests in regional and local history and literature; Africana; Judaica; film and television studies; fairy tales and folklore; speech and language pathology; citizenship studies; and gender and ethnic studies.

Journals: *Criticism*; *Discourse*; *Framework*; *Human Biology*; *Marvels and Tales*; *Merrill Palmer Quarterly*; *Jewish Film & New Media*

Special series: African American Life; Citizenship Studies; Contemporary Approaches to Film and Media; Fairy Tale Studies; Great Lakes Books; Made in Michigan Writers Series; Painted Turtle Books; Raphael Patai Series in Jewish Folklore and Anthropology; TV Milestones; William Beaumont Hospital Series in Speech and Language Pathology;

Joint imprints, copublishing, and distribution programs: Hebrew Union College Press; Cranbrook Institute of Science; Detroit Institute of Arts; Lotus Press; University of Alberta Press

Wesleyan University Press

Editorial Offices:

215 Long Lane

Middletown, CT 06459

Phone: 860.685.7711

Fax: 860.685.7712

Email: (user I.D.)@wesleyan.edu

Book Distribution Center:

Wesleyan University Press

c/o University Press of New England

1 Court Street, Suite 250

Lebanon, NH 03766-1358

Phone: 800.421.1561

Fax: 603.643.1540

Website and Social Media:

Website: www.wesleyan.edu/wespress/

Facebook: www.facebook.com/pages/Middletown-CT/
   Wesleyan-University-Press/101994439844863

Twitter: weslpress

UK/European Representative:

Eurospan

Canadian Representative:

University of British Columbia Press

Staff

Director/Editor-in-Chief: Suzanna Tamminen (860.685.7727; email: stamminen)

Acquisitions Editor: Parker Smathers (860.685.7730; email: psmathers)

Marketing: Leslie Starr, Assistant Director/Marketing Manager (860.685.7725; email: lstarr)

Publicist: Stephanie Elliott (860.685.7723; email: selliott)

Full Member

Established: 1957

Title output 2011: 31

Titles currently in print: 468

Admitted to AAUP: 2001

(Former membership: 1966-1991)

Title output 2012: 30

Editorial Program
The current editorial program focuses on poetry, music, dance, science fiction studies, film/
TV/media studies, regional studies, and American studies.
Special series: Early Classics of Science Fiction; Music/Culture; Music/Interview; Wesleyan
Poetry; Wesleyan Film; Garnet Books

University of the West Indies Press

7A Gibraltar Hall Road
Kingston 7
Jamaica West Indies

Phone: 876.977.2659
Fax: 876.977.2660

Website and Social Media:
Website: www.uwipress.com

UK/European Distributor:
Eurospan

US and Caribbean Orders:
Longleaf Services
P.O. Box 8895
Phone: 800.848.6224

Canadian Distributor:
Scholarly Book Services

Staff
Director: Linda Speth (email: lspeth@cwjamaica.com)
Editorial & Production Manager: Shivaun Hearne (email: shivearne@gmail.com)
Marketing & Sales Manager: Donna Muirhead
   (email: uwipress_marketing@cwjamaica.com)
Finance Manager: Nadine Buckland (email: nbuckland@cwjamaica.com)

International Member
Established: 1992
Title output 2011: 27
Titles currently in print: 300

Admitted to AAUP: 2005
Title output 2012: NR
Journals published: 1

Editorial Program
Scholarly books in the humanities and social sciences with lists emphasizing a Caribbean
context in the fields of cultural studies, gender studies, history, literature, economics, education, environmental studies, sociology, and political science.
Journal: *Journal of Caribbean History*

West Virginia University Press

Street Address:
Bicentennial House
1535 Mileground Road
Morgantown, WV 26506

Mailing Address:
PO Box 6295
Morgantown, WV 26506-6295

Phone: 304.293.8400
Fax: 304.293.6585

Order Fulfillment and Distribution:
Chicago Distribution Center
11030 South Langley Ave.
Chicago, IL 60628
Phone: 800.621.2736
Fax: 800.621.8476

Website and Social Media:
Website: www.wvupress.com
Facebook: www.facebook.com/
  westvirginiauniversitypress

Staff
Director: Carrie Mullen (ext. 202; email: carrie.mullen@mail.wvu.edu)
Marketing Manager: Abby Freeland (ext. 206; email: abby.freeland@mail.wvu.edu)
Production Manager/Art Director: Than Saffel (ext. 204; email: than.saffel@mail.wvu.edu)
Journals Manager/Editor: Hilary Attfield (ext. 205; email: hilary.hattfield@mail.wvu.edu)
Office Manager: Floann Downey (ext. 201; email: floann.downey@mail.wvu.edu)

Full Member
Established: 1963
Title output 2011: 15
Titles currently in print: 145

Admitted to AAUP: 2003
Title output 2012: 15
Journals published: 5

Editorial Program
Serious works of nonfiction in American history, with an emphasis on West Virginia and Appalachia; art history, economic history; ethnic studies; West Virginia and Appalachian fiction; medieval studies, especially Anglo-Saxon studies; regional studies in Appalachia; American studies; natural history. A second imprint, Vandalia Press, publishes fiction and non-fiction of interest to the general reader concerning Appalachia and, more specifically, West Virginia.
Journals: *Education and Treatment of Children; Essays in Medieval Studies; Tolkien Studies; Victorian Poetry; West Virginia History*
Special series: Medieval European Studies; Regenerations: African American Literature and Culture; Rural Studies; West Virginia University Sound Archive Series; West Virginia and Appalachia Series, West Virginia Classics

Wilfrid Laurier University Press

75 University Avenue West
Waterloo, ON N2L 3C5 Canada

Phone: 519.884.0710 ext. 6124
Fax: 519.725.1399
Email: press@wlu.ca
Indiv: (user I.D.)@press.wlu.ca

<u>Canadian & US Distributor:</u>
UTP Distribution

<u>UK/European Distributor:</u>
Gazelle Book Services Limited

<u>Website and Social Media:</u>
Website: www.wlupress.wlu.ca
Blog: nestor.wlu.ca/blog/
Facebook: www.facebook.com/wlupress
Twitter: wlupress

Staff

Director: Brian Henderson (ext. 6123; email: brian)
Acquisitions Editors: Lisa Quinn (ext. 2843; email: quinn); Ryan Chynces (ext. 2034; email: rchynces)
Managing Editor: Rob Kohlmeier (ext. 6119; email: rob)
Production and Editorial Projects Manager: Heather Blain-Yanke (ext. 6122; email: heather)
Marketing Manager: Penny Grows (ext. 6605; email: pgrows)
    Web Page and Marketing Coordinator: Leslie Macredie (ext. 6281; email: leslie)
    Publicist: Clare Hitchens (ext. 2665; email: clare)
Coordinator, Distribution & Journals: Cheryl Beaupré (ext. 6124; email: cheryl)
Financial Administrator: Phillip McTaggert (ext. 6030; email: phillip)
Information Systems: Steve Izma, Computing Systems Administrator (ext. 6125; email: steve)

Full Member

Established: 1974
Title output 2011: 37
Titles currently in print: 421

Admitted to AAUP: 1986
Title output 2012: 40
Journals published: 7

Editorial Program

Art and art history; Canadian literature; cultural studies; environmental studies; family studies; film and media studies; history; indigenous studies; life writing; literary criticism; literature in translation; military history; music; philosophy; poetry; politics; religious studies; social work; sociology/anthropology; women's studies.

Journals: *Anthropologica; Canadian Bulletin of Medical History; Canadian Journal of Community Mental Health; Canadian Military History; Canadian Social Work Review; Florilegium; Indigenous Law Journal; Topia: A Canadian Journal of Cultural Studies*

Special series and joint imprints: Bahá'í Studies (with the Association for Bahá'í Studies); Canadian Commentaries; Canadian Corporation for Studies in Religion; Collected Works of Florence Nightingale; Comparative Ethics; Cultural Studies; Editions SR; Environmental Humanities; Film and Media Studies; German Studies; Indigenous Studies; Laurier Military History; Laurier Poetry; Laurier Studies in Political Philosophy; Life Writing; Studies in Childhood and Family in Canada; Studies in Christianity and Judaism; Studies in International Governance (with the Centre for International Governance Innovation); Studies in Women and Religion; TransCanada

The University of Wisconsin Press

1930 Monroe Street, 3rd Floor
Madison, WI 53711-2059

Phone: 608.263.1110
Fax: 608.263.1120
Email: uwiscpress@uwpress.wisc.edu
Indiv: (user I.D.)@wisc.edu

Orders:
Chicago Distribution Center
11030 South Langley Ave.
Chicago, IL 60628-3892
Phone: 800.621.2736; 773.702.7000
Fax: 800.621.8476; 773.702.7212

Website and Social Media:
Website: uwpress.wisc.edu
Facebook: university of wisconsin press

UK Distributor:
Eurospan

Staff

Director: Sheila Leary (608.263.1101; email: smleary)
  Subsidiary Rights: Anne McKenna (608.263.1131; email: rights@uwpress.wisc.edu)
  Permissions: permissions@uwpress.wisc.edu
Acquisitions Editorial: Senior Acquisitions Editor: Raphael Kadushin (608.263.1062; email: kadushin) (biography and memoirs, Classical studies, dance, fiction, film, folklore, gay/lesbian interest, 20th-C European history, Jewish interest, poetry contest, travel)
  Acquisitions Editor: Gwen Walker (608.263.1123; email: gcwalker) (African studies, American history, botany, environmental studies, Irish history, human rights, Latin American studies, Russian/East European studies, Southeast Asian studies, regional Wisconsin and Great Lakes history and natural history)
Manuscript Editorial: Managing Editor: Adam Mehring (608.263.0856; email: amehring)
  Editor: Sheila McMahon (608.263.1133; email: samcmahon)
Design and Production: Terry Emmrich, Production Manager (608.263.0731; email: temmrich)
  Assistant Production Manager: Carla Marolt (608.263.0732; email: marolt)
  Senior Compositor: Scott Lenz (608.263.0794; email: sjlenz)
Marketing: Andrea Christofferson, Marketing Manager (608.263.0814; email: aschrist)
  Advertising: (608.263.0733; email: advertising@uwpress.wisc.edu)
  Publicity Manager: Elena Spagnolie (608.263.0734; email: publicity@uwpress.wisc.edu)
  Exhibits and Data Coordinator: Lindsey Meier (608.263.1136; email: lnmeier)
Journals: Jason Gray, Journals Manager (608.263.0667; email: jmgray5)
  Production and Assistant Manager: Susan Kau (608.263.0669; email: szkau)
  Advertising: Adrienne Omen (608.263.0534; email: amomen)
  Marketing: Toni Gunnison (608.263.0753; email: gunnison)
  Customer Service: Debra Rasmussen (608.263.1135; email: dlrasmussen)
  Bookkeeper: Beth Johnson (608.263.0654; email: bajohnso)
Business: Dave Stange, Accountant: (608.263.1137; email: dmstange)

Office Manager: Jim Hahn (608.263.1128; email: jhahn3)
Business office fax: (608.263.1120)

Full Member

Established: 1937

Title output 2011: 60

Titles currently in print: 2,070

Admitted to AAUP: 1945

Title output 2012: 61

Journals published: 11

Editorial Program

Scholarly and general-interest works in African studies; American cultural and intellectual history; Classical studies; environmental studies and botany; fiction; film studies; folklore; dance; gay/lesbian studies and memoirs; human rights; Jewish studies; Latin American studies and Latino memoirs; modern European and Irish history; Russian and East European studies; Southeast Asian studies; and Wisconsin and the Upper Midwest (all aspects). For the Brittingham, Felix Pollak, and Four Lakes Poetry series, contest guidelines are available online at www.wisc.edu/wisconsinpress/poetryguide.html

Journals: *American Orthoptic Journal; Arctic Anthropology; Contemporary Literature; Ecological Restoration; Journal of Human Resources; Land Economics; Landscape Journal; Luso-Brazilian Review; Monatshefte; Native Plants Journal; SubStance*

Special series: Africa and the Diaspora: History, Politics, Culture; Brittingham Prize in Poetry, Felix Pollak Prize in Poetry, Four Lakes Poetry Series; Critical Human Rights; Folklore Studies in a Multicultural World; George L. Mosse Series in Modern European Cultural and Intellectual History; Harvey Goldberg Series for Understanding and Teaching History; History of Ireland and the Irish Diaspora; Languages and Folklore of the Upper Midwest; Living Out: Gay and Lesbian Autobiographies; New Perspectives in Southeast Asian Studies; Print Culture History in Modern America; Publications of the Wisconsin Center for Pushkin Studies; Sources in Modern Jewish History; Studies in American Thought and Culture; Studies in Dance History; Wisconsin Film Studies; Wisconsin Land and Life; Wisconsin Studies in Autobiography; Wisconsin Studies in Classics; Women in Africa and the Diaspora; Writing in Latinidad

Imprints: Terrace Books, Popular Press

The Woodrow Wilson Center Press

Woodrow Wilson International Center for Scholars
One Woodrow Wilson Plaza
1300 Pennsylvania Avenue, N.W.
Washington, DC 20004-3027

Phone: 202.691.4042
Fax: 202.691.4001
Email: press@wilsoncenter.org
Indiv: (user I.D)@wilsoncenter.org

Website and Social Media:
Website: www.wilsoncenter.org/press

Staff

Director: Joseph Brinley (202.691.4042; e-mail: joe.brinley)
Editor: TBA
    Editorial Assistant: Cherie Worth (202.691.4029; email: cherie.worth)

Associate Member

Established: 1987
Title output 2011: 15
Titles currently in print: 262

Admitted to AAUP: 1992
Title output 2012: 16

Editorial Program

Woodrow Wilson Center Press publishes work written at or for the Woodrow Wilson International Center for Scholars, the official memorial of the United States to its twenty-eighth president. The Center was created by law in 1968 as a living memorial "symbolizing and strengthening the fruitful relation between the world of learning and the world of public affairs." The Press's books come from both the work of the Center's scholars in residence and from some of the eight hundred meetings held at the Center each year.

The Center's interests range widely in areas associated with questions of public policy. The Press has published in American studies; history; international relations; political science; economics and finance; religious studies; urban studies; women's studies; and the study of Africa, Asia, Europe, Latin America, and the Middle East.

All the Press's books are copublished. Partners include Johns Hopkins University Press, Stanford University Press, Indiana University Press, University of California Press, University of Pennsylvania Press, and Columbia University Press. The Cold War International History Project Series is copublished with Stanford.

Yale University Press

Street Address:
302 Temple Street
New Haven, CT 06511

Mailing Address:
PO Box 209040
New Haven, CT 06520-9040

Main: 203.432.0960
203.432.6129 (Receptionist)
203.432.0900 (Acquisitions Editorial)
203.432.4060 (Design/Production)
203.432.0961 (Marketing)
203.432.0163 (Publicity)
Email: (firstname.lastname)@yale.edu

Distribution/Customer Service:
Triliteral LLC
Customer Service Toll Free: 1.800.405.1619
Customer Service Fax 800.406.9145

Yale Press Fax Numbers
203.432.6862 (Accounting)
203.432.0948 (Administration)
203.436.1064 (Acquisitions 1st Floor)
203.432.2394 (Acquisitions 2nd Floor)
203.432.8485 (Marketing 3rd Floor)
203.432.5455 (Promotion)
203.432.4061 (Design/Production)
401.658.4193 (Warehouse)

London Office:
47 Bedford Square
London WCIB 3DP
United Kingdom
Phone: 9-011-44-20-7079-4900
Fax: 9-011-44-20--7079-4901
Email: firstname.lastname@yale.co.uk

Website and Social Media:
Website: www.yale.edu/yup/
Blog: yalepress.typepad.com/yalepresslog/
Facebook: www.facebook.com/yalepress
Twitter: yalepress

Staff

Director: John E. Donatich (203.432.0933)
  Executive Assistant to the Director: Danielle Di Bianco (203.432.4301)
  Margellos Series Coordinator: Elina Bloch (347.282.9568)
  Chief Operating Officer: Katherine Brown (203.432.8496)
  Chief Financial Officer & Assistant Director: John D. Rollins (203.432.0938)
  Permissions and Ancillary Rights Manager: Donna Anstey (203.432.0932)
  Acquisitions Editorial: Christopher Rogers, Editorial Director/Executive Editor, History, Current Events (203.432.0935); Jean E. Thomson Black, Executive Editor, Life Sciences, Physical Sciences, Environmental Sciences, Medicine (203.432.7534); Eric Brandt, Senior Editor, Humanities, Literary Studies, Cultural Studies, History of Ideas, Performing Arts (203.432.8010); William Frucht, Executive Editor, Law, Political Science International Relations, and Economics (203.432.7571); Patricia Fidler, Art Publisher, Art and Architectural (203.432.0927); Jennifer Banks, Senior Editor, Religion, Classics, Philosophy (203.432.6807); Joseph Calamia, Editor, Physical Sciences, Environmental Sciences, Geology, Applied Mathematics, Engineering (203.432.0904); Laura Davulis, Digital Projects Editor; Associate Editor, History (203.432.5701); Michelle Komie, Senior Acquisitions Editor, Art and Architecture (203.432.8420); Sarah Miller, Editor, College Course-books

(203.432.0901); Tim Shea, Editor, Foreign Languages and ESL (203.432.4921); Vadim Staklo, Associate Editor, Annals of Communism, Reference List (203.432.0631); Steve Wasserman, Executive Editor at Large, Trade List (203.432.9698)

Director of Publishing Operations: Christina Coffin (203.432.4062)

Manuscript Editorial: Jenya Weinreb, Managing Editor (203.432.0914)

  Assistant Managing Editor: Mary Pasti (203.432.0911)

  Editors: Laura Jones Dooley (804.714.4466); Dan Heaton (203.432.1017); Ann-Marie Imbornoni (203.432.0903); Phillip King (203.432.1015); Susan Laity (203.432.0922); Margaret Otzel (203.432.0918); Jeffrey Schier (203.432.4001); Heidi Downey (203.432.2390)

Production: Associate Production Manager: Maureen Noonan (203.432.4064)

  Reprint Controller: Orna Johnston (203.432.4060)

  Production Manager Art Books: Mary Mayer (203.432.0925)

  Production Controller: Katherine Golden (203.436.8022)

  Senior Production Controller: Aldo Cupo (203.432.7484)

  Design: Art Director: Nancy Ovedovitz (203.432.4067)

  Designers: Lindsey Voskowsky (203.432.4065); James L. Johnson (203.432.4068); Sonia Scanlon (203.432.4066); Mary Valencia (203.432.8092)

Sales: Jay Cosgrove, Sales Director (203.432.0968)

  General Sales Queries: (203.432.0966)

  Academic and Library Sales Manager: (203.432.7350)

  Art & Digital Sales Manager: Stephen Cebik (203.432.2539)

Marketing and Promotions Director: Heather D'Auria (203.432.8193)

  Publicity Director: Brenda King (203.432.0917)

  Publicists: Robert Pranzatelli (203.432.0972); Alden Ferro (203.432.0909); Elizabeth Pelton (410.467.0989); Jennifer Doerr (203.432.0969); Julia Haav (718.715.1081).

  General Publicity Inquiries: Daniel Blanchard (203.432.0163)

  Online Marketing Coordinator: Ivan Lett (203.432.0961)

  Educational Marketing Manager: Debra Bozzi (203.432.0959)

  Academic Discipline Marketer: Karen Stickler (203.436.8467)

  Direct Mail Assistant: Lisa Scecina: (203.432.0957)

  Exhibits/Advertising Manager: Ellen Freiler (203.432.0958)

  Assistant Marketing Director: David Wilfinger (203.432.0974)

Digital Publishing: David Schiffman, Director of Digital Publishing (203.432.2619)

  Digital Product Manager: Sara Sapire (203.432.0965)

  Digital Production Editor: John Carlson (203.436.9298)

Business: John D. Rollins, Chief Financial Officer & Assistant Director (203.432.0938)

  Accounting Manager: Timothy Haire (203.436.1924)

  Senior Accountant: Wendy DeNardis (203.432.0951)

  Accounting Assistant: Stephanie Pierre (203.432.0949)

  Database Analyst: Marc Benigni (203.432.8446)

  Operations Coordinator: Theresa Donroe: (203.432.0952)

  Inventory & Building Operations Manager: Jim Stritch (203.432.0939)

  Computer Information Services Manager: Milton Kahl (203.432.0937)

London Office:

Managing Director, London and Editorial Director (Humanities): Robert Baldock

Publisher, Art and Architecture: Gillian Malpass, History of Art, History of Architecture and Fashion

Publisher, Trade Books, London: Heather McCallum, History, Politics, Current Affairs, International Affairs, Biography, History of Science
Publisher, Pevsner Architectural Guides: Sally Salvesen, Decorative Arts, Art and Architecture
Head of Marketing: Noel Murphy
Foreign Rights Manager: Anne Bihan
Editor: Phoebe Clapman, Politics, Economics, Current Affairs

Full Member

Established: 1908   Admitted to AAUP: 1937
Title output 2011: 466   Title output 2012: 490
Titles currently in print: 5,688

Editorial Program

Humanities, social sciences, natural sciences, physical sciences, medicine. Poetry is not accepted except for submissions to the Yale Series of Younger Poets contest, held annually. Festschriften and collections of previously published articles are not invited and very rarely accepted.

Special series, joint imprints and/or co-publishing programs: Agrarian Studies; Anchor Bible and Commentaries; Annals of Communism; The Annotated Shakespeare; Babylonian Collection; Bard Graduate Center; Carnegie Endowment for International Peace; The Castle Lectures in Ethics, Politics, and Economics; A Century Foundation Book; Complete Prose Works of John Milton; Complete Works of St. Thomas More; Council on Foreign Relations; Cowles Foundation; Culture and Civilization of China; Darden Innovation and Entrepreneurship; David Brion Davis Lectures; Democracy in America; The Diary of Joseph Farington; Dodge Lectures; Dura-Europos; Economic Census Studies; Economic Growth Center; Economic History; Elizabethan Club; English Monarchs; Faith and Globalization; George Elliot Letters; The Henry McBride Series in Modernism and Modernity; Henry Roe Cloud Series for American Indigenous Peoples and Modernity; History of the Soviet Gulag System; Horace Walpole Correspondence; Institute for Social and Policy Studies; Institute of Far Eastern Languages; Institution of Human Relations; Intellectual History of the West; Italian Literature and Culture; James Boswell; Jewish Lives; Lamar Series In Western History; Library of Medieval Philosophy; Neighborhoods of New York City; Margellos World Republic of Letters; New Directions In Narrative History; The New Republic; Oak Spring Garden Library; Okun; Open University; Page Lectures; The Papers of Benjamin Franklin; The Papers of Benjamin Latrobe; Papers of Frederick Douglass; Papers on Soviet & East European, Economic & Political Science; Paul Mellon Centre for Studies in British Art; Pelikan History of Art; Percy Letters; Petroleum Monographs; Pevsner Series: Buildings of England, Scotland, and Ireland; Phillips Andover Archaeology; Philosophy and Theory and Art; Poems of Alexander Pope; Posen Library of Jewish Culture and Civilization; Psychoanalytic Study of the Child; The Relations of Canada and the United States; Rethinking the Western Tradition; Russian Classics; Science in Progress; The Selected Papers of Charles Willson Peale and His Family; Silliman Lectures; Society and the Sexes; Stalin Archives; Storrs Lectures; Studies in Comparative Economics; Studies in Hermeneutics; Studies in Modern European Literature and Thought; Terry Lectures; Theoretical Perspectives in Archaeological History; Walpole Series in Eighteenth Century Studies; Why X Matters; The Works of Jonathan Edwards; The Works of Samuel Johnson; Yale Classical Monographs; Yale Classical Studies;

Yale Contemporary Law Series; Yale Drama Series; Yale Edition of the Unpublished Works of Gloria Stein; Yale French Studies; Yale Guide to English Literature; Yale Health and Wellness; Yale Historical Publications; Yale Judaica; Yale Law Library Publications; Yale Law School Studies; Yale Library of Military History; Yale Liebniz; Yale Linguistics; Yale New Classics; Yale Publications in Religion; Yale Romantic Studies; Yale Series of Younger Poets; Yale Studies in Economics; Yales Studies in English; Yale Studies in History & Theory of Religious Education; Yale Studies in Political Science

AAUP PARTNERS

The AAUP Partner Program was launched in 2008. For more details about the AAUP Partner Program, visit www.aaupnet.org/about/partners. The following companies enrolled as Partners in 2012.

Attributor

119 S. B Street, Suite A
San Matero, CA 94401

Phone: 650.340.9601
Fax: 800.851.6536

Website and Social Media:
www.attributor.com

Staff Contacts
CEO: Matt Robinson (650.224.3294; email: matt@attributor.com)
Office Manager: Maricar Baylor (650.340.9601; email: maricar@attributor.com)

Year enrolled as AAUP Partner: 2012

Company Description
Attributor is the global leader in book and document anti-piracy, leak protection and marketing services. The company's software and services protect book revenues and authors' rights by finding and removing pirated content across the Internet.

Baker and Taylor

New Jersey Office:
1120 US Highway 22 East
Bridgewater, NJ 08807 BakerandTaylor

New Hampshire Office:
999 Maple Street
Contoocook, NH 03229

Website and Social Media:
Website: www.baker-taylor.com
Facebook: www.facebook.com/pages/Baker-Taylor/140688295944178
Twitter: BakerandTaylor
YouTube: www.youtube.com/user/BakerandTaylorTV?feature=mhw5

Staff Contacts

Vice President-Academic & Higher Education Library Merchandising: David Hetherington
(908.458.5928; email: david.hetherington@baker-taylor.com)
Divisional Merchandising Director: Sally Neher (908.541.7460; email:sally.nehere@baker-taylor.com)
Co-Op & Advertising Manager, Merchandising Division: Lynn Bond (908.541.7374;
email: lynn.bond@baker-taylor.com)

NH Contacts:

Vice President, Operations and Publisher Relations, YBP Library Services: Nat Bruning
(603/746-3102 x3304; e-mail: nbruning@ybp.com)

Year enrolled as AAUP Partner: 2009

Company Description

Baker & Taylor is a leading distributor of books, videos, and music products to libraries, in-stitutions and retailers. We have been in business for 181 years and have developed long-term relationships with major book publishers, movie studios and music labels. We have more than 44,000 customers in more than 120 countries. Baker & Taylor is also committed to being an industry leader in digital media delivery. Through best-of-breed technologies, Baker & Taylor offers its publishers and customers bundled physical and digital media distribution services.

BookMasters

Compose. Create. Connect.

30 Amberwood Parkway
Ashland, Ohio 44805

Phone: 419.281.5100 Toll-free: 800.537.6727
Fax: 419.281.0200
Email: info@bookmasters.com

<u>Website and Social Media:</u>
Website: www.bookmasters.com
Blog: blog.bookmasters.com/
Facebook: www.facebook.com/bookmastersgroup
Twitter: BookMasters

Staff Contacts
Vice President, Global Development: Deb Keets (800.537.6727 ext. 1140; email: dkeets@bookmasters.com)

Year enrolled as AAUP Partner: 2009

<u>Company Description</u>
Bookmasters, based in Ashland, Ohio, is the largest integrated provider of editorial and design services, eBook conversion, printing, distribution, and marketing services for publishers and authors. The organization has remained a publishing industry leader for more than 40 years.

BookMobile

5120 Cedar Lake Road
Minneapolis, MN 55416

Phone: 800.752.3303
Fax: 763.398.0198
Website: www.bookmobile.com

Staff Contacts

CEO: Don Leeper (763.398.0030, ext. 124; email: dleeper@bookmobile.com)
National Sales Manager: Jeanne Weinkle (312.330.8036; email:
jweinkle@bookmobile.com)
Marketing Director & Publisher Services Manager: Nicole Baxter (800.752.3303, ext. 126;
email: nbaxter@bookmobile.com)
Design & Digital Services Manager: Rachel Holscher (800.752.3303, ext. 112; email:
rholscher@bookmobile.com)
Distribution Manager: Mark Jung (800.901.3480; email: mjung@itascabooks.com)

Year enrolled as AAUP Partner: 2008

Company Description

BookMobile provides innovative digital services and solutions, with a reputation of excellent quality and great customer service. BookMobile provides: short run digital printing; automatic replenishment programs; true print-on-demand; automatic inventory replenishment; Direct-to-Consumer services; eBook conversion; app development; website development; design and typesetting; content management; and eBook and print distribution.

Books International, Inc.

22883 Quicksilver Dr.
Dulles, VA 20166

Phone: 703.661.1500
Fax: 703.661.1501
Website: www.booksintl.com

Staff Contacts
Vice President: Vartan Ajamian (703.661.1519; email: vartan.ajamian@booksintl.com)
Director of Business Development: Ellen Loerke (703.661.1512; email: ellen.loerke@booksintl.com)
Director of Database Management: Beth Prester (703.661.1525; email: beth.prester@booksintl.com)
MIS Director: Sal Signorino (703.661.1514; email: sal@booksintl.com)
Customer Service Manager: Todd Riggleman (703.661.1527; email: todd@booksintl.com)

Year enrolled as AAUP Partner: 2009

Company Description
Books International provides third-party fulfillment services to publishers and distributors using Cats Pajamas software and the new Elan suite of programs. All activity is done under the publisher's name. EDI, PUBNET, website interface all supported. Publishers have daily to their live database to view and export data. On-site digital printing with Integrated Book Technology Inc. (IBT) offers print-to-order and short print run advantages.

Cushing Malloy, Inc./C-M Books

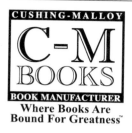

1350 North Main Street
Ann Arbor, MI 48104

Phone: 734.663.8554
Fax: 734.663.5731

Website and Social Media:
Website: www.cushing-malloy.com, www.c-mbooks.com
Twitter: @CM_Books
Facebook: www.facebook.com/CushingMalloyBooks
Pinterest: pinterest.com/cmbooks/

Staff Contacts
President: Thomas F. Weber (734.663.8554; email: tfweber@cushing-malloy.com)
Marketing Director: Meg Souza (734.663.8554; email: msouza@cushing-malloy.com)
Sales/Customer Care: Adam Hieber (734.663.8554; email: ahieber@cushing-malloy.com)

Year enrolled as AAUP Partner: 2012

Company Description
C-M Books is a leader in the world of book manufacturing specializing in the making of soft and hard cover books in short to medium runs. Contact C-M Books today for all of your book production needs (offset, digital, eBooks) and experience our One Contact Customer Service. Where Books Are Bound For Greatness™

codeMantra, LLC

600 West Germantown Pike, Suite 400
Plymouth Meeting, PA 19462

Phone: 610.940.1700
Fax: 215.243.6421
Email: cminfo@codemantra.com

Website and Social Media:
Website: www.codemantra.com

Staff Contacts

President: Anantha Tirupati (610.940.1700; email: andy@codeMantra.com)
Director of Content Solutions: Merv L. Samuels (203.357.8150:
   email: merv@codemantra.com)
Director of Technology: Scott Cook (646.290.7557; email: scook@codemantra.com)
Director of Publishing Services: Walter W.J. Walker (914.310.6205; email: wwjwalker@
   codemantra.com)
Director of Global Client Services: Paul DeMarco (508.497.2500; email:
   pdemarco@codemantra.com)

Year enrolled as AAUP Partner: 2008

Company Description

codeMantra brings a managed approach to digital publishing with, people, processes and
technology. Our reputation is built on quality conversion services, which are complemented
with Collection Point ™ our hosted DAM and DAD (digital asset distribution) offering.
Our Universal PDF ™ is widely embraced as the one format that meets requirements for all
web PDF applications. With pubXML, we offer flexible data modeling and the creation of
XML workflows to deliver all viable digital formats, including ePub, mobiPocket, HTML,
XHTML, PDF, BBeB (Sony), PDB (Palm), NFO (net library),OEB and ASCII. Our complete system enables publishers to fully manage the publishing opportunities in the digital
aftermarket. codeMantra is a Mark Logic technology partner.

Copyright
Clearance
Center

222 Rosewood Drive
Danvers, MA 01923

Phone: 978.750.8400
Fax: 978.646.8600

Website and Social Media:
Website: www.copyright .com
Twitter: copyrightclear

Staff Contacts
Alliances Director: Stephanie Fox (978.646.2531; email: sfox@copyright.com)
Channel Marketing Manager: Julie Estrada (978.646.2613; email: jestrada@copyright.com)

Year enrolled as AAUP Partner: 2012

Company Description
CCC provides smart solutions that simplify the licensing of content that allows businesses and academic institutions quickly get permissions to use copyrighted materials.

Credo Reference

Smart Research Starts Here

201 South Street, Fourth Floor
Boston, MA 01890

Phone: 617.426.5202
Fax: 617.426.3103

Website and Social Media:
Website: www.credoreference.com, corp.credoreference.com
Twitter: credoreference

Staff Contacts
President: John Dove (617.292.6111; email: dove@credoreference.com)
Content Product Specialist: Ingrid Becker
   (617.292.6130; email: ingrid.beck@credoreference.com)

Year enrolled as AAUP Partner: 2012

Company Description
Credo is a completely customizable online reference solution for learners and librarians. Credo's General Reference Collection, Publisher Collections and Subject Collections combine extensive content from multiple publishers with unique cross-referencing technology, effortlessly delivering authoritative answers to millions of researchers worldwide.

Crossref

50 Salem Street
Lynnfield, MA 01840

Phone: 781.295.0072
Fax: 781.295.0072

<u>Website and Social Media:</u>
Webiste: www.crossref.org
Twitter: CrossRefNews

Staff Contacts
Business Development and Marketing: Carol Ann Meyer (email: cmeyer@crossref.org;
   781.629.9782)
Assistant Marketing Manager: Anna Tolwinska (781.295.0072; email: annat@crossref.org)

Year enrolled as AAUP Partner: 2012

<u>Company Description</u>
CrossRef is a not-for-profit association of publishers. Since 2000, it has provided reference
linking services for 54 million content items, including journal articles and books chapters
among others. CrossRef's other services include Cited-By Linking, CrossCheck plagiarism
screening, and CrossMark update identification.

De Gruyter INC.

 DE GRUYTER

121 High Street, Third Floor
Boston, MA 02110

Phone: 857.284.7073
Fax: 857.284.7358
Email: usinfo@degruyter.com

Website and Social Media:
Website: www.degruyter.com
Facebook: www.facebook.com/degruyter.publishers

Staff Contacts
CEO: Dr. Sven Fund (+49 30 260 05 211; email: sven.fund@degruyter.com
Editorial Director, North America: Michiel Klein-Swormink (857.284.7073, ext. 118; email: michiel.klein-swormink@degruyter.com
Director Operations: Andy Paminger (857.284.7073, ext. 109; email: andy.paminger@ degruyter.com)

Year enrolled as AAUP Partner: 2012

Company Description
The academic publishing house De Gruyter can look back on a history spanning over 260 years. The Berlin-based group of companies releases over 800 new titles each year in the fields of medicine, the humanities, natural sciences, social sciences, and law, in addition to more than 600 journals and digital media publications. De Gruyter's mission is the widest possible dissemination of scholarship of the highest academic standards for the international academic community. Outside Germany, De Gruyter has offices in Boston and Beijing.

Ebrary

 ebrary

318 Cambridge Ave.
Palo Alto, CA 94306

Phone: 650.475.8700
Fax: 650.475.8881

<u>Website and Social Media:</u>
Website: www.ebrary.com
Facebook: www.facebook.com/pages/ebrary/154346767012
Twitter: ebrary

Staff Contacts

Director, Content Marketing and Development: Anna Bullard (650.475.8748; email: abullard@ebrary.com)
Director, Publisher Relations: Marc Fawwaz (650.475.8784; email: marc@ebrary.com)
Publisher Relations Manager: Matthew Kull (650.475.8794; email: mkull@ebrary.com)
VP, Content Devlopment: Leslie Lees (650.475.8757; email: leslie@ebrary.com)

Year enrolled as AAUP Partner: 2009

<u>Company Description</u>

ebrary offers libraries the widest variety of models for acquiring e-books from over 500 leading publishers. By partnering with us, publishers can easily and effectively take advantage of the growing e-book market using the same PDF files and metadata that are created in the process of publishing books in print. A member of the ProQuest family of companies.

finitiv

finitiv®

1730 S. El Camino Real Ste 480
San Mateo CA 94402-3079

Phone: 650.212.0400

<u>Website and Social Media:</u>
www.finitiv.com

Staff Contacts
President: Andrew Brenneman (andrew@finitiv.com)
Vice President Technology: Blair Cummins (blair.cummins@finitiv.com)
Vice President Strategy: Robert Lynch (robert.lynch@finitiv.com)
Director of Operations: Wendy Angus (wendy.angus@finitiv.com)

Year enrolled as AAUP Partner: 2011

Company Description
Finitiv drives digital publishing success through the delivery of consulting, technology development, and cloud services. With FinitivPCS™, The Publishers Cloud Suite, Finitiv delivers strategic cloud-based solutions to enable publishers to drive revenue and gain control of their digital initiatives.

Glatfelter

Corporate Headquarter:
96 South George Street
York, PA 17401

Phone: 717.225.4711
Fax: 717.846.7208

Website and Social Media:
www.glatfelter.com

Chillicothe Facility
232 E. Eighth Street
Chillicoth, OH 45601

Phone: 740.772.3111
Fax: 740.772.0024

Staff Contacts
Director of Marketing & Book Publishing Product Manager: Melissa Klug (740.649.3005;
   email: melissa.klug@glatfelter.com)
Key Account Manager: Ken Miller (908.889.4175; email: kenneth.miller@glatfelter.com)

Year enrolled as AAUP Partner: 2011

Company Description
Glatfelter manufactures book publishing papers for university presses; free-sheet papers that
meet all ANSI permanence standards. We believe that if a book is important enough to go in
print, it's important enough to deserve great paper.

Ingram Content Group

INGRAM.

Ingram Content Group
One Ingram Blvd.
LaVergne, TN 37086 USA

Phone: 615.793.5000
Email: inquiry@ingramcontent.com
Website: www.ingramcontent.com

Staff Contacts
Lead Buyer – University Presses: Ron Watson (615.213.5375;
   email: ron.watson@ingramcontent.com)
VP, Content Acquisition, North America: Joe Thomson (615.213.5129; email:
   joe.thomson@ingramcontent.com)
Content Acquisition Account Executive: Jim Heuer (330.220.6552;
   email: jim.heuer@ingramcontent.com)
   VP, Digital Products: Marcus Woodburn (615.213.5628;
   email: marcus.woodburn@ingramcontent.com)

Year enrolled as AAUP Partner: 2010

Company Description
Ingram Content Group Inc. is the world's largest and most trusted distributor of physical and digital content. Thousands of publishers, retailers, and libraries worldwide use our products and services to realize the full business potential of books, regardless of format. Ingram has earned its lead position and reputation by offering excellent service and creating innovative, integrated solutions while anticipating industry changes and creating opportunities for our customers. Our customers have access to best-of-class digital, audio, print, print-on-demand, inventory management, wholesale and full-service distribution programs.

I T H A K A

J S T O R | P O R T I C O | I T H A K A S + R

Addresses:
ITHAKA: JSTOR, Portico, and Ithaka S+R
151 East 61st Street
New York, NY 10065
Phone: 212.500.2600
Fax: 212.500.2366

ITHAKA: JSTOR, Portico , and Ithaka S+R
2 Rector Street, 18th floor
New York, NY 10006
Phone: 212.358.6400
Fax: 212.358.6499

Website and Social Media:
Websites: www.ithaka.org, www.about.jstor.org
Facebook: www.facebook.com/JSTOR.org
Twitter: JSTOR

Staff Contacts:
EVP, JSTOR Managing Director: Laura Brown (212.500.2600;
  email: Laura.brown@ithaka.org)
Director, Books at JSTOR: Frank Smith (212.358.6400;
  email: Frank.smith@ithaka.org)
Director, Current Journals Program: Mary Rose Muccie (609.986.2200;
  email: Maryrose.muccie@ithaka.org)
Associate Director, Marketing & Communications: Sarah Glasser
  (212.358.6400; email: Sarah.glasser@ithaka.org)
Associate Director, Archive Collections: Barbara Chin
  (212.358.6400; email: Barbara.chin@ithaka.org)

Enrolled as AAUP Partner: 2011

Company Description
JSTOR (www.jstor.org) is a research and teaching platform for the academic community. With more than a thousand journals and one million primary sources, JSTOR is one of the world's most trusted sources for academic content. JSTOR is part of ITHAKA (www.ithaka.org), a not-for-profit organization that also includes Portico and Ithaka S+R.

Klopotek North America

klopotek.

Klopotek North America Inc
2001 Route 46
Parsippany, NJ 07054

Phone: 973.331.1010
Fax 973.331.0042

Website: www.klopotek.com

Staff Contacts:
CEO: Ulrich Klopotek (email: u.klopotek@klopotek.com)
SVP Operations: Susan Lehrhaupt (email: s.lehrhaupt@klopotek.com)
VP Sales & Marketing: George Logan (email: g.logan@klopotek.com)
VP Business Development: Steve Waldron (email: s.waldron@klopotekcom)

Enrolled as AAUP Partner: 2011

Company Description
Klopotek's mission is to provide software solutions built on standardized business processes to publishers worldwide. Klopotek is dedicated to develop solutions offering publishers the best strategic and commercial advantages in their ever changing business models.
Over 350 book and journal publishers on four continents are using the Klopotek Standard Software Solution

Lehigh Phoenix
18249 Phoenix Drive
Hagerstown, MD 21742

Phone: 800.632.4111 or 301.733.0018

Website: www.lehighphoenix.com

Staff Contacts

VP-National Sales: Michael Wettstein (917.841.5900;
  email: mwettstein@lehighphoenix.com)
VP-Sales Western Region: Sandy D'Amato (510.688.1954;
  email: sdamato@lehighphoenix.com)
VP-Sales Midwest Region: Eric Henze (614.323.4420;
  email: ehenze@lehighphoenix.com)
Sales Executive (Mid-Atlantic): Michael Cassells (201-707-5715; email: mcassells@lehigh-
  phoenix.com)
Sales Executive (Southeast Region): Trudy Mullendore (240-818-1104; email: tmullendore@
  lehighphoenix.com)

Year enrolled as AAUP Partner: 2012

Company Description

Lehigh Phoenix, with the largest sheet-fed facility in the United States, is the leader in providing book components for all markets. With our technologically advanced prepress and press operations, a knowledgeable customer service team, an array of innovative special effects and finishing operations, and dependable freight services, we are committed to producing distinctive products, including case covers, paperback covers, book jackets, inserts, brochures, and catalogs.

Manila Typesetting Company (MTC)

12th Floor, Pet Plans Building 4444 EDSA
Guadalupe Viejo, Makati City 1212, Philippines 1211
Phone: +632 8976629
Website: www.mtcstm.com

Staff Contacts
Owner & Operations: Paul Hartley (+6328976629; email: phhartley@gmail.com)
Owner & Sales: Michael Angless (+441993709513; email: mangless@mtcstm.com)
Operations: Myrna Ting
Customer Service: Amor Nanas

Year enrolled as AAUP Partner: 2012

Company Description

Sampaguita, a jasmine, comes from the Filipino "sumpa kita," in English, "I promise you." Everyone on staff promises their best for every project.

MTC, dedicated to providing high quality, reasonably priced, and timely service to publishers of professional, scholarly, scientific, technical, and medical research, offers:

Journal and Book Production
Project Management
Copy Editing
Typesetting, Layout and Design
XML Conversion
Data Processing
Non Destructive/Destructive Scanning
Legacy Projects – large and small
Image Editing and Enhancement
EBook/ePub Creation and Conversion

Newgen North America
2714 Bee Cave Road, Suite 201
Austin, TX 78746
Phone: 512.478.5341
Fax: 512.476.4756

Website: newgen.co

Newgen KnowledgeWorks
60/3 Lattice Bridge Road
Thiruvanmiyur
Chennai – 600041, India
Phone: +91 444 202 0548
Fax: +91 442 443 0740

Staff Contacts:

President: Maran Elancheran (512.870.7106; email: maran@newgen.co)
Vice President - Customer Support: Bill Grosskopf (cell: 512.294.1011;
   email: bill@newgen.co)
Composition Manager: Angie Sheltz (512.478.5341; email asheltz@newgen.co)

Enrolled as AAUP Partner: 2011

Company Description

Newgen is a complete solutions provider to books and journals publishers in the US, UK, and Europe. Our project managers in the US and India offer the services of copyeditors, proofreaders, indexers, illustrators, XML coders, and pagers to process an author's manuscript from submission to print-ready, XML, and e-book files. We are a leading provider of digital archiving, data conversion, electronic publishing, and state-of-the-art e-book conversion services.

Helping you put your best book forward®

7300 West Joy Road
Dexter, MI 48130

Phone: 734.426.3939
Fax: 800.706.4545
Email: info@thomsonshore.com

Website: www.thomsonshore.com

Staff Contacts
VP of Sales & Marketing: Terri Barlow (734.426.6214; email:Terrib@thomsonshore.com)
Sales Manager–University Press Market: Mark Livesay (734.426.6207; email: markl@thomsonshore.com)
Customer Service Representatives: Kelley Jones (734.426.6237; email: kelleyj@thomsonshore.com); Dawn Rice (734.426.6299; email: dawnr@thomsonshore.com)

Year enrolled as AAUP Partner: 2008

Company Description
Thomson-Shore is a renowned book manufacturing company. We offer POD, digital and offset printing in black and white to full color with full binding capabilities. We also offer e-book conversion, distribution/fulfillment and publicity services.

International Sales Agents and Distributors

Baker & Taylor International
1120 Route 22 East
Bridgewater, NJ 08807 USA
Phone: 800.775.1800; 908.541.7000
Email: btinfo@btol.com
Website: www.btol.com/international.cfm

Bay Foreign Language Books Ltd.
Unit 4, Kingsmead
Park Farm, Folkestone
Kent CT19 5EU United Kingdom
Phone: +44 (0) 123 720 020
Fax: + 44 (0) 123 721 272
Email: sales@baylanguagebooks.co.uk
Website: www.baylanguagebooks.co.uk

Boydell & Brewer, Ltd.
Whitwell House
St Audry's Park Road
Melton Woodbridge
Suffolk IP12 1SY United Kingdom
Phone: +44 (0) 1394 610600
Fax: +44 (0) 1394 610316
Email: trading@boydell.co.uk
Website: www.boydellandbrewer.com

Canadian Manda Group
165 Dufferin Street
Toronto, ON M6K 3H6 Canada
Phone: 416.516.0911
Fax: 416.516.0917
Email: general@mandagroup.com
Website: www.mandagroup.com

Codasat Canada Ltd.
3122 Blenheim Street
Vancouver, BC V6K 4J7 Canada
Phone: 604.228.9952
Fax: 604.222.2965
Email: info@codasat.com
Website: www.codasat.com

Combined Academic Publishers, Ltd.
15a Lewin's Yard, East Street Chesham
Buckinghamshire HP5 1HQ
United Kingdom
Phone: +44 (0) 1494 581601
Fax: +44 (0) 1494 581602
Email: nickesson@combinedacademic.
  demon.co.uk
Website: www.combinedacademic.co.uk

David Brown Book Company
PO Box 511 (20 Main Street)
Oakville, CT 06779 USA
Phone: 860.945.9329
Fax: 860.945.9468
Email: queries@dbbconline.com
Website: www.oxbowbooks.com/dbbc

D.A.P. | Distributed Art Publishers, Inc.
155 6th Avenue, 2nd Floor
New York, NY 10013 USA
Phone: 212.627.1999
Fax: 212.627.9484
Website: www.artbook.com

Eurospan Group
3 Henrietta Street, Covent Garden
London WC2E 8LU United Kingdom
Phone: +44 (0) 2072 400856
Fax: +44 (0) 2073 790609
Email: info@eurospangroup.com
Website: www.eurospan.co.uk

Footprint Books
Footprint Books Pty Ltd,
1/6a Prosperity Parade,
Warriewood, NSW 2102,
Australia
Phone: +61 2 9997 3973
Fax: +61 2 9997 3185
Website: www.footprint.com.au/

Forest Book Services
6 Forest Road,
Milkwall, Coleford
Gloucestershire GL16 7LB United Kingdom
Phone: +44 (0) 1594 833858
Fax: +44 (0) 1594 837573
Website: www.forestbooks.com

Gazelle Book Services, Ltd.
White Cross Mills
Hightown, Lancaster
Lancashire LA1 4XS United Kingdom
Phone: +44 (0) 1524 68765
Fax: +44 (0) 1524 63232
Email: sales@gazellebooks.co.uk
Website: www.gazellebookservices.co.uk

Georgetown Terminal Warehouses Ltd
34 Armstrong Avenue
Georgetown, Ontario
Canada L7G 4R9
Phone: 905.873.2750
Fax: 905.873.6170
Email: info@gtwcanada.com
Website: www.gtwcanada.com

Hargreaves, Fuller & Paton
Email: harful@telus.net

Herder Editrice e Libreria
Piazza Montecitorio 117-120
I-00186 Roma Italy
Phone: + 39 (06) 679 46 28 / 679 53 04
Fax: +39 (06) 678 47 51
Email: distr@herder.it
Website: www.herder.it

Lexa Publishers' Representatives
Phone: 718.781.2770
Email: mical.moser@verizon.net

Libro Co. Italia s.r.l.
Via Borromeo, 48
50026 San Casciano V.P.
Florence, Italy
Phone: +39 055 8228461
Fax: +39 055 8228462
Email: libroco@libroco.it
Website: www.libroco.it

Login Brothers Canada
300 Saulteaux Crescent
Winnipeg, Manitoba R3J 3T2
Phone: 800.665.1148 or 204.837.2987
Fax: 800.665.0103 or 204.837.3116
Email: orders@lb.ca
Website: www.lb.ca

Marston Book Services, Ltd.
PO Box 269
Abingdon Oxfordshire OX14 4YN
United Kingdom
Phone: +44 (0) 1235 465504
Fax: +44 (0) 1235 465555
Website: www.marston.co.uk

NBN International
10 Thornbury Road
Plymouth PL6 7PP
United Kingdom
Phone: +44 (0) 1752 202301
Fax: +44 (0) 1752 202333
Email: cservs@nbninternational.com
Website: www.nbninternational.com

Orca Book Services
160 Milton Park
Abingdon OX14 4SD United Kingdom
Phone: +44 (0) 1235 465500
Email: tradeorders@orcabookservices.co.uk
Website: www.orcabookservices.co.uk/

Oxbow Books
10 Hythe Bridge Street
Oxford, OX1 2EW United Kingdom
Phone: +44 (0) 1865 241249
Fax: +44 (0) 1865 794449
Email: oxbow@oxbowbooks.com
Website: oxbowbooks.com/oxbow

Oxford Publicity Partnership
5 Victoria House, 138 Watling Street East,
Towcester, NN12 6BT, United Kingdom
Phone: +44 (0) 1327 357770
Fax: +44 (0) 1327 359572
Email: info@oppuk.co.uk
Website: www.oppuk.co.uk

Publishers Group UK
63-66 Hatton Garden
London EC1N 8LE United Kingdom
Phone: +44 (0) 207 4051105
Fax: +44 (0) 207 2423725
Email: info@pguk.co.uk
Website: www.pguk.co.uk

Renouf Books
22-1010 Polytek Street
Ottawa, ON K1J 9J3 Canada
Phone: 866.767.6766
Fax: 613.745.7660
Email: orders@renoufbooks.com
Website: www.renoufbooks.com

Roundhouse Group
Unit B
18 Marine Gardens
Brighton BN2 1AH United Kingdom
Phone: +44 (0) 1273 603 717
Fax: +44 (0) 1273 697 494
Email: sandy@roundhousegroup.co.uk
Website: www.roundhousegroup.co.uk

Scholarly Book Services, Inc.
289 Bridgeland Avenue, Unit 105
Toronto, ON M6A 1Z6 Canada
Phone: 800.847.9736; 416.504.6545
Fax: 800.220.9895; 416.504.0641
Email: customerservice@sbookscan.com
Website: www.sbookscan.com

University of Toronto Press Inc. Distribution
5201 Dufferin St.
Toronto, ON M3H 5T8 Canada
Phone: 416.667.7791
Fax: 416.667.7832
Email: utpbooks@utpress.utoronto.ca
Website: ww.utpress.utoronto.ca/
    UTP_Distribution/index.ph

University Presses Marketing
The Tobacco Factory
Raleigh Road,
Southville, Bristol BS3 1TF
United Kingdom
Phone: +44 (0) 117 9020275
Fax: +44 (0) 117 9020294
E-mail: sales@universitypressesmarketing.
    co.uk
Website: www.universitypressesmarketing.
    co.uk

Yale Representation, Ltd.
Andrew Jarmain
47 Bedford Square
London WC1B 3DP United Kingdom
Phone: +44 (0)207079 4900
Fax: +44 (0) 20 7079 4901
Website: www.yalebooks.co.uk/

THE ASSOCIATION

The Association of American University Presses (AAUP) was established by a small group of university presses in 1937. In the subsequent years, the association has grown steadily. Today AAUP consists of 130 member presses, ranging in size from those publishing a handful of titles each year to those publishing more than a thousand.

AAUP is a nonprofit organization. Its sources of financing are limited to membership dues and to revenues derived from such activities as organizing national conferences and seminars, producing publishing-related books and catalogs, and operating cooperative marketing programs. In addition, grants provided by foundations and government bodies help to finance special projects.

AAUP's member presses provide much of the personnel that guide the association and carry out its work. A board of directors sets policy for the organization. Many individuals serve on committees and task forces. Their activities reflect the diverse concerns of the membership, including keeping up with emerging electronic publishing technologies, production and analysis of industry statistics, maintaining copyright protections, professional development, marketing, and scholarly journals publishing.

The AAUP Central Office, located in New York City, consists of an executive director and a small professional staff. The office manages member programs and coordinates the work of the board and committees.

AAUP members currently fall into four categories—full, international, associate, and introductory. For a complete description of membership requirements, consult the "Guidelines on Admission to Membership and Maintenance of Membership," on page 243.

AAUP Central Office

Association of American University Presses
28 W. 36th Street, Suite 602
New York, NY 10018

Phone: 212.989.1010
Fax: 212.989.0275
Email: info@aaupnet.org

<u>Website and Social Media:</u>
Website: www.aaupnet.org
Facebook: www.facebook.com/universitypresses

Staff
Executive Director (until March 1, 2013): Peter J. Givler (ext. 29; email: pgivler@aaupnet.org)
Executive Director (after March 1, 2013): Peter Berkery (ext. 29; email: pberkery@aaupnet.org)
Assistant Director and Controller: Timothy Muench (ext. 28; email: tmuench@aaupnet.org)
Administrative Manager: Linda McCall (ext. 30; email: lmccall@aaupnet.org)
Marketing and Communications Director: Brenna McLaughlin (518.436.3586; email: bmclaughlin@aaupnet.org)
Membership Manager: Susan Patton (ext. 25; email: spatton@aaupnet.org)
Marketing and Membership Coordinator: Kim Miller (ext. 26; email: kmiller@aaupnet.org)
Communications Coordinator: Regan Colestock (ext. 24; email: rcolestock@aaupnet.org)
Office Assistant: Michael Valcic (email: mvalcic@aaupnet.org)

2012-13 AAUP Board of Directors

Peter Dougherty, Princeton, President (2012-2013)
Philip Cercone, McGill-Queen's, President Elect (2012-2013)
MaryKatherine Callaway, Louisiana State, Past President (2012-2013)
Timothy Doyle, Harvard, Treasurer (2012-2013)
Erik Smist, Johns Hopkins, Treasurer Elect (2012-2013)
Meredith Babb, Florida (2010-2013)
Ellen Faran, MIT (2011-2014)
Garrett Kiely, Chicago (2012-2015)
Sheila Leary, Wisconsin (2012-2015)
Darrin Pratt, Colorado (2010-2013)
Mark Saunders, Virginia (2012-2015)
Charles Watkinson, Purdue (2011-2014)
Anna Weidman, California (2012-2013)
Peter J. Givler, ex officio

2012-2013 AAUP Committees and Task Forces

Admissions and Standards
Susan Doerr, Minnesota
John Byram, New Mexico
Garrett Kiely, Chicago
Leila Salisbury, Mississippi
Eric Schwartz, Princeton

Annual Meeting
Brian Halley, Massachusetts, Chair
Claire Evans, Alabama
Jane Hoehner, Wayne State
Rachael Levay, Washington
Jessica Pellien, Princeton
Nathan Putens, Nebraska
Janet Rossi, MIT

Book, Jacket, and Journal Show
Lindsay Starr, Texas
Regina Fuentes, Texas
Jennifer Hill, Duke
Todd Lape, Mississippi
Nathan Putens, Nebraska

Business Systems
Tom Johnson, New England, Chair
Mike Bieker, Arkansas
Timothy Doyle, Harvard
Tom Hellenberg, New York
Roger Hubbs, Cornell
John Rollins, Yale
Rebecca Schrader, MIT
Ioan Suciu, Georgetown

Copyright
Mike Schwartz, Princeton, Chair
Peggy Garry, Columbia
Kay Hechler, US Institute for Peace
Laura Leichum, Georgetown
Eve Sinaiko, Special Advisor
Amanda Steele, Temple
Sandy Thatcher, Special Advisor
Clare Wellnitz, California
Vicky Wells, North Carolina
Laura Young Bost, Texas

Design and Production
Terri O'Prey, Princeton, Chair
Marianne Jankowski, Northwestern
John Long, National Gallery of Art
Kenneth Reed, Princeton
Carol Stein, ASCSA

Digital Publishing
Krista Coulson, Chicago, Chair
Susan Albury, Duke
Joy Adreakis, Indiana
Toni Gunnison, Wisconsin
Mick Gusinde-Duffy, Georgia
Bonnie Russell, Wayne State
Bryan Shaffer, Purdue
Annette Tanner, Michigan State

Marketing
Laura Baich, Indiana, Chair
Caitlin Churchill, Texas A&M
Emily Grandstaff, Virginia
Jessica Pellien, Princeton
Elizabeth Scarpelli, Rutgers
Amelia Wise, Cornell

Nominating
Alex Holzman Temple
Richard Brown, Georgetown
David Hamrick, Texas
Nicole Mitchell, Washington
Joanne O'Hare, Nevada
Rebecca Schrader, MIT

Library Relations
Jane Bunker, Northwestern, Chair
Donna Dixon, SUNY
Julia Gammon, Akron
Jennie Gavacs, Chicago
Suzanne Guiod, Syracuse
Alex Holzman, Temple
Peter Mickulas, Rutgers
Peter Potter, Cornell
Lisa Quinn, Wilfred Laurier
Leila Salisbury, Mississippi
Lynda Schuh, Illinois
Charles Watkinson, Purdue

Professional Development
Alisa Plant, Louisiana State, Chair
Amanda Atkins, MIT
Jonathan Haupt, South Carolina
Larin McLaughlin, Illinois

Scholarly Journals
Alicia Vonderharr, Wayne State, Chair
Elizabeth Brown, Johns Hopkins
Lauren Crocker, Wayne State
Dave Lievens, Pennsylvania
Astrid Meyer, Penn State
Katherine Purple, Purdue
Jill Rodgers, MIT
Ann Snoeyenbos, Johns Hopkins

University Press Week Task Force
Will Underwood, Kent State, Chair
Colleen Lanick, MIT
Melissa Pitts, British Columbia
Michael Roux, Illinois
Leila Salisbury, Mississippi
Mark Saunders, Virginia

By-Laws (As revised June 17, 2010)

ARTICLE I: PREAMBLE

This Corporation, existing under the Not-for-Profit Corporation Law of the State of New York, shall be known as the Association of American University Presses, Inc. (hereinafter referred to as the "Association"). The Association expects members to recruit, employ, train, compensate, and promote their employees without regard to race, ethnic background, national origin, status as a veteran or handicapped individual, age, religion, gender, marital status, or sexual preference.

ARTICLE II: PURPOSES

The purposes of the Association shall be:

a) To encourage dissemination of the fruits of research and to support university presses in their endeavor to make widely available the best of scholarly knowledge and the most important results of scholarly research;

b) To provide an organization through which the exchange of ideas relating to university presses and their functions may be facilitated;

c) To afford technical advice and assistance to learned bodies, scholarly associations, and institutions of higher learning; and

d) To do all things incidental to and in furtherance of the foregoing purposes without extending the same.

ARTICLE III: MEMBERSHIP

The Association admits members in four categories: (1) full membership, (2) associate membership, (3) international membership, and (4) introductory membership.

Section 1: Definition of Full Membership.

The full membership of the Association shall consist of those members who were in good standing at the time of the incorporation of the Association in 1964, except those who have since resigned or whose membership has been otherwise terminated, and all other members who have since been admitted in accordance with the procedures set forth in Section 3 of this Article. Presses with affiliate status as of June 2007 will be instated as full members upon approval of the membership.

Section 2: Definition of a University Press.

A university press eligible for full membership is hereby defined as the nonprofit scholarly publishing arm of a university or college, or of a group of such institutions within a state or geographic region, located within the Americas and publishing primarily in English. A university press as here defined must be an integral part of one or more such colleges and universities, and should be so recognized in the manual of organization, catalogue, website, or other official publication of at least one such parent institution. The organization and functions of the university press must lie within the prescription of its parent institution or institutions.

Section 3: Eligibility for Full Membership.

Any university press satisfying the requirements set forth in the "Guidelines on Admission to Membership and Maintenance of Membership" (hereinafter, the "Guidelines") that are in force at the time of application shall be eligible for election to full membership in the Association. A university press shall be elected to membership by a majority vote of the membership on the recommendation of the Board of Directors at the Annual or a Special Meeting of the membership. Such action shall be taken by the Board only on the prior recommendation of the Committee on Admissions and Standards, which shall be responsible for determining that the applying university press satisfies the minimum requirements for membership. Annual dues for full members shall be set from time to time by the Board of Directors.

Section 4: Associate Membership.

The associate membership of the Association shall consist of those associate members who have been admitted since the time of the incorporation of the Association in 1964, in accordance with the procedures in force at the time of application.

Presses of non-degree-granting scholarly institutions and associations may apply for associate membership, provided that those institutions are incorporated as not-for-profit and that the presses satisfy the requirements for full membership, except that the auspices and structures of the parent organizations of such presses will in all instances be those of non-degree-granting institutions or scholarly associations rather than those of universities. Associate members should be located within the Americas and publishing primarily in English. In the absence of an editorial committee or board, an applicant for associate membership shall observe commonly accepted standards of editorial review.

Admission to associate membership shall be by a majority vote of the membership at an Annual or Special Meeting, a quorum being present, on the prior recommendation of the Committee on Admissions and Standards and the Board of Directors. Associate members shall enjoy such rights and privileges as determined by the Board of Directors, including the right to serve on the Board of Directors or on the Standing Committees of the Association and the right to vote on any business conducted by the Association. Associate members shall not be eligible to participate in the Association's statistical programs for full members. Annual dues for associate members shall be set from time to time by the Board of Directors. The number of associate members shall not exceed thirty-five percent of the number of full members of the Association and no more than one associate member representative may serve on the Board at any one time.

Section 5: International Membership.

The international membership of the Association shall consist of those international members who have been admitted since the time of the incorporation of the Association in 1964, in accordance with the procedures in force at the time of application.

International membership may be applied for by (a) university-affiliated scholarly publishers and presses of non-degree-granting scholarly institutions and associations in parts of the world not embraced by the Americas and (b) such presses within the Americas that publish primarily in languages other than English. To qualify for international membership in the Association, a publisher in either class must submit the same application as applicants for full and associate member status but will not be expected to meet precisely the staffing and organizational requirements for those members. Admission to international membership shall be by a majority vote of the membership at an Annual or Special Meeting, a quorum being present, on the prior recommendation of the Committee on Admissions and Standards and the Board of Directors.

International members shall enjoy all rights and privileges of membership except the right to vote in any business being conducted by the Association, the Board of Directors, or the membership. Any reference elsewhere in these By-Laws to a voting right, therefore, shall be read so as to exclude international members. Annual dues for international members shall be set from time to time by the Board.

Section 6: Introductory Membership.

Eligible for introductory membership are nonprofit scholarly publishers that intend to apply for AAUP membership in one of the other categories either during their introductory term or at the end of that term. Presses may not stay in the introductory category for more than three years.

Candidates for introductory membership will be expected to provide evidence concerning the scholarly character of their publishing programs and information about present staffing, reporting relationships, review processes, and also any changes or developments proposed in these areas, but they will not be expected to meet the publication rate, staffing, or organizational requirements of full membership. Admission to introductory membership shall be made at the discretion of the Executive Director of the Association in consultation with the Board upon receipt by the Membership Manager of a letter of application that includes the requested information.

At any time during the introductory period introductory members may apply for regular membership in the appropriate category. After three years, the introductory membership is automatically terminated.

Introductory members shall enjoy such rights and privileges as determined by the Board of Directors, but in no event shall their rights and privileges extend to service on the Board of Directors or on the Standing Committees of the Association or voting in any business conducted by it. Any reference elsewhere in the By-Laws to a voting right, therefore, shall be so read as to exclude introductory members. Annual dues for introductory members shall be set from time to time by the Board.

Section 7: Voting and Other Privileges.

Each full member and each associate member of the Association shall be entitled to one vote in such business as may come before the Association. Only members in good standing shall be entitled to vote or otherwise enjoy the privileges of membership in the Association.

Section 8: Cancellation of Membership and Resignation.

A university press, by its very nature, must be devoted to scholarly and educational ends; the failure of a university press to pursue such ends as its fundamental business shall constitute grounds for canceling its membership in the Association. Any accusation of such a failure will be brought to the Committee on Admissions and Standards for a recommendation to the Board.

A membership may also be canceled for continued nonpayment of dues or for continued failure, after admission to membership, to meet the minimum requirements set forth in the Guidelines.

Cancellation of full, associate, or international membership shall be effected, on recommendation of the Board of Directors, by a two-thirds vote of the members present and voting at the Annual Meeting or a Special Meeting, a quorum being present.

Any member may resign at any time if its current annual dues are paid, provided its resignation is confirmed in a written communication to the Executive Director and President of the Association from a responsible officer or group of officers of the parent institution or institutions.

Should a member in any class of membership resign after the due date of the annual dues payment and before the next annual dues payment date, the member is responsible for the payment of such dues at the time of resignation.

ARTICLE IV: MEMBERSHIP MEETINGS

Section 1: The Annual Meeting.
The Annual Meeting of members shall be held at such time and place within or without the State of New York as may be designated by the Board of Directors after giving due weight to preferences expressed by members. Such meetings shall be held for the purpose of electing the Board of Directors, approving the annual budget, and transacting such other business as may be properly brought before the meeting. At each Annual Meeting of members, the Board of Directors shall cause to be presented to the membership a report verified by the President and the Treasurer, or by a majority of the Board, in accordance with the requirements of Section 519 of the New York Not-for-Profit Corporation Law.

Section 2: Special Meetings.
Special Meetings of the members shall be held at such time and place within or without the State of New York as may be designated by the Board of Directors. Such meetings may be called by (a) the Board of Directors; or (b) the Executive Committee; or (c) the President, the President-elect, or the Executive Director acting on a request received in writing that states the purpose or purposes of the meeting and is signed by 30 percent or more of the members of the Association.

Section 3: Notice of Meetings.
Notice of the purpose or purposes and of the time and place of every meeting of members of the Association shall be in writing and signed by the President, President-elect, or the Executive Director, and a copy thereof shall be delivered personally or by the U.S. Postal Service not less than ten or more than fifty days before the meeting, to each member entitled to vote at such meeting.

Section 4: Representation by Proxy.
A member may authorize a person or persons to act by proxy on all matters in which a member is entitled to participate. No proxy shall be valid after the expiration of eleven months from the date thereof unless otherwise provided in the proxy. Every proxy shall be revocable at the pleasure of the member executing it.

Section 5: Quorum.
Except for a special election of Directors pursuant to Section 604 of the New York Not-for-Profit Corporation Law, the presence at a meeting in person or by proxy of a majority of the members entitled to vote thereat shall constitute a quorum for the transaction of any business, except that the members present may adjourn the meeting even if there is no quorum.

Section 6: Voting.
In the election of members of the Board of Directors and the election of Officers, a plurality of the votes cast at an Annual Meeting shall elect. Any other action requires a majority of votes cast except as otherwise specifically provided in these By-Laws. A vote may be taken without a meeting if a majority of the members in good standing submit written votes in response to a request to this effect from the President, the President-elect, or the Executive Director.

ARTICLE V: DIRECTORS AND OFFICERS

Section 1: The Board of Directors.

The Association shall be managed by its Board of Directors, and, in this connection, the Board of Directors shall establish the policies of the Association while considering the wishes of the membership and the constituency of the Association (which constituency consists of the employees of the member presses), and shall evaluate the performance of the Executive Director. The Board of Directors shall meet at least three times each year, once in the fall and once in the winter and in conjunction with the Annual Meeting of the membership of the Association. The Board of Directors shall consist of not fewer than nine or more than thirteen Directors, all of whom shall be at least nineteen years of age, at least two-thirds of whom shall be citizens of the United States, four of whom shall be the elected Officers of the Association. Directors other than Officers (Directors-at-Large), like Officers, must be on the staff of a member press, except that the Executive Director is an ex officio (nonvoting) member of the Board of Directors and the Executive Committee.

Section 2: Election Procedure and Term of Office.

Directors shall be elected by a plurality vote of the members present at the Annual Meeting. Candidates may be nominated by the Nominating Committee appointed by the Executive Committee, or from the floor. Officers shall be elected for a one-year term, except that the President shall remain on the Board of Directors for an additional year as Past-President; Directors-at-Large shall be elected for a three-year term. Directors shall not succeed themselves except that (a) Directors who are elected Officers shall continue as Directors as long as they remain Officers, and (b) the Treasurer shall remain on the Board for an additional year as a Director-at-large. Each newly elected Director and Officer shall assume office at the close of the Annual Meeting at which the election is held. Any Director or Officer may resign by notifying the President, the President-elect, or the Executive Director. The resignation shall take effect at the time therein specified. Except as provided for in Article IX ("The Executive Director"), Directors shall not receive any compensation for serving as Directors. However, nothing herein shall be construed to prevent a Director from serving the Association in another capacity for which compensation may be received.

Section 3: Officers.

The elected Officers of the Association, each of whom must be on the staff of a member press, shall be a President, a President-elect, a Treasurer, and a Treasurer-elect, each to be elected for a one-year term by a plurality vote of the members present at the Annual Meeting. Between Annual Meetings of members, a Special Meeting of members may elect, by a plurality vote of the members present, an Officer to complete the term of an Officer who has resigned or otherwise ceased to act as an Officer.

Section 4: Duties of Officers.

The President shall serve as presiding officer at all meetings of the membership and all meetings of the Board of Directors and the Executive Committee. The President, with the Executive Director, serves as spokesperson for the Association. At the Annual Meeting of members, the President and the President-elect shall provide a forum for the Association membership and constituency to discuss and assess the Association's program. The President-elect shall discharge the duties of the President in the President's absence, and shall succeed to the office of President in the event of a vacancy in that office, filling out the unexpired term as well as the term to which he or she is elected President.

The Treasurer shall be custodian of the Association's funds, shall be responsible for the preparation of its financial records as the basis for an annual audit, and shall report at the Annual Meeting of members on the Association's financial condition. The Treasurer-elect shall discharge the duties of the Treasurer in the Treasurer's absence, and shall succeed to the office of Treasurer in the event of a vacancy in that office, filling out the unexpired term as well as the term to which he or she is elected Treasurer.

Section 5: Removal from Office and Replacement.
Any Director or elected Officer may be removed from office at any time, for cause or without cause, by a majority vote of the membership or may be removed for cause by a majority vote of the Board acting at a meeting duly assembled, a quorum being present. If one or more vacancies should occur on the Board for any reason, the remaining members of the Board, although less than a quorum, may by majority vote elect a successor or successors for the unexpired term.

Section 6: Board Meetings.
Meetings of the Board of Directors shall be held at such place within or without the State of New York as may from time to time be fixed by resolution of the Board, or as may be specified in the notice of the meeting. Notice of any meeting of the Board need not be given to any Director who submits a signed waiver of such notice. Special Meetings of the Board may be held at any time upon the call of the Executive Committee, the Executive Director, the President, or the President-elect.

Section 7: Board Quorum.
A majority of the members of the Board of Directors then acting, but in no event less than one-half of the entire board of Directors, acting at a meeting duly assembled, shall constitute a quorum for the transaction of business. If at any meeting of the Board there shall be less than a quorum present, a majority of those present may adjourn the meeting without further notice from time to time until a quorum shall have been obtained. The "entire Board of Directors" shall mean the total number of Directors that the Association would have if there were no vacancies.

Section 8: Board Voting.
Except as otherwise specified in these By-Laws, all decisions of the Board shall be by majority vote of the Directors in attendance, a quorum being present. Any Board action may be taken without a meeting if all members of the Board or committee thereof consent in writing to the adoption of a resolution authorizing the action. The resolution and the written consents thereto shall be filed with the minutes of the proceedings of the Board. Any member of the Board or of any committee thereof may participate in a meeting of such Board or committee thereof by means of a telephone or similar communications equipment allowing all persons participating in the meeting to hear each other at the same time. Participation by such means shall constitute presence in person at a meeting.

ARTICLE VI: EXECUTIVE COMMITTEE
The Executive Committee of the Board of Directors shall consist of the Past-President and President of the Association and the President-elect, Treasurer, Treasurer-elect, and the Executive Director (ex officio, nonvoting). The Executive Committee shall advise and confer with the Executive Director, call Special Meetings of the Board of Directors as necessary, appoint committee members not otherwise appointed pursuant to these By-Laws, and serve as the investment committee for the Association. The Executive Committee shall, if necessary, act for

the full Board of Directors between meetings of the Board, but only in those matters not establishing policy or not requiring a vote of more than a majority of Directors in attendance.

ARTICLE VII: STANDING COMMITTEES

The Standing Committees of the Association (in addition to the Executive Committee) shall be the Committee on Admissions and Standards, the Committee on the Annual Meeting Program, and the Nominating Committee. The Committee on Admissions and Standards shall be constituted as provided in the Guidelines. Appointments to the Committee on the Annual Meeting Program and the Nominating Committee shall be made in accordance with Article VIII of these By-Laws.

ARTICLE VIII: OTHER COMMITTEES AND TASK FORCES

Other committees and task forces may be established by agreement of the Executive Director and the Board. The President-elect shall appoint chairs of said committees (and the Standing Committees) and such of their members as the Executive Committee may care to designate. The President-elect shall charge the said committees with such duties, including reporting duties, as he or she may deem appropriate. Task forces shall be established for a limited time to accomplish a specific goal. The President shall appoint chairs of task forces and provide their charges. Reports of standing and all other committees and task forces shall be made to the Board of Directors, in writing or orally, as requested by the Executive Director.

ARTICLE IX: THE EXECUTIVE DIRECTOR

The Board of Directors may appoint at such times, and for such terms as it may prescribe, an Executive Director of the Association who shall report to the Board of Directors and who is responsible for implementing policy through fiscally sound programs; monitoring the work of committees and task forces; and managing the Central Office (such Central Office consisting of salaried employees hired by the Executive Director in order to carry out the business of the Association). The Executive Director shall prepare an operating plan and budget and shall participate in meetings of the Board of Directors and Executive Committee in an ex officio nonvoting capacity as appropriate. Under the authority of the Board of Directors, the Executive Director shall have responsibility for the execution of Association policy, for the furtherance of the Association's interests, and for the day-to-day operation of the Association's business and programs. The Executive Director shall act as secretary at all Board meetings, Executive Committee meetings, and Annual and Special Meetings of the Association, and shall prepare and distribute minutes of the same. The Executive Director shall serve as Corporate Secretary. The Executive Director's salary shall be fixed annually by the Board.

ARTICLE X: REGIONAL ORGANIZATIONS

The Board of Directors may recognize geographical regions within which members of the Association and others may organize themselves for regional meetings to further the aims of the Association.

ARTICLE XI: DUES

The amount of the annual dues payment by members shall be voted each year at the Annual Meeting on recommendation of the Board of Directors. The fiscal year of the Association shall be April 1 to March 31. Dues shall be payable by September 30, at which time any member press that has not paid its dues shall be subject to suspension at the Board's discretion. When a member is suspended for nonpayment of dues, the President of the Association shall so notify the director of the said member and the responsible officer or officers of its parent institution or group of institutions, and shall further advise them that if such member has not paid its dues by the end of the Association's fiscal year its membership shall be subject to cancellation.

ARTICLE XII: BOOKS AND RECORDS

The Association shall keep at its office within the State of New York correct and complete books and records of account; minutes of meetings of the members, of the Board of Directors, and of the Executive Committee; and an up-to-date list of the names and addresses of all members. These books and records may be in written form or in any other form capable of being converted to written form within a reasonable time.

ARTICLE XIII: CHANGES IN BY-LAWS AND GUIDELINES

Members may propose changes to these By-Laws and Guidelines by submitting the proposed change and its rationale to the Executive Director. S/He will arrange for the Board's review of any such proposal at the next appropriate Board Meeting. If the Board recommends Association approval of the proposed change, the change will be presented with at least thirty days advance notice to the membership at the next Annual or Special Meeting called for that purpose at which a quorum is present. A change to the By-Laws requires a two-thirds majority of all Members eligible to vote (in person or by proxy). A change to the Guidelines requires a majority of all Members eligible to vote (in person or by proxy). Whenever there is a conflict between these By-Laws and the Guidelines, any Statement of Governance, or a resolution of the membership, Board of Directors, or Executive Committee, or any other document published by the Association, these By-Laws shall prevail.

In the event the Board recommends against approval of a proposed change, the member proposing the change may call a vote on the measure at the Annual Meeting or at a Special Meeting for that purpose, provided thirty days notice is given and thirty percent of the Association's voting members sign a request that sign a request that said proposal be voted upon. Requirements for adoption of the measure are as stated in this Article.

Guidelines on Admission to Membership and Maintenance of Membership

As revised June 14, 2007

A. Preamble

The purposes of the Association are to encourage dissemination of the fruits of research and to support university presses in their endeavor to make widely available scholarly knowledge and the most important results of scholarly research; to provide an organization through which the exchange of ideas relating to university presses and their functions may be facilitated; to afford technical advice and assistance to learned bodies, scholarly associations, and institutions of higher learning; and to do all things incidental to and in furtherance of the foregoing purposes without extending the same.

B. Types of Membership

The Association admits members in four categories: (1) full membership, (2) associate membership, (3) international membership, and (4) introductory membership.

1. Full Membership

Eligible for full membership are nonprofit university presses, defined as the scholarly publishing arm of a university or college or a group of such institutions within a state or geographic region, located within the Americas and publishing primarily in English, that satisfy the following criteria:

(a) Eligible presses must be an integral part of one or more such colleges and universities, and should be so recognized in the manual of organization, catalogue, website, or other official publication of at least one such parent institution. The organization and functions of the university press must lie within the prescription of its parent institution or institutions.

(b) A committee or board of the faculty of the parent institution or institutions shall be charged with certifying the scholarly quality of the publications that bear the institutional imprint.

(c) Publication of ten or more scholarly titles in the twenty-four months preceding the date of application shall be required for admission to full membership. Scholarly books, journals, and digital projects that include original scholarly content will all be counted to satisfy this requirement. The word "scholarly" is used here in the sense of original research of a character usually associated with the scholarly interests of a university or college. (Textbooks, manuals of a synthetic character or intended for class use, and publications for which the press serves primarily as a printer and/or distributor for other departments or divisions of the university or college are not to be included in the aforementioned minimum scholarly publishing requirement.)

(d) An acceptable scholarly publishing program shall have the benefit of the service of not fewer than three full-time equivalent employees, of whom one shall have the rank and functions of director. This official shall report, organizationally, to the President of the university or college, or to an officer at the vice-presidential or decanal level (i.e., an officer reporting either to the President or to the chief academic officer) having both academic and fiscal authority, or to the designated representative of a group of such institutions who shall have both kinds of authority.

Any press satisfying these requirements shall be eligible in principle for election to full membership in the Association.. Annual dues for full members shall be set from time to time by the Board.

2. Associate Membership
Presses of non-degree-granting scholarly institutions and associations may apply for associate membership, providing those institutions are incorporated as not-for-profit and that the presses satisfy the requirements for membership, except that the auspices and structures of the parent organizations of such presses will in all instances be those of non-degree-granting institutions or scholarly associations rather than those of universities. Applicants for associate membership should be in a state or geographic region located within the Americas and publishing primarily in English. In the absence of an editorial committee or board, an applicant for associate membership shall observe commonly accepted standards of editorial review.

Associate members shall enjoy such rights and privileges as determined by the Board of Directors, including the right to serve on the Board of Directors and on the Standing Committees of the Association and the right to vote on any business conducted by it. Associate members shall not be eligible to participate in the Association's statistical programs for full members. The number of associate members shall not exceed thirty-five percent of the number of full members of the Association and no more than one associate member representative may serve on the Board at any one time. Annual dues for associate members shall be set from time to time by the Board.

3. International Membership
International membership may be applied for by (a) university-affiliated scholarly publishers and presses of non-degree-granting scholarly institutions and associations in parts of the world not embraced by the Americas and (b) such presses within the Americas that publish primarily in languages other than English.

Candidates for international membership will be expected to provide evidence concerning the size and scholarly character of their publishing programs but will not be expected to meet the staffing or organizational requirements of full membership.

International members shall enjoy all rights and privileges of full membership except the right to vote in any business conducted by the Association. Any reference elsewhere in the By-Laws to a voting right, therefore, shall be so read as to exclude international members. International members shall not be eligible to participate in the Association's statistical programs. Annual dues for international members shall be set from time to time by the Board.

4. Introductory Membership
Eligible for introductory membership are nonprofit scholarly publishers that intend to apply for AAUP membership in one of the other categories either during their introductory term or at the end of that term.

Candidates for introductory membership will be expected to provide evidence concerning the scholarly character of their publishing programs and information about present staffing, reporting relationships, review processes, and also any changes or developments proposed in these areas, but they will not be expected to meet the publication rate, staffing, or organizational requirements of full membership. Presses may not stay in the introductory category for more than three years.

At any time during the introductory period introductory members may apply for regular membership in the appropriate category. If a press does not wish to continue as an introductory member for three years, it may resign from the Association after payment of its current annual dues. After three years, the introductory membership is automatically terminated.

Introductory members shall enjoy such rights and privileges as determined by the Board of Directors, but in no event shall their rights and privileges extend to service on the Board of Directors or on the Standing Committees of the Association or voting in any business conducted by it. Any reference elsewhere in the By-Laws to a voting right, therefore, shall be so read as to exclude introductory members. Annual dues for introductory members shall be set from time to time by the Board.

C. Application, Admission, and Cancellation

1. Application

All inquiries from prospective applicants for membership in the Association are to be directed to the Membership Manager of AAUP. The Membership Manager shall advise the candidate of the substance of these Guidelines on Admission to Membership and Maintenance of Membership, and shall require as evidence of satisfactory compliance with them for all membership categories, except the Introductory Membership, the following materials for submission to the Committee on Admissions and Standards:

(a) One copy of each of 10 or more different scholarly titles published by the applicant and certified by its faculty editorial board or committee in the twenty-four months preceding the date on which the application for membership is filed, and full runs of the issues of any journals for the year or years in which a journal serves as one of the titles. If original digital publications are submitted, the applicant will provide access to committee members.

(b) A list of the peer reviewers (names and affiliations) for each of the books or original digital publications submitted as part of the application. Published reviews of the titles and information about scholarly awards received may be submitted as part of the application.

(c) Copies of the applicant press's catalogs for the past two years for each member of the Committee on Admissions and Standards.

(d) A complete list, by name and title, of the staff of the applicant press, to be prepared in that form in which such information is given for active members in the most recent edition of the Directory of the Association of American University Presses. For part-time staff the list should indicate the percentage of time each person devotes to the press.

(e) A statement from a senior administrative officer of the parent institution, or the designated representative of a group of institutions, outlining the immediate and long-term intentions and financial expectations of the institution or group of institutions for its press, and reflecting a realistic appreciation of the cost of supporting a serious program of scholarly publication.

(f) Copies of its financial operating statements for the two most recently completed fiscal years.

With respect to the scholarship of published works, the Association will in general accept the certification of the press's own faculty board or committee and will not pass judgment on the scholarship of any individual work. However, the Committee on Admissions and Standards will take into account the observance by the press of commonly accepted standards of editorial review, ordinarily including at least one positive evaluation by a qualified scholar not affiliated with the author's own institution.

2. Admission

Following the filing of a formal application for full, associate, or international membership and notification by the Membership Manager of AAUP to the applicant of its acceptance for consideration, the candidate press shall be regarded as having entered a period of probation, which will last for a period of time no longer than one year, at the end of which, if not sooner, its candidacy will be acted upon as prescribed under the By-Laws, and during which it shall enjoy the following privileges of membership: (a) the right to send delegates to the Annual Meeting at the member rate, and (b) the right to send representatives to all training sessions, workshops, symposiums, and conferences dealing with professional activities of scholarly publishers and enjoying the support of the Association.

A press shall be elected to full, associate, or international membership by an affirmative vote of a majority of the Association's full members at the Annual Meeting or a Special Meeting, a quorum being present, on the recommendation of the Board of Directors. Such action shall be taken by the Board only on the prior recommendation of the Committee on Admissions and Standards, which shall be responsible for determining that the applying press satisfies the minimum requirements for membership. Admission of a new full, associate, or international member to the Association shall take effect immediately following an affirmative vote of a majority of the Association's full membership at the Annual Meeting or a Special Meeting.

Admission to introductory membership shall be made at the discretion of the Executive Director of the Association in consultation with the Board upon receipt by the Membership Manager of a letter of request that includes information about present staffing, reporting relationships, review processes, and any changes or developments proposed in these areas.

To maintain its active membership status, each member press shall be required to submit each year to the Central Office of the Association, for publication in the annual Directory of members, both a roster of its current staff and an indication of the number of books, journals, and original digital publications that it has published in each of the two calendar years preceding and that have been certified as to scholarship by its editorial board or committee.

3. Cancellation

A university press, by its very nature, must be devoted to scholarly and educational ends; the failure of a press to pursue such ends as its fundamental business shall constitute grounds for canceling its membership in the Association. Any accusation of such a failure will be brought to the Committee on Admissions and Standards for a recommendation to the Board. Cancellation of membership shall be effected, on recommendation of the Board of Directors, by a two-thirds' majority vote of the members present and voting at the Annual Meeting or a Special Meeting, a quorum being present.

It shall be the responsibility of the Membership Manager to review each listing of an active press in each annual edition of the membership Directory, and to undertake action as follows when any member seems to have fallen below the qualifying criteria for membership: (a) to notify the Executive Director and the Committee on Admissions and Standards of a member's apparent delinquency under the Guidelines so that the Executive Director may make an inquiry and, if current standards are not being met, offer the assistance and cooperation of the Association in bringing about satisfactory solutions to the member's problems; (b) to advise the President, the Committee on Admissions and Standards, and the Board when notification of an apparent delinquency has been sent and an offer of assistance made; (c) to inform the President, the Committee on Admissions and Standards, and the Board of any response received from the member press following the offer of assistance.

Should the delinquent press fail to resolve its difficulties within one year of the Executive Director's notice, the Committee on Admissions and Standards shall submit to the Board of Directors a full report of the situation, and recommend, for endorsement by the Board and transmission to the membership for ratification, that the membership of the delinquent press be terminated. Two years from the date of its expulsion, a press shall be entitled to apply for readmission through initiation of the application procedures herein prescribed.

E. The Committee on Admissions and Standards

The official agency for the administration of these guidelines shall be the Committee on Admissions and Standards, which shall operate under authority delegated by the Board of Directors, and which shall consist of between four and six members, two of whom, at least, shall be the director of a member press. The incoming President will appoint the chair of the committee from among members of the current committee with at least one year of service. The chairs shall each serve a term of one year as part of their three-year term on the committee and may not succeed themselves in office. The chair shall appoint the remaining committee members. Terms of the committee members will normally be three years each except that in the year that these revised Guidelines take effect shorter terms may be established for some of the members. Committee members will not be eligible to serve more than two successive terms.

PERSONNEL INDEX

Hoppel, Lynn	170	Jacques, Kelly Chrisman	91
Horn, Vernon	26	Jajunga, Elise	109
Horst, Ines ter	52	Jankowski, Marianne	132, 232
Horton, Karen	141	Janssen, Karl	91
Hoskins, Beth	63	Jarrad, Mary Beth	127
Houck, Anna	49	Jemison, Lisa	182
Hough, Marcia	170	Jerome, Jennifer	57
Howard, Jesse	109	Jestis, Cheryl	80
Howard, Meredith	57	Jiambalvo, Jane	53
Howarth, Jessica	103	Joerschke, John	71
Howells, Richard	75	Johnson, Aaron	45
Hoyt, Chris	176	Johnson, Bailey	93
Hozier, Sherri	125	Johnson, Beth	199
Hruska, Libby	117	Johnson, Crissie	23
Hu, May	42	Johnson, Harmony	38
Huang, Irene	37	Johnson, Jackie	129
Hubbard, John	143	Johnson, James L.	203
Hubbart, Dustin	79	Johnson, Kimberly F.	88
Hubbell, Norma E.	92	Johnson, Robert	120
Hubbs, Roger A.	60, 61, 232	Johnson, Seth	108
Huber, Molly	111	Johnson, Sharon	161
Hudson, Christopher	116	Johnson, Sonya	64
Hudson, Tricia	141	Johnson, Thomas	123, 124, 232
Huff, Regan	71	Johnston, Orna	203
Hughes, Allison	50	Johovic, Kelley	148
Hughes, Eileen	40	Jolley, Marc A.	106
Huijstee, Ryan van	103	Jolluck, Christine	62
Hull, Stephen P.	123	Jones, Ben	187
Hulsey, Dave	83	Jones, Bessie	27
Humphrey, Harv	133	Jones, Briony	125
Hunt, Jenny	36	Jones, Christopher	53
Hunt, Val	75	Jones, Elizabeth	163
Hunter, Sian	66	Jones, Jamie	194
Hunter, Sylvia	183	Jones, Kathleen Pike	191
Husband, Len	183	Jones, Kelley	226
Hutchins, Jamie	45	Jones, Lesley	63
Hwa, Karen T.	60	Jones, Parneshia	132
Hyzy, Karen	53	Jones, Renee	169
Iaffa, Elena	57	Jones, Tim	74
Igali, Monika	26	Jones, Valerie	113
Iguchi, Yasuyo	100	Jones, Zina	117
Ikeda, Masako	76	Jordan, James D.	56
Ilacqua, David	103	Jung, Mark	209
Imbornoni, Ann-Marie	203	Juniko, Siobhan	183
Imperio, Irene	173	Kachergis, Anne	50
Inscoe, John	72	Kadair, Catherine	96
Ireland, Brad	118	Kadis, Linda	34
Izma, Steve	198	Kadushin, Raphael	199
Jackson, Bea	63	Kaemmer, Beverly	112
Jackson, David	167	Kageff, Karl	164
Jackson, Erika	187	Kahl, Milton	203
Jackson, Joe	52	Kalett, Alison	149
Jackson-Whyte, Debra	171	Kalish, Ilene	126
Jacob, Mary Ann	178	Kallet, Jeff	135
Jacobi, Sarah	83	Kane, Adam	119
Jacobs, Donald	70	Kane, Sonia	156
Jacobs, Joanna	23	Kaneshiro, Norman	76
Jacobson, Tanjam	50	Kanter, Greg	37
Jacobson, Tony	88	Kanyama, Vertelle	52
Jacqmin, Hilary	88	Kaplan, Anne	111

Macklem, Ann	38	Mazzocchi, Jay	128
MacNeil, Lela Scott	32	McAdam, Matt	87
Maco, Mary Kate	167	McArdle, Jeff	80
Macredie, Leslie	198	McBeath, Kasey	180
Madara, Susan	161	McBeth, Barbara	124
Madden, Kyla	103	McBride, David	140
Magoulias, Michael	53	McCall, Linda	231
Mahalek, Gina	129	McCallum, Heather	204
Mahrt, Kim	121	McCarthy, Juliana M.	88
Maikowski, Steve	126	McCarthy, Shannon	66
Mainville, Lara	138	McCaull, June	101
Maisner, Elaine	128	McCay, Deanna	170
Majdalani, Tara	65	McClanahan, Pamela	111
Malar, Gregory	157	McConnell, Melissa	40
Malcolm, Frances	166	McCormick, Mack	93
Malcolm, Reed	43	McCormick, Monica	127
Malcolm-Clark, Darja	83	McCormick, Wynona	178
Malcom, Ian	74	McCoy, Anne	57
Males, Myndee	141	McCoy, Jim	85
Malley, Lawrence J.	33	McCreary, Courtney	114
Malpass, Gillian	203	McCullough, Michael	63
Manaktala, Gita	100	McDermott, Kathleen	74
Mandel, Robert	180	McDonald, Leigh	32
Maner, Ron	128	McDonnell, Kate	169
Manning, Linda	188	McDuffie, John	27
Manning, Shaun	108	McEntire, Ila	93
Mao, Ling	64	McFadden, Ray	141
Marcotte, Kay	125	McGandy, Michael J.	60
Markova, Lyudmila	125	McGann, Michaen	171
Marolt, Carla	199	McGlone, Jonathan	108
Marr, Marie	186	McGraw, Tom	53
Marshall, Carmen	63	McGuire, Kristi	52
Marshall, Julie	86	McGuire, Laurie	61
Marshall, Kate	43	McHugh, Elise	125
Marshall, Melissa	144	McIntire, Karyn	108
Marshall, Stewart	125	McIntosh, Susan	104
Marsland, Joanna Ruth	128	McKee, Sarah	72
Martin, Annie	194	McKeigue, Emily	95
Martin, Barb	164	McKenna, Anne	199
Martin, Carolyn	163	McKie, Ellen	175
Martin, Dawn	109	McKnight, Emily	133
Martin, Katherine	140	McLaughlin, Brenna	231
Martin, Larisa	91	McLaughlin, Larin	79, 233
Martin, Mike	178	McLeod, John	175
Martin, Pieter	112	McMahon, Sheila	199
Martin, Shari	39	McMenemy, Siobhan	183
Martinelli, Theresa	194	McMillen, Wendy	133
Marting, Bill	141	McPhie, Miriam	71
Masiulis, Nida	52	McTaggert, Phillip	198
Mason, Jacqueline	103	Means, Allison Thomas	85
Matheson, Laurie	79	Mehring, Adam	199
Mathias, Ashley	163	Meier, Lindsey	199
Matsuo-Chun, Julie	76	Meijer, Margreet	94
Matthen, Kate	83	Melton, Mardee	76
Matthews, Alicia	63	Melvin, Terrence	40
Mautner, Stephen M.	117	Merzlak, Paul	120
May, Theresa	175	Mesker, Louis W.	80
Mayer, Dariel	189	Metro, Judy	118
Mayer, Loomis	67	Metz, Isabel	114
Mayer, Mary	203	Mevis, Chandra	83

OTHER PUBLICATIONS AND RESOURCES

AAUP Announce

An informational bulletin for AAUP's wider community. Interested scholarly communications, academic, and publishing professionals are invited to subscribe to this email bulletin to stay up-to-date on Association news and events

AAUP Annual Report

The report provides a summary of association activities.

AAUP Book, Jacket, and Journal Show Catalog

The purpose of the Show is to recognize achievement in the design, production, and manufacture of books, book jackets, and journals. The catalog displays and critiques all titles selected in this annual competition. Gratis to members, $20.00 to non-members.

AAUP bulletin

The bulletin is a monthly news brief on the programs and activities of the association, distributed electronically to AAUP members only.

AAUP Digital Digest

A blog of news and commentary from AAUP, featuring the "Books That Matter" essay series. *aaupdigitaldigest.wordpress.com*

AAUPNET.ORG

The association's website features information about AAUP programs, activities, and upcoming events; news about our member presses; a job list; resources for scholars, publishers, and librarians; and much more.

AAUPWiki

The AAUPWiki is a collaborative site designed to help AAUP members learn and share best practices, conference materials, and professional development tools. Hosted by Princeton University Press, and editable by registered AAUP members, the AAUPWiki is open to interested members of the scholarly communications field at: *aaupwiki.princeton.edu/*

Books for Understanding

Books for Understanding is an online resource for anyone looking for in-depth background and expertise on today's news. This service features subject-specific bibliographies on critically important news stories. New bibliographies are compiled when a major news story breaks or heated public debate takes place. This resource is available at: *www.booksforunderstanding.org*

The Exchange

The association's quarterly public newsletter is now an online-only publication. *The Exchange* is available free to interested members of the public and the scholarly communications community on the AAUP website.

University Press Books for Public and Secondary School Libraries

An annual bibliography that lists more than 400 university press titles in a wide range of disciplines. A committee of public and secondary school librarians selects the titles. The bibliography is published with support from the American Library Association (ALA) and is now also available in print and online at: *www.aaupnet.org/librarybooks*